WHEN I FALL IN LOVE

Miranda Dickinson has always had a head full of stories. From an early age she dreamed of writing a book that would make the heady heights of Kingswinford Library. Following a Performance Art degree, she began to write in earnest when a friend gave her The World's Slowest PC. She is also a singer-songwriter. Her first three novels, *Fairytale of New York*, *Welcome to My World* and *It Started with a Kiss*, have all been *Sunday Times* bestselling titles.

To find out more about Miranda visit www.miranda-dickinson.com

By the same author:

Fairytale of New York
Welcome to My World
It Started with a Kiss

MIRANDA DICKINSON

When I Fall in Love

AVON

AVON

A division of HarperCollins*Publishers*
77–85 Fulham Palace Road,
London W6 8JB

www.harpercollins.co.uk

A Paperback Original 2012

1

A catalogue record for this book is
available from the British Library

ISBN-13: 978-1-84756-236-4

Set in Sabon LT Std by Palimpsest Book Production Limited,
Falkirk, Stirlingshire

Printed and bound in Great Britain by
Clays Ltd, St Ives plc

As I write this, I am looking back at four extraordinary years of excitement, fun and lots of hard work. I would like to thank all the lovely team at Avon for everything they have done to make these the most exciting of my life so far: my fab editor Sammia Rafique, Caroline Ridding, Claire Bord, Rhian McKay and Jim Blades.

Big thanks to my wonderful agent, Hannah Ferguson, for being one of the most positive people I know and for believing in the crazy stuff in my head (wombats included!) For crucial draft reading and confidence boosts, unending thanks to Kim Curran-Goodson. Thanks also to Kate Harrison for her expert Brighton knowledge and knowing her Laine from her Lanes.

I love my tweethearts on Twitter who keep me going, make me giggle and occasionally make me cry. I would especially like to thank Trish Hills, Cressida McLaughlin, Gem Fletcher, Natalie Hewis, Kayla Staniland, Kath Eastman and Joanna Cannon for being wonderful friends and cheerleaders.

As ever, real people have inspired parts of this novel.

So thanks to the gorgeous Gemma Perkins for inspiring Elsie, Chris Armfield for inspiring Woody's rock wisdom, and the lovely Cupcake Genie team in Crawley whose awesome shop and cupcakes inspired Sundae & Cher's menu (www.cupcakegenie.co.uk). Thanks as ever to my fab Peppermint massive – watch out for your cameo!

And finally, to my wonderful new husband Bob – thank you for being my unexpected future and for making everything sparkly again.

Life can throw you spanners, curveballs, opportunities and surprises. This book is about going forward, regardless of what lies behind . . .

For Kim.
Because this story wouldn't have been as brave
without you.

A dream you dream alone is only a dream.
A dream you dream together is reality.
John Lennon

CHAPTER ONE

Not supposed to be like this

'Excuse me, miss?'

Elsie Maynard looked up from her half-crossed-out shopping list to see the hulking figure of a security guard blocking her way. 'Hi. Sorry, I'm in a bit of a rush, actually, so if you'll just . . .'

'I'm going to have to ask you to come with me, please.'

This was the last thing she needed today. Not only had her lunch break been delayed by forty-five minutes by a particularly persistent wafer-cone salesman but also, in her haste to complete all the shopping tasks on her list, she had left work without her umbrella just as the heavens opened. And now *this* . . .

'I've *told* you, I don't have time to stop.'

The huge security guard gave a world-weary sigh and clamped an enormous hand rather too heavily on her shoulder. 'I must insist, miss. I believe you have goods you have not paid for, so if you will just accompany me back into the shop, please . . .'

What on earth was this man-mountain on about? *Of course* she had paid! What kind of person did he think she was? Incensed at the very notion, Elsie opened her mouth to protest, when a new voice interrupted her.

'Hey. Can I help?'

He was young, arguably handsome, with dark brown hair and green eyes. Everything about him gave the impression of someone in complete control: from his neat haircut to the well-cut suit and overcoat he wore, together with the fact that, frustratingly, he was apparently immune to the large splats of rain Elsie could feel soaking through her too-thin work uniform and tights. Over his shoulder Elsie caught sight of a blonde-haired young woman dressed in a turquoise and black Fifties diner waitress outfit, looking as if somebody had just tipped a bucket of water over her head – and her heart sank as she realised it was her own reflection in the shop window.

Mr Impervious-to-Rain's smile would probably have been welcome, were it not for Elsie's sneaking suspicion that he was *enjoying* the sight of her, bedraggled, flustered and now squirming with embarrassment on the steps of the high street chemist's.

'I'm fine, thank you. It's just a misunderstanding . . .' she began, but Mount Kilimanjaro had turned his attention from her to seek solidarity with the recent male addition to the street spectacle.

'She hasn't paid,' he confided, pointing a thick finger at the haemorrhoid preparation and earwax softener in Elsie's hand, 'for *those* items.'

Oh. My. Life. In her fury at being accused of theft, Elsie had completely forgotten the two quite possibly most embarrassing items in the whole world that she now held. But of course she had paid for them! Hadn't she?

The young man suppressed a smile and Elsie felt her stomach lurch again as cold raindrops permeated her collar

2

and began to run down the back of her neck. 'I'm sure it's just a small misunderstanding,' he smiled affably at the gargantuan unsmiling man still gripping Elsie's shoulder. 'Look, here's twenty quid. Can't be any more than that, can it?'

A brief glimpse of softness flashed across the security guard's steely expression. 'Well . . .'

Sensing his opponent weakening, the young man's smile eased wider. 'I imagine you see this kind of thing every day, huh? Lunchtime shoppers, brains left at the office, so many shiny things to buy that they make one tiny slip of judgement . . .' He turned the whiteness of his sincerity on Elsie, a move which may have been intended to comfort but had the directly opposite effect. 'I mean, this girl seems very lovely and not really your average shoplifter, eh?'

The steel returned as Mountain Man surveyed her. 'Takes all sorts.'

'I'm sure it does, officer. But, trust me, I see all manner of felons in the course of my job and I can spot a wrong 'un a mile off. This, sir, is not one of them.'

This? Despite the help obviously being offered by the smartly dressed stranger beside her, being referred to as an inanimate object was a step too far for Elsie. 'Now *hang on* a minute . . .'

Her planned tirade was halted by a raised, gloved hand and a look that threatened dire consequences if she defied his gesture. Fuming, she dug her drenched heels into the pavement and glared at him.

'Come on, twenty quid?' he continued. 'I'll even go back into the shop with you to get a receipt. Can't say fairer than that, can I?'

To Elsie's amazement, the security guard shrugged his bulky shoulders and released her. 'All the same to me,' he muttered, pocketing the twenty-pound note and turning back towards the store. 'Just tell your girlfriend to pay a bit more attention next time.'

'What? I'm *not* his gir—'

'Absolutely. Stay there, *darling*. I'll be back in a moment.' Smiling like an advert for tooth whitening toothpaste, he winked at Elsie as he accompanied the guard inside the shop.

Gazing down in utter disbelief at the questionable items in her hand, Elsie remained frozen to the spot trying to process what had just happened. One minute she had been dashing around the huge high street chemist on the corner of Brighton's North Street and Queen's Road looking for baby wipes and mascara, the next she had been interrupted by her father calling to ask her to pick up some embarrassing but necessary items for him . . . Maybe her mind had been elsewhere – especially given the important decision she had made that morning – but she had *paid* for the items, she was sure. Who would try to steal pile preparation and earwax remover anyway? Certainly not Elsie Maynard, assistant manager of Sundae & Cher ice cream café, upstanding citizen of Brighton and the last person on the planet to ever consider shoplifting. Even as a teenager she had always maintained an unblemished record, her fear of getting into trouble only strengthened by witnessing the fallout from minor misdemeanours involving her two older sisters (more often than not involving overindulgence in alcohol and trips home in panda cars . . .)

'There, all sorted.' The smiling man was back, a triumphal glow from his recent chivalrous endeavours lighting his face. He handed her a receipt. 'Busy day, eh?'

'I paid for these,' Elsie insisted, the sting of injustice still smarting.

'You didn't. But it's OK, I sorted it for you.'

Pushing the receipt back at him, Elsie grabbed her purse from her damp handbag and angrily flicked through the receipts in the wallet section. 'Look, I don't know who you are, and I'm not being ungrateful, but that bloke was mistaken. I distinctly remember paying for these things with a twenty-pound note. I know this because I only had one twenty in my wallet that I'd just taken out from the cash machine and now, as you can see, it's not . . . Oh . . .' Her heart plummeted to her soggy toes as she pulled out a folded twenty-pound note, exactly where she'd put it at the cash point before she entered the shop.

The young man's voice softened. 'Honestly, it's fine. It happens to the best of us.' He held out his hand. 'I'm Torin, by the way. Torin Stewart.'

Still reeling from the revelation of her unwitting descent into petty crime, Elsie shook his hand. 'Elsie Maynard.'

'Pleasure to meet you, Elsie Maynard,' Torin grinned. 'Under different circumstances would've been preferable, of course, but I'm glad I was able to help. So, how about a coffee? You look like you need one and it'll get you out of this rain.'

Thoroughly mortified and filled with a compelling urge to remove herself from the situation, Elsie pushed the twenty-pound note into his hand and began to leave. 'I'm sorry, I really have to go . . .'

'Hey, why the rush?'

'I'm on my lunch break, which ended about twenty minutes ago,' Elsie returned, hoping that the pace she injected into her steps would deter him from following her down the street.

Unfortunately for Elsie, Torin was not one to be brushed off so easily. 'Now come on. I just saved your life back there.

Surely that entitles me to at least a coffee with you? It can be my treat if money's a bit tight . . .?'

That was the final straw. Blood pumping furiously in her ears, Elsie spun round to face him. 'Excuse me? I *have* money, actually. What part of "I have to go" do you not understand? I'm late for work and I'm soaked through from this *stupid* rain and, believe me, the very last thing I would like to do right now is go anywhere with you. I've paid you back so I don't owe you anything.'

'Is that the way you thank all your rescuers?' The twinkle in his eye sent a second wave of fury pumping through Elsie.

'Who do you think you are, Lancelot? And *where* do you get off interfering in other people's business, anyway? I am entirely capable of looking after myself, you know. I am not a damsel in distress that needs rescuing by a big, strong bloke. I would have *sorted* the situation, without your help. I would have *managed*. So thank you very much for jumping in, but I really didn't need you to.'

Torin was stopped in his tracks and Elsie felt the smallest glint of satisfaction as she walked away. Fair enough, he had helped to release her from the iron grip of the security guard, but he didn't have to make a virtue of the fact. Or attempt to turn the situation into some kind of emotional blackmail to go with him for coffee, either. Honestly, the cheek!

'Un-be-*lievable!*' a voice shouted behind her.

Elsie groaned as she pressed on, dodging lunchtime shoppers hurrying through the insistent mid-March rain. *Does this bloke ever give up?*

'I *thought* you looked like somebody in need of assistance,' Torin continued, drawing level with Elsie as they stormed together down the street. 'And all I did was try to save you from an embarrassing and potentially litigious situation. Well, more fool me!'

'You said it,' Elsie muttered, wishing with all her heart that he would get the message and leave her alone.

'Talk about ungrateful! *Some* women would see what I did just now as chivalrous.'

'And *some* women would think you were a pathetic male on an ego trip, making yourself appear superior. "Stay there, darling . . ." as if I was some dumb-nutted bimbo! Chauvinism is not chivalry, mate.'

'Oh, so stopping a security guard from hauling you back into a shop in full view of half of Brighton was *patronising*, was it?'

Of course it wasn't. But Elsie was tired, embarrassed, soaked to the skin and not likely to give in to the annoying man who *still* seemed impervious to rain. 'I'm sorry, I really don't have time for this.'

'Time for what? For being told how unreasonable you are?'

Elsie gave a hollow laugh as she skirted round a café A-board placed unwisely in her path. 'Oh right, *I'm* unreasonable . . .'

'Yes, you are. May I remind you that there was every chance that security guard wouldn't have let the situation go?'

'How do you know that? You can't possibly know that!'

He was matching her pace, step for step, his reddening face pulling closer to hers. 'It was obvious to anybody! You only had to see the gleam in his eye to know that he intended to make an example of you. It could have involved the police, a magistrates court visit, a fine . . . a *criminal record*?'

Halting suddenly, Elsie faced him. 'OK, enough! Believe it or not, I have more important things to think about today than whether or not I would have ended up with a criminal record if you hadn't intervened. I've said thank you, I've paid you back, what more can you possibly want from me?'

Breathing heavily, Torin held up his hands. 'Nothing. Obviously nothing.' Then, to Elsie's surprise, instead of hurling a clever comeback at her, he backed away, turned and disappeared into the crowd.

If she hadn't seen the look of sincere disappointment in his eyes, Elsie would have just dismissed the whole thing. But the unexpected impact of it sent a whisper of conscience cutting like a scythe through her consternation. Blinking away the raindrops dripping from the edges of her fringe, she stood in the middle of milling shoppers, the events of the past ten minutes replaying over and over in her mind.

The insistent ringing of her mobile brought her sharply back to the present.

'Hello? Oh hi, Dad. Yes, I have your things. I'll bring them over after work.'

Taking one last glance up the street, Elsie shook the nagging doubt from her mind.

'Weirdo,' she told herself. 'Clearly a weirdo.'

CHAPTER TWO

Moving on . . .

By the time Elsie parked her car outside her father's three-storey townhouse later that day, thick grey clouds had laid siege to Brighton's skies, emptying their weight of rain on the streets of the seaside city. Despite her best efforts to shield herself from the torrential downpour by holding her handbag above her head as she dashed from the car, she arrived at the purple wood and stained-glass front door soaked once more.

The tinkle of a small wind-chime over the door and heady smell of warming patchouli oil and Nag Champa incense sticks were immediately soothing as she walked into the hallway and headed towards the Indian bead curtain that covered the entrance to the kitchen. It had been many years since she had moved out of this place but it still always felt like home when she returned.

Jim Maynard beamed when Elsie walked into the kitchen. He was out of his work clothes already, his respectable business suit replaced by his favourite Nepal striped patchwork shirt, baggy combat trousers and bright orange Doc Marten boots. Elsie smiled back. She always preferred the sight of her father in his relaxed attire, with his much-beloved gold earring back in his ear: it was a truer version of himself than his well-respected Brighton businessman persona that he had adopted since taking over his father's classic furniture store business.

'It's my favourite youngest daughter!' he exclaimed, wrapping her up in one of his famous Dad-hugs, which was even more welcome today than usual. 'Good day?'

Elsie opened a brightly painted enamel tea caddy and popped two ginger and cinnamon teabags into a hand-painted kingfisher-blue teapot, a gift to Jim from his middle daughter Guin when she set up her pottery business in Shoreham-by-Sea four years ago. 'Annoying day, actually.' She smiled at her father. 'But it's better now I'm here.'

'I'm glad, darling. I knew there was a reason we needed patchouli oil today. Sit down, take a deep breath and tell your old dad about it.' Jim took the whistling kettle from the gas stove and made the tea. 'What happened?'

'Oh, nothing, really. I just had a bit of an ordeal at lunchtime.'

Her father was about to enquire further when the kitchen door opened and a chorus of 'Shoplifter!' filled the kitchen, followed by loud shrieks of laughter.

Elsie groaned as her two older sisters piled onto her, shouting, laughing and ruffling her hair. Sometimes being so close to your sisters (and texting them as soon as anything happened in your day) was a bad thing . . .

'Our little sister, the petty thief!' Daisy Maynard laughed, flicking back her perfectly coiffed blonde hair and clapping slender hands at the sight of her sister's chagrin. 'I'm so proud!'

'We were going to get you a swag bag and mask from the fancy dress shop on the way here but Junior decided to play up,' Guin added, patting her burgeoning belly. 'You seem to have this one on side already, Els.'

Elsie grinned despite her embarrassment and reached out to stroke her sister's considerable baby bump. 'You've got taste, kid. Just stick with your Auntie Elsie and you'll stay relatively sane.'

'Although she'll have you signed up to the family crime business before you know it,' Daisy added as she and Guin descended into hilarity.

'What's this about crime?' Jim looked from one daughter to the others, trying to keep up. After their mother had removed herself from the family unit when all three girls were little. Jim had assumed the role of sole referee of the whirlwind known as the Maynard sisters and was often left bewildered by their endless energy and the breakneck speed of their conversations.

'Our little sister was almost arrested for shoplifting today,' Guin said, groaning as she lowered herself carefully onto a chair by the kitchen table. Her blue eyes flashed with mischief as she pulled a hairband from her wrist and wound her wavy blonde hair into a loose bun at the nape of her neck. 'Who'd have thought it, eh? Goody-Two-Shoes Elsie a criminal mastermind!'

'It was a misunderstanding,' Elsie protested. 'I handled the situation.'

'Really? *You* handled it?' Daisy asked, eyebrows raised.

'Yes,' Elsie replied firmly, wishing again that she hadn't informed them so comprehensively of the event in a string of texts that afternoon. 'I had a lot on my mind and honestly thought I'd paid. It was obvious in the end that I had made a mistake.'

'Oh.' Jim handed out mugs of tea, not really sure how to respond to this revelation. 'Well, we live and learn, eh?'

Filled with a rush of love for her father, Elsie squeezed his hand as she accepted a mug from him. 'We do. So you see, Dad, everything's good now.'

'I'm glad to hear it. Now, I did a bit of baking last night. Don't suppose I can interest any of you girls in a slice of banana and walnut bread, can I?'

This was met by a chorus of appreciation and, delighted, Jim opened an old Roses tin to serve up his recent culinary triumph. As he and Guin began to chat, Daisy grabbed Elsie's hand and pulled her into the small hallway at the back of the kitchen.

'So?' she demanded, folding her slender arms and giving Elsie a classic Older Sister Stare.

Elsie was having none of it. She had outfaced her eldest sister many times over the years and she wasn't about to be intimidated by her today. 'So what?'

'You *know* what, Elsie Maynard. Why didn't you mention *the chap*?'

Elsie shrugged. 'Dad didn't need to know.'

'How do you figure that? That handsome stranger saved you from being *arrested*, for heaven's sake!'

'*Shh!* Keep your voice down . . . And I never said he was handsome.'

Dropping her voice to a harsh whisper, Daisy eyeballed her sister. 'I beg to differ. Anyway, why are you so het up about this? It's OK to admit you needed help, you know. It's no reflection on you. It doesn't mean you can't cope or anything . . .'

Elsie had heard enough. 'Drop it, Dais! Let's just . . . talk about something else for a bit.'

Daisy relented and wrapped an arm around Elsie's shoulder. 'Fair enough, lovely. I'm sorry. So, was he fit?'

'Daisy!'

'Oh come on, Elsie, humour me!'

'I suppose he was, in an annoying, waterproof way. I wasn't looking too closely at the time.'

An indeterminable look passed across Daisy's face. 'Good. That's good.'

Later, when the Maynards were sitting around the dining room table in the large, first-floor living room eating vegetable tagine with tabouleh and pearl couscous (a particular favourite of Jim's), Elsie decided to announce the decision that she had been distracted by when she inadvertently became a lunchtime shoplifter. It had been on her mind all week, ever since she had decided to finally open the small, chocolate satin-covered box by her bed after eighteen months of waiting. This morning, she had made her decision: the first part of moving on . . .

'Right, everyone, I'm glad you're all here – and sitting down – because I've something I want to say.' She smiled at the apprehensive looks of her nearest and dearest. 'Don't panic, it's good news, I think.' She took a breath to steady herself. 'I've decided to start dating again.'

'Oh *Els* . . .' Guin's face reddened and she burst into tears, much to the amusement of her sisters. Since she had discovered she was pregnant, the normally pragmatic middle Maynard sister had become an emotional wreck, sobbing uncontrollably at everything from songs on her car radio to television adverts for pet food and sofas. Laughing at her own emotional state, she accepted the box of tissues her father always kept close for such occasions and wiped her eyes. 'Man, I am such a *wuss*! I hope all this sobbing isn't going to traumatise my baby. I'm just so – *happy* for you, honey.'

Jim reached across the table and took Elsie's hand. 'My brave girl. And you feel all right about it all?'

Elsie could feel herself shaking, but she knew she was. 'I'm terrified – I mean I've no idea how to go about it, or even how it's done now – but it feels right.'

'We can help,' Daisy said, nodding furiously – a suggestion which slightly alarmed Elsie. Daisy prided herself on being a bit of a matchmaker, even though several of her match-ups for friends had ended in dreadful dates and acrimonious splits. But then, as Elsie reasoned, when you were as effortlessly gorgeous as Daisy Maynard with a successful career and a wealthy property developer boyfriend, what would you really understand about the perils of dating?

'Promise me one thing, darling: steer clear of those dreadful dating sites,' Jim interjected, his assertion eliciting shock from his three daughters. 'No, I'm serious. I signed up for two of them last year and they were most disappointing.'

The unexpected revelation of Jim's secret online dating history temporarily hijacked the conversation, and Elsie allowed herself to relax a little as the incredulous reaction flowed around her. After this week's apprehension of telling her family what she was planning, she now felt strangely peaceful. It was the right decision and it was an important one.

I love you because you're brave and strong and you always know what to do.
xx

It was the first message in the pile stacked neatly inside the former chocolate box the subject of Number 50 on The List:

50. Read the box messages – all of them.

It had taken Elsie eighteen months to bring herself to open it, the thought of its unread contents strangely comforting. When she made the decision last Monday to fulfil the last-but-one item on The List, it had felt like being reunited with an old friend. And as soon as she read the first message, Elsie knew it was the right time. The message made perfect sense – and instantly she knew what to do.

'Wow,' said Cher Pettinger, owner of Sundae & Cher, when Elsie told her the news a week after the shoplifting incident. 'And you're sure you're ready to dive into the shark-infested dating waters again?'

Elsie pulled a face. 'Well, when you put it like *that*, how can I resist?'

'No, no, that's not what I meant,' Cher shook her head, the tall ebony beehive atop it shaking wildly. 'It's just, you know, when you've three divorces under your belt like me the whole dating scene becomes more of a moron-dodging exercise than anything else.'

Elsie smiled at her boss, noting again how at odds her lack of dating success was with the confident forty-something dressed head to toe in vintage Dior. 'I'll bear that in mind. How is the latest flame?'

Cher grimaced as she dropped a newly mixed tub of house speciality Apple, Cinnamon and Nutmeg ice cream into the glass-fronted display cabinet. 'He *was* looking promising until I realised he still lived with his mother. Forty-two years old and still sleeping in a bedroom with He-Man wallpaper.'

'Blimey.'

'Believe it, sister. It's a *jungle* out there. But you know me: ever the optimistic adventurer.'

Cher Pettinger's relationship history read like a cautionary

15

tale on the perils of dating. Married and divorced three times, she had since endured a string of hopeless beaus, from the owner of the local amusement arcade who had a strange penchant for life-sized dolls, and the toyboy estate agent who was convinced that he was being stalked by MI5, to the ageing lothario hotelier who turned out to be a serial bigamist. But Cher was nothing if not committed to her dating cause, gamely braving the 'jungle of morons' in pursuit of true love.

Elsie liked her boss immensely, despite Cher's infamously dry sense of humour, which had earned her a fearsome reputation in North Laine. She was sassy and assured and undaunted by life – and in Elsie she had found a kindred spirit. Together, over the past three years, they had turned the once hippy vegan café in colourful Gardner Street that Cher inherited from her dotty aunt, Lucy 'Skyflower' Pettinger, into a retro-themed ice cream café that the great and good of Brighton flocked to, irrespective of the season.

Sundae & Cher was filled with 1950s and 1960s memorabilia, from the gold-framed Elvis and Frankie Valli photographs on the wall behind the green glass counter, to the black and white harlequin tiles on the floor, replica Wurlitzer jukebox, black and white checked tablecloths and red leather and chrome chairs. It had the air of being simultaneously retro and chic, and modern and cool – and Elsie loved to see people's expressions when they walked in for the first time. Of course, the killer detail was that all the ice cream sold in the café was made onsite, in the basement kitchen with its large ice cream mixing machine and large freezer cabinet. This meant that Sundae & Cher could offer flavours nobody else in Brighton could match, changing them regularly to keep the ever-enthusiastic customers coming back for more. From Toasted Popcorn to Blue

Cheese and Walnut, Maple Banana and even a Tomato, Basil and Olive combination, Sundae & Cher's unique ice cream flavours had become a talking point in the famous seaside town. Add to this the effortlessly relaxed and fun atmosphere and it was easy to see why Sundae & Cher fitted into colourfully bohemian Gardner Street perfectly.

Cher was obsessed with 1950s and 1960s fashion, proudly wearing vintage finds from the retro clothing boutiques that lined the streets of Brighton's famous shopping district. Her home, too, was a shrine to retro kitsch, her love of which was evident wherever she was.

As such, she looked every inch the part behind the glass counter of Sundae & Cher – as did Elsie in her black short-sleeved blouse with white collar and cuffs, turquoise satin circle skirt and white frilled apron. It was fun to dress up for work and even though the days were long and busy, Elsie adored being part of Cher's throwback business vision. It was as if Cher's trademark dynamism was infused into the very fixtures and fittings of the ice cream café – a sense of optimism and fun pervaded everything, something which had proved precious to Elsie during the last eighteen months.

Today, as she scooped colourful balls of handmade ice cream into deep blue sundae glasses, Elsie felt more positive about her decision than ever.

'So, want me to set you up?' Cher asked, popping Belgian chocolate-filled wafer sticks into the top of the sundaes. 'Because I'm sure I know some suitable gents. Not that I'm saying you won't find anyone under your own steam, you know, but every little helps and that.'

The door opened and a middle-aged man bounded across the harlequin-tiled floor towards them. 'Morning, lovely ladies!'

17

'And here's one of them now,' Cher winked. 'Dennis, my lovely. How's our favourite morning customer?'

Dennis' ample cheeks flushed. 'Always the better for seeing you, m'dear.'

Cher feigned coyness and batted her false eyelashes at him. 'Such a charmer! So what can I tempt you with today?'

His eyes made a greedy survey of the generous swirling mounds of rainbow-hued ice creams before him (and, arguably, a wider reconnoitre of Cher's generous chest in the process). 'Ah, decisions, decisions. I think I will have one of your excellent breakfast pastries, considering the early hour.'

'Good choice. Anything *with* that, Dennis?'

Elsie knew the script of this conversation by heart. Every Monday and Thursday morning, at nine o'clock precisely, Dennis Keith would visit Sundae & Cher on his way to the small accountancy office where he worked. His ultimate goal was to have three scoops of ice cream with his breakfast *pain au chocolat*, but his sense of British propriety and conscience would never allow him to ask for this outright. Instead, a well-practised bartering ensued, after which he could rest easy that he was not being greedy but, in fact, merely accommodating Cher's culinary suggestion. It wouldn't do to hurt her feelings by refusing ice cream, would it?

'I wonder if I might have a scoop of your excellent *gelato* with my breakfast?'

'Of course, lovely. Which one would you like?'

Dennis made a grand show of indecision, hopping left to right as he surveyed the selection. 'Vanilla – no, wait – Mango and Ginger Swirl looks most inviting . . . But then there's Chocolate Space Dust . . . oh, it's *so* hard to choose!'

Cher leaned over the counter just low enough to

momentarily lure his eyes away from the ice cream. 'Dennis, you know I'll be offended if you don't try all three . . .'

Mission accomplished, his eyes twinkled as he pretended to be surprised. 'Really? In that case, how can I refuse?'

As he walked away happy, Cher twirled her ice cream scoop like a Wild West sharpshooter. 'See? Do I know men or what?'

Elsie grinned and picked up a menu covered in vivid pink Post-it notes. 'No doubting that fact. You thinking of redesigning the menus again?'

Cher handed Elsie a cup of tea. 'Not the menus. The *menu*.'

'Sorry?'

'I've been thinking about being a bit more adventurous with what Sundae & Cher offers. Try to extend our reach a bit. Now we're heading towards Easter I thought it was as good a time as any to have a bit of a spring clean.'

Elsie looked at the written suggestions on the menu stickies. 'I like the idea of porridge and pancakes for the Breakfast list. After all, not everyone can face ice cream first thing in the morning like Dennis.'

'I've asked our friends at Cupcake Genie to do us some seasonal specials, too, and I can tie in the ice cream flavours with some of their ideas,' Cher continued, her eyes ablaze with inspiration. 'And there's more . . .' She hurried into the kitchen behind the counter and returned a few moments later with a frosted Tupperware box. She cracked open the lid and scooped a spoonful of palest lilac-coloured gelato from inside, handing it to Elsie. 'Try that.'

The taste was unbelievable – like crushed Parma Violets and rose petals. 'Wow, that's amazing.'

'It's organic and dairy-free,' Cher beamed. 'I made it using almond milk. It works with any of our flavours and it's something we can offer that nobody else in Brighton does. Then I've ordered a crêpe hotplate, so we can offer handmade crêpes on site with scoops of ice cream, fresh fruit and pretty much any of our toppings. It'll look fantastic and the smell of freshly cooked crêpes will fill the place! If that works, who knows? Waffles made in-house, takeaway ice cream, more of your awesome cookies . . . *anything's* possible.'

'Sounds like you've thought of everything. So when are all these menu changes taking place?' Elsie asked.

'Not for a while. I'm still working on bringing everything together. I want your ideas, too. This needs to be a joint effort, OK?' She looked over to the corner of the café where Dennis was blissfully engrossed in his guilt-free breakfast. 'If only all our customers were as easy to please as Dennis, eh?'

Elsie grinned. 'Maybe we should appoint him Chief Menu Consultant.'

'You're kidding, aren't you? He'd never leave!'

'Fair point.' Elsie placed the menu on the counter. 'So, being more adventurous it is then.'

The wink Cher blessed Elsie with was pure filth. 'In as many ways as we can, girl.'

On Saturday morning, Elsie met Daisy for breakfast in the Driftwood Café on the beach near the Palace Pier. As usual, Daisy looked as if she had been expertly dressed and prepared by a team of beauticians and fashion stylists: her simple white shirt was completely crease-free and elegantly teamed with dark, slim-fitting jeans and brogues, with a large silk pashmina scarf completing her outfit. Elsie had always been in awe of her eldest sister and had spent much of her early teens trying to emulate Daisy's style, until she reached the age of sixteen and discovered the kooky fashion boutiques in North Laine, which helped her to develop her own style. Today she was wearing a sweet, cherry-print dress over loose-fitting jeans, her beloved red Converse trainers and a bright green cardigan to fend off the cool sea breeze, her hair tied into a ponytail with a length of scarlet ribbon. A good four inches shorter than her sister, Elsie nevertheless bore a striking resemblance to her, both of them taking after their absent mother with their high cheekbones and large, denim-blue eyes, while their sibling Guin was the spit of Jim – tall and athletically built with a mass of thick, wavy blonde hair, the envy of her sisters whose tresses wouldn't know a curl if they saw one.

The late morning sun was warming the deck of the café as Daisy poured tea from a quirky spotted teapot into two oversized cups.

'I hope you realise this is the first Saturday I've taken off in five months,' Daisy said, sliding a cup across the mosaic table-top towards her sister. 'You should feel highly honoured.'

'I do.'

'Good.' Daisy stirred her tea, observing Elsie carefully. 'So, how are you with everything? And I mean really, Els, not the Wonderwoman impression you put on for Dad and Guin.'

'I'm good. Don't give me that look, I'm honestly fine with all of this.'

Daisy was far from pacified with this answer. 'Then tell me – because I'm not sure I understand – what brought about your decision to date again?'

'I've started to read the box messages.'

Daisy's spoon dropped onto the saucer with a clank. 'Oh. *Wow.*'

'I know. And it feels good. The right time, you know? In fact, I read the second one this morning and it's brilliant. Look . . .' She took the folded paper from her purse and passed it across the table.

I love you because you're fearless
and never afraid to start something new.
xx

For someone whose emotional control was legendary, Daisy looked dangerously close to tears. The paper shook gently in her fingers as she read the message and she was silent for some time. 'What a beautiful thing to say . . .'

'Not that we should be surprised.'

'No, I suppose not.' Daisy handed the paper back to Elsie. 'I know this will sound strange, considering, but you really are incredibly lucky. André's never said anything like that to me in all the time I've known him.'

'Do you wish he would?'

'Oh, I don't know. Sometimes I think it would be nice to hear how he feels about me, but other times I just think we're one of those couples who don't work that way. Not that it's important, really.' She flicked the topic away with a wave of her long fingers as if it were a troublesome fly. 'So, what are you going to do with this message?'

'I need to start something new.'

'Like what?'

Elsie inhaled the salty air rising from the waves crashing on the pebble beach in the distance as a pair of squawking seagulls circled above. 'I've no idea. But I think starting something new would help me to begin to think of myself as a person in my own right, you know?'

'You *are* a person in your own right . . .' Daisy began to protest.

'No, I know that. But I have this whole unexpected life stretching out in front of me now and I should work out what to do with it. I just need to discover what happens next.'

Daisy shook her head. 'You're amazing. The way you've coped with all this . . . well, I think it's wonderful.' Embarrassed by her own emotion, she quickly moved on. 'Have you thought about what you'd like to do?'

'A little. The only thing I've come up with so far isn't really a new thing, though.'

'Tell me.'

Elsie felt a rush of excitement as she spoke. 'OK, do you remember when we were growing up and we used to put on those dreadful musical shows for Dad?'

'On Sunday afternoons! I'd forgotten those!' Daisy clapped her hands and laughed so loudly that a passing waiter almost dropped his tray.

Around the time of Elsie's eighth birthday, Sunday afternoons in the Maynard household became musical spectaculars. Daisy, then twelve, had just joined a kids' drama club at the local Methodist church hall and was convinced she was destined for the bright lights of the West End. As with most things during their childhood, the Maynard sisters' productions were instigated by Daisy, largely as a vehicle for showcasing her own performing skills, dragging middle sister Guin and little sister Elsie in as supporting cast. Not that either of them minded, as both were in constant awe of their confident, headstrong sibling. Each week, the Sunday Spectacular would become more enthusiastic and elaborate, with Elsie and Guin introducing costumes, wonky-eyed sock puppets and, eventually, music to the proceedings. By the time Elsie was twelve, she had attained the position of Musical Director, playing the family's forever-out-of-tune piano in the dining room as her sisters danced and hammily acted their way through lengthy self-penned productions.

'Poor Dad,' Daisy laughed, 'I can't believe he actually sat through those week after week.'

'He was a very good audience, though. Standing ovations every Sunday, remember?' Elsie grinned.

'How could I forget? You're not thinking of resurrecting the Sunday Spectaculars, are you?'

'Hmm, I'm not sure even Brighton is ready for that much theatrical experimentation. But I was thinking I might join a drama group or an operatic society. I'd quite like to do musicals – even though the old vocal cords haven't had an outing for years. And it would be good to meet new people, get "out there" again. I need to start somewhere, and doing something I enjoy seems like a good enough place to start. Even if my voice isn't up to scratch after all this time.'

Daisy stared at her sister as though she had just proclaimed the sea to be pink. 'Don't be ridiculous! Your voice is brilliant. Far better than anyone else in the family – including Uncle Frank, and he's been making a living in local pubs for years trashing the Great American Songbook. I reckon you could sing anywhere and people would listen.'

'That's kind of you to say but I think I might need to work on it a little before I let it out in public.'

'Nonsense. Hang on a minute . . .' Daisy's eyes widened as a thought occurred to her. 'You could sing *right here*.'

She pointed to the corner of the café's boardwalk, where a rainbow-painted upright piano sat. It wouldn't have looked out of place at a Coldplay gig and had been a feature of the café since the previous summer when a six-week arts project had left it behind. Its lid bore the invitation: *Play me – I'm yours!* and occasionally someone would accept the challenge, meaning that at any time your organic, Fairtrade coffee could be accompanied by a rock'n'roll medley, a Chopin piano concerto or a terrible rendition of 'Chopsticks'.

'*Shh*, don't be daft!' Elsie gave a nervous laugh and looked around, praying that none of the café's customers had heard Daisy's suggestion. Thankfully, the other people on the boardwalk appeared to be blissfully unaware of it, enjoying their leisurely breakfasts in the spring sunshine.

But Daisy Maynard was an impossibly gorgeous woman on a mission. 'I mean it, Els! Do it now – go on, sing something!'

'I can't . . .'

'Yes, you can. You're *fearless*, remember?' A glint of pure mischief flashed in her dark-blue eyes as she sat back in her chair, a victorious smile on her face. 'I *double-dare* you.'

Elsie stared at her sister. If there was one irrefutable truth that the three Maynard sisters knew, it was that a double-dare was the ultimate challenge. To ignore it was to practically betray the Maynard family honour – and incur the unending jibes of the entire clan: Dad, Daisy, Guin, and even their late Grandma Flo, who had been a stickler for it when she was alive. No matter the potential consequences of the double-dare subject, nothing was worth facing the repercussions of turning it down . . .

Elsie pulled a face at her sister, but the die was cast. As she rose slowly, the sudden jolt of adrenaline caused by the sheer audacity of what she was about to do almost made her squeal out loud. Daisy nodded eagerly as Elsie walked across to the piano. Flexing her hands over the multi-coloured keys, she took a deep breath and dived in.

The first couple of bars of 'I Will Survive' were a little shaky – understandably so, given the instantly bemused faces of the customers. But as Daisy began to provide percussion by slapping the stainless steel table, Elsie's confidence grew. By the time she neared the chorus, her heart was pumping like a steam train and she was singing at full throttle.

And then, something amazing happened.

A bespectacled man in a slim-fitting check shirt at the far end of the boardwalk suddenly got to his feet and joined in the chorus, followed by a lady at the next table. As people began to join in, the shared thrill of their spontaneous performance reverberated around the space. Diners inside the café crowded by the windows and open door to watch this spectacle and a group of dog walkers gathered to observe the extraordinary sight. Joggers along the promenade stopped and peered over the sea-green railings; a gaggle of teenage girls abandoned their texting and turned their camera phones towards the boardwalk café; older couples enjoying ice cream pointed and laughed. Smiles were everywhere, and as Elsie led her improvised band of singers in the final chorus, she felt more alive than she had in a long time.

When the song ended, an enormous cheer went up from performers and onlookers alike, the shared emotion bringing tears to Elsie's eyes as the café staff wolf-whistled and applauded like maniacs. Then, this being Brighton, the unwitting flashmob performers self-consciously returned to their tables as if nothing had happened.

Elated, Elsie high-fived her grinning sister. 'How was that?'

Daisy gave a low bow. 'You are my official hero, Elsie Maynard! Heck of a way to start something new.'

'I thank you.'

'This calls for cake – no, I'm sorry, you can't protest, sis. You've just attained legendary status. Cake is the only fitting tribute to your genius.' Daisy hurried into the café.

Elsie smiled to herself, a strong feeling of fulfilment rushing through her. The stunt had been daft in the extreme, but it had awakened something deep within her. She had been looking for something new: and, while she wasn't altogether sure that this discovery actually meant anything, she couldn't shake the feeling that something significant had just been achieved. And she wasn't wrong. For unbeknownst to Elsie Maynard, someone had been watching her spontaneous appearance carefully from the promenade railings. Someone who was about to change her life completely . . .

CHAPTER THREE

Pleased to meet you . . .

He was dressed entirely in black: from his too-tight jeans (slightly inadvisable for a man of his age), scuffed leather boots studded with silver stars and torn T-shirt emblazoned with a white skull that appeared to be winking, to his well-worn leather jacket and dented Stetson hat. The only exception was the crimson red kerchief knotted at his neck. A long, greying ponytail languished down his back and silver chains jangled at his wrists. Watching the remarkable scene unfolding on the boardwalk café below him, he leaned against the promenade railing, chewed his cinnamon gum thoughtfully and nodded slowly as an undeniably genius plan began to form in his mind.

When the onlookers from the promenade around him began to disperse, he took a pair of blue-tinted, round-lens sunglasses from his back pocket, placed them ceremoniously on his nose, tipped his hat-brim forward and sauntered down the stone steps to the boardwalk.

Daisy returned with a tray, her face flushed from laughter. 'They love you in there,' she gushed. 'Cake's on the house!'

'Seriously? Blimey, I should do this more often.'

'The manager asked if you can come back next Saturday. I think he was serious . . .'

'Not sure being a café singer is really me, but it's nice of him to ask,' Elsie said, clinking cups with Daisy.

'A-a-a-ngel!' said a voice over their heads.

Elsie and Daisy looked up to see a middle-aged man in black standing beside their table.

Daisy frowned at the newcomer. 'Sorry?'

'You're a vision, a miracle, a *mystical sign*, babe.'

Elsie stifled a giggle, but Daisy took an instant dislike to the unwelcome stranger interrupting their conversation. 'No, *thank you*,' she stated.

He appeared to be momentarily knocked off guard. 'Say what?'

'Whatever it is you're selling, we're not interested.'

'Lady, do I look like a common beach merchant to you?'

'I have no idea who you are. But my sister and I are enjoying a relaxed morning together, so if you don't mind, we . . .'

'Your sister? Your sister is a gift from the *gods*, girl.'

'You're very kind,' Elsie replied, far more amused by the man in black than Daisy was. 'But I think you're mistaking me for someone else.'

'On the contrary,' he replied, pulling a chair from a nearby table and sitting down without an invitation. 'You're the one I've been looking for!'

'Erm, excuse *me*,' Daisy began, but the man in black wasn't listening.

'Woody,' he said, jutting a jangling hand towards Elsie. 'Woody Jensen. You may remember me from hit Eighties rock band Hellfinger.'

It was clear from the identical expressions of the Maynard sisters that neither did. Unperturbed, Woody pressed on.

'I co-wrote the global hit "Hard Rockin' Summer" – 1987? It's still a leading light on the *Kerrang!* Radio playlist . . .'

Elsie shrugged. 'I was two in 1987 and my sister was six – sorry.'

Visibly deflated, Woody removed his hat and plonked it on the table. 'It was a *seminal hit*, man . . . World tour, groupies – the whole nine yards. Are you sure you don't remember?' He began to sing in a throaty falsetto voice, drumming his be-ringed fingers on the table top: '*Heart beatin' faster than a-Olympic runn-uhh, we're livin' the dream for a hard rockin' summ-uhh . . . Oh-oohh, hard rockin' summ-uhh . . .*' He looked hopefully at Elsie and Daisy. 'Ring any bells?'

'Only alarm ones,' Daisy muttered.

'Say again?'

'Look, it's been a blast meeting you, obviously, but I'd really appreciate it if you left us alone now?'

Woody folded his arms. 'Not until your sister's heard my *attractive* proposition.' He grinned lasciviously at Elsie.

Quick to defend her sister from what she perceived to be a scruffy rocker's dodgy advances, Daisy flew to her feet and leaned threateningly over Woody. 'Listen, I've asked you nicely to leave. If you insist on staying I'm going to have to ask the manager to eject you from the premises . . .'

'Hey, babe, chill. All I want is to ask your sister one question and then I'm gone. Acceptable?'

Suddenly feeling sorry for the former global rock star at their table, Elsie placed her hand on her sister's arm. 'I think we should hear what Mr Jensen has to say, hun.'

Daisy sank back onto her chair. 'But he's . . .'

Ignoring her sister's protest, Elsie turned to Woody. 'Ask away.'

A look of pure reverent awe washed across Woody's stubble-edged face. 'A-a-a-a-ngel,' he breathed, before composing himself. 'I need your help. You see I'm a man burdened with ambition and creative skill beyond anything what a man should have to carry. But it's a cross I bear for my creativity, babe. Point is, I'm on the edge of a rebirth – a spiritual readjustment, if you will – and I have a feeling that this new phase of my life will be my strongest yet. If I can only get my project off the ground, that is.'

Daisy was staring at him like he was a three-headed alien. Elsie gave him a patient smile. 'And what is your question, exactly?'

'Well, I was up on the prom, considering my next move, when a *vision* appeared to me – just like in '84 when I dreamed of a rock band that would take over the known world and Hellfinger was born. And the vision was *you* – here, on this humble boardwalk – like a musical shaman, charming the Brighton faithful to do your mystical will.'

Elsie laughed. 'It was "I Will Survive", not a religious chant.'

'But that's the point, girl! You took a humble song and made it magical. That's what I want to do.'

'I'm sorry, I really don't know what you're asking me to . . .'

Woody grasped her hand, taking her by surprise. 'I'm talking about a *choir*, babe! But not a goody-goody, saccharine sweet choir in a church hall. I'm talking a band of vocal believers, faithfully bringing classic tunes to the masses. Hendrix, Lennon, McCartney, Gaga. But I can't do this alone: I need a musical director – a collaborator, if you will – to bring my dream to reality. I was asking the universe for a sign – just as you started to sing. It's *fate*, babe! So what do you say? Will you jump into the abyss of chance and play destiny's piano?'

'With an offer like that, how can you refuse?' scoffed Daisy.

'How indeed . . .?' Elsie answered, her mind suddenly racing with possibilities.

Daisy gripped her arm. 'Wait – you're not seriously considering this, are you?'

Elsie couldn't lie. Despite all the good reasons there were for her not accepting, she *liked* this middle-aged rocker with his crazy idea. The hint of something beyond the norm intrigued her intensely. This week's note had said she was fearless: surely pursuing this was evidence of the fact?

'I was looking to start something new. This might be it.'

'No way! I'm sorry, Elsie, I can't let you do this.'

Woody's brow lowered. 'I think you'll find *Elsie* can . . .'

'Daisy, I think this could work. I wanted to do something musical and this could be fun. Imagine the people who would respond to a non-conventional choir. People I might have something in common with and be able to build something with . . . Come on, Dais, you said you'd support me in whatever I chose to do. If I'm going to start something new and maybe begin to date again, this could be a perfect opportunity.'

'Yeah, *Daisy*, lighten up and catch the vision,' Woody added, perhaps unwisely given the murderous look in Daisy's eyes.

'Nobody has introduced us so you shouldn't use my name!' she exclaimed, the utter Britishness of her argument only serving to make Elsie giggle.

'Daisy Maynard, meet Woody Jensen. Woody, meet Daisy. And I'm Elsie. Now we're all formally introduced. Happy?'

'Not particularly.' Irritated, Daisy wrapped her long

pashmina scarf around her shoulders and glared at them both. 'If you want to do this, fine. But I'm coming too. I'm not letting you go anywhere alone with this – this – *person*.'

Woody scooped up the Stetson and replaced it on his head. 'Cool with me, babe. The more the merrier.'

They arranged to meet the following Tuesday evening at Sundae & Cher, Woody clearly relishing the prospect of 'dreams and ice cream'. Daisy waited until Woody had left to reveal her true feelings to Elsie.

'I can't believe you'd even consider doing anything with *that man*,' she said, as they picked their way slowly across the pebbled beach. 'He's a nutjob!'

Elsie bent down to pick up a smooth, grey pebble. 'I know he's a little . . . eccentric, but isn't everybody in this town? You have to admit, it sounds like fun.'

'It sounds like a *nightmare*,' Daisy retorted. 'Els, are you sure this is what you want? Because there are all manner of perfectly decent choirs in Brighton that you could join instead. The DreamTeam are meant to be wonderful – and they perform at the Theatre Royal every year. Imagine singing on that stage! You'd love it, I'm sure . . .'

Elsie shot her sister a wry look. 'Be in a choir run by Jeannette Burton? The only choirmistress who grabs more of the spotlight than her choir? No, thank you. I don't want to be led in musical medleys by a fifty-something woman in skin-tight red leather trousers. It would be most off-putting . . .' She smiled, remembering Cher's damning verdict on the woman: '*Just like Simon Cowell in red leather*' . . . 'Besides,' she continued, turning the pebble over and over in her hands, 'the kind of choir Woody and I could create would be fun and definitely not conventional.'

Change was a good thing, Elsie decided, as she mulled over the events of the past week. Deciding to date again – even if right now it was a theory rather than a plan of action – and the possibility of participating in whatever type of mystical musical happening Woody had in mind filled her with a sparkling sense of excitement. On the surface neither decision was particularly world-shaking, but they represented significant steps forward for her.

Later that afternoon, when Daisy had left to meet her friends for lunch, Jim called to ask Elsie to pop into his shop. With nothing else to do, Elsie was glad of the invitation; besides, she always loved visiting her father at work.

Jim Maynard was the proprietor of Brighton Home Stores – Brighton's premier furniture and home furnishings emporium in the centre of town. He had inherited the business from his father and grandfather before him, and was consequently a well-known figure in Brighton. It amused Elsie to see him in a suit and tie – because she knew the truth about him. Outside work, Jim shunned convention more than any of his children (even New Age vegan and self-confirmed Earth Mother, Guin) and, when at home, he was the embodiment of all things alternative. He had lived in a hippy commune for four years in his teens and never quite lost his love of peace, love and tie-dye. The family home was an explosion of colour, each room swathed in jewel-hued Indian fabrics and bright stencilled painted walls. He ate homemade vegetarian meals from hand-thrown pottery plates (made by Guin), burned incense and joss sticks in the living room and kitchen and possessed a penchant for hypnotic sitar music, which was usually floating through the house from one of his many CD players.

Yet at work, Jim Maynard was the model businessman, the only clue to his closet-hippyness being the small gold ring he wore in one ear – something which his well-heeled (and decidedly conventional) customers hardly even noticed. It had been a conscious decision of his when he first took over the business, a sign of respect for his father who had convention stamped through his core like a stick of Brighton rock. And, while Jim would never express it, this work persona defined another side of his character: the dutiful, committed side, which characterised his all-conquering love for and devotion to his daughters.

Elsie loved the family shop – the smell of polish and new fabric mingling with the scent of fresh coffee, which Jim insisted on having available for his customers all day. As a small child she had spent many happy hours watching her father work, pretending that the entire shop with its elegant room displays was her own home. When her mother had deserted the family, Elsie and her sisters had spent even more time in the shop, arriving after school and waiting until closing time to go home with Jim. As they grew up, each was given a Saturday job in the store and, consequently, all three had fallen in love with interior decorating, something that was reflected in all of their homes today.

Elsie often wondered which of them – if any – would one day inherit the shop from their father. Guin was busy building her home, managing her pottery studio and preparing for a family which she planned to expand to at least three children; Daisy had her partnership in the interior design practice and was unlikely to want to trade that in to run a provincial furniture store; which only left Elsie, who right now was more than happy to remain as assistant manager of the ice cream café. Jim appeared unworried by the prospect, however; content instead to see his three girls making their own way in the world.

He was filling in an order form for an elderly customer when Elsie entered. He raised his hand and winked and

Elsie waved back, busying herself by inspecting the new display of cushions by the side of the counter. She loved watching her father interact with his customers. Jim was a natural entertainer, eliciting smiles from the hardest-faced visitor, and this skill had earned him a place on the local town council where he was renowned as a peacemaker in the squabbling ranks.

He escorted the old lady to the door and returned to hug Elsie. 'My, are *you* a sight for sore eyes! How's your day been, darling?'

'Great, actually. It looks like I'm starting a choir.'

Jim's expression clouded until Elsie explained about the song in the beach café and her meeting with Woody, at which point an enormous grin spread across his face.

'Woody Jensen from Hellfinger? Wow, kid, that guy's a legend! And you'll be working with him?'

Elsie gave her father a look. 'I didn't know you were a closet rocker, Dad?'

'Ah, there's plenty you don't know about me, pudding,' he replied, tapping the side of his nose. 'I saw Hellfinger in '88 at Knebworth, the year after "Hard Rockin' Summer" went to number one. Awesome, they were. Such a shame how it all ended for them. Their drummer killed himself while they were touring Japan and it turned out he'd been the glue holding them all together. With him gone, the band began to fall apart. I think they tried to replace Woody as lead singer after their gig in Cologne the following year and that was the final nail in Hellfinger's coffin.'

'Who knew my dad was the font of all things Hellfinger?' Elsie marvelled, ignoring her father's mock offence. 'So, did you want anything particular or just to see your favourite daughter?'

'I *always* love to see you,' he replied, walking across to

the company coffee machine that was steaming away in the small kitchen behind the counter. 'Coffee?'

'Love one, thanks.'

'There you go.' Jim handed her a mug and they moved to a display of two turquoise velvet chaise longues to sit down. 'Now, I hope you aren't going to be angry with me, darling, but I've been thinking about what you said and I've done something I probably shouldn't.'

'Oh?' Amused, she noted her father's sheepish expression. 'Don't worry, Dad, I'm not going to disown you. What have you been up to?'

'Well, I happened to mention your big decision to Marty this morning and, well, we came up with a bit of a plan.'

At that moment, Elsie knew her face belied her feelings at the mention of Jim's business partner. Marty Hogarth had been in business with Jim since the mid-1990s and was the exact opposite in terms of his demeanour, attitude to customers and world-view. Where Jim believed the best of everyone, however misplaced this belief might be, Marty scrutinised the world with a cynical squint, believing that everyone was working to a hidden agenda. But Jim remained firmly fond of Marty, so for his sake Elsie and her sisters remained civil whenever he was in the room. What they said once he *left* was a different matter . . .

'And what did Captain Cynical have to say about that?'

Jim gave her a reproachful stare. 'Now, there's no need for that. Marty is a good man, Elsie – no, he *is*. In any case, he was most supportive of your decision.'

'Really?'

'Yes. You see, he's not as dark as you like to paint him. I told him that you were thinking of dating again and he suggested someone who would be interested to meet you.'

'Ah . . .'

'Now, before you say no, hear me out. Marty's nephew Oliver is a genuinely lovely chap. I've been working with him on the new company website for the past month and we get on like a house on fire. I really think you two might have a lot in common.'

Elsie loved her father completely for his enthusiasm but couldn't stifle the note of dread that sounded in her mind. 'That's a lovely thought, Dad, and I really appreciate it, but I don't know anything about him, so . . .'

Jim folded his hands in his lap. 'I know you don't. That's why he's coming for coffee.'

'When?'

'Any minute.'

'*Dad* . . .'

'I *know* I probably should've asked you first. But Olly said he would pop in today and I knew you wouldn't be busy this afternoon, so I thought . . . Please don't look at me like that, Els, I was only trying to be helpful.'

If someone had asked Elsie which of her family and friends were most likely to attempt a matchmaking coup, her father probably wouldn't have made the list. And yet now she found herself ambushed by him! She was about to respond when the door opened and Jim jumped up.

'This is him, now. Promise me you'll be nice?'

Accepting the inevitable, Elsie nodded. 'Of course I will.' She rose slowly and prepared herself. This was not what she'd had in mind to be doing today. Looking over towards the door, she saw Jim chatting happily with a tall, blond-haired man. He had the relaxed air of someone who had just strolled off the beach, wearing a dark grey hooded sweatshirt, faded jeans and blue Converse trainers. But as he approached, Elsie noticed his smile – broad and friendly

38

– and it instantly reminded her of someone she had known before. An unexpected ball of emotion formed at her throat and she had to momentarily look down at her feet until it passed.

'Elsie, this is Oliver Hogarth, Marty's nephew. Olly, I'd like to introduce you to my daughter, Elsie,' Jim beamed proudly. 'She's assistant manager at an ice cream café in North Laine.'

'Great to meet you, Elsie,' Olly replied, holding out his tanned hand. When Elsie accepted, she noticed how warm his handshake was.

'Nice to meet you, too. Dad was saying you're working on his website?'

Olly smiled. 'Yes, I am. It's been fun, hasn't it, Jim?'

'Indeed it has. Olly is a partner in a very successful web design company, Els, did I tell you? He's *very* talented.'

Way to go on the subtlety, Dad . . .

Olly gave a bashful smile. 'Your dad is too kind. It's something I've done since uni and I'm lucky enough to do it for a living now.'

'Splendid he is at it, too. Now, Olly, can I leave you with my daughter for five minutes? I just have to – erm – *check* something in the stockroom. Won't be a tick!' Jim was so excited by his matchmaking skills that he practically skipped away.

Elsie shook her head. 'You'll have to forgive my father. He doesn't get out much these days. Um – do you want to sit down?'

'Yeah, thanks.'

They sat on the velvet chaise longues and all of a sudden it was as if every sound in the whole furniture store ceased. Elsie smiled politely and desperately racked her brain for something to say. From the slight tension of Olly's smile, it was clear he was doing the same. After a few gut-wrenchingly awful minutes, Olly laughed and relaxed a little.

'Look, shall we start again? I feel as if we've been ambushed and I really wouldn't want you to think I was in on Jim's plan.'

Elsie felt the tension easing in her shoulders. 'Good idea. I'm sorry, the first I heard about you was about five minutes before you arrived.'

'It's cool, honestly. My uncle called me at lunch time and said I should come to see Jim because there was something important he wanted to show me. I didn't realise he meant you.' His laugh was as warm and inviting as his handshake and Elsie instantly liked him for it.

'Let's just forget how we ended up here, then. Would you like a coffee? There's a machine in the staff kitchen – it's not exactly the best in the world, but I can recommend it for providing a talking point during embarrassing meetings?'

He laughed again and slapped his hands on his knees. 'I have a better idea,' he said, rising and walking over to the stockroom door at the back of the shop. Opening it slightly, he called, 'Jim! We're just popping down the road for a coffee. Can we get you anything?'

'No, no, I'm fine,' Jim's disembodied voice came floating through from the stockroom. 'You two have fun!'

Olly returned to Elsie's side and held out his hand. 'Is that OK? I just thought it might be less – er – *intense* if we chatted somewhere else?' While still a little shell-shocked by her sudden introduction to him, Elsie couldn't help feeling intrigued by the easy-natured young man with his handsome face and friendly smile. Accepting his hand to stand up, she called goodbye to Jim and they left the store.

Five minutes later, they were sitting in cosy armchairs in a small café, surrounded by shelves of second-hand books.

Elsie had often walked past BiblioCaff but had never before ventured inside. As she sipped her mocha, she noticed how at home Olly appeared here. The relaxed nature of the café, where fellow customers helped themselves to books from the shelves as they enjoyed coffee and cake, seemed to suit his easy-going appearance.

'I love this place,' he said, stirring chocolate dust into his cappuccino foam. 'I found it about a year ago when my business moved nearby. Can't beat decent coffee and books – the best combination in the world. So, you work in an ice cream café?'

Elsie nodded. 'Sundae & Cher in Gardner Street. It's my friend Cher's business and I'm assistant manager. It's a retro place, so a lot of fun to work there.'

'I've been, actually. A mate of mine is a particular devotee of the Cream Tea ice cream – the one with the bits of real scone and strawberry jam in it?'

'Ah, one of our bestsellers, that is.'

'I'm not surprised. The way Cam goes on about it you'd think it was elixir from the gods. We go kitesurfing together at weekends and he always insists on an ice cream when we get back into town. That's what I've been doing this morning, as a matter of fact. Hence the . . .' He pulled the front of his hoodie to indicate his clothing. 'I usually try to smarten myself up for work, of course.'

Elsie laughed. 'Oh I don't know, I think the "cool surfer dude" look for business is highly underrated.'

'Why, thank you.' Olly's green eyes twinkled and to Elsie's surprise she felt a slow blush claiming her cheeks.

'You're welcome.'

'Can I interest you in a sample of our coffee and walnut cake?' a waitress asked beside them, the suddenness of her arrival making them both jump a little.

Olly accepted but Elsie refused, her stomach suddenly tight. Once the waitress had moved to the next table, Olly took a sip of coffee and appeared to be selecting his words carefully.

'It really is good to meet you. I mean that. Look, this might be a bit forward, so feel free to tell me to get lost, but I was just wondering if you might like to do coffee with me again sometime? I'm usually free on Saturday afternoons. You know, if you happen to be in town and at a loose end.'

Elsie considered his suggestion for a moment. The thought of dating again – now that it was a distinct possibility and not just a theoretical decision – was scary in the extreme. But then Olly wasn't really asking her on a date, was he? He was interesting, witty and intelligent, possessed a similar sense of humour to hers and was undeniably good-looking: surely meeting him occasionally for coffee wouldn't hurt? Elsie had to admit she was enjoying his company and the prospect of more of it was very appealing. This week's note had insisted she was fearless: perhaps this was as good a time as any to take a risk . . .

'Yes. I'd love to.'

CHAPTER FOUR

Altogether now . . .

'You have a *date*!'

'I do *not*. All I said was that I might meet him for coffee. It's hardly an acceptance of marriage, is it?'

Daisy was unremitting in her delight, dancing around the chic kitchen of her expensive Hove apartment. 'I'm so proud of you, Els! And of Dad, too – who knew he was such a matchmaker, eh?'

Elsie sighed as she swirled a jasmine teabag around in her mug by its string. 'I shouldn't have told you. I knew you'd react like this.'

Daisy came to a breathless halt and flopped onto a high stool by the glass breakfast bar. 'But he's gorgeous, right?'

Elsie shrugged. 'He's nice-looking I suppose.'

'Good. That's good, isn't it?'

'Yes, it's good. Now can we talk about the choir, please?'

Daisy groaned. 'We can. But I need a favour first.'

'Go on then, but only if you grovel.'

'You are an evil little sister, Elsie Maynard. Fine, have it your way.' She adopted a pleading expression, folding her perfectly manicured hands in front of her. 'O great and noble sister of mine, I bring but one petition to your door. Grant me an audience in my time of need and do not turn me into the darkness where there will be much weeping and gnashing of teeth.'

Elsie laughed. 'Are you sure you wouldn't rather be an actor than an interior designer? There's still time for a career change.'

'Behave, you.' Daisy made a swipe at her sister. 'Seriously, I need help after the meeting tomorrow evening.'

'Anything for such hammy acting,' Elsie giggled.

'The thing is, I was wondering if you could drive me to Croydon.'

'Croydon? That's a two-hour round trip!'

Daisy gave an apologetic smile. 'I know, and ordinarily I wouldn't bother but I'm doing a pitch for a potentially massive client account on Friday and we need to style a concept room. It's all a little last-minute but there's a particular type of look we're going for. So I need to visit . . .' she lowered her voice, as if she was about to divulge some potentially dangerous information '. . . a *certain* Scandinavian home furnishing store.'

Highly amused by her sister's admission, Elsie feigned shock. 'Daisy! *No!*'

'I know.'

'Whatever would Dad say if he knew you were patronising *that* place?'

Daisy visibly paled. '*Promise me* you won't tell him? I can hardly believe I'm heading there myself. The thing is, my car's out of action all week – the re-spray the garage did when I hit that bollard last month wasn't satisfactory, so I told them I expected it to be rectified. I think I scared them sufficiently to do a proper job this time. You know I wouldn't ask unless it was really necessary. Please?'

'No problem,' Elsie replied, seeing the relief on her sister's face. 'But I hope you realise you'll owe me. For a *long* time . . .'

Daisy hugged her. 'I'll find a way of repaying you, don't worry.'

On Wednesday evening, when the last customer made a reluctant exit from the delights of Sundae & Cher, Elsie flicked the Open sign to Closed and headed to the kitchen where Cher was busy going through her order sheets for the next day.

'Last one out?' Cher asked, nibbling on a teddy-shaped wafer as she worked.

'Finally. I think Mrs Annick has almost managed to demolish the tub of Sticky Toffee Pudding ice cream single-handedly this week. And she always looks so crestfallen when I tell her we're closing. I think she'd quite like to live here if she could.'

Cher's throaty laugh ricocheted around the lemon-yellow kitchen tiles. 'Obviously I'm missing a trick there. I should make the place an ice cream B&B.' She cast a critical eye over Elsie. 'You OK, kid?'

Elsie rubbed her forehead and drew a chair up to the preparation table. 'A bit tired, but otherwise I'm good.'

It was only a partial truth, but the rest of it was difficult to put into words. Ever the pragmatist, Elsie had put it down to all the new things that were happening in her life and the significant decisions she was making, all of which were bound to carry an emotional cost. Being able to look objectively at everything was a step forward in itself – eighteen months ago her view of the future had been mark-edly different. So, while she would admit to feeling more than a little apprehensive about meeting Daisy and Woody this evening to set the wheels of the choir project in motion, it was a good thing. 'A little bit of fear can get you moving forward,' her father always said, himself not immune to the unexpected twists and turns of life.

'What time are the others turning up?'

Elsie checked her watch. 'In about ten minutes. Right, what do you want me to do before they arrive?'

Cher dismissed the suggestion with a wave of her scarlet-painted nails. 'Don't you worry about that. Pop the kettle on and let's have a cuppa. Mine's a Rooibos, please.'

Elsie smiled. 'Yes, boss.' She flicked the switch on the kettle and fetched one Rooibos teabag for Cher and a peppermint teabag for herself. 'Thanks for letting us meet here this evening, hun. I didn't trust Daisy in a pub setting. One glass of red wine and she'd be likely to tell Woody exactly what she thought of him: the choir would be over before we'd even started.'

'Not his biggest fan, eh?'

'You could say that.'

Cher stretched and pushed her order sheets away. 'I might hang about and meet this famous Woody, then. If he can wind your perfect sister up that much then I'm intrigued.'

Elsie handed Cher a mug of tea. 'Be my guest. In fact, I can sign you up as our first official member if you fancy it?'

'No fear,' Cher snorted. 'My loopy mother might've named me after a singer but that's as far as the association goes. My voice could curdle our entire stock.'

Daisy was on time, of course. Despite the fact that she had worked a long day, she looked fresher than Elsie did first thing in the morning, dressed in a well-cut grey trouser suit, her long blonde hair swept to one side in a low pony-tail and one of her many pashmina scarves draped expertly

46

around her shoulders. For the umpteenth time, Elsie marvelled at her older sister. No wonder she had reputedly left a string of broken hearts across Brighton and beyond during her twenty-eight years on the planet: Daisy Maynard was one of life's beautiful people. Not that she realised it, of course. But then that was one of her most endearing qualities. Her partner André, while not the most demonstrative of men, had said as much to Elsie when she had last seen him, at Jim's birthday party a couple of months ago:

'She's stunning. Every day I wake up beside her I'm amazed she can't see it.'

Daisy's choice of partner had been the source of great consternation to her father, especially when he knew how often they were apart, but André's successful business life seemed to suit Daisy's strong independence and somehow they made the relationship work. Recently, however, Elsie had detected a tiny note of dissatisfaction creeping into Daisy's comments about her boyfriend. Perhaps she was beginning to want more – but, as with most things in her life, she was remaining tight-lipped.

Elsie was closer to Daisy than she was to Guin, largely because she had idolised her eldest sister for as long as she could remember, but also because, with their mother out of the picture during most of her childhood, Daisy had assumed an almost maternal role in the Maynard household. Now they were simply best friends who happened to be siblings, and Elsie was fiercely proud of their relationship.

'I take it our former rock star hasn't arrived yet?' Daisy asked, already prepared for battle.

'He'll be here.'

'Hmm.' She sat down at one of the tables and produced an expensive Moleskine notebook from her handbag. 'Maybe it would be better for all of us if he didn't bother.'

Irritated, Elsie sat opposite her sister. 'I told you that you didn't have to be here this evening. I don't expect you to hold my hand, you know. Besides, Cher's in the kitchen – any trouble from Captain Hellfinger and she'll manhandle him off the premises.'

Daisy had to smile at the mental picture of retro Cher ejecting the rocker from her ice cream café. At that moment, the brass bell above the door jangled to herald Woody's arrival. He stopped in the doorway, looked up and nodded sagely at the bell.

'Cool. For whom the bell tolls, yeah?' He walked over to Elsie, grabbed her hand and blessed it with a bristly kiss. 'Angel.'

'Hi, Woody. Great you could make it.'

He nodded again, his eyes making a considered survey of the café interior from behind his sunglasses as he shrugged off his fringed black leather jacket to reveal a faded grey Mötley Crüe T-shirt beneath. 'Good vibe here. I sense the satisfied souls of generations, man. Ice cream is a great healer of hearts and hurts.'

'It certainly is.' Cher had entered from the kitchen and was observing Woody with a wry smile. 'I'm Cher Pettinger. I own this place.'

With one move, Woody removed his sunglasses, hooked them over the back pocket of his jeans and slid across the harlequin tiles to Cher's side, his eyes eagerly drinking in the sight of her enviable figure in her low-cut white blouse and turquoise circle skirt with matching heels. 'Then you must be an angelic visitation into this poor rocker's life. If your wares are as inspirational as your establishment, I wouldn't mind sampling them.'

Cher lowered her false eyelashes and purred, 'Easy, tiger.'

Daisy rolled her eyes heavenwards and picked up her pen.

'Much as I hate to break up the party, can I suggest we get started? Els and I have to go to Croydon straight after this meeting.'

'Croydon? Who goes to Croydon for anything?' Woody frowned but Daisy's interruption had achieved its purpose, bringing him back to the table.

'Thank you. Now I think we should discuss what we're trying to achieve with this choir. What songs will we sing? Are we forming for a particular performance opportunity or simply as a social gathering?' Daisy looked up from her list at Elsie and Woody's bemused expressions. 'What?'

Elsie placed her hand gently on Daisy's. 'This is Woody's vision. And I'm helping him with it. You're here for moral support, remember?'

'Well, I was only trying to help . . .'

'I know and, believe me, you're being a great help. Lots of important things to consider there, which we will, *after* we've heard what Woody has to say.'

Open-mouthed, but remembering that Elsie stood between her and the questionable Swedish home décor she needed for work, Daisy folded her arms and nodded at Woody.

'Good girl,' he grinned, oblivious to the killer death stare Daisy shot back. 'This choir – and I don't even want to call it a choir because it's more like a meeting of musical minds – it needs to be *meaningful*, yeah? None of that *Ave Maria* shizzle. No offence, Daisy, if you like that kinda stuff. I'm just working to a higher calling. We're gonna represent the greats – bestowing their music on this generation so the legends live on in hearts and minds. We'll be like undercover agents for the forces of music: choir ninjas, if you will. We'll strike fast and hard, leaving minds reeling with musical missiles, man. It'll be a spiritual awakening for the masses, through the medium of musical mash-ups. So whaddya say?'

Elsie didn't really know how to respond. Woody's vision didn't sound like any choir she'd ever encountered – more like an underground resistance movement than a group of people getting together to enjoy singing songs. It was immediately obvious to her what she could bring to the table in this partnership: sanity, mostly.

'It all sounds very impressive. But to get to where you want this to be, I think we need a more – um – *practical* strategy. What type of people are we looking for to be part of this? And, perhaps most importantly, where are we going to rehearse? I called a couple of church halls and community centres today and I have to say it's not looking promising. Those that aren't booked up completely during the week are either too far out of town or ridiculously expensive.'

Woody looked as if he had just lost the award for Best Band 1984 to Black Lace. 'But this thing has *gotta* happen, Elsie! I *saw* it in my dream . . .'

'How many people do you think you're looking for?' asked Cher.

'It depends who responds when we put the call out for singers,' Elsie replied. 'We can try to get a story in the local papers and I thought I'd make some posters and see if I can get the shops and pubs in North Laine to display them. My guess is we'll probably get five or six people to begin with.'

'So meet here,' Cher suggested. 'I presume you have a keyboard or something you can bring?'

Elsie nodded, thrilled at Cher's kind suggestion. But not as thrilled as Woody Jensen was. For at that very moment he had leapt from his chair and scooped Elsie's boss into a dramatic Hollywood clinch, as Daisy looked on in sheer horror. Breathless and laughing, Cher broke free from Woody's embrace and straightened her blouse.

'Blimey, if that's the reception I get for offering you a venue for the choir, I'd like to see what happens when I offer you something you really need.'

Woody's grin was pure lechery. 'Stay around for long enough and you might find out, treacle.'

Cher winked at Elsie. 'Ooh, I like this one. You can bring *him* again!'

An hour later, as Elsie and Daisy drove towards Croydon, Daisy was still struggling to cope with the outrageous flirting she'd witnessed.

'Talk about *overt*. I thought they were going to ignore us completely and just go *at it* right in the middle of the café,' she shuddered.

Keeping her eyes on the building traffic ahead, Elsie smiled. 'I thought it was sweet.'

'It was *obscene*. I'm not surprised he acted that way but I would've thought Cher had more sense.'

'It was nice to see her having fun,' Elsie replied. 'She's had a bit of a rough run lately with her latest flame.'

Daisy tutted and stared out of the passenger window. 'And she thinks *that man* is going to be any better? Well I'm glad I was with you. Who knows what kind of moves he might have pulled on *you* otherwise? You know what they say about rock'n'roll stars and their *liberal* behaviour . . .'

The traffic lights ahead changed to red and the car came to a halt in a long line of early evening traffic. Elsie let out a sigh and turned to her sister.

'Dais, you're going to have to find something to like about Woody if you want to be a part of this choir project. Or else it might be best for you to bow out now.'

Her sister stared at her. 'Is that what you want?'

The traffic inched forwards, anticipating the signal change.

'Of course it's not. But I also don't want to have a battle raging between the two of you. The choir is meant to be fun, remember? Either sort it out or don't be involved.'

The green light framed Elsie's flint-like expression as the car pulled away from the junction. For a long time, neither sister spoke, the only sound the robotic tones of the sat-nav lady.

'*In. Point-five miles. Turn. Left. On. Beddington Farm Road. Then. Turn. Right.*'

The familiar yellow and blue warehouse came into view and Daisy took the opportunity to break the silence. 'Looks like we're here.'

'*Arriving. At. C-R-0. 4-U-Z.*'

'It would seem we are.'

'Els, look, I'm sorry. He just seems to bring out the worst in me. But I'll try to get on with him, I do want to be involved in this project.'

Elsie reached across and patted her sister's knee. 'Then that's good to hear.' She surveyed the busy car park before them. 'My life, I wasn't expecting it to be this busy.'

The vast car park sprawled around the superstore was heaving with cars as they crawled at a snail's pace along the rows. Some vehicles had clearly given up looking for actual spaces and were jacked up at awkward angles on the surrounding pavements, while others lurked ominously behind parked cars with open boots being packed by grim-faced shoppers. It was every person for themselves today it seemed, a reality quite at odds with the relaxed Scandinavian images the chain displayed on its enormous billboard signs across the car park.

'Maybe we should have set off earlier,' Daisy mumbled, the smallest hint of panic beginning to sound in her voice.

'We'll find a space, don't worry,' Elsie assured her,

scouting the lines of parked cars ahead for any glimpse of a departing vehicle or vacant space.

'I beg to differ. This is worse than Christmas.'

'We'll *find* one,' Elsie repeated. Suddenly, she saw it: at the end of the row, barely visible behind the boot of a tank-like four-by-four. But it was a *space* . . . Putting her foot down, Elsie sped towards it and practically handbrake-turned her car in. Flushed with pride at her daredevil parking skills, she whooped loudly and turned to a pale-faced Daisy, just as a car horn blared loudly behind her.

'Did you see that? Am I the Queen of Parking Space Spotting or what? Daisy? What's wrong?'

'I think that car was waiting.' Daisy nodded towards a sleek black Jaguar that was furiously screeching away.

Elsie was unrepentant. 'Their fault for not claiming it quickly enough.'

'But they were indicating . . .'

'Daisy. You wanted to come to this highly questionable home store – despite what Dad would say if he ever found out – and if I hadn't parked in this space we could well have not been able to stay. It was a genuine mistake on my part. I didn't see there was a car waiting. But this kind of thing happens all the time, so stop worrying and let's go inside, OK?'

Reservations thus laid to rest, Daisy agreed and they stepped out of the car.

'That was a pretty nifty bit of parking, I'll give you that.'

Elsie locked the door and grinned at her sister. 'High speed stunt-parking is one of my many specialities.'

'Oi! You should drive with your eyes open, love,' an angry voice shouted behind them. Elsie and Daisy turned to see a man storming in their direction. Never a fan of confrontation, Daisy groaned and hurried quickly towards the store entrance. Elsie made to follow, then froze as the features of the fuming figure came into view. *Oh no. Surely not . . .*

At exactly the same time, the man recognised Elsie and skidded to a halt inches away from her. 'You!'

'I don't believe this.'

'Un-be-*lievable*!'

Elsie sighed and stared at him. 'I didn't realise you were waiting, OK? I'm sorry.'

'You're sorry.'

'Yes, I am.'

'But you still stole *my* space.'

'Your space? Oh, forgive me, I didn't see *"Torin's Space"* painted across the piece of public tarmac I just parked in.'

Torin raised an eyebrow. 'So, you remembered my name?'

Irritated, Elsie folded her arms. 'I happen to have an excellent memory.'

'So do I, *Elsie Maynard*. Man, it seems like you just can't keep away from me, doesn't it? First that awkward incident with your pile cream and now this . . .'

'Whatever.' Elsie had heard enough. Her blood boiling, she slung her handbag on her shoulder and headed quickly towards the entrance to the store.

'This isn't the end of this,' Torin called after her, an annoying chime of amusement in his voice that made her cringe even more. 'Mark my words!'

Reaching the vast entrance where Daisy was waiting, Elsie virtually yanked her sister up the escalator into the shop. 'Do you have your list? Good. Let's find what you need and get out of here as soon as possible.'

As they raced around the room layouts, Elsie was aware that Daisy was staring at her. When she was sure they had gained enough distance from Torin (who was no doubt following in their wake), Elsie came to a halt by a bright purple kitchen display.

'You're never going to believe this,' she said, her breath shortened by their speedy circuit of the shop floor, 'but that was *him*.'

'Him who?'

'The bloke – the one who was there when the *stealing* thing happened – the annoying one I was telling you about.'

Daisy's eyes were wider than the glossy white dinner plates artfully arranged on the black granite worktop beside them. 'No!'

'Yes. And he wasn't particularly impressed with my parking.'

'Well I never. How funny! You have to laugh at this, Els, I mean, what are the chances of us driving forty-three miles and you bumping into the same guy?'

Elsie sank onto a black plastic bar stool by the breakfast area mock-up. 'It beggars belief,' she replied, willing her heart rate to slow. 'He wasn't happy, I can tell you.'

'I could see that – oh, watch out, Els, he's coming!'

Horrified, Elsie looked across the store to see Torin walking quickly past the living room layouts. Grabbing Daisy, she ducked down behind the breakfast bar and peered around the side as he approached.

'What do you think you're doing?' Daisy protested, yelping when Elsie jabbed her in the ribs with her elbow. '*Shh!*'

'Elsie, we're *hiding* in a kitchen display . . .'

'I know!' Elsie hissed back. 'We're just waiting until he goes past. Then he'll be following the arrows like all the other shoppers and we'll be sufficiently behind him.'

Daisy shot her an incredulous look. 'You're mad, you realise that?'

Elsie ignored her sister's amusement and waited until Torin was out of sight. When she was satisfied he had gone, she rose slowly to her feet, coming face to face with a very bemused store assistant.

'Er – do you need any help?' he asked, his acne-strewn brow furrowing.

Adopting her brightest, most innocent smile, Elsie patted the beechwood-effect top of the breakfast bar. 'Excellent workmanship. Truly. Even at floor level, you can see the quality.' With Daisy in tow, she maintained her grin until they were clear of the kitchen display and out in the space of the walkway once more.

Daisy laughed, 'Shopping with you is never dull.' She pulled a typed list from her bag. 'We'd better find these items before there's any more excitement.'

So they continued circumnavigating the store, with Daisy taking her time to select cushions, vases, table lamps and rugs, while Elsie kept a vigilant eye out for any sign of Torin. For the next twenty minutes, he was nowhere to be seen and she began to relax.

Despite her merciless mocking of Daisy about this contro-versial visit, she relished the opportunity to spend time with her sister. Watching Daisy at work was fascinating. The items she selected – most of which Elsie would have walked straight past – created an eye-catching mix in her yellow woven plastic store bag. It was so much fun to watch that Elsie completely forgot her irritation at seeing Torin again.

But then, it was as if a switch flicked and suddenly he was *everywhere*. Twice they had to duck into room displays, several times behind affordably priced sofas and even once into a mock shower cubicle when he was spotted in the vicinity. Feeling her hackles rising, Elsie made a momentous decision that shocked her sister even more than her recent revelation about dating again:

'Right. We're going *against the arrows*.'

'But you're meant to follow the arrows, Els! It's what you do when you come here. It's *understood*.'

Eyes wild with panicked determination, Elsie faced her. 'I am *not* bumping into that man again, you hear me? I'm tired, we have an hour's journey home and I really don't want another awkward confrontation today.'

Much to the consternation of the shoppers behind them, Elsie and Daisy began to pick their way back, finding the recklessness of the act surprisingly liberating. They had almost reached the stairs to the ground floor when someone stepped into their path from behind a ceiling height advertising hoarding – and Elsie's heart hit the floor.

'Funny. I never pictured you as an "against the arrows" kind of girl.' Torin's green eyes were sparkling like the crystal lampshade over his head, the same half-amused smile playing on his lips.

Daisy was looking from Torin to Elsie and back like an overexcited Wimbledon spectator.

Elsie closed her eyes. '*Please* go away.'

He laughed – a sound that made all of Elsie's defences instantly build. 'Oh come on, you nicked my parking space. At the very least that should win me some gloating rights?'

Daisy nudged her. 'That seems fair to me, Els.'

Elsie stared at her sister. 'Thanks for nothing.'

Surprised, Torin held his hand out to Daisy. '*Thank you*. I'm Torin Stewart.'

'Daisy Maynard. I'm Elsie's sister.'

They shook hands, Torin holding Daisy's for a moment longer than she was expecting.

'Ah, a pleasure to meet another of the Maynard clan,' he said, glancing sideways at Elsie. 'Especially a *polite* one.'

Daisy ignored the muttered remark from Elsie and smiled back at Torin. 'Oh, Elsie's usually the picture of politeness. I guess there must be something about you that brings out her bad side.'

'Oh and I expect you know all about that, being her sister?'

'You'd be *amazed* at the stories I could tell you . . .'

They're enjoying this, Elsie moaned to herself, *they're both flipping enjoying it*. 'Pleasant though this attack on my character is for both of you, we really should be going.'

Daisy shook her head. 'No hurry, hun.' She smiled her famous Daisy Maynard Smile™ at Torin – the one that had set many a man on a course towards heartbreak over the years – and Elsie knew this was far from over. 'Actually, we were thinking of having a coffee before we head home. Don't suppose we could tempt you to join us? As our way of apologising for the car park incident?'

Torin looked at Elsie, who averted her eyes. Right now all she wanted was to leave as soon as she could. Her expression must have betrayed her true feelings because, quite unexpectedly, Torin declined.

'I'd love to, but I'm on a bit of a tight schedule. It was good to meet you, Daisy. Elsie, nice to see you again. I hope you find everything you're looking for. Good evening.'

Elsie watched him walk away and, for the second time in as many weeks, felt the small pang of conscience in her stomach. Shaking it away, she faced Daisy.

'Thanks for the help there, sis.'

'I'm sorry, he just seemed like a really nice guy. I was *trying* to be polite . . . Oh, don't look at me like that. It was an awkward situation and I thought maybe if we all sat down over coffee it might be a little less so.'

'Believe me, it would have been a hundred times worse. He is the most arrogant, jumped-up individual I've ever had the misfortune to run into. *Twice* now.'

Daisy nudged Elsie's arm. 'My mistake, lovely. He did seem to be a little too pleased with himself, now you mention it. Let's pay for this contraband and get the heck out of here, shall we?'

Two days later, Jim called Elsie at work and asked her to meet him at his house for tea. Always a fan of a Dad-cooked meal, Elsie was happy to oblige, heading straight over when her workday ended.

The most delicious aroma of cinnamon, onions, rosemary and pomegranate filled the kitchen when Elsie entered. In the middle of an industrious cloud of steam, Jim emerged, carrying a huge earthenware tagine.

'We're going Moroccan tonight!' he announced, holding the pot aloft as if it was a sporting trophy. 'There's a bowl of couscous on the counter and a nice bottle of Chilean red. Be a dear and bring them over, would you?'

'It smells amazing, Dad. New recipe?'

Jim set two places at the table and accepted a glass of wine from her. 'Yep. Excellent Moroccan cookbook I bought from that second-hand bookshop café Olly loves so much. In fact, I was having coffee with him when he spotted it.' His awful attempt at slipping this into the conversation made Elsie giggle.

'Dad. That was terrible.'

Jim's face fell. 'I thought I was being subtle.'

'No offence, but perhaps you'd better stick to cooking?'

'Point taken. Sit, sit! We should have this while it's hot.

Preserved lemon? Found these in a wonderful deli that's opened near the Theatre Royal.'

'You're such a foodie.'

Pleased by this, Jim winked at her. 'Next stop *MasterChef*, eh?' He served the aromatic vegetable stew and handed her a multi-coloured plate. 'Now, tell me what you think.'

It was wonderful – warm, spicy flavours that made Elsie's palate tingle and reminded her of a holiday they had taken to Marrakech when she was fourteen, Jim determined that his daughters should have every opportunity to visit new and exciting cultures. She could still remember his brave but ultimately fruitless attempts at bartering over a rug in the souk, as the sights, sounds and smells of the bustling market laid siege to their senses.

She had to hand it to Jim: he was a tremendous cook. But more than the chance to sample his excellent food, Elsie relished the opportunity to spend time with her father. The past two years of her life had often demanded her attention to the point where she had neglected time with her family; only now was she feeling like she was reclaiming some of it. Growing up as one of three siblings, with the added complication of her mother's absence, time alone with her father had always been invaluable; even now, as each of the Maynard sisters lived out their lives, Jim's time was divided. A fair man in everything, he tried to give each of them an equal portion of his attention, although Guin's impending motherhood meant this was likely to change soon.

'So what was it you wanted to tell me?' Elsie asked, when the meal was over and they were sitting in the comfortable lounge watching soft candlelight bathe the walls from the collection of oil burners and pillar candles on the coffee table. Patchouli and lavender incense pervaded the air and

Jim's favourite Bollywood chill-out album provided an exotic soundtrack.

'Ah yes. It's *very* exciting. You know that I'm on the Traders' Association committee for the Brighton Carnival this year?'

Elsie didn't, but this was nothing new. Jim was nothing if not committed to his town.

'Well, I am. Never learn, will I? Anyway, the point is, we were discussing community music for the street stage we're sponsoring and I suggested your choir! I told them how much of a community endeavour it's going to be, and they thought it was a fantastic idea! What do you think?'

'I think it's great, Dad, but don't you think it might be better to wait and hear the choir we put together before you start booking us?'

'It's not till July, so there's plenty of time to prepare for it.' Jim hugged her. 'I have every faith in you.'

Whether or not the choir would be able to take up Jim's offer, Elsie was encouraged by the vote of confidence. She walked the streets of Brighton delivering choir recruitment posters to local businesses, handed out leaflets to customers at Sundae & Cher and persuaded a journalist at the local free paper to write a story, thus saving her the expense of placing an advert. She and Woody discussed their plans at length, determined to create something that stood out from the other choirs in the area.

'It'll be fun and inclusive, more than anything.'

'Babe – we can't lose. We'll be the only choir with destiny on our side.'

'And we'll make the songs interesting and different. Try to avoid some of the choir clichés and create a repertoire

61

that they *want* to sing.' Elsie hesitated, as a thought occurred. 'People *will* come, won't they?'

Woody's conviction was Jedi-like. 'If we ask them, they will come.'

The day of the widely advertised first choir meeting arrived, and Elsie spent most of it wrestling with nerves and trying her best not to dwell on the possible outcomes for the evening. It was as if she was at the edge of a tall precipice, her toes dangling over a two-thousand-foot sheer drop, waiting to take a step of faith: thrilling and utterly terrifying in equal measure.

Daisy arrived a little after seven that evening, with an unapologetic Woody appearing twenty minutes later.

'I was seeking inspiration,' he shrugged. 'You can't rush that.'

By eight, Elsie was trying not to check her watch, Daisy was pacing the floor and even Woody was beginning to show signs of apprehension.

'What time was on the posters?' Cher asked.

'Seven-thirty,' Daisy and Woody chorused.

'Ah.' She looked uneasy. 'Perhaps they're caught in traffic. Wednesday nights, you know . . .' Unconvinced by her own argument, she fell silent.

'Nerves, man. That's what it is. Deep down the whole town knows this choir is about to shake the establishment.'

'It's a choir, Woody, not a political movement.'

Woody regarded Daisy with disdain. 'So you say.'

Daisy ignored him. 'This is ridiculous. They're not coming, Els. Let's just call it a night.'

Elsie considered the disheartened group. Part of her wanted to pack up and go home, but she had been so sure people would respond – surely that level of certainty counted for something?' 'You can go, if you like. I'm going to wait to see if anyone turns up.'

'Suit yourself. If you don't mind, I'll head off.' Daisy picked up her coat.

'Yeah, you go, girl,' Woody replied. 'Leave the believers keeping the dream alive.'

Incensed, Daisy pointedly dropped her coat over the back of a chair and sat down again. 'Then I'm staying, too.'

Elsie groaned and stepped outside, leaving the Mexican standoff in the ice cream café behind her. The early-April evening was clear and a slight breeze sent goosebumps along her arms as she gazed up the quiet street. While she didn't want to admit it to the group inside, she could feel her optimism fading like the light in the early evening sky above. Maybe the venue was wrong, or the night of the week? She shivered as a gust of wind whipped along Gardner Street. If there was one thing that could be said about her, she reminded herself, it was that Elsie Maynard wasn't a quitter. This was, she told herself, merely a blip. It may not be the establishment-rocking, quasi-revolutionary idea that Woody seemed to think it was, but starting this choir was something she wanted to do. Therefore, she *had* to find a way to make it happen . . .

'Am I too late?'

Elsie turned her head to see a tall figure approaching. As the light from the café window illuminated his face she felt her heart lift.

'Olly! I'm so pleased to see you.'

Olly's smile was easy and completely welcome. 'That's the best reception I've had all day. So, how's it going?'

Elsie's shoulders dropped. 'It's not. The only people here are my sister, my boss and Woody.'

'Ah.'

'I know. But now you're here, so that's a step in the right direction.'

'Mmm. Only *slight* problem is that I can't stay, I'm afraid. I was on my way to a family thing and thought I'd look in.'

The bright glimmer of hope in Elsie's heart spluttered out. 'Oh, I see. Thank you, though – for thinking of me.'

His brow furrowed and he held up his hand. 'Wait there.'

Elsie watched as he raced off, ducking into a doorway about fifty yards down the street. Taken aback, Elsie remained obediently outside the shop, pulling her thin cardigan around her shoulders to ward off the evening chill. For a full five minutes, she waited, peering in the direction Olly had disappeared for any sign of his return. Finally, just as the tips of her fingers were beginning to numb, a shaft of light flooded into the street from the doorway and Olly stepped out, accompanied by five others. Elsie could hear their excited conversation as the group approached.

'Here you are: choir volunteers!' he announced happily.

'But how did you . . .? Where . . .?'

Olly dismissed her questions. 'Doesn't matter. You can buy me coffee when we meet on Saturday.'

Elsie frowned. 'Which Saturday?'

'Whichever Saturday you like. As long as it's *soon*. Not saying you owe me or anything but . . .' he indicated the small group of people around him. 'Deal?'

It was impossible not to smile at his brazen cheek. 'Fine, deal.'

'Excellent. I'll call you. Now, don't you have a rehearsal to run?' With a grin so wide it would make the Cheshire Cat envious, he left Elsie on the street surrounded by the volunteers. She watched him leave, the surprise of this new development tingling through her, before bringing herself back to the present and ushering the group inside.

Daisy and Woody's faces were a picture when she appeared with the new choir members and they sprang into action, shaking hands, taking names and contact details and arranging the chairs into a circle in the middle of the room. The first members of the choir were a diverse group of people indeed: nineteen-year-old Danny Alden and his bird-like girlfriend Aoife McVey; self-assured twenty-nine-year-old Sasha Mitchell; fifty-something taxi driver Stan Goodson and quiet pensioner Irene Quinn. It transpired that they had all been drinking in the pub at the end of the street when Olly had burst in and silenced the patrons with an impassioned appeal for choir members. Whether he had offered anything in return was unclear, although Elsie suspected money might have been placed behind the bar to quench the thirst of potential volunteers. But it didn't matter – whatever his modus operandi, Elsie was immensely thankful for Olly's assistance and, she had to admit, more than a little thrilled by it.

Once the group had assembled and had been furnished with coffee by Cher, Elsie motioned for the meeting to begin.

'Thank you all, so much, for being here this evening. I know that none of you were expecting to join a choir today.'

A ripple of laughter passed around the room.

'But let me explain why I think this project will work. Firstly, there are no auditions, no prerequisites for joining and no charge for being a choir member. We'll all decide the songs we want to sing and try to include something for everyone. The most important thing for me is to create something we can all be a part of and enjoy. All I need from you, if you're interested, is enthusiasm. Everything else will come along the way.'

Woody coughed loudly, causing all eyes to turn towards him.

Elsie took the hint. 'I won't be doing this alone. Ladies and gentlemen, may I present Woody Jensen . . .'

The assembled group murmured their hellos as Woody stood, his Matrix-style leather coat and skull T-shirt beneath giving him what he hoped was a suitably imposing appearance. Silver chains jangled at his wrists as he raised both hands in a red carpet greeting. 'Greetings. You may remember me from the hit Eighties rock band, Hellfinger?'

Daisy stifled a giggle at the uniformly blank looks that met this question.

'No bother, you can Google me later. I'm proud to say this choir was my idea and the universe itself sent me this wonderful woman to be a minstrel to my musical wizardry. Together, friends, we can shake the very foundations of this town, infuse the collective psyches of the people with mystical tunes and bring power back to the proletariat through the medium of music . . .'

'. . . Or just have a lot of fun making music,' Elsie added quickly, noting the relief on several of the group's faces.

Woody nodded. 'Well, yeah, that too.'

'Does that sound good?'

Danny raised his hand. 'Could we do some up-to-date stuff? I was part of The DreamTeam for six months and the most modern thing we did was "Mr Postman" by The Carpenters.'

Sasha sniggered. 'Talk about lame. I vote we do Gaga.'

'Gaga is *great*, man! We can mash her up with Led Zep or Hendrix . . .' Woody's grey eyes were alive as a million musical possibilities flashed before him.

'We can do whatever you want,' Elsie said, trying her best to rein Woody in. 'It's important that we find music we all like and have fun performing it.'

Stan raised his hand. 'Well, you can count me in, girl. I

love a bit of warbling, me.' He nudged Irene, who was sitting beside him. 'What d'ya reckon, Reenie? Up for showing these whippersnappers how it's done?'

Irene smiled but said nothing, her downy cheeks turning the tiniest bit pink.

'Don't let her fool you,' Stan said. 'Irene used to be on the stage, back in the day. One of Brighton's finest, she was. Sang with Vera Lynn on a concert tour for the troops in Canada at the end of the war when she was just seventeen.' He patted her knee. 'Bit of a hoofer in your day, weren't you, girl?'

'Stop it, Stanley,' she replied, and Elsie noticed how bright her eyes shone as she smiled. 'I haven't sung for years.'

'It doesn't matter. It'll be good to have another Brighton great in our ranks,' Daisy remarked, pointedly nodding at Woody.

'So what happens now?' Aoife asked, the sudden arrival of her voice surprising everyone in the room.

Elsie shrugged. 'It's really up to you all. I suppose the first thing is to find an evening to meet that suits everybody and then we start work proper next week.'

After much discussion – and several random veerings off-course with Woody's Hellfinger references – Wednesday evenings were deemed to be perfect for choir rehearsals, and the inaugural meeting of the choir came to an end.

Elsie thanked them as they began to leave, wondering how many would return the following week.

'It sounds like a bit of a laugh,' Sasha said at the door, long false eyelashes fluttering beneath her razor-sharp, bleached-blonde fringe. 'Will we be able to do solos and stuff? Only people say I have a bit of a solo voice.'

Elsie shrugged. 'I don't see why not. This choir can be whatever we want it to be.'

'Sweet. See you next Wednesday.'

Stan and Irene shook Elsie's hand. 'Lovely evening,' Irene smiled. 'Most unexpected, but lovely.'

'I hope you're ready for our vocal delights, girl,' chuckled Stan.

'I'm looking forward to experiencing them.'

Daisy joined Elsie by the door as the last of the choir members filed out into the chilly night. 'Do you think that went well?' she asked, clearly not all that convinced that it had.

'I think so. I suppose we'll find out next week.'

Walking home, Elsie took a deep breath and looked up at the starlit sky. The night might not have taken the course she was expecting, but it felt good nevertheless. Positivity seemed to sparkle around her as she walked: the lights from the homes she passed were brighter, the night sky was a beautiful midnight blue and her heart felt lighter than it had for years.

'This choir could well be the making of you, Elsie Maynard,' she said to herself.

CHAPTER FIVE

Hello again, hello . . .

It was still dark when Elsie awoke next morning, pools of light from the streetlights outside her windows pooling in through the half-closed curtains in the bedroom of her Victorian terraced house. The dream from which she had stirred was the same that had brought her to daylight many times before: not a nightmare as such, more a captured moment of time playing on a perennial loop in her subconscious. She had dreamed it so often that it was strangely comforting now, almost reassuring in its reliability. There were never any words, only sensations. Oddly enough, the locations regularly changed, but the essence of the dream remained constant: the touch of a hand on hers followed by a tiny squeeze – barely perceptible to the naked eye but as powerful as a one-hundred-thousand-volt shock. And then, nothing but the feeling of being suspended in a pitch-black void, as if hanging above the earth before the lights of morning appeared. At first, Elsie had been unnerved by the dream but now it was an accepted part of her new life: a last vestige of the past to remind her of how far she had come.

Slowly rising from sleep-tossed sheets, she padded down white wood-stained stairs to her kitchen and leant against the beechwood countertop as the kettle bubbled up into life. She rubbed her eyes and caught sight of the list of possible choir songs she had scribbled on the back of an electricity bill by the phone hours before. Instantly, she felt her heart lift as the thrill of potential struck her like it had last night walking home from the choir meeting.

There was a mixture of material – from well-loved musical numbers to a smattering of recent chart songs and a couple of choir classics she remembered singing at school. Woody had, of course, suggested a few that she had so far success-fully avoided – including an intriguing medley of Blue Oyster Cult 'Don't Fear the Reaper' and Katy Perry's 'I Kissed a Girl', performed to a stomping glam rock-style beat. Something told Elsie that Brighton, however bohemian it liked to appear, wasn't *quite* ready for that musical delight to be unleashed . . .

She made tea in a mug Guin had made for her and smiled as she read the legend in vivid pink paint-strokes surrounded by blue and orange flowers:

Do it, or Elsie!

It was a bad joke, typical of her sister's humour – but this morning it assumed a feeling of greater significance. Taking her tea back upstairs, Elsie sat on the side of her high, iron-framed bed and reached over to pick up the silk-covered box from her bedside table. Lying on top of the pile of papers inside it was the next message:

I love you because you love surprises xx

Not all surprises, Elsie thought. *Some surprises I could live without.* As she sipped her tea, watching the dawn begin to peek over the rooftops of her street, she couldn't have known how timely her thoughts would prove to be . . .

As soon as she arrived at Sundae & Cher, Elsie knew that something was up. For a start, Cher was already in, which was most unlike her, and had uncharacteristically restocked the ice cream cabinet – a job normally reserved for Elsie on account of the fact that Cher disliked lifting the bulky tubs from the freezer. This task completed, Cher now appeared to be pacing the kitchen floor.

Elsie smiled as she entered the kitchen. 'Morning. Is everything OK? Only I didn't think seven-thirty a.m. existed in your vocabulary.'

'It doesn't, usually. But I thought I'd break with tradition today,' she replied, fiddling with a box of sugar sachets and failing in her attempt at nonchalance. 'I had that new batch of Kiwi and Gooseberry to mix downstairs and there's a ton of Cookie Dough waiting for you to work your magic on. Not right now, obviously. Just – um – whenever you're ready.'

'Right.' Frowning slightly, Elsie passed Cher to put her coat and bag in the cupboard by the back door. 'I'm going to check the freezer stock levels downstairs.'

Cher's guilty smile did nothing to remove Elsie's growing suspicion. 'Absolutely. Yes. Great idea.' She paused as if to say something else, then clapped her hands. 'In fact, I'll come down with you.'

'Fine.' Leading the way, Elsie walked to the stairs at the back of the kitchen that led to Sundae & Cher's ice cream lab in the small basement of the café. The smell of vanilla filled the air as she entered the chill of the basement and

Elsie momentarily forgot Cher's strange behaviour as she revelled in the magic of the room. She loved it here: not just because of the sweet aroma or large industrial mixer (the sight of which always brought out the kid in her, reminding her of standing on a stool next to Jim learning how to use the food processor on one of their many Saturday baking sessions), but because this place signified the heart of Sundae & Cher. This was where the magic happened – taking a basic ice cream mix and adding weird and wonderful ingredients to create brand new taste experiences.

She opened the door of the enormous freezer cabinet and began to count the stacked tubs inside. 'Looks like we're running low on Vanilla. We should probably get another batch made today.'

'I'm on it. We can't be running out of our top-selling flavour, can we?'

Elsie lifted out two heavy tubs of pale green gelato. 'Is this the new flavour?'

'Yes. Mixed it earlier. Good, huh?'

'I think this is going to be really popular,' Elsie replied, turning to Cher. 'It might be an idea to put one of them out straight away. Shall I swap it for one of the regular flavours today and see how it sells?'

'Yes. Good. Er – actually, before you do that, there's something you should know . . .'

Elsie ignored the tightening in her stomach. 'Yes?'

'Now don't be mad at me, but I might have just *maybe*, set you up on a date . . .'

'*Cher* . . .'

Cher shrugged apologetically. 'I know, I'm sorry. I just happened to be chatting with an old friend of mine and she mentioned that her brother would be fun for a date – if you were interested, of course.'

'Well, that's very kind of you, but right now I'm not really in a position to . . .'

'Of course. I mean, no pressure, obviously. Although I did tell her that we were going to The Feathers for a drink after work this evening.'

Elsie felt her backbone bristling. 'I might not be able to make it.' She picked up one of the tubs and began to ascend the stairs.

Cher followed her with the other tub, hurried past her in the kitchen and stood across the entrance to the café, blocking Elsie's way. 'Actually, I think you should.' Her forthright assertion was fatally undermined by her uncertain expression.

'You do?'

'Yes.'

'OK. Why?'

Cher sighed. 'Because it would be good for you. And because my friend might have arranged for her brother's boss to be there too, who happens to be rather gorgeous.'

Elsie couldn't believe what she was hearing. 'So you've set us up on a double date?'

'Don't say it like that, Els, you make me sound conniving.'

'Well, maybe that's because you are . . .'

'I really like him. I mean, I think he has serious potential. And I've been trying to score a date with him for over a year.' She lowered her voice and clasped her hands together like a plaster saint. 'He has his *own house*, Elsie! Not like the last one. And his own teeth! He's normal and has no strange hobbies or questionable personal habits. Do you *know* how hard it is to find someone that sane in this town?

Practically impossible! Not to mention the fact that he's successful and interesting and I know he thinks I'm attractive. You know how rubbish my dating life has been. This one is *normal*! So I'm not even going to ask you: I'm going straight to pathetic begging. *Please?'*

Elsie knew she had no choice. If Cher could have the chance to enjoy a normal date for once, perhaps it was worth one uncomfortable evening in presence of a 'someone's brother'.

'I don't have anything to wear,' Elsie replied slowly.

'I'll give you cash to buy an outfit at lunchtime,' Cher answered. 'Shoes too, if you like.'

'I haven't brought my make-up with me.'

'You can borrow mine. Or buy new. *Please?'*

Elsie weighed up her options. 'Fine. But I'm only staying for an hour.'

Cher beamed like a kid at Christmas. 'One hour is all I need.'

The day passed with excruciating tardiness, every minute outstaying its welcome. The more she thought about it, the greater Elsie's dread of what could lie ahead became. By four-thirty, her nerves were beginning to get the better of her, and there was only one person she knew who could help to keep her resolve strong. Leaving Cher manning the counter, Elsie grabbed her mobile and stepped outside. Gardner Street was a buzz of busyness, the warm hum of chat and countless footsteps reverberating the length of the street. She smiled at Emma from the Vegetarian Shoe Shop as they passed one another and watched as a group of Goths crowded with surprising enthusiasm in the doorway of Cybercandy. Smiling to herself, she dialled her sister's number.

'Hello, Daisy Maynard speaking?'

'Daisy, it's me. Can you chat for a minute?'

'No problem. Wait there . . .' Elsie could hear the click-clack of her sister's heels as she walked from her office to somewhere more conducive to a private conversation. 'OK. What's up, lovely?'

Elsie moved to let a dog walker hurry past. 'Cher's set me up on a completely daft double date tonight. I agreed at first but now I'm freaking out about it. I mean, it's too early – I haven't had any time to prepare, or make sure my head is in the right place. What was I thinking? This is the craziest idea. I can't go through with it, can I?'

Daisy's laugh was not unkind. 'Slow down, Speedy Gonzalez! Take a deep breath and let's look at this practically. Where are you meeting the bloke?'

'At The Feathers, this evening.'

'Right, a public place, that's good. So, what do you know about him?'

'Only that Cher fancies his boss, he's a brother of someone she knows and he's supposed to be a nice guy.'

'Anything else? What he does for a living? What he looks like?'

Elsie kicked a screwed-up crisp packet at her feet. 'Nothing. That's the problem, Dais. How on earth am I meant to know whether I have anything in common with him or not?'

'Well, you don't. But that's kind of the point of dating, isn't it? All you are doing is meeting someone who may or may not be interesting enough for you to want to get to know him. It's hardly rocket science, is it?'

Daisy was making sense and, as so often happened when Elsie talked things over with her sister, the situation began to look less like a forty-foot-high brick wall. 'Thanks, honey. I don't know what happened there.'

'You were scared. And it's totally understandable. Blind dates are notorious for dodgy dating encounters. But I know you'll be fine. It's been a long time since you last dated. Things have changed – and you've changed too, remember. I think you should try not to over-think this and just see it for what it is. You're doing a favour for a friend and possibly meeting a nice bloke in the process. It's a step, not an entire journey.'

Daisy's words were still resounding in Elsie's mind as she changed in the small cloakroom at the back of the café an hour later. The kooky bluebird-print dress she had hastily purchased from the small boutique a few doors away from Sundae & Cher in her lunch break with a bunch of notes thrust into her hand by a very excited Cher was sweet but casual and, teamed with her favourite red ballerina pumps, felt comfortable. Cher had loaned her a red cardigan, which completed the look. She gathered her blonde, shoulder-length bob into a relaxed up-do and held it in place with a couple of black combs. It wasn't the most inspired dating attire, but it felt like *her*.

Cher went a little over the top with her enthusiastic reaction when Elsie walked into the kitchen, but Elsie accepted the compliments anyway. She needed to feel confident and, after Daisy's pep talk, she was determined to enjoy the experience. *You love surprises*, she reminded herself, her fingers closing around the piece of paper from the satin box in the pocket of her coat, as she and Cher walked to the green-tiled pub near the Theatre Royal where many local shopkeepers headed after work for a drink.

The pub was already packed with post-work revellers, the loud buzz of conversation peppered with stabs of raucous laughter. Elsie had always loved this place and liked the way it had stubbornly resisted the urge to succumb to gastro-pub tweeness as so many others in the area had done. It was her father's favourite watering hole and she had often accompanied him there in her mid to late teens when he met fellow councillors or furniture suppliers.

They squeezed through the bodies to reach the bar and waited for a full five minutes before catching the attention of Nick, the cheerful, red-faced landlord.

'Evening, girls,' he shouted. 'What can I get you?'

'Just an orange juice for me and a red wine for Cher, please.'

'Right you are.'

'Is Jake Long in yet, Nick?' Cher asked.

'Not yet.' He placed a glass of wine in front of her and flicked the top off a bottle of orange juice to pour into a glass of ice for Elsie. 'Early, though. He's normally in about six. Why, you looking for him?'

'Might be.' Cher winked at Nick and disappeared into the crowd to find a seat as Elsie paid for the drinks.

'Hot date,' Elsie confided.

'Serious? He's too normal for Cher, isn't he?'

Elsie laughed. 'It's a bit of a new direction for her.'

Nick gave an overdramatic sigh. 'I've told her: if she's looking for a real man, she knows where I am.'

'I'll pass the message on,' Elsie replied, taking the drinks and winding through the throng of bodies until she found Cher proudly guarding a table with four chairs by the window. 'Nick offered to be your real man again.'

Cher rolled her eyes heavenwards and took a large gulp of wine. 'He can go on dreaming. I've heard too many rumours about Nick Plass to go there.' She looked at her watch. 'Jake shouldn't be long. Aren't you drinking?'

'I might have one later.' Elsie might have been thankful for a little Dutch courage, but she fully intended to go into this without the aid of alcohol.

They made themselves comfortable and chatted aimlessly about work for twenty minutes, neither of them really thinking about the subject, as the prospect of the evening ahead loomed large over them. When Cher's glass was empty, she stood to head back to the bar but was stopped in her tracks by the sight of two men weaving through the standing drinkers. Jake Long strode in front, his impeccable suit standing out amongst the casually dressed locals, an expensive overcoat folded over one arm. He was handsome for his age – his kind dark eyes and lightly tanned skin contrasting with the flashes of silver at his temples and running through his lustrous brown hair. Cher was suddenly all coy eyelashes and shy smiles as he approached the table.

Elsie was so busy being impressed by Jake's appearance that she forgot to look at her own date for the evening, who was waiting behind his boss, obscured from view by the crush of pub customers.

'Delighted you could make it,' Jake smiled at Cher, an obvious twinkle in his eye. 'Apologies for our lateness – we had a last-minute meeting at the office.' He extended his hand to Elsie. 'Nice to meet you.'

'You too.'

'I have a feeling this is going to be a most pleasant evening,' Jake replied, moving to one side. 'Let me introduce you to our most brilliant junior partner in the practice . . .'

As he was speaking, the young man beside him stepped forward, and instantly Elsie's breath deserted her. *Surely not . . .*

'. . . Torin Stewart.'

Jake and Cher were grinning like a pair of hungry hyenas, but as Elsie's eyes met Torin's, neither of them was smiling.

Forced by propriety to be civil, Elsie held out her hand. 'Elsie Maynard. Nice to meet you.'

'Is it?' Torin briefly shook her hand, the shock of his warm skin on hers causing her to pull away as quickly as she could. The briefest of smiles passed across his lips before he turned to Jake. 'I'll get the first round in, shall I?'

Jake clapped his hands together. 'Excellent idea. Mine's a single malt with water, no ice. Ladies?'

'Red wine for me. Elsie?'

Struggling to stop the room from spinning around her, Elsie wrestled her way back into the moment. 'Same, please. Large.'

Cher raised an eyebrow and Elsie managed a weak smile in return. As Jake sat opposite Cher, she quickly turned her attention squarely onto him and Elsie sank back into her chair. How was it possible for Torin to be her blind date? After their initial meeting and the excruciating second round in Croydon, Elsie had felt sure that she and Torin Stewart were never destined to cross paths again. Yet here he was – for the third time in as many weeks. What was she going to say to him?

All too quickly, Torin returned with a tray of drinks, seemingly charmed when it came to being served quickly in the only pub in Brighton that made a virtue of its long bar waiting times – a fact attested to by a large sign over the bar bearing the legend:

We don't do 'fast'. Our beer is worth the wait.

'Blimey, we'll send you to the bar again,' Cher remarked, raising her glass to Torin. Grinning, he clinked his pint glass against hers and then held it towards Elsie.

'To a pleasant evening?'

Reluctantly, she accepted the toast. 'A pleasant evening.' Pleasant, she added to herself, meaning *short* . . .

Jake and Cher immediately launched into animated conversation, their body language screaming attraction as they did so. Torin sipped his beer slowly, his eyes never leaving Elsie. Doing her best to present an unaffected air, Elsie returned his gaze, smiling pleasantly as she desperately scrabbled for suitable topics of conversation to make the evening pass quickly.

'I take it you're a solicitor?'

'I prefer lawyer – bit of a fan of the US terminology, I'm afraid. But yes, that's what I do. How about you?'

'Assistant manager of a retro ice cream café.'

This appeared to surprise him. 'Oh? Whereabouts?'

For a split second, Elsie was tempted to concoct a fake address to ensure he couldn't find her, but then common sense prevailed as she realised Jake or Cher would gladly furnish him with the correct information in any case. 'In North Laine – Gardner Street. I work for Cher.'

'I see. So, who'd have thought us two would meet up again like this, eh?'

Instantly, Elsie felt her insides clench into a knot and she looked down into her already half-empty wine glass.

Torin gave an almighty sigh and muttered something into his beer.

Suddenly irritated by this, Elsie glared straight at him. 'Sorry? Didn't catch that.'

'I *said* it's a shame you can't be more civil, given the circumstances.'

'Excuse me? I am being civil, thank you very much. I'm having a drink with you and making polite conversation. I fail to see what else I need to do to increase my civility.'

Torin held up his hands. 'Well – not do *that*, for a start.'

'Do what?'

'Fly off the handle. Totally overreact to everything I say.

You've done it every time we've met and it hasn't once been warranted.'

'Everything good with you two?' Jake interjected, the glow of a successful date illuminating his expression.

Elsie and Torin smiled politely and, satisfied, Jake returned his attention to Cher.

Elsie lowered her voice and leant towards Torin. 'I beg to differ. You were completely full of yourself when you "rescued" me from the security guard and then you proceeded to stalk my sister and me around that store.'

'I was pleased to *help* you,' Torin hissed back. 'And I wasn't stalking anyone. You were the one walking against the arrows and your sister was perfectly charming, as I recall.'

Elsie ignored him and drank her wine, looking across to the clock above the bar. *Twenty minutes? She had only endured twenty minutes so far?* Elsie had promised Cher an hour – but if their conversation continued to head down the dicey road it was careering along, it would be impossible to keep her promise. Reeling in as much of her anger as she could, she took a breath and returned her stare to his.

'This is getting us nowhere. I think we should change the subject. I don't want another fight and I would hazard a guess that you don't, either.'

The fury in his eyes softened. 'I don't. What else can we talk about?'

At a loss for anything more creative to suggest, Elsie said, 'Tell me about your job,' instantly reprimanding herself for sounding like advice from a 1950s manual on successful dating conversation topics: *Show an interest in his career . . .*

So Torin explained about the kind of law he practised, what it meant to be a junior partner, what his ambitions

81

for the future were and how he had made the decision while at primary school that he would study law.

'Classic case of going into the family business,' he explained. 'Only my mother's side of the family, not my father's. Dad owns a music shop in Hove – about as far removed from law as you can get.'

'And you knew from the age of – what – eight or nine that you wanted to be a lawyer?' Elsie momentarily forgot her consternation, the fact of his early conviction startling her.

'Yes. Why, is that so surprising?'

'It's not, I suppose. But I didn't have a clue what I wanted to do with my life when I was that age, apart from have fun and maybe one day appear in *Neighbours*. In many ways, I still don't really know if there's a career that would fit me perfectly. But I love what I do, so that's fine for me for now.'

She could see him relax and was surprised at how much relief this brought her.

'There's a lot to be said for job satisfaction. I see many people struggling in my profession because they're trying to live out someone else's expectations for their career, not pursuing something they are passionate about. Kids fulfilling their parents' ambitions at the cost of their own.'

'And you?' The question was out before she realised it, far more personal than she was intending.

'Thanks for asking. I count myself as one of the lucky ones because I love what I do.'

'I'm going to attempt to beat Torin's bar time,' Jake grinned. 'Same again for everyone?'

All agreed apart from Elsie, who decided it was safest to revert to orange juice for the remainder of the evening. As Jake left, Cher grinned at Torin.

'I hope Elsie's told you about the new exciting venture she's embarking on?'

'No, not yet. Tell me.'

'A community choir!' Cher replied before Elsie had the chance to speak. 'And they're meeting in my café.'

'I'm impressed,' Torin replied, and Elsie could have sworn she saw a flicker of genuine sentiment in his expression. 'Is this something you're experienced in?'

'No. But then the point of it is to create something new, not regurgitate an old method that has been used before. We're going to sing a variety of songs and the emphasis will be on fun.'

Sensing their conversation was safely set up, Cher made her excuses and headed towards the Ladies'. Torin folded his arms and leant back in his chair. 'So, you know how to have fun, after all?'

So much for your sincerity, Elsie thought, her hackles rising. However much she might have hoped they could have a civil conversation, it was obviously not going to happen. Ever. 'I do, as a matter of fact. Which just proves that you know nothing whatsoever about me.'

'It was merely an observation. I guess everyone else must see a different side of you than I have so far.'

Go figure, Torin. 'I guess they must.' She looked at the clock again. Five minutes had dragged their heels past since she last checked. This was going to be the longest hour of her entire life . . .

'Please don't be offended. I just have a knack of getting the measure of people very quickly, which I know can be unnerving. It's an occupational hazard, I'm afraid. I can accurately sum up someone's character often within a few minutes of meeting them.'

Elsie couldn't believe his smugness. 'You mean you're

quick to judge people? I don't see that as a skill. I see that as a flaw.'

'Oh really? Well, I've already worked *you* out, Elsie Maynard.'

'Don't be ridiculous. You can't possibly know that much about me.'

'I think you'll find I can.' He sipped his pint and scrutinised her for an uncomfortable moment. 'Are you challenging me to prove it?'

The gall of him! Well, Elsie reasoned, there was only one way to haul him off his high horse. 'Yes. Yes, I am.'

Rubbing his hands together, he began. 'Right. Well, from your blatant misunderstanding of me and misreading of my motives, I can conclude that you have had very little experience of men – one or two serious boyfriends at most. From the small indentation on the third finger of your left hand I can see that one of those relationships resulted in marriage; from the absence of a ring now and your noticeably prickly nature towards men in general I assume that this marriage came to an end, perhaps some time ago. Am I correct?'

'I—'

Elsie swallowed hard as a groundswell of emotion threatened to sweep her off her feet. Torin had unwittingly broken through the layers of carefully constructed defences and his observations stabbed deeply. Momentarily blindsided, she struggled for control and he saw it, the same glint of triumph in his eyes as before.

'What? Nothing to say? Surely this can't be the great Elsie Maynard, queen of the lightning comeback? I must say, I thought you'd have retaliated by now.'

He was goading her, she knew it, but the pulse of shock was fast turning to anger within her and she needed a moment to formulate her reply.

'Just – just give me a minute . . .'

Torin took a celebratory glug of beer and slapped the table. 'Aha! Admit it – I totally summed you up! I am *too good* at this.'

'Fine. You want to know?' With every last scrap of resolve within her, Elsie rose to her feet. 'You were correct when you said I'd only had one serious relationship. It did lead to marriage and that marriage ended, eighteen months ago.'

He spread his hands wide. 'Hey, it's what I do. Please don't be offended. Sit down, would you? We were just beginning to have fun.'

'No, thanks. I think I've stayed long enough.'

'Oh come on, Elsie. There's no need to be embarrassed about it. Plenty of women your age are divorcees.'

Elsie fixed him with a stare that could freeze sunbeams. 'That's true. But not many women my age are *widows*.'

With that, she turned her back on a visibly shocked Torin and walked with purpose out of the pub and onto the street beyond. Her promise to Cher was completely forgotten: the only impulse driving her steps was to escape.

CHAPTER SIX

Just the way you are . . .

Lucas would have loved it. He would have thrown back his lovely black hair and guffawed so loudly that even half-deaf Mrs Rafferty next door would have heard it. And Elsie would have laughed with him – it was impossible not to when faced with a laugh as infectious as his. Even towards the end of his battle, when every movement required concerted effort, his laugh was the one part of him that never succumbed to the cancer claiming his body. Jim often said he heard Lucas laugh more during the last year of his life than in all the years he'd known him. But then the last year was something Lucas was determined to enjoy. He had a point to prove – a list to fulfil. And each of the items on The List he created for their final year together was designed to amuse them both, to squeeze every last drop of joy out of the time they had left.

Lucas Webb was a lover of the absurd, his sense of humour one of the things Elsie loved the most about him. He could find the ridiculous, hilarious side of any situation, no matter how grim it first appeared. The bleak diagnosis of his cancer was no exception to this: and his coping mechanism was the spark for The List.

When Dr Hayes had delivered the devastating news to Lucas and Elsie in the too-small, too-warm consulting room in the Royal Sussex County Hospital, their first reaction had been mind-numbing shock and disbelief, quickly leading to body-shaking sobs as they both broke down. Twelve months, at most – a meagre allocation for someone who loved life as much as Lucas did. All their plans – travelling, a business of their own, children – now lay screwed up and discarded like the balls of paper strewn in the dull grey metal bin beneath Dr Hayes' regulation NHS desk. The sense of injustice was immense, a crushing weight of hopelessness robbing the room of oxygen, deeper than Elsie had ever experienced.

But an hour later, when they were walking hand-in-hand along Brighton Pier, a remarkable transformation began in Lucas. Elsie remembered him stopping, near the entrance to the amusements, hope blazing in his dark brown eyes.

'Elsie, I've had quite possibly the most brilliant idea!'

So startling was the sea change in his mood that Elsie gave an involuntary laugh. 'What is it?'

'OK. Hear me out. When I heard the diagnosis this morning I was like, "Only twelve months?" But I've thought about it and I realised – we *have* twelve months. Twelve months to do whatever we like and nobody can argue with us! So, here it is: we make a list of things we have to do. And I'm not talking about naff stuff like swimming with dolphins because, frankly, I think they're overrated. In fact, that should be our criteria: nothing overly sentimental, nothing expensive and nothing predictable. We pick, say, fifty things we have to complete before I . . . you know . . .'

He was shaking when he suggested it, but his smile was all the persuasion Elsie needed to agree. And so the idea for The List was born: fifty tasks unique to them, a personal mandate for fun in their final year together. Such as sneaking into Brighton Library to stick smiley-face sticky notes within the pages of classic novels that Lucas had deemed to be so depressing that readers would be in need of some guerrilla-placed light relief (to Elsie's knowledge, some of those notes might still be lying in wait amid the leaves of *Jude The Obscure*, *The Mill on the Floss* and *War and Peace* . . .); decorating the rubbish bins along Brighton promenade with tinsel at midnight on a balmy July night; paddling in wellies in the ornate Victoria Fountain in Victoria Gardens in the centre of town; and spending the night in a neighbour's son's tree house with a large bottle of Jack Daniel's, snuggled up, drunk and sniggering like school kids under layers of blankets.

Every item on The List conformed to the three criteria. All except one.

'Oh, and Paris,' Lucas had added, when fifty items had been listed.

She observed him with amusement. 'Hang on a minute, you said nothing overly sentimental, nothing expensive and nothing predictable, right?'

'Right.'

'So what's Paris, then? Surely it's all three.'

His grin was pure Lucas Webb mischief. 'Paris is *geographical*.'

'Lucas . . .'

'Humour me, Els? I'm a dying man, remember? You have to honour my wishes.'

And so The List that should only ever have contained fifty items became fifty-one, the last task destined to become the only one never to be fulfilled in time . . .

Standing on the dark beach as the inky ocean lapped the

shore below her, Elsie found herself laughing now, despite her tears. Lucas would have applauded her parting shot in the pub: the ultimate way to win an argument.

'If all else fails, play the death card, kid. It gets them every time.'

What Lucas would have loved the most, though, was that Elsie had been in the pub in the first place tonight. For the entire twelve months they had planned until the end, Elsie's mandate to carry on afterwards had been Lucas' recurring theme.

'You have a whole life ahead of you, darling. And I will be expecting you to live it. No moping around like you've died, too. Promise me. Promise me you'll live life for us both?'

Of course she missed him. He was in every thought, every action of the day, and he had loved Brighton so much that even the bricks and streets of the town seemed to be infused with his spirit. But a strange thing had happened when he finally passed away after their extraordinary last year: the overriding emotion Elsie experienced was thankfulness for the years she had been blessed with Lucas in her life. Some of her extended family put it down to an anomaly of grief: she was in denial, obviously, and the pain and anguish would surely follow. But it didn't – or, at least, not the debilitating grief that she had expected to feel. Deep sadness and a longing to be close to him again, yes: often and sometimes entirely without warning. Tiny, insignificant things that induced unexpected tears, absolutely. But so much deep grieving had assaulted her during their final year together, catching her off-guard in the middle of the crazy tasks on The List, that it was almost as if the most profound part of her grieving was done during this time. Maybe it was because Lucas had talked with her so much about what life would be like once he was gone:

'Wait six months after I leave and then take your wedding ring off. And no longer than that. I mean it, Els. Consider it a gift to me, OK? In return I'll be giving some other lucky chap the chance to have you in his life.' . . . 'You'll be fine, honey. I believe in you, remember? You're beautiful and so strong – that's what I love about you. So I'm expecting you to get out there again, whenever you're ready.' . . . 'And none of this "black widow" shizzle, OK? Black isn't your colour anyway. Dress like Queen Victoria and I'll haunt you until you change it!'

In the months since his death, Elsie had followed his wishes to the letter and, as with so many of the things Lucas had suggested, it made her feel better. It was almost as if each act was a gift to him, her strength his reward for the faith he had placed in her to carry on.

Even so, she hadn't meant to reveal her past to Torin this evening, and she was angry with herself for using it as such a trivial point-scoring act. Torin's inference that she was merely a bitter, betrayed divorcee had incensed her. Especially when the truth was so markedly different. But Lucas was worth more than that. And no matter how much her parting shot would have amused him, he deserved his memory to be treated with more respect.

Leaving the sea behind, she crunched across the pebbled beach back to the steps leading to the promenade, her mind awash with thoughts.

'Babe. The Led Zep mash-up will work, I'm telling you.'

'I'm not having this conversation again, Woody. We've got a list of six songs and that's plenty to be going on with. And we only have six members, remember? I don't want to lose any of them before we've even begun.'

Woody tutted and pushed his sunglasses up his nose,

despite the Saturday morning greyness surrounding the beach café. 'I expected more of you, girl. I thought we were meant to be different.'

'We are different! Your Lady Gaga medley is still in – it's the first thing we're doing.'

'Gaga is merely an interesting aperitif, an *amuse bouche* to the real event, if you will,' he sniffed, twisting his espresso cup in its saucer.

'Fair enough. So let's make sure it's the best it can be before we ask the choir to tackle the *greats* . . .'

Woody signalled his assent and Elsie congratulated herself for finding the correct phrase to pacify the ex-rocker's concerns. It was good to think of something other than her encounter with Torin yesterday, the memory of which had plagued her mind all night. She looked down at the list before her and tapped the notebook with her pen.

'Now, Dad says that the offer to perform at Brighton Carnival in July is pretty much confirmed, so that gives us three months, give or take a week, to create something worth watching. Do you think we can do it?'

Woody held up a hand, the silver rings clinking together as he did so. 'Wait. Let me consult the Oracle.' He raised his forefingers to his temples and closed his eyes.

Elsie made a quick check around her to see if the other customers in the Driftwood Café were watching this spectacle: thankfully, newly purchased pages of the *Guardian* and *The Times* were occupying most of them, and those without newspapers were either deep in conversation or transfixed by mobile device screens. Thanking heaven for small mercies, she returned her attention to Woody, who now appeared to be muttering and chuckling under his breath. After a few minutes of this, he opened his eyes and folded his hands slowly on the table in front of him.

'I have duly consulted. The answer is yes.'

'Right. Good, then.' Elsie resisted the temptation to ask which celestial being had bestowed this information on her fellow choirmaster, reasoning that it was probably safer not to know.

He picked up his cup again and gazed over its rim towards the clouded horizon out at sea. 'But we must work hard to make them the music warriors destiny has ordained.'

'Sorry, do *what*?'

With unhidden pity at his companion's obvious lack of insight, Woody stared at her. 'They ain't gonna get far if they don't *sing* something, babe.'

Even considering his dubious connections to mystical guides, Woody could not have foreseen the wisdom this statement would have.

The following Wednesday, Elsie sat behind her keyboard and motioned for the small choir to stop talking and listen.

'Right, so it's time we got started. Woody has put together a great medley of three Lady Gaga songs, which I think we can have a lot of fun with. Daisy's going to hand out some music sheets so hopefully everyone will be able to follow along. Does anyone know what they sing?'

Danny raised his hand. 'Um, songs?'

'Yes, we'll definitely be singing *songs*,' Elsie replied in her best encouraging tone, which bore more than a hint of Joyce Grenfell. 'What I meant was, do you all know which parts you sing? Alto? Tenor? Soprano?'

'I watch *The Sopranos*,' Stan grinned, affecting the most appalling impression of an Italian-American accent, 'cos you gotta love a bit of Tony and *duh family*, eh?'

'Ooh, I love that show,' Sasha agreed as she and Stan launched into an excited commentary on their favourite episodes.

Daisy smiled helpfully at Elsie as she handed out music. Elsie inhaled deeply and hoped that her smile wasn't drooping as much as her spirits were. It was nearly nine p.m. already and so far all that had been accomplished was an elongated discussion of where they could find customised T-shirts for a choir uniform, and a small fracas over Sasha's curt reaction to Woody's suggestion that a medley of Hellfinger hits could be a better opening gambit for the choir:

'Bit difficult to make a medley out of only one song, isn't it?'

'I'll have you know our debut album sold over eighty thousand copies!'

'Really? I wonder how many of those are now landfill?'

'How *dare you* besmirch the name of England's seminal Eighties rock gods!'

'Seminal rock gods? Don't make me laugh! Most of you are dead, in rehab or so drunk you can't stop shaking. That's what Wikipedia reckons. Only the chap who had the good sense to leave and become a record producer got anything out of your *seminal* band!'

'I won't have his name uttered in this space, you hear me, girl?'

The argument had only been halted by Cher's timely intervention with freshly baked dark chocolate and espresso cookies from the kitchen served with scoops of white chocolate ice cream, but now a distinct atmosphere hung over Sasha and Woody who had assumed disgruntled positions at opposite sides of the room.

Elsie took a deep breath and smiled brightly at everyone. 'OK, I'm going to play some notes and ask you to sing them. I should be able to work out from that which parts everyone should be taking.'

Initially, the collective sound made by the gathered

singers was anything but encouraging. Danny came in way too high and continued in a strained falsetto for several minutes until Elsie sang the note in the correct key for his voice. Sasha's instrument proved a powerful one, although she clearly thought singing a single note was beneath her, opting instead for a set of vocal acrobatics that even Beyoncé would have considered a little over-the-top. Aoife just looked terrified and Elsie had to stop everyone else singing just to hear the young girl's whispered tone. Stan got a fit of the giggles and couldn't sing for laughing. Irene managed a note at least, which shrank away to nothing when Elsie complimented her on it. Woody sat next to Elsie, eyes wide in sheer horror at the ear-gratingly awful sound, and even Daisy looked as if she was ready to throw in the towel.

Elsie clapped her hands and surveyed the mournful choir before her. 'OK, take a break, everyone. Now I'm going to come round and just sing with each of you to give you the notes you need, and then we'll try it again all together when everyone's happy.'

Twenty minutes later, Elsie had arranged the group into something resembling choral order. Aoife and Sasha represented the sopranos, Irene was designated the alto part, while Danny was the sole tenor and Stan somewhere between baritone and bass. Elsie patiently sang each part in turn for the group (who mumbled in return) then raised her hand to quiet them again.

'OK, that's good. Not very loud, but I appreciate we're all still finding our voices . . .'

Sasha tutted. 'Some of us more than others.'

Danny glared at her. 'What is *that* supposed to mean?'

'Irene doesn't speak at all, let alone sing, and your girlfriend couldn't make a noise if her ass was on fire.'

'Sasha, there's no need for that,' Elsie jumped in. 'I think you should apologise . . .'

'I will not. I've been holding back my voice all night to let this lot sing and none of them have bothered even trying.'

Stan's face reddened. 'Easy on, now. It's the first time we've all sung, remember.'

'Well *sing*, then!'

Woody stormed over to Elsie. 'I think we made a mistake with these people. None of them understand their *destiny* . . .'

'What would you know about destiny, you failed rocker *freak*?' Sasha retorted as the room became a mass of raised voices, angry words and wild gestures.

Elsie stood and was about to speak when a booming voice pierced through the din.

'Ee-e-e-e-e-e-e-*enough*!'

The room fell silent and all heads turned to see an uncharacteristically ruffled Daisy breathing heavily by the counter.

'I can't believe what I'm seeing. Grown men and women acting like spoilt children – no, *worse* than that because I'm pretty sure even children would draw the line at such pettiness. Now you listen to me, my sister has put so much effort into making this choir something fun, something different – something you'll want to be a part of. You've not even given her the courtesy of your attention to complete one song yet! If you knew what she has been through in the last few years . . .' she swiped at a tear that dared to show itself at the corner of her left eye '. . . if you had *any* idea . . .'

Elsie shook her head. 'Daisy, don't . . .'

'. . . The point is that this choir is Elsie's baby, her new adventure. And she does *not* deserve to have it trampled on by people who care more about their own egos than someone else's dream. So I suggest that if you aren't willing to participate in this choir in a spirit of co-operation and fun, you leave now because, quite frankly, we don't need you.'

Elsie closed her eyes, fully expecting to hear the departing scrape of six chairs. But, to her surprise, the café fell silent. Daring to look, she saw the chastened eyes of each member observing her. Even Sasha Mitchell appeared to be momentarily hushed.

Irene cleared her throat. 'Well said, Miss Maynard. I think maybe we should begin?'

Later that evening, Elsie linked arms with her sister as they walked down Gardner Street. 'Thank you.'

'What for?'

'For organising us all.'

Daisy smiled. 'It's the least I could do.'

'All the same, if you hadn't said something we could have had a war on our hands. Listen, how would you feel about being assistant musical director?'

Daisy's eyes shone. 'Really?'

Elsie hugged her arm. 'Yes. You sorted us all out tonight, Dais. I have a feeling we're going to need to do that regularly.'

'Well, then I would be honoured. I just hope tonight will have given them food for thought. I still think Sasha is going to be a troublemaker, mind.'

'Maybe. But did you hear her voice?'

'What voice? As far as I could tell the only volume that woman can achieve is when she's insulting someone.'

Elsie laughed. 'She's certainly got a tidy sideline in put-downs. No, I mean when she was singing. She was holding back tonight, but I couldn't miss the purity of her tone when we were working out the parts. She's hiding an impressive instrument behind all that hot air. I just have to work out how to coax it out.'

'And what about Silent Irene? And Whispering Aoife? I don't think either of them managed a note that wasn't solely audible to dogs tonight.' Daisy paused as they reached her mint-green Figaro, clicking the remote on her keys to unlock it. 'I'm not saying you can't do it, Els, I just don't envy you the task.'

Secretly, Elsie didn't relish the prospect much either. But as she waved goodbye to her sister, she felt the burn of irritation at tonight's lack of progress giving way to something else: determination. The events of the evening had initially bruised her confidence, but now a firm resolve began to set like molten steel in her bones. She *had* established a choir as she and Woody had planned and they *were* going to perform as one if it was the last thing she did.

'People are like doors. You just have to find the right key.'

Lucas had whooped when he read the words printed on the cheap and cheerful fridge magnet they found in a gift shop in Whitstable as he and Elsie embarked on item number 3 of The List:

3. Buy embarrassing fridge magnets from seaside towns and display on home fridge.

'This is perfect! Tacky and garish and blessed with a pomposity of its very own!'

Seeing the disgusted look from the shop owner, Elsie had begged him to lower his voice, but Lucas had ignored her, purchasing the small plaster item while roundly condemning its offensiveness.

It caught her eye as she made coffee next morning and

Elsie found herself struck by its sentiment. Maybe it had a point – no matter what Lucas would think of this assertion. Perhaps everyone had a key.

Lucas certainly had. For him it had been Elsie's knowledge of lesser-known Morrissey songs, as demonstrated during the tense final minutes of their sixth-form college's End of Year Quiz, a tradition set by a previous principal years before and upheld by each successive intake of students as a near-sacred event. The teaching staff took pride in the complexity, scope and trickiness of the questions they prepared each year, covering everything from modern cultural references to classic art, philosophy, history, literature and current affairs. In her first year of college, a few months past her seventeenth birthday, Elsie had been unexpectedly promoted to the Lower Sixth team when her then best friend Clara had fallen sick with German Measles days before the end of term. Clara had urged her to participate during an impassioned phone call the night before the quiz was due to take place.

'I know you don't think so, but you know more stuff than the rest of us put together. The Upper Sixth team are terrifying – we need all the help we can get and you're the only person I've got left to ask. Say yes, please!'

Reluctantly, Elsie had accepted, keeping her eyes behind the long veil of her then-henna-reddened mane and praying that no one noticed her flushed cheeks behind the pale foundation she wore as she took her place at the table with her teammates. Her heart had sunk when she saw the captain of her team – the boy with the long dark hair who she had gazed at across her history classroom all year. Lucas Webb was beautiful: high cheekbones and dark, piercing eyes that viewed the world in a way Elsie had never encountered before; a unique sense of style that at once set him apart but also garnered respect from his fellow classmates; and a smile that lit up the room for everybody but her. Because to Lucas, Elsie was invisible, her longing looks lost on him as he wowed his friends with witticisms and endeared himself to his teachers with his startling intellect. She had watched it all as if from behind a plate-glass barrier, unable to reach out to him yet spellbound by his character. And now the vacant chair next to him was hers as the two teams assembled for the End of Year Quiz, the honour of their respective years on the line. What would she say to him? Would he even acknowledge her existence?

As it transpired, she needn't have worried. In later years, Lucas confessed that this was the day his life changed forever – when, in the final throes of the most closely fought competition for years, with the Upper Sixth team poised for victory at 78 points to the Lower Sixth's 77, a question on Morrissey's second solo studio album was passed to his team.

'Name the fifth track on Morrissey's second album, *Kill Uncle*.'

Blank looks met Lucas as he turned to his team for help.

'Come on, we have to get this or we lose! Does anyone know anything by Morrissey?' More blank looks and shaking heads greeted him.

Mr Henley, the college principal, tapped the question cards impatiently on the table. 'I'm afraid I'm going to have to hurry you, Lower Sixth.'

Elsie had felt giddy as she raised her hand, an act which seemed to require every shred of confidence she possessed. She was almost one hundred per cent certain of the answer, having seen the album in question on Guin's bedroom floor when her sister had recently gone through a period of self-loathing after a particularly bad break-up, but the thought of being wrong terrified her. What if she was mistaken? Lucas would be sure to ignore her then, remembering her merely as 'the girl who lost the End of Year Quiz'. But it was too late: eagle-eyed Henley had spotted her hand.

'Elsie Maynard?'

'"King Leer",' she had said, her voice a cracked whisper when it first appeared. Glancing sideways at the beautiful dark eyes now intent on her, she cleared her throat and repeated, louder: 'The song is "King Leer".'

Pausing for dramatic effect, Mr Henley eventually relieved the tension by shouting, 'Correct! Lower Sixth wins by two points!'

And that had been it: from that day on, Lucas had noticed nobody else but the quiet history student with her dyed hair and supreme knowledge of obscure musical trivia. He had followed her around Brighton that summer: appearing at the family furniture shop where she was working with a highly dubious cover story of searching for a particular brand of beeswax polish; persuading a mate to ask Clara out to give him an excuse to request a double date (which Elsie refused out of sheer embarrassment) and timing his walks along the beach to coincide with hers. Eventually his persistence paid off and Elsie agreed to a date – without the company of Clara or Lucas' spot-endowed friend. Lucas took her to a burger bar for lunch, followed by a long walk around the town. They talked for hours, slowly discovering a shared love of art films, Douglas Adams novels and U2, the August Saturday slipping past until, at eight-thirty p.m., he kissed her in the porch of the Maynard family home and Elsie knew immediately she had found The One that she had heard so many authors and songwriters describing.

'Penny for 'em?' Cher appeared at Elsie's side.

'Sorry?'

'Well, I know mixing your Popping Candy Cookie dough can be fascinating, but I'm pretty sure it doesn't warrant your current level of deep thought.'

Elsie smiled. 'Ah. I was just remembering how Lucas and I met.'

'Oh honey.' Cher squeezed Elsie's arm.

'No – it's all good. You know it is. I don't know why it's been on my mind this morning. I was looking at one of his daft fridge magnets and it brought it all back.'

'And after that awful date I made you go on . . . I'm so sorry, Els. I had no idea Jake's colleague was going to insult you.'

'Cher, I've already said it's OK. You couldn't have known what would happen.'

'All the same, he had no right to make you upset.' She sighed. 'You know, it's odd. Even now I still expect Lucas to walk into the café. I miss him.'

'I know you do. You two were always thick as thieves. Especially when you let him play with the ice cream mixer.'

Cher laughed. 'Big kid. This place has a lot to thank him for. That Blueberry Choc Chip ice cream he concocted has been one of our best sellers. Heck, I'm still buying our cupcakes from Crawley because Lucas loved them so much.'

Elsie smiled. Lucas had fallen in love with the small cupcake café in Crawley town centre when he had been working for a large technology company on the outskirts of the town and had insisted Elsie and Cher accompany him to the vivid pink café one Saturday to taste their wares. As a result, Cher had placed a regular order for Cupcake Genie's beautiful handmade cupcakes, despite the distance from Brighton, and the association had remained ever since. But then, that was typical Lucas: he made anything seem possible.

'I wonder what he would have made of your choir,' Cher said, scooping a teaspoonful of cookie dough and popping it into her mouth. 'I reckon he'd have given that Sasha short shrift. The thing I remember about your Lucas is that he didn't suffer fools gladly.'

Elsie had to laugh at that. The thought of Lucas unleashing his merciless wit on Sasha Mitchell was one she would definitely store up for the next time the brassy young woman kicked off at choir practice. 'All the same, there has to be some way to encourage her to connect with the others. She's probably the most talented singer we have but if she keeps causing trouble like last night she could be counter-productive to the choir's success.'

The little brass bell above the door rang out as a customer entered. Cher frowned. 'Blimey, they're early this morning. I've only just flicked the sign over.'

'What it is to be a woman in demand, eh?'

'Oh yeah, fantastic.' Cher pulled a face as she walked through into the café. Moments later, she reappeared, an odd expression on her face. 'Someone for you, sweets.'

Intrigued by Cher's expression, Elsie grabbed a cloth to wipe her hands and followed her boss. There, standing by the counter dressed in a smart suit and grinning broadly, was Olly.

'Morning, Elsie.' He looked around the empty café interior. 'I'm not too early, am I?'

'Hi. No, you're our first customer of the day.'

There was a pronounced cough and Elsie turned to see Cher's conspiratorial smile.

'Ah, sorry. This is Cher, my boss.'

'Charmed,' Cher smiled, extending her hand a little too far to reveal a view of her ample chest perhaps not particu-larly appropriate considering the early hour of the morning. 'Elsie's told me nothing at all about you, I'm afraid.'

Elsie sighed. She was never going to hear the end of this all day, judging by Cher's delight. 'Olly's building a website for my dad's business.'

'Ooh, handsome *and* clever,' Cher gushed. 'And presumably *hungry* too?'

For a split second, Olly seemed mystified until Cher seductively waved a menu in front of her too-low-cut blouse. 'Oh. Right. Yes, breakfast would be good.'

'Well, you just rest your cute bum somewhere and Elsie will take your order,' Cher purred, turning on her stilettos and tip-tapping back into the kitchen, swinging her hips dramatically as she went.

Elsie smiled at the visibly shaken young man by the counter. 'The table by the window is a good one.'

Olly laughed as he sat down. 'Your boss is *ferocious*! Is she like that with everyone?'

'Only the good-looking ones.' Instantly, Elsie felt herself flush as Olly smiled at her.

'Why, thank you.'

'You're welcome. So, what would you like?'

He held her eyes for a moment before turning his attention to the menu. 'The maple and bacon muffins sound fantastic. And a coffee, please – cappuccino would be great.'

As Elsie wrote his order on her pad, she could feel her hand shaking. *Pull yourself together, Elsie*, she scolded herself, annoyed at her reaction. 'Right, I'll just go and . . .'

'Actually, there was another reason I came,' Olly said suddenly, looking up at her.

'Oh?'

'Yes. The thing is – well – I haven't seen you since the evening of your first choir meeting and you did promise we would meet up for coffee a few weeks back . . . I'm sorry, forgive my ramblings. I'm just going to ask you

103

straight because, frankly, I've gone over and over this all the way here and I couldn't come up with anything better, so . . .' he took a breath, his eyes fixed on hers '. . . how about dinner? With me, that is? Not a "sometime in the future" thing that'll never happen. This week? Like, say, tomorrow evening?'

'Oh.' The suddenness of Olly's question, coupled with the fog of thoughts in her own mind this morning, rendered Elsie temporarily speechless.

Olly's face fell, interpreting her reaction as the precursor to a rejection. Dropping his gaze from hers he did his best to appear uninjured. 'Look, it's fine. I just thought I'd ask.'

Elsie felt her pulse jump into life. 'No,' she said quickly – and a little too loudly, her word causing a slight echo in the café. Lowering her voice, she placed her hand lightly on his warm shoulder. 'Actually, I'd love to. And tomorrow evening would be great.'

Olly's delight was impossible to hide. 'You would? Great!'

Elsie flipped over the page with his breakfast order on her pad and scribbled something else before tearing it off and handing it to him.

'That's my address. Want to pick me up about seven-thirty?'

His fingers brushed against hers as he accepted the piece of paper. 'Wonderful.'

'Yes?'

'Yes.'

'You said yes?'

Elsie frowned at her middle sister. 'I did. So what do you think?'

Guin smiled. 'I think Dad'll be over the moon. He's been

going on about that bloke for weeks. More importantly, how do you feel about it?'

Elsie shrugged. 'Good. I mean, I sort of surprised myself when I agreed to it, but after that awful blind date with Torin I figured the worst had already happened. I like Olly. He's charming, funny, interesting . . .'

'And *fit as*, according to what you said to Daisy,' Guin interjected, wincing as her baby kicked inside her. 'Oh, great, now I'm being censored by my own unborn child. Just what I need.'

'Well, I think it's fabulous,' Daisy said, bringing a Bodum teapot over to the elegant glass table in her luxurious apartment where the Maynard sisters had gathered after work that day. 'You said you were going to start dating and you've done it. Never let it be said that Elsie Maynard doesn't finish something she begins.'

'Talking of which,' Guin added, winking at Elsie, 'I can't believe you ended up on a blind date with your knight-in-shining-armour. What are the chances, eh?'

Elsie turned to Daisy. 'Thanks for that, sis.'

'What? I couldn't *not* tell Guin, could I?'

While Elsie couldn't really object to her sisters sharing stories, the topic of her exchange with Torin was still decidedly uncomfortable. There had been no word from him since the event and Cher – who Elsie knew for a fact was still seeing Jake – had remained tight-lipped about the details of the aftermath of her flight from the pub. 'I suppose not. Let's talk about something else, though.'

'I bet he felt awful,' Guin said, ignoring her. 'I mean, he obviously had you down as some man-hating woman and then you slapped that on him.'

Elsie looked out across the harbour where a small speedboat was leaving a silver trail across the calm ocean waters.

She didn't want to consider what Torin's reaction to her revelation had been. The events of last week had served to show her that she didn't like the person she became when Torin was around. She wasn't a mean person, didn't enjoy verbal combat and was unused to having to avoid people. The reason why these traits reared their ugly heads whenever she was in Torin's presence was beyond her – but what she did know was that the best way to avoid it happening again was to steer well clear.

'I can't imagine he would have intended to say what he did,' Daisy was saying to Guin. 'Even though he was a bit too pleased with himself when we met him.'

'You mean when you and Els crossed over to *the dark side*,' corrected Guin, the opportunity to rib her older sister obviously even more alluring than continuing to embarrass Elsie was. 'If *only* Dad knew . . .'

To her considerable relief, Elsie watched the conversation steer safely from Torin onto safer ground. She didn't want to think about him any more. Dismissing him from her mind, Elsie settled back to enjoy the Maynard sibling banter.

CHAPTER SEVEN

Getting to know you . . .

I love you because you're everybody's friend
xx

Elsie stared at the new piece of paper in her hand. How could Lucas have written that? Even given her general lack of enemies, Elsie would never have classed herself as *everybody's* friend when they were married. And especially not now, given her recent run-in with a certain too-smug lawyer. But then, compared with her late husband, Elsie would probably appear to make friends easier than Snow White in a forest full of woodland creatures . . .

Lucas was known for forming opinions of people at lightning speed – and holding fast to those opinions despite their best efforts to prove him wrong. He was rarely unkind, but, as Cher had observed, he was unwilling to pander to people's vanity or thoughtlessness. Following his diagnosis, it was as if this trait had been magnified within him, fuelled perhaps by the realisation that it didn't matter any more – or his new theory that he could be forgiven any failing on account of his new life-status.

'I'm a dying man. Who is likely to pick a fight with me now?'

His bloody-mindedness had always been a flashpoint between him and Elsie and, while in many ways it made him who he was, his ability to maintain his ground to the bitter end was a constant irritation to her.

'Why can't you back down, just this once?'

'And celebrate their ignorance? Not likely!'

In light of this, what did his message in the Box of Love mean? Had he secretly admired Elsie's peacekeeping ability over the years? Was this evidence of end-of-life regrets or just his acceptance of how different they were in this respect?

One thing Elsie had always been careful to do after Lucas died was to ensure she remembered the annoying things about him alongside the lovely. She had witnessed, first-hand, the unwarranted canonisation of her maternal grand-mother who had died years before. Friends, family and neighbours had gathered at the wake and spoken in glowing terms about a benevolent, saintly woman who bore abso-lutely no resemblance whatsoever to the mean-spirited, cantankerous old lady who had made her father's life a living hell for years. Granny O'Shaughnessy had actively encouraged Elsie's mother to desert her family in favour of an acting career in London that never happened and, when Jim had sought to maintain his relationship with the woman for the sake of his girls, she had taken great delight in using each visit as an opportunity to remind him of his unsuit-ability for her beloved daughter.

'Moira's glad she left you, James,' she would sneer, in full earshot of his three young girls as they played at her house. 'Her life is so much better now she doesn't have the shackles of you and those kids around her feet.'

At Granny's wake, Elsie had listened to people who had

108

undoubtedly hated her grandmother in life praising her in death and, when she questioned a neighbour about it, was told in hushed tones that it was 'not good to speak ill of the dead'. Lucas had laughed when Elsie had relayed the events of the day to him. 'Well, if you go before me, I'll make sure everyone knows about all your failings.'

Now, it gave Elsie a great deal of comfort to remember her annoyances with Lucas. It made his memory more real, more tangible. Making him into some plaster saint in her mind would only have served to take him further away, to make him untouchable and distant.

His latest message sat uncomfortably in her pocket as she walked along Gardner Street towards Sundae & Cher. Tonight was the night of her date with Olly and her heart was a mix of anticipation and anxiety about it. As the peppermint-green façade of the ice cream café came into view, she decided to focus on positive things for the rest of the day. Her mind had been occupied by doubts too much recently.

With no sign of Cher, she set about preparing the café for the day's custom. Down in the basement work kitchen she considered the latest batch of new ice cream flavours in the freezer, deciding on tubs of Mint and Apple, Clotted Cream and Honey and Ginger Snap Biscuit. She placed the selection in the glass display cabinet before firing up the coffee machine. At nine a.m. she turned the door sign to Open and picked up the brightly painted A-board from its overnight resting place in the kitchen to carry it outside.

Elsie loved the early morning busyness of working here, especially when she did it alone. This was always the moment when the day seemed most promising, full of unseen delights yet to happen. Gardner Street had an air of expectancy about it this morning, its brightly painted buildings

109

sparkling with a sheen of morning dew under a cold blue sky. Elsie had stood here many times before, but every day she found something new in the street. Today, a collection of slightly bedraggled pigeons were doing their best to balance on the neck of the enormous guitar mounted on the yellow and red frontage of the Guitar, Amp & Keyboard Centre on North Road at the bottom of the street. As they tiptoed up and down the neck it looked like they were attempting to play a group version of a rock classic. She smiled to herself. Woody would definitely approve.

Her positivity thus restored, she paused on the quiet street to wave to Sandra who owned the fabric shop opposite, when a voice suddenly spoke behind her, making her start.

'Elsie.'

She turned to see Torin standing in the doorway of the café. He was dressed in his work suit and held a folded copy of *The Times* under one arm with a heavy-looking rucksack slung over the opposite shoulder. His face was slightly flushed as if he had just sprinted and Elsie noticed the pronounced rise and fall of his chest underneath his suit jacket. His sudden presence shook her recently-found equilibrium and she felt intense irritation prickling across her shoulders. Averting her eyes, she said nothing, walking past him into the café.

He followed her inside, his footsteps quick on the black and white floor tiles. 'Elsie, *please* . . .'

'I'm really busy.'

'Yeah, I can see that from the complete lack of customers.'

'Go away.'

'Not until you *talk* to me.'

She stepped behind the counter, keen to put a physical barrier between her and him. 'I don't have anything to add to my last statement.'

110

He dropped his newspaper and rucksack on the nearest table. 'Well I want to say something.'

Suddenly vulnerable, Elsie crossed her arms in front of her body. 'So, say it and go.' She cursed herself for recognising conviction in his eyes as he faced her. It would be so much easier to dismiss whatever it was he was about to say if she hadn't seen sincerity there.

'I came here because I wanted to apologise. For last week. I had no idea of your loss and, believe me, if I had I would never have suggested that you . . .'

'You couldn't have known. I don't generally introduce myself with that fact. I find it scuppers polite conversation.'

'Elsie, I . . .'

'Torin, I really don't have time for this.'

'All the same, I think you need to listen.'

Elsie glared at him, wishing with every fibre of her being that he would disappear and let her return to the safety of her work.

Taking her silence as an invitation, Torin began. 'I don't blame you for hating me. I completely took advantage of the situation and, to be honest, made a total prat of myself. Ordinarily I would just have ignored the whole thing and not sought to make amends but . . . You see, the thing is, I've felt so dreadful about it since our date, and—'

'It wasn't a date.' The words tumbled out of her mouth before her head could stop them. Frustrated with her outburst, she grabbed a blue sundae glass from the dishwasher tray on the counter and started to dry it on her apron.

Torin stared at her. 'Our *meeting*, then.'

'Right.' She put the sundae glass on the counter, grabbed a Tupperware box and began to pile peach and raspberry cupcakes onto a glass cake stand on the counter, the tongs in her hand shaking as she did so. Why wouldn't he just go away? Couldn't he see how awkward he was making her feel?

'I wanted to say sorry. Whatever else I might have said, or implied in recent weeks, I never meant to make a point of your loss.' He held up his hands. 'That's all I wanted to say.' He nodded, picked up his newspaper and bag and walked to the door.

'Wait.'

Despite her intense vexation with the man, Elsie couldn't let him leave without acknowledging how difficult his apology must have been to make. She didn't have to like him, but she knew she wasn't a mean person and couldn't bear the possibility of anyone thinking of her as such – even Torin Stewart.

Surprised, he turned back. 'What?'

'Thank you. It can't have been easy for you to come here and I appreciate the gesture.'

'Er – thanks.'

'And, for the record, I don't hate you. I've never hated anyone, actually. Not really. We're never going to be friends – that much is evident – but I'm not the person you seem to think I am. I'm better than that.'

'I don't think . . .'

Elsie reached under the counter and produced a large mug. 'Look, the machine's ready and I'm guessing you might not have had time for coffee this morning. Can I interest you in one?'

For someone so used to keeping his personal feelings concealed in the course of his job, Torin was making a complete mess of doing it now, his shock as plain to see as the bespoke suit he wore. 'Yes. Yes, that would be good.' He placed his paper on the counter and sat at one of the red leather and chrome bar stools, dropping his rucksack to the floor, watching her all the time.

She put the last peach and raspberry cupcake from the box onto a plate and slid it across the counter towards him, avoiding his stare. As she turned towards the coffee machine, Elsie took advantage of the hiss of steaming milk and buzz of percolating espresso to calm herself and assess the unexpected situation. Making coffee for Torin Stewart had definitely not been on her To-Do list for today, but it felt right to be doing it. He could have one coffee and a cupcake, and her act of mercy would be complete. Then he could walk away for good. Layering steamed milk and dark, glossy espresso in the mug, she caught a brief image of Lucas in her mind's eye, sitting beside the coffee machine as he always did when waiting for her shift to finish, leaning back on one of the tall bar stools procured from the window bar and grinning at her.

'Whatcha doin', Elsie?' he would ask, in his best Forrest Gump impression. 'Tell me whatcha up to?'

'I have no idea,' Elsie said out loud.

'Sorry?'

Snapping back to the present, she returned to the counter and placed the coffee before Torin. 'Nothing. You realise your acceptance of this makes us quits for your helping me with that security guard?'

He raised the mug to his lips. 'Absolutely. Verbal agreement thus sealed. Wow, good coffee. I shall come here again.' He stopped when he saw her expression. 'Or, maybe I won't.'

Elsie poured a mug of steamed milk for herself and added a dash of almond syrup. 'Glad we have an understanding.'

'I'm not sure I understand it. Nevertheless, while I'm here on what will therefore be my only visit to your good establishment – mind if I ask you a question?'

Fair enough, Torin. It'll be the last time we talk anyhow.
'Be my guest.'

'How long ago did . . .? I'm sorry, feel free to tell me to get lost.'

Elsie took a deep breath, still not sure whether she wanted him to know these details about her life. 'Lucas – my husband – died eighteen months ago after a twelve-month battle with pancreatic cancer. He was twenty-five.'

Torin winced. 'That's no age at all, I'm sorry. So Maynard is your married name?'

Elsie shook her head. 'My maiden name. Lucas didn't believe I should change it when we married.'

'I see. How long had you been married?'

'Four years. But we'd been together since we were seventeen.'

'Wow. Such a tragic thing to lose a love like that.'

Elsie pulled up a stool behind the counter and sat down. 'I don't see it that way. I was loved by the most amazing guy in the world for eight wonderful years. Most people don't get to enjoy that kind of love their whole lives. I count myself as one of the lucky few.'

Torin looked at her for a long time, the clicking of the cooling coffee machine the only sound in the café. Then, he dropped his gaze towards the froth on his coffee. 'That's . . . I haven't heard someone talk about loss like that.'

'I suppose a lot of people don't feel that way. But I do.'

He picked a wooden stirrer from the countertop display and pushed the froth around in his mug with it. 'Right. Forgive me for asking, then, but if you think you already found the love of your life, how come you agreed to go on a double date with your boss last week?'

Elsie took a sip of sweet, warm milk and gazed out towards the street beyond the large windows of the café, which was beginning to fill with morning commuters and shoppers. 'It's time to start again,' she replied, the thought of it sending a pulse of trepidation through her core. 'Besides, Cher wanted to meet Jake so much that I could hardly refuse.'

His eyes met hers. 'And if you'd known it was me you'd be meeting?'

Elsie smiled. 'Then I'd have refused, naturally.'

A moment of understanding passed between them. Then, as soon as it had arrived, it vanished as Torin drained his mug in one long gulp and stepped down from the stool.

'Well, I have clients to see, the law to upkeep, et cetera.' He swung his rucksack over his shoulder and nodded at Elsie. 'Thank you for my one-and-only excellent coffee in Sundae & Cher.'

'You're welcome.'

'I'd like to say I'll see you later but . . .' he raised his hand in surrender '. . . that's unlikely.'

'It is.'

The brass bell rang out as he stood in the open doorway, a broad smile illuminating his features. 'Thank you.'

Elsie looked down at the folded newspaper still on the counter where he had dropped it. 'Don't forget your paper.'

He waved his hand. 'Keep it. Consider it a peace offering.' And with that, he was gone, the door closing fast behind him.

Staring at the door, Elsie realised she felt relieved. Lucas would have been proud of her. Turning her mind back to her morning chores, she picked up a handful of serviettes and began to set the tables.

The day passed uneventfully, mercifully so given its unexpected and unsettling start, the details of which Elsie

115

continued to mull over, as morning became lunch and afternoon. She chose not to tell Cher or her sisters about her conversation with Torin, deciding it was best they didn't know. For now, she was satisfied that they had parted as never-to-be-friends.

Standing in her bedroom at seven p.m., she turned her attention to tonight's date. She had chosen a plain blue flared dress with matching heels and a beautiful scarf Cher had brought her from one of her many trips to Paris, covered in tiny pale pink rosebuds on a sky-blue background. Consulting the full-length mirror on the back of her bedroom door, she was pleased with the combination. She didn't look like she was trying too hard, but felt feminine enough to remind herself that she was a woman out on a date – a fact she figured would both boost her confidence and help her to relax enough to enjoy the evening.

Just before seven-thirty, her mobile lit up with a text from Daisy:

Have a fantastic time tonight, lovely!
Let me know how it goes ☺ D xx

The doorbell rang at exactly seven-thirty-one and Elsie couldn't help grinning at the thought of Olly waiting one minute longer to ensure he didn't appear too keen. He was dressed in a white shirt with khaki trousers and wore a simple leather band around one wrist. When he stepped across the threshold into her home he brought a small bunch of orange and yellow ranunculus blooms from behind his back to present to her.

'I know flowers are a bit of a lame gesture, but I thought you might like them.'

'They're lovely. Thank you.'

He checked his watch. 'Table's booked for seven-forty-five, so we should probably get going, if that's all right with you?'

They made their way down the small path from Elsie's front door towards Olly's Mazda, which was parked on the street. He held open the passenger door for her and half-sprinted round to the driver's side. To her relief, Elsie found herself enjoying this chivalry as she settled into the cream leather seats. It was charming and thoughtful – unlike her first date with Lucas, which had begun with stilted awkwardness, fraught with teenage nerves. She remembered the way he had shaken her hand stiffly, as though she was interviewing for a job rather than stepping out on a date with him, and it had taken him a full thirty minutes to make any kind of eye contact. But this evening her suitor was relaxed and chatty, putting her delightfully at ease.

Olly drove them along the coast road until they pulled in at a small restaurant overlooking a secluded bay. The evening light was fading as a waitress took them to their table by a set of French doors overlooking the jetty outside.

'I hope this is OK,' he said, consulting the menu. 'A friend of a friend owns this place and the seafood here is so fresh it's practically still swimming. You do like seafood, don't you?'

Elsie smiled. 'Love it.'

Olly blew out a whistle. 'That's a relief! By the way, you're looking lovely tonight . . .' He pulled a face and slapped his hand against his forehead. 'I'm sorry, that was the worst line ever.'

Elsie reached across and placed her hand over his. 'Olly, stop apologising. This is a great place and I'm looking forward to spending time with you. OK?'

He hooked his thumb over hers to keep her hand on his.

'Thank you. I'll be honest, your dad told me at lunchtime that this was your first proper date since . . . and I wanted to make sure it was perfect for you.' He let go of her hand. 'I promise I'll relax now. Let's order, shall we?'

From that point on, their conversation flowed freely, Elsie enjoying the opportunity to find out more about the good-looking man opposite her. She discovered that he, like her, was the youngest of three children, the son of a veterinarian father and legal secretary mother. He had fallen in love with kitesurfing while on a year out in Australia before university and had recently purchased an aged Volkswagen camper van, which he hoped to restore and take on trips to Cornwall and North Devon. He loved reading spy thrillers, was a big fan of films adapted from John Grisham novels, but disliked action films with no plot. His dream was to set up his own design studio and he hoped to one day run a marathon.

In return, Olly asked about the choir, Elsie's job and Lucas – and, unlike her conversation with Torin that morning, Elsie encountered no reservations about sharing her past with him. In fact, everything about Oliver Hogarth made Elsie feel at home. When he took her hand during dessert, she didn't object, the closeness of their interlacing fingers completely welcome and not alien as she had anticipated it might be; and later outside, when he draped his jacket across her shoulders, she found herself leaning against his warm body as they walked together along the shingle beach before returning to his car.

A comfortable silence settled between them on the journey back, the glow of a good evening filling Elsie with a surprising sense of peace. When they reached her front door, Elsie looked up into Olly's eyes that were sparkling in the light of the porch lamp, and felt her heartbeat quicken.

'So, how did I do?' he asked, the joke of his earlier eagerness now firmly established between them.

'Not bad,' she grinned back. 'But I think perhaps I should let you try again, just to see if you improve.'

He raised an eyebrow and moved closer. 'Is that so?'

'Mm-hmm.'

'You think I have potential?'

'Yes, I think maybe you do.'

Smiling, he wrapped his arm around her waist and drew her to him, the softness of his lips on hers as soothing as a blanket on a winter's night. It was quite unlike the insistence with which Lucas had kissed her – the intensity and hunger of his kisses never waning from their first date to their last goodbye. Olly's kiss was gentle and new, respectful of the occasion but entirely heartfelt. Slowly, Elsie returned it, the unhurried luxury of the kiss drawing her in as their embrace deepened. When it ended, they shared a nervous giggle, suddenly tentative again.

'I'll call you, soon?' he asked, stroking her face gently.

'Yes. Thank you for a lovely night, Olly.'

He paused to look at her, his face flushed and his eyes alive. 'Thank you. Goodnight.'

Elsie was still smiling as she turned the key in the front door lock and walked slowly into her home. As first dates go, she thought to herself, it had been a very good night indeed.

'I don't see why *she* should be singing soprano if she isn't planning to *sing*,' Sasha Mitchell growled, sending an accusatory glance at Aoife, who blushed fiercely and stared at the floor.

Elsie surveyed the assembled choir members in the café and witnessed the same frustration on their faces that was currently gnarling at her insides. By now she had imagined her fledgling choir would be well on the way to working together as a closely-knit team – their lack of experience compensated for by the rise in confidence as they discovered the joy of singing together. So much for *that* theory.

'Sasha, forget Aoife for a minute, will you? All I want you to do is to sing the line so that she can hear it. Beginning at the top of the chorus of "Bad Romance", here we go . . .'

Sasha Mitchell had to be one of the most frustrating women ever to grace the streets of Brighton, Elsie grumbled to herself as she started to play. From the sheer speed of Sasha's sarcastic retorts it was obvious that her mind was quick, but all too often she chose to hide her intelligence behind the loud, obnoxious façade of a woman more concerned with peroxide blonde hair extensions, fake tan and skirts so short that even the bravest teenager would think twice about wearing them in public. Her heels were so high and pointed that they could quite conceivably be handed in to the police during a dangerous weapon amnesty and leopard-print was a perennial feature of any outfit she (almost) wore. She spoke her mind without hesitation, rarely smiled (unless she was ruthlessly massacring someone else's character) and appeared to relish every opportunity to be outspoken and controversial.

But – she had a voice, well concealed as it was behind the vitriol, that hinted at skill beyond its current use as a weapon of mass destruction. And it was this single fact – this tantalising glimpse of something more – that right now was the only thing preventing Elsie from personally ejecting the objectionable creature from Sundae & Cher.

Sasha tutted and began to sing quietly, her voice strained by the effort of holding it back.

120

'*Louder*, Sasha!' Elsie urged, turning up the volume on the keyboard in a vain attempt to coax the singer into a competition.

Stubbornly, Sasha retained her current volume, rolling her eyes heavenwards as if the very act of singing was beneath her.

Elsie was about to give up when a loud, falsetto voice began to sing the soprano line. She looked up from her music to see Woody springing to the centre of the floor, his legs spreading wide into a rock-star stance as he threw back his head and gave a full-on rendition that would have had Gaga herself rising to her platform heels with applause. When the chorus ended, Stan, Danny and Aoife clapped and whistled, the spectacle of the ageing rocker strutting his stuff instantly uniting them. Even Irene, knitting quietly by the counter, lowered her needles to her lap and joined in the ovation with polite applause. Sasha glowered as Woody took a bow.

'Why, thank you, fellow musical adventurers,' he said, tipping his Stetson. 'Now *that's* how you do a soprano line, girl.'

'Your trousers must be too tight, mate,' Sasha shot back. 'I think your balls need air.'

'Woody has a point, Sasha,' Elsie interjected.

'There was a point to *that*?'

'Yes, actually. He was demonstrating how to perform a song.'

Sasha pulled a face. 'I know how to perform.'

'Do you? Do you really?' Elsie stepped away from her keyboard, irritation at Sasha's tone intensifying with every word. 'Because after hearing your lacklustre attempt I'm starting to wonder if you're able to sing at all, or if you're just bluffing in a pathetic attempt to get attention.'

The café fell silent – even Woody was taken aback by the sudden change in Elsie's attitude. Sasha pointed at the keyboard. '*Play.*'

'Why? So you can whisper the song and waste more of our time?'

Sasha's over-plucked, pencilled-in brows knotted and she lowered her voice to a menacing growl. 'Play the song and I'll show you.'

Elsie walked back to the keyboard and began to play. Closing her eyes, Sasha took a breath and began to sing, the power and tone of her voice making everyone in the room stare open-mouthed at her. Thrilled with the confirmation of her suspicions, Elsie carried on playing past the chorus, and Sasha, rising to the challenge, continued the song until the end, when a stunned choir rose to their feet to applaud her.

'Now *that*,' Elsie said, watching Sasha's flushed face break into a smile in the midst of the applause, 'is what I call a performance!' Keen to build on the moment, Elsie quickly assembled the choir together in their requisite parts and began to play the introduction to the Lady Gaga medley. 'Now that Woody and Sasha have shown us how it's done, we're going to go for a full performance of the medley. Don't worry about what anyone else is doing, just sing your part as we've practised, and let's see what happens. Here we go, two, three, four . . .'

What happened next was as imperfectly close to a miracle as it was possible to be. The notes were shaky, the parts even more so, but the essence of a performance was there. Everybody felt it, evident in the steady swell of volume and the broadening smiles spreading across the choir members' faces as they sang. Stan began to sway jerkily as the medley progressed and even Aoife and Irene's voices became audible in the mix. But above all, the unique thrill of shared performance began to permeate the room, building to a natural crescendo and breaking like a wave over the choir as the medley reached its end. Woody slung his arm around Elsie's shoulders as they watched their delighted choir clapping and congratulating one another.

'The magic is starting, babe. Gaga has had her mystical way with all of us.'

Elsie did her best to remove the mental picture she had just been blessed with and allowed herself a small moment of celebration. Her strategy for reaching Sasha Mitchell hadn't gone as she'd planned, but at least she'd proved that the loud-mouthed woman could achieve a similar volume when she sang. Now all she had to do was to find the key for the rest of them. Aoife surely just needed a confidence boost to perform – and Elsie hoped this would come with time. What Danny lacked in technical skill he more than made up for with enthusiasm, so with a little practice he could become a solid member of the choir. Stan, too, had a steady voice that would hold its own in the lower ranges. Looking across the room, Elsie saw Irene quietly returning to her knitting, the effect of her recent participation apparently dissipated already. What would unlock Irene's performance, Elsie wondered? The pensioner certainly seemed to enjoy spending time with the choir, and could often be seen engaging in quite lengthy conversations with each one of the members during the tea breaks in rehearsals. Elsie also knew, from a brief conversation she had shared with Irene that evening before everyone else arrived, that she loved the music. Occasionally – as had happened this evening – Irene joined in with the singing and seemed to love it. But how could Elsie encourage Irene to become a full participant in the choir's fledgling repertoire?

Daisy brought a mug of tea over to her. 'I think we've made progress tonight.'

'I think we have.'

'Thanks to Woody,' Daisy grinned. 'The way he wound Sasha up was nothing short of brilliant. And then you sealed the deal. Don't tell him I said so, but I think the two of you have the makings of a great leadership team. I'm proud of you, sis.'

Elsie hugged Daisy. 'I'm so glad you're here. I know we have a long way to go, but I really think this could become something a bit special.'

'With you steering it, it's bound to be.' Daisy surveyed her. 'You look happy.'

'I am.'

A brief memory of Olly's smile and gentle kiss flashed across her mind. *A good start all round*, she congratulated herself. *Onwards and upwards, Elsie . . .*

CHAPTER EIGHT

Baby steps . . .

April arrived with a rush of sunshine, the weather forecasters on TV confirming the promise of a mini-heatwave over the Easter holiday. Brighton was suddenly abuzz with impromptu holidaymakers from London and the Home Counties, students enjoying their extended spring break and local residents determined to make the most of the unseasonably mild weather.

Sundae & Cher saw its usual takings double overnight, the offer of refreshing ice cream too enticing for passers-by to resist. The ice cream mixer in the basement kitchen was on almost permanent service as the café struggled to keep up with demand. Lucas' Blueberry Choc Chip, their Classic Vanilla and the new Hazelnut Oreo Swirl flavour completely sold out within an hour of being made and Cher worked late into the night creating new batches of ice cream for the increased custom. For four days in a row, Cher and Elsie opened the ice cream café an hour earlier and still, when they arrived each morning, they encountered queues of customers pressed against the windows and already claiming the tables and chairs set outside in the street.

'I know it's a bit hotter than usual, but who in their right mind wants to eat ice cream at eight o'clock in the morning – apart from Dennis?' Cher grumbled as she piled large scoops of Pink Sugar Bubblegum gelato into the café's signature handmade chocolate-dipped waffle cones.

'Hey, don't knock it. Just enjoy the rush,' Elsie grinned, handing change back to another satisfied customer.

'You should be on TV,' the lady gushed. 'I've never tasted ice cream as good as yours.'

'Now there's a thought, Cher,' Elsie grinned, scooping balls of Melon and Grape sorbet into a bowl with two mango cupcakes for the next customer. 'You could be the Nigella of the ice cream world!'

The increased custom was undoubtedly a boost for the business, but by half past three that afternoon, Cher and Elsie were exhausted. Taking advantage of a brief lull in the flow of customers, Cher poured them each a glass of homemade lemon and peppermint cordial over ice and they collapsed at the table nearest the counter.

Cher kicked off her shoes, pulled up a chair and swung her aching legs onto it. 'Even in the height of the summer season last year I don't recall people queuing like that.'

'What it is to be popular, eh? It's good to see the place packed.' Elsie stretched her arms above her head to unknot the muscles in her shoulders. 'I just wish it could be this full for choir practice tonight. Perhaps we should bribe them with free ice cream.'

'Still no new members?' Cher asked, flicking open a copy of the local free paper.

Elsie shook her head. 'I don't understand it. I've run three adverts in the newspaper, given a couple of interviews to local radio and Stan even handed out flyers to the mums at his granddaughter's school gate last week. With all the

126

choir programmes there have been on TV lately you'd think the interest would be higher than usual.'

'Oh for the intervention of Saint Gareth Malone.' Cher raised her eyes to heaven and clasped her hands together, making Elsie giggle. 'I wonder if we could stalk him on Twitter until he agrees to help.'

'Now there's a thought.'

'Or perhaps we should unleash the full force of Woody Jensen's creativity on the choir. One of his The Doors-slash-Beyoncé mash-ups might just do the trick.'

Elsie grimaced. 'Please don't encourage him. It's difficult enough to keep him reined in without granting him carte blanche with our repertoire. I'll ask everyone again this evening for ideas and hope we come up trumps.'

'Oh.' Cher's smile faded as she pointed at the open paper. 'I don't suppose this will help.'

Elsie moved her chair to Cher's side to look at the story she had found.

AWARD-WINNING CHOIR LAUNCHES TALENT SEARCH

Budding singers are being invited to audition for Brighton's premier show choir.

The DreamTeam, which last year won the coveted South-east Choral Cup, has launched ChoirStar – an X-Factor-style search for new members aged 18–35. Auditions are being held over the next three Saturdays at St Mary's Church Hall, Hove, culminating in a lavish final to be held at Brighton's Theatre Royal in June, which will feature a celebrity judge.

Choir leader, Jeannette Burton, told The Argus, 'ChoirStar is a fantastic opportunity for Brighton's best amateur singers to join the top choir in the Southeast. We are bracing ourselves for an unprecedented response.'

Ms Burton refused to either confirm or deny rumours that TV's popular choirmaster, Gareth Malone, is due to appear at the grand final . . .

'Turncoat,' Cher scoffed. 'Good job we didn't seek his assistance.'

'This shouldn't affect our potential members,' Elsie said. 'The DreamTeam is as far removed from the spirit of a true choir as you can get. Our choir is all about fun and inclusivity – not about looks and rigidity. We might be few in numbers, but at least all of them are starting to enjoy singing.'

'All the same, attracting people here could be tricky.'

'Well, we need to think of something.'

Elsie mulled over the issue for the rest of the day, but by seven p.m. had drawn a total blank. When Woody arrived at Sundae & Cher, he thrust a crumpled newspaper page at her in disgust.

'Have you seen this?'

'I have.'

'It's not cool with my soul, Elsie. I sense the Greats are not happy with this development, either. We need a radical happening, a call to arms for the musical faithful of this great town . . .'

Elsie rubbed her aching temples. 'Or maybe just a few more people to join us?'

'That too. Now, I've been thinking about this all day and I've come to the conclusion that we have to make a stand against the plastic, bland, *doh-ray-me* crap that woman serves up. We need to be the Banksy of show choirs, man! Sticking musical art to the masses and leaving them in *total awe* while we slink away . . .'

'Woody, what on earth are you talking about?'

'You need to widen your mind, Elsie! There's no law says choirs can't rock it large.' Woody grinned a gold-toothed smile, tapping his rings on the table as if to drive home whatever point it was he was attempting to make. He pulled a chair over from a neighbouring table and sat astride it, leaning his arms on its backrest. 'So, we up the ante. Offer something that red-trousered woman and her Stepford Children clones couldn't even dream of.' He waved his hands in a mystical manner and closed his eyes. 'Gaga is just the beginning. Now is the time for the big guns: Floyd, Lennon, The Carpenters. I've been working on a meeting of ABBA's "Summer Night City" and Deep Purple's "Smoke on the Water" that will blow their tiny minds. I've even recorded a blistering backing track in my personal bedroom studio . . .'

'OK, fine.'

'Eh?'

Woody's suggestion was the closest thing Elsie could see to a way forward. 'Go for it. But you have to take charge of promotion. Surely someone of your musical stature can bring us some publicity?'

Woody's grey eyes lit up like a slot machine. 'Just leave it to me, babe. I'm going to float like a butterfly and *sing* like a bee!'

'Do bees sing?'

He tutted and stood up, as Irene, Stan and Danny arrived. 'You're totally missing the point, babe.'

The prospect of Woody's unusual musical amalgamation was dodgy in the extreme, but as Elsie saw him explaining his vision to half of the choir, she couldn't help smiling. At least it would be fun to see the small band of would-be choristers tackling the distinct nuances of Scandinavian pop and stadium rock. Inevitably, her thoughts strayed to Lucas. If only he could see this . . .

'Nice place, is it?'

Elsie opened her eyes to see Irene Quinn's face gazing up at her. 'Sorry?'

'Where you were in your mind. It seemed like a nice place. You looked very peaceful.'

A little taken aback, Elsie nodded. 'I suppose it was.'

Irene smiled. 'I have a place like that. Often end up there when I'm knitting.' She lifted the knitted length of blanc-mange-blue and orange striped wool to emphasise her point. 'Jumper, this is, for my grandniece's little one. Not that I'm making much progress.'

'It looks lovely.' Elsie decided to take the opportunity to ask the question she had been pondering since the choir's first meeting. 'If you don't mind me asking, are you enjoying being part of the choir?'

Irene didn't miss a beat before answering. '*Love* it.'

'Oh – er, *good*. It's just that I haven't really heard you sing much and I was wondering if perhaps you had a particular song you thought we should do?'

'No need to worry about me, dear. You and Woody are doing an excellent job with us all. And more people will come, of that I'm sure.' Seeing Elsie's confusion, she leaned closer and added, 'Isn't about the singing for me, you see. It's the company. Long time since I felt so much a part of something.' She placed a blue-veined, parchment-skinned hand on Elsie's arm. 'For us that have *lost*, company is important.'

Elsie's breath caught in her throat. Had someone told Irene about Lucas? 'How did you . . .?'

'I recognised it in you, dear.' She smiled in the direction of the choir members, who were gathered around a small CD player watching Woody with a mixture of amusement and fascination as he acted out his vision for the new songs, the bobbles around the edge of the buff scarf wrapped around his neck jumping with every movement. 'This project'll bring you more than you expect. It's a good thing, Elsie. A comfort, for you as much as for them – perhaps more.' Smiling to herself, she left Elsie and resumed her favoured seat by the counter, her attention claimed once more by the half-knitted jumper in her hands.

Elsie watched the tiny old lady settling herself, her blush rose cardigan matching the rouge on her downy cheeks as her watery blue eyes sparkled. She wasn't sure whether to be comforted by Irene's perception, or unnerved by it. A loud whoop from Woody summoned her attention.

'Magic! The magic is here, dudes! *Now* we're getting somewhere . . .'

Later that week, Elsie joined her sisters for a family dinner at Jim's. As usual, Jim had been scouring his extensive recipe book collection for a suitably exotic meal and tonight they were enjoying a feast of grilled halloumi cheese with apricots, flaked almonds and allspice on a bed of fluffy basmati rice, with homemade chapattis and mango chutney.

'Dad, your chapattis are always so good,' Guin said, tearing one in half and dipping it in the sweet chutney. 'I haven't had any cravings with this pregnancy but I reckon I should invent one for these.'

Jim laughed. 'It would be my pleasure to supply you, Guinie. I learned how to make them when I spent time in Goa before I met your mother. Maybe one day I'll teach your little one to make them, too.' He smiled at his daughters gathered around the carved wood dining table in the small dining room that was bedecked in jewel-like Indian silks and illuminated by tiny candle lanterns. 'This is so nice. All my girls together.' His eyes glistened in the candlelight.

Daisy reached across and patted his hand. 'We wouldn't miss it, Dad.'

'Oh blimey, don't you start, Dad, or we'll all be in tears,' Guin laughed.

'Well, I mean it. You three are my proudest achievements. I look at all of you and I'm so unbelievably amazed at the wonderful young women you've grown into. My Daisy, successful and beautiful; my Guin, about to become a mum; my strong little Elsie, moving on with her life. It does this old heart good.'

'Talking of moving on,' Daisy said, turning to Elsie. 'How is that gorgeous designer of yours?'

'He isn't *my* designer,' Elsie retorted, feeling the full force of the Maynard family stares falling on her. At that moment, her mobile began to ring and she caught her breath as Olly's name appeared. *Fantastic timing, Mr Hogarth.* 'Um, I just – I'd better take this. Sorry, Dad.'

Jim grinned at her. 'I'll make an exception to the "no mobiles at the dinner table" rule if that's who I think it is.'

Ignoring the excited chatter of Jim and her sisters, Elsie walked out into the kitchen to take the call.

'OK, we can speak now.'

'I'm sorry, do you have guests?'

'No, I'm at Dad's with Daisy and Guin. So you can imagine their faces at this precise moment.'

'Oh no, hope I haven't made things awkward for you?'

Elsie laughed. 'Not at all. You'll have made their day. So, how are you?'

'I'm good, thanks. Sorry for not calling sooner, I've been snowed under at work and, you know, after my embarrassing

132

eagerness last Friday I didn't want to scare you by calling before.'

'Well, I'm glad you called.' She hesitated, unsure whether to say more. It was lovely to hear his voice and she realised she was grinning as she spoke to him.

'I'm glad I called, too. Listen, how about meeting up on Saturday – in town? We could have lunch or coffee or whatever?'

'Sounds good.'

'OK. So, how about brunch on Saturday at BiblioCaff at, say, eleven-ish?'

'That would be fine.'

'Excellent. Hey, I had a great time on Friday.'

A sliver of joy wriggled down to Elsie's toes. 'Me too.'

Daisy accosted her the moment she set foot back in the dining room. '*So?* Was it who we think it was?'

'Probably. That was Oliver Hogarth and we're meeting on Saturday for brunch. Happy?'

Jim clapped his hands and swept Elsie up in an enormous bear hug. 'Wonderful news! I'm so thrilled for you, darling!'

'Dad, it's only brunch,' Elsie protested.

'Ah, but it's a *start*,' he beamed.

As the conversation around the dining table progressed to different territory, Elsie sat back, suddenly presented with a new sensation. Something was building within her – a note of caution, an unexpected question that, as yet, she couldn't decipher. Maybe it was the unanimous vote of confidence in Olly from her family, or the speed with which their friendship appeared to be progressing. Or maybe it was her own fear at what might lie ahead. But then, all she had agreed to was one more date, she told herself. And Olly was a wonderful man. The safety she had felt with him, and the peace his closeness and kiss had brought her,

133

had been unexpected gifts. She was excited at the prospect of seeing him again – and that must be a positive thing, mustn't it?

As she observed the familiar Maynard family dynamics playing out around the dining table, she realised her father was smiling at her. Whether this was due to being in the presence of his girls or the promise Oliver Hogarth offered, Elsie wasn't sure, but she resolved to put her concerns to rest.

'Excuse me, is this the right place to sign up for the choir?' The lanky teenager kept his hands firmly shoved in the pockets of his hoodie as he spoke, his body slouched into an elongated 'S' as he stood by the counter in Sundae & Cher.

'Yes, it is,' Elsie replied, handing him a clipboard that already bore the names of three new recruits. 'I'm Elsie, by the way. I lead the choir with Woody Jensen – he was the lead singer of Hellfinger in the 1980s?' She cringed as the words came out. *Blimey, I'm beginning to sound like Woody* . . .

The teenager nodded sagely. 'My dad knows him. That's why I'm here. He said I should come.'

'Good, um, *great*. Just pop your details on this list so we can contact you and I'll see you at choir rehearsal next Wednesday at seven-thirty.'

'Is that another one?' Cher asked, passing with a tray of dirty dishes en route to the dishwasher.

'Yes. So far every one seems to know Woody in one way or another.'

'See, I told you he was useful.'

'No, you didn't. You said he was *fit*. In my dictionary that doesn't mean the same thing.'

'Whatever. He's certainly proving himself.'

By the end of the day, the choir's number had more than doubled and Elsie gazed happily at the list of new members. Quite how Woody knew all these people remained a mystery. They ranged from Dee, a fourteen-year-old girl who was already a member of two local choirs and was looking for a new challenge – to Juliet, a retired headmistress who had never sung a note in public before. Kathy, a twenty-something estate agent who had blushed and changed the subject when Elsie asked how she knew Woody, and Graeme, a local butcher with secret operatic ambitions joined Lewis, the lanky teenager, and Sheila, a forty-something matronly dental nurse to complete the new recruits.

'Think you can make it work?' Cher asked, peering at the clipboard list.

'I reckon we could have the makings of a nicely rounded sound here.'

Cher sniffed. 'One suggestion? You need a name. That Burton dragon has The DreamTeam – wanky, I grant you, but it's a name you remember. The choir needs a title everyone can get behind. How about The Sundaes?' Cher suggested, as she lifted a steaming tray of newly washed sundae glasses from the dishwasher. 'It's a bit like The Saturdays, with a link to this place. I mean, I don't know any other choir that meets in an ice cream café.'

'Cher, you're a genius!' Elsie declared.

The Sundaes. Elsie loved the name and, when she relayed it to Woody on Saturday morning, his immediate reaction confirmed her confidence:

'We'll be the smooth sauce of musical splendour, with layers of decadent brilliance building on the irresistible sweetness of the Greats . . .'

Daisy and Elsie stifled their amusement as Woody twisted

his hips alarmingly with each syllable, the act earning a disapproving tut from an elderly lady walking towards them on the promenade.

A fresh breeze from the sea was a welcome addition to the already considerable heat of the morning as they strolled towards town, Elsie tryng not to think about the minutes ticking away before her arranged meeting with Olly.

'We should get T-shirts,' Woody continued, 'now our baby has a name. There's a possibility I could secure us some funds . . .'

'All legal, I hope?' Daisy asked, a little too quickly.

Woody observed her with disgust. 'Always. The law and I are good friends, girl. You should know that by now.'

'What sort of funds?' Elsie asked, careful to keep her tone light to avoid any hint of concern.

'A benefactor – a sponsor, if you will. I happen to know someone who is keen to support us as a community venture.' He glared at Daisy. 'If no one has any objections, that is.'

Daisy pretended not to notice. 'None here.'

'I am also good friends with an old roadie of the band who now runs his own T-shirt printing business. Handy, wouldn't you say?'

'That's wonderful, Woody,' Elsie reassured him. 'It would be good to have T-shirts by the time we perform at the Carnival.' An alarm beeped on her mobile and she felt her heart jump. 'That's my cue to leave. Woody, I'll see you on Wednesday evening. Thanks for all your hard work.'

'A pleasure as always, a-a-a-angel.'

'Have a great time,' Daisy said, hugging her tightly. 'And call me later. I want to know *all* the details, OK?'

CHAPTER NINE

I'm sorry, have we met?

The interior of the small café was heaving with bodies taking advantage of BiblioCaff's air-conditioning. Outside, already perspiring shoppers passed by its windows gazing in on the artificially cooled customers with barely concealed envy. Olly raised his hand in greeting when Elsie entered the café.

'Come and enjoy the air-con,' he smiled, as she sat down at his table. 'I bet this place has never seen so many people desperate to get in before.'

Elsie felt a shiver of excitement as she basked in his smile. 'It's been crazy all week at work, too. We've never seen an April like it.'

They ordered coffee and Eggs Benedict and settled down for a leisurely brunch. As they talked about their week, Elsie noticed how Olly watched her constantly. Even when the food on his plate momentarily called his gaze away, it returned to her at the earliest opportunity. It had been a long time since she had commanded so much of somebody else's attention and it felt good, if slightly alien, to experience such scrutiny again.

'How's the choir?' he asked.

'Good. Woody brought some new people, so the next practice should be fun.'

'It's bound to be fun with the combined magic of you and Woody,' Olly grinned.

Elsie felt the back of her neck prickle and turned her attention to stirring the froth into her latte.

'I was chatting with your dad first thing,' he continued, oblivious to Elsie's reaction. 'He's incredibly proud of you, you know. I think he'd join the choir in an instant if he didn't think it might cramp your style.'

Elsie looked up. 'He said that?'

'Not in so many words, no. But I know how he feels.'

'You do?'

The intensity of his stare was back again, and this time Elsie couldn't look away. 'The way you talk about the choir – it's infectious.' He dropped his gaze and gave a self-conscious laugh. 'Heck, I sound like a complete groupie, I'm sorry.'

She was aware of tension now creeping along her spine. 'No you don't.'

His smile returned, along with the searching stare. 'Thanks. Listen, about the other night . . .'

Why was she feeling like this? When she had spoken to him a few days ago she couldn't wait to see him. What had changed now? 'Olly . . .'

'I just wanted to say, I had fun. And I haven't stopped thinking about our kiss. It was – *incredible* . . .'

Elsie kept her smile steady, despite the silent screaming of her limbs to move away. 'I've thought about it a lot, too.'

'You have?'

'Isn't it always the case that you run into someone you

know when you come into town?' someone said beside them.

I recognise that voice, Elsie thought, turning to see Torin Stewart standing by their table. He was dressed casually in jeans, red T-shirt and blue trainers and appeared to be highly amused by the surprise his interruption had caused.

So much for keeping away from me, Elsie thought. 'I didn't know you knew this place.'

'Know it? I *love* it! Although, I must confess, today that's mainly due to the air-con. If you ask me, the coffee can be a little hit-and-miss . . .'

Olly cleared his throat a little too loudly and Elsie was quick to respond.

'Well, it's excellent today. Olly and I are very impressed.'

'Really? I stand corrected.' Torin held out his hand to Olly. 'I'm sorry, I didn't introduce myself: Torin Stewart.'

'Oliver Hogarth, good to meet you.'

They shook hands and Elsie was acutely aware of something else lurking beneath their politeness.

'I hope the proprietors of this place know how fortunate they are to receive your vote of approval,' Torin grinned at Elsie, increasing her discomfort. 'Considering the excellent coffee you make.'

'How do you know each other?' Olly asked, his smile covering much.

'I advised Elsie on a certain legal matter recently.' His lie was deftly delivered.

'Oh.'

Torin smiled. 'And how does she know *you*?'

He was goading Olly, of that Elsie was sure, and she wasn't about to let that happen. Forgetting her own reticence, she spoke. 'We're here on a *date*, actually,' she stated, seeing victory and defeat register simultaneously opposite her and to her right. 'So, if you don't mind . . .?'

Chastened, he took the hint, stepping back. 'Certainly. Good to see you "getting out there" again. Have a good day.'

Turning back to Olly, Elsie smiled. 'I'm sorry about that,' she said, meaning every word. 'He's a bit intense. Lawyers, you know.'

'Don't apologise, it's fine. I'm sorry if I embarrassed you – before your friend came over, I mean.'

'You didn't. And for the record, he isn't my friend. Look, Olly, what you said was lovely, I'm just . . . This is all very new for me. I might take some time to . . .'

'It's cool. We're both trying this thing on for size. It must feel odd considering what you've been through.'

Unwittingly, he had hit the nail on the head. Even though Elsie knew this was what Lucas wanted her to do, she still felt as if she were betraying him, somehow. In all the time they'd been together, it had never even occurred to her to look at another man, and while she accepted his assertions that she would find love again, putting it into practice was proving more emotionally challenging than she had anticipated.

Olly sensed the struggle within her and lowered his voice. 'I'm not trying to replace your husband. I'd just like to spend some time with you. No pressure, no expectations. Just you and me having fun together. Deal?'

His words meant more than he could have ever realised. 'Deal.'

For the rest of the afternoon, they talked and laughed, the earlier atmosphere all but erased from memory. Elsie had to admit that she was liking Olly more as the hours passed. His view of the world was similar to hers and he

140

possessed a startling ability to make her laugh. As they wandered around the specialist shops in North Laine, she caught herself glancing at the handsome young man at her side, and when his tanned hand bumped against hers she let his fingers slip briefly between her own before pulling away. It became an unspoken game between them – stealing glances at each other and finding excuses for contact while appearing unaffected by it all. The way he looked at her – with a mixture of bashfulness and attraction – thrilled her, and his every action appeared to be designed to put her at ease. She liked his easy nature, his laidback worldview – so different from Lucas, yet somehow familiar. When she laughed at his jokes he lit up and it felt good to be the centre of his attention. Oliver Hogarth was quietly breaking down Elsie's carefully built boundaries and she knew it.

At four-thirty p.m., they walked to the entrance to the pier, where they would part company. Olly took Elsie's hand and raised it to his lips.

'Thank you for a wonderful afternoon.'

'Thank you.'

'Look, I meant what I said: I have no intention of rushing things here. So let's say we'll meet up in a couple of weeks – I'll wait for your call this time. But you have my number: if you want to make it sooner, you just have to say.'

'I will call you,' she assured him.

'I know you will.'

They hugged, the sensation of peace that Elsie had experienced on their first date returning like a flood. When Olly pulled back, Elsie hesitated for a moment, then dismissed her cautiousness and reached her hand to rest gently on his cheek. He accepted the invitation and leaned down to kiss her.

'Incredible,' he whispered, his breath brushing across her lips before he moved away.

Willing her heart to stop thudding quite so hard, Elsie waited until he had disappeared from view before reaching into her bag to find her mobile phone. She was about to call Daisy for the required post mortem, when she noticed a new text message:

Babe. T shirts are go.
Sponsor says we can ask him for anything.
Magic! Woody ☺

Elsie smiled at the message. The reach of Woody's influence was impressive to say the least. He certainly was a surprising character – but then several people in Elsie's life were surprising her lately.

Elsie found an unoccupied bench under the white-painted wooden canopy running along the length of the pier and sat down, compelled by a sudden familiar urge to take stock of all that had happened. She felt the movement of the pier boarding as people walked past – a sensation that always surprised her. How odd that you never realised how much the boards shook when you were walking along them! Gazing down at her feet she looked through the gaps in the boards to the swirling grey-green waves far beneath the pier, her thoughts drifting out to another place in time . . .

In the last year of Lucas' life, Elsie had often come to the pier alone to think and it had become an important place for her ever since. One of the few outward signs of the changes that had occurred in her life since his death had been her discovery of her own ability for introspection. Previously she had never thought to question her actions, always relying on her gut reaction to guide her – but when the challenges of supporting Lucas arrived, Elsie found greater comfort in the few moments she could be alone to let it all wash over her. Lucas was the first to notice it, concerned by the change he witnessed in his young wife.

'You're becoming such a thinker these days,' he had observed one day from where he lay on their bed, as she folded freshly laundered clothes for him. 'I hate that I'm the cause of it.'

'Are you saying that you don't want me to be thinking about you?' she had joked, wishing with all her heart that she couldn't see the regret etched into his features.

'Of course not. You should be obsessed by my very beauty, obviously.'

'Which I am, obviously.'

He had held her for a long time then, saying nothing, the insistent beat of his heart betraying his emotion. From that moment, Elsie was careful to hide this new side to her character, waiting until Lucas was asleep, or spending time with members of his family, to slip away to think.

'Elsie? Hi!'

Elsie shielded her eyes from the sun and saw a tall, slender teenager walking towards her.

'Hi, Danny. Nice to see you.'

'I'm on my break – can I join you?'

'Be my guest.'

'Thanks.' He opened a bottle of spring water and took a long swig. 'It's so hot today. And all the customers are cranky. I hate Saturdays like this.'

'Where do you work?'

'On my uncle's deckchair pitch, just down the beach. I swear some of those people visiting have forgotten they're not in London. I mean, it's the weekend, don't they know they can chill out?'

Elsie smiled. 'I don't suppose this heat is helping, either.'

'Probably not. But it's always like this once Easter arrives.

Start of the season, you know.' He twisted the cap back onto his water bottle and wiped his brow. 'I'd rather be with Aoife, of course. But I have to take every opportunity to make some money for us.'

'How long have you been together?'

Danny flushed. 'Next Saturday is our three-year anniversary. I asked her out on the last day of school when we were sixteen. She's amazing – completely different when it's just us. I love her so much.'

A familiar flutter passed across Elsie's heart. 'The One, eh?'

'Absolutely The One. I'm going to marry her, you know. I'm saving up for a ring – that's why I work weekends on the deckchairs as well as bar work in a club in town.'

It was impossible not to draw parallels between this young couple and the pair of young lovers she and Lucas had been at their age. Elsie remembered Lucas talking about their future together as early as their second date. They had been so in love, with all of their lives yet to happen – so full of positivity and unshakeable hope. Maybe she could feel like that again. Maybe with Olly . . . Elsie smiled at Danny. 'That's wonderful.'

A man appeared at the entrance to the pier and shouted across the heads of the visitors milling around. 'Oi, Danny-boy! Customers!'

'Better go,' Danny grinned. 'Uncle Eric's like Genghis Khan with a hangover today. See you Wednesday!'

Standing slowly, Elsie found her mobile again, dialled a number and began to walk home.

'Hi, Dais, it's me. Checking in as promised . . .'

The heatwave passed after a week, much to the relief of Brighton's workers, and as the Easter holidays ended the

144

town settled back into an easy routine. Woody's sponsor – a local business owner who was one of the few remaining faithful members of Hellfinger's fan club – provided the choir's T-shirts as promised. Barring a slight design fault (namely two unfortunately-placed ice cream cones with cherries on the women's T-shirts, which caused great hilarity), the new uniform succeeded in bringing the choir closer together – a fact borne out by the significant improvement in their performance.

To Elsie's surprise, Woody's ABBA/Deep Purple medley proved very popular indeed, and while Stan and Graeme's shockingly energetic rendition of the famous "Smoke on the Water" riff was a dubious feature of Woody's direction, Elsie was pleased to see the choir having so much fun. Kathy and Dee's vocals were making a real difference in the alto section, boosting the volume, while Juliet's initially shaky attempts at singing gradually developed into a respectable sound.

In an effort to provide something for everyone in The Sundaes' growing musical repertoire, Elsie introduced a couple of older songs – 'I'll Walk Beside You' (after she discovered this was Irene's favourite song) and 'What a Wonderful World' – together with Alicia Keys' 'Empire State of Mind Part II' and Coldplay's 'Paradise'. It was wonderful to work at home on choral arrangements using the small Bentley piano that Lucas had bought her for her twenty-first birthday and as she worked she realised how much she had missed playing. After his death, she had always seemed to have a hundred other things to do and was forever conscious of the piano sitting idle in the front room of their house.

'Cool instrument,' Woody observed, leaning on the side of the piano as Elsie played him her new vocal arrangement of Cee Lo Green's 'Forget You'.

'Thanks. It was my twenty-first birthday present.'

'Sweet. You play like a many-fingered enchantress,' he grinned. 'Always intended to learn the magic of the keys myself.'

Elsie stopped playing and scribbled a pencil change on the manuscript paper. 'It's never too late to learn, Woody.'

'Nah.' He flopped down into a nearby armchair. 'I discovered long ago that the only instrument I was destined to master was this one.' He patted his throat. 'Designed by a deity to call the faithful to revere the notes of the Greats. Not that I'm bragging, you understand.'

Elsie stifled a giggle. 'Of course not.'

'So what about you? You don't mind just singing from the piano?'

It was an odd question. 'What do you mean?'

'Well, girl, the way you sang the first time I saw you – that's a gift you have.'

'Actually, I'm enjoying creating the sound of the choir,' she admitted. 'I've never had superstar ambitions for my singing, you know. I always preferred to be part of something bigger. This suits me fine.'

Woody nodded slowly. 'Sweet.'

She dropped her pencil on the music stand and stretched the stiffness from her arms. 'So what do you think of The Sundaes' progress?'

'Not bad. But we've got to kick them out of their comfort zones. They've never known the fear of setting foot on a stage. How do you think they're going to kick it when they have to sing for the town?'

It was a good observation. In a little over six weeks they would stand at Brighton Carnival in front of what could potentially be a couple of hundred people who expected to

146

see a polished performance – an experience that could strike fear into the heart of the most seasoned professional.

'What did you have in mind?'

Woody fixed her with a determined stare. 'We go *public*, babe.'

CHAPTER TEN

Feel the fear . . .

'Where are we going?'

'You'll see.' Woody strode ahead of the small band of singers along the promenade towards Brighton Pier.

'I don't see why we should follow you anywhere, *freak*.'

'And that, Sasha, is why I am the musical visionary and you are the mindless minion in this scenario.'

'It's going to be fun,' Elsie assured the worried choir members as they hurried to keep up with Woody's long, cowboy-booted strides. 'Trust us.'

'Yeah, *Sasha*, live dangerously for once,' Danny grinned as he passed his furious choirmate.

It was ten-thirty-five a.m. on the dull Saturday morning following Elsie and Woody's conversation and their plan was taking shape. Woody made a sharp left-hand turn onto the pier and the others followed. He carried a small, battery-powered karaoke machine under one arm and Elsie had a camcorder hidden in her bag. Just the other side of the amusement dome, Woody raised his hand, Moses-like, for the choir to halt.

'This is the place.'

Stan and Graeme – who had struck up such a firm friendship that they had earned the nickname 'Tweedledum and Tweedledee' from the rest of the choir – exchanged identical confused expressions.

'Why? What for?' Graeme asked, staring warily at the doughnut stand beside him.

'Nothing,' Woody replied, adding with a wink, '*yet.*'

Recognising growing fear within the members of the choir, Elsie took the initiative. 'We're here because we want to try something. Now don't worry, it's going to be fun, but you have to trust us, OK?'

Sasha snorted. 'Trust *him*? You must be joking . . .'

'*Philistine!*'

Elsie glared at them both. 'Woody, Sasha, if you don't mind . . .? Thank you. What's going to happen is this: I'm daring you to sing. Now. Right here. In fact, I'm *double-daring* you,' she looked over at Daisy and they shared a smile, 'which in my family means a *fait accompli.*'

'Come again?' Lewis, the lanky seventeen-year-old, asked, bemused.

'It means you have to do it, loser.'

'*Sasha . . .*'

Sasha raised her hands. 'What? I'm just saying . . .'

Aoife turned to Danny. 'I'm not doing this.'

'It'll be fine, hun.' He put his arm around her as Kathy and Dee smiled nervously in a vain attempt at reassurance.

'What do you want us to sing?' Juliet asked. 'We haven't warmed up, or prepared anything.'

'I thought we could do "What a Wonderful World",' Elsie replied. 'You all know that one and you sang it brilliantly on Wednesday night. I know we've sprung this on you. But when we sing at the Carnival, there will be a lot more people than this watching us. Now I believe we can do this – who's with me?'

There was a decidedly uncertain murmur of agreement and Woody arranged The Sundaes into their choir formation before hitting the Play button on the Barbie-pink karaoke machine. The slightly shaky recording Woody had made of Elsie's piano accompaniment began to play and a man walking his excitable springer spaniel stopped to watch. Elsie stood facing The Sundaes and raised both hands to count them in.

For all her previous complaining, Sasha appeared pacified enough to sing her first verse solo, her voice gaining in confidence with each line. Behind her, the assembled choir swapped worried glances, entering the song with tentative 'oohs' midway through the first verse. A few more onlookers gathered, watching the strange spectacle playing out halfway along Brighton Pier with amused smiles.

Elsie's face was beginning to ache from the encouraging smile she wore, but she pressed on regardless. *Come on*, she urged them silently, *just sing!* Woody stood to one side, shoulder to shoulder with Danny and Lewis, his 'oohs' considerably louder than theirs, closing his eyes for greater effect. Irene watched Elsie's every direction like a beady-eyed hawk, although Elsie couldn't tell from the tiny movements of her mouth whether any sound was coming out or not. The second verse arrived and The Sundaes began to sing along with Sasha. At last, the volume was increasing – and Elsie's spirits lifted when she heard it. It was far from perfect: recent recruit, Sheila (a dental nurse in her forties), Juliet the retired headmistress and Graeme the butcher all sang noticeably sharp; Danny often forgot the lyrics as his attention wavered; Sasha's harmony lines were so loud that the

150

melody was lost; and all of the singers dropped off into embarrassed mumblings at the end of each line. But it was a *performance* – and it represented a major step forward for The Sundaes.

The end of the song met with brief, polite applause from the makeshift audience before the spectators dispersed, leaving The Sundaes elated and congratulating each other.

Elsie flushed with pride at the sight of *her* choir, laughing and revelling in their recent shared experience. A bittersweet flicker of pain hurt her when Danny drew Aoife into an elongated embrace and she looked away to see her sister's smiling face.

'It's happening, Elsie. *You* did this!'

Elsie closed her eyes as Daisy's arms encircled her. 'It's wonderful.'

'I think we deserve a reward for that,' Stan said. 'Who votes we head to Sundae & Cher for ice cream?'

'Reward,' Woody scoffed. 'Your reward is the opportunity to fulfil your destiny. Van Gogh didn't demand ice cream. Jim Morrison never wailed for a choc ice at Woodstock.'

Laughing at Woody, the choir headed off towards their reward, while Daisy and Elsie hung back a little. 'Lucas would be so proud of you, sis.'

'You think so?'

'I know so. And he would have adored Woody.'

Elsie smiled. 'I know. I think it's a blessing the pair of them never met. I'm doing the right thing, aren't I?'

Daisy understood the deeper significance of the question. 'Yes, you are. With the choir *and* with Olly.'

An hour later, when the still-buzzing choir members had finally gone their separate ways, Elsie pushed open the door of Brighton Home Stores and smiled when Jim rushed up to greet her.

'Hi, Dad.'

'It's *so* good to see you! To what do I owe this honour?'

Elsie explained about the choir's challenge, the details of which Jim lapped up with attentive delight.

'I'll bet their faces were a picture when you sprang that on them!'

'Some of them took a bit of persuading, yes.'

Jim shook his head. 'My little Elsie, the strict choirmistress. I don't think I could have predicted that.'

'Actually, I'm the "good cop" in the outfit. If they start causing trouble I unleash the full force of Woody Jensen on them.'

They sat down on a red leather corner sofa and Elsie noticed how tired her father looked today. A few months before Lucas was diagnosed with cancer, Jim had endured a health scare of his own. He had collapsed at work complaining of chest pains and was rushed to A&E, his daughters fearing the worst. For a scary twenty-four hours, Elsie and her sisters waited for news as countless tests were performed. Eventually, it transpired that, rather than the heart attack his symptoms had suggested, Jim had suffered an infection of the fluid around his heart. A week later, the family returned home, celebrating Jim's escape from serious illness – little knowing that within weeks they would be facing the worst possible news about another of their own.

While Jim made a full recovery, the virus had left its mark on his body and now, if he grew overtired, under the weather or overworked, dark circles would appear beneath his eyes to betray him.

'Have you been working late again?' Elsie asked him. 'You look exhausted.'

'I had a meeting last night that overran. Olly and I had to go through the website with a fine-toothed comb to iron out some technical issues.' He paused, his eyes full of concern. 'Have you spoken to him lately?'

Olly. It had now been over two weeks since she had last seen him – a fact that sat uncomfortably within her. While it had in one sense been easier to throw herself into the choir, she had missed his company and had caught herself several times in recent days wondering how he was. But each time she had attempted to call him, nerves had inexplicably held her back. Would she seem too eager? What was the correct amount of time you were supposed to wait before calling anyway?

'I've just been so busy,' she said, hating the way her words appeared, like a blasé excuse thrown out to protect herself.

'He asked after you.' Jim's personal opinion was as visible as the bright red leather on which they were sitting. 'I think he'd appreciate a call.'

'Dad . . .'

He held up his hands. 'I'm just saying, it could be good for you both. I thought you were getting along so well.'

'We were – we *are*, Dad. It still feels strange to be thinking of another man instead of Lucas. I know this is what he wanted and I'm trying but something keeps holding me back.'

Jim stroked her face. 'My darling, darling girl. Of course you'll feel strange, but this is a whole new chapter of your life that you're embarking on. Any kind of change naturally brings its own fears and trepidation.' He was silent for a moment, his thoughts moving to another place in time. 'When your mother left . . .' he faltered and instinctively Elsie squeezed his hand. Nodding, he cleared his throat and continued. 'When she left, I felt as if the rug had been snatched from beneath my feet. Even though I knew it was coming, even though I had long suspected it and understood that it was the inevitable conclusion of all our fighting, I still felt robbed of the decision. But while I knew there was no hope of her ever coming back, I still struggled when I tried to get on with my own life. It's taken all these years for me to finally feel ready to pursue a relationship again.' He smiled. 'And I know my forays into internet dating have been a source of horror and amusement for you girls, but for me it's my first step. Just like you're making. Oliver is a wonderful young man, and I think it could be good for you to be looked after for a while. You've spent so long coping, being the one in charge. And that's admirable, but, darling, it's fine to need somebody else. You like Olly, don't you?'

Elsie nodded.

'Then tell the boy, Elsie. He deserves to know.'

He was right, of course he was. She knew she was thinking about this too much – like Daisy had said. But there still remained a concern that she wasn't sure she was able to express. Lucas was a tough act to follow. And he had been so adamant that she would find someone else that she felt she should take extra time to make sure whoever that was would be worthy. Of course, Lucas had known this would be the case . . .

'You will find someone else,' he had said to her, a month before he died. 'No, don't argue, I know you will. But I also know that it's going to take someone pretty special to win you.'

'Lucas, let's not talk about this now,' she had begged him, the subject both inappropriate and abhorrent to her as the precious days left with her husband slipped away.

He was unrepentant, digging his heels in as he'd always done. Stubborn, single-minded, beautiful man . . . 'I know you. You won't settle for anything but the best. *When* you fall in love again . . .'

Her hand had silenced him as it rested on his lips. 'I'm in love. With you. And that's all that matters.'

He had dropped the subject on that occasion, but weeks later it emerged again.

'There will be someone after me. I know you don't want to hear it, but I need to say it, and I'm the dying one so I get the casting vote. You're too amazing to keep all of your potential locked away in some misguided attempt at remembering me. I don't want that kind of memorial, Elsie. And you know full well that if the tables were turned, you'd be saying exactly the same to me. The next guy is going to have a battle on his hands because I know you'll need him to be your equal, and not many blokes are capable of that. Just promise me that when opportunity arrives and the time is right, you won't hold back?'

'I'll call him,' Elsie assured Jim. 'I promise.'

I love you because you never give up, no matter what.
xx

The latest message from the silk-covered box made Elsie smile as she prepared the interior of Sundae & Cher for the next choir rehearsal, the following Wednesday. Right now when it came to the choir, it was easy not to give up: despite the occasional rumblings between Woody and Sasha (and Sasha in general), Elsie could see the choir becoming something worth belonging to. It felt good to have been part of it from the very beginning and as Elsie set out the

155

chairs, picturing each of The Sundaes as she did so, she realised how much she needed to feel this way. Before Lucas died it was her relationship with him that gave her a sense of belonging – a shared experience where both of them had begun in the same place. After his death, much of Elsie's life felt as if she had entered conversations midway, being at a disadvantage from the others who had been there from the beginning. Of course, she belonged to her family; the Maynard family unit was as tight and secure as it was possible to be. But while she and Lucas had built a life together, a certain amount of her family's life had carried on without her, leaving her with the smallest inkling that she had somehow missed important happenings – special conversations, landmark events like new jobs, wedding plans and house-hunting – that Jim, Daisy and Guin had shared.

Her impulse to begin something new – fuelled by the first message from Lucas – had been correct, she now realised. More than simply a new way to meet people, the choir was becoming a vital tool for reconnecting her to a sense of community. She wondered if this were true for Woody, Sasha, Danny and the others. Was the choir filling a gap in their lives?

Reaction from the pier performance was still percolating through The Sundaes when they arrived. Woody took charge of the first song of the night, blessing the assembled singers with a lengthy dose of his rock 'n' roll wisdom before they sang. When, after ten minutes, Daisy politely suggested that perhaps the best way to impart his knowledge to his 'musical faithful' was through practice rather than words, he grudgingly conceded – the sigh of relief amongst the choir was audible at the other end of the room where Elsie was making last-minute changes to another vocal arrangement.

'I've noticed something about Irene,' Daisy said, joining Elsie when Woody and the choir were safely singing.

'What about her?'

'I've watched her at rehearsal over the past three weeks. Do you realise she's managed to chat with everyone individually during that time? Every time you look over at her she's deep in conversation with someone else. I think it's great – especially that she feels comfortable enough here to do it.'

'She has a real insight with people,' Elsie agreed. 'She said something to me recently about us both having lost someone we loved. Nobody told her about Lucas – she just saw it in me, I suppose. And Danny mentioned he'd been telling her about his plans to propose to Aoife. Even Sasha was talking with her after the pier performance on Saturday.'

Daisy smiled. 'I love the sense of community that's growing now. Actually, I think that might be the main point of The Sundaes, regardless of Woody's ambitions for covert world domination.'

Elsie had been feeling the same way for weeks and it was good to hear her sister's confirmation. 'I know what you mean. In many ways I wouldn't mind if the Carnival was our only public performance. Although,' she pointed to the opposite side of the room, where Woody was demonstrating a routine of hip-thrusts to Lewis and Danny that, given the tightness of his trousers, could best be described as inadvisable, 'do we really want to rob the world of *that* view?'

When the rehearsal was over and the café locked up for the night, Elsie and Daisy walked down to the seafront.

'It's still early,' Daisy said, as they reached her car. 'Fancy getting a late bite to eat or a drink somewhere?'

Elsie shook her head. 'Mind if we do it another night? I have things to do this evening.'

'Your loss, sis.' Daisy hugged her. 'I'll call you tomorrow.'

The promenade was quiet, a couple of dog walkers and a late-night jogger the only other people around as Elsie walked under the streetlights, running her hand along the cool iron of the railings. In her other hand, a contact name and number glowed stubbornly up at her from her phone screen. There was no way around this, she told herself. She had put off the moment for long enough.

'*Hi, this is Olly Hogarth. Sorry, I'm not available at the moment. Leave a message and I'll get back to you.*'

The release of tension on hearing his voicemail message caused Elsie to laugh out loud, clamping her hand over her mouth apologetically when a passing dog walker stared at her. Well, she had tried. When he next looked at his phone, Olly would see her missed call and call her back. It would then be up to him to make contact and at least Elsie would be prepared to take the call. In the meantime . . .

Brrrrrrrrringgg!

Elsie jumped as the old-fashioned telephone ringtone sounded on her mobile. 'Hello?'

'Hello, stranger.' His voice was warm as maple syrup over pancakes and made her skin tingle. 'Sorry I missed your call.'

'That's OK. How are you?'

'Good, thanks. Better now I know I haven't completely offended you.'

Elsie bit her lip. 'I'm sorry. I should have called before . . .'

'Hey, it's fine. Look, I'm actually at the office at the moment, working late. Don't suppose you fancy picking up some fish and chips and heading over? It would be great to see you – not to mention the fact that I haven't eaten all day.'

Surprised by the ease with which the conversation had

restarted between them – and her reaction to hearing Olly's voice again – Elsie agreed.

Twenty minutes later, she stood by a darkened doorway not far from her father's shop and pressed the intercom button next to a label that read 'Freebird Design'.

'Hey. Door's open. Come on up.'

Olly's studio was situated on the first floor, reached by climbing a narrow staircase and entering through a full-glass door emblazoned with a bright orange bird logo. Its white walls contrasted with lime-green sofas in the small reception area and bright orange picture frames which hung around the walls displaying Freebird's recent work – websites, magazine adverts and photographic assignments.

'Bit bright, isn't it?' Olly smiled, as he rose from his chair to greet her. 'I keep telling Kieran, my business partner, that we should provide every visitor with a pair of sunglasses. One of these days, somebody's going to sue us for eye damage.' He walked into a lime-green kitchen area at the far end of the studio and returned with plates and cutlery.

Elsie sat at the next desk to his, handing him a steaming packet of fish and chips and a bottle of water. 'How come you're still working? It's nearly ten o'clock.'

'Tough client,' he replied, mid-mouthful. 'They've made so many changes on a campaign that we're now running scarily close to the deadline. Necessary part of the business, I'm afraid.'

'I hope you're charging them extra.'

He took a swig of water. 'Doesn't work like that, unfortunately. Wish it did. It's a good contract, despite them being so awkward. So, how's the choir?'

'You mean The Sundaes?' Elsie smiled, opening her coat to reveal her choir T-shirt.

'Good name.' Amused, he peered closer. 'Interesting design feature, there.'

Remembering the unfortunately placed cherries, she reddened slightly and laughed. 'Ah, yes. That would be a Woody Jensen innovation.'

'Nice. And how is our resident rock'n'roll guru?'

'As full of his mystical rock wisdom as ever. It's quite endearing, actually.' She put her fork down and wiped her hands on a tissue. 'For all his strangeness he's a good person and he really cares about the choir. It's taken a bit of time for everyone to get used to his ways but I think they're all growing closer to him now.'

'I'm glad.'

There was a pause and Elsie took the opportunity to say what she had been rehearsing in her head for the past three days. 'Look, Olly, I really am sorry that I didn't call you before tonight.'

'Hey, you called. That's all that matters.'

'No, I think I need to explain.' She took a deep breath, praying that the words she needed would appear as she began. 'I don't want you to get the wrong idea about me. I don't lead people on and I never intended to hurt you at all. I've really enjoyed the time we've spent together and I think you're wonderful . . .'

Olly's smile faded and he looked down as if accepting the inevitable. 'Elsie, don't . . .'

'Wait. I haven't finished. I like you, Olly. A lot. You're great company, and I like the person I am when I'm with you. Part of me wants to see what could happen if we took things further, but part of me is too terrified to try. I know you know about Lucas and I think the way I'm feeling has a little to do with him. More than anything I just want you to know that this isn't a No.'

160

He lifted his head. 'It isn't?'

'I admit that I put off calling you because I honestly couldn't work out what I was feeling. There is a lot of change going on in my life right now and I'm still trying to process everything.'

'You should have just told me, like we agreed last time, remember? I'm not expecting the world, and I'm not expecting you to fall into my arms, either. It's been a while for me, too. My last relationship ended three years ago – we lasted five years – and I've only had the odd date since then. When I was with you on our first date, it seemed so familiar – like slipping back into an old routine – and I forgot that in reality we hardly knew each other. Does that make sense?'

It did and Elsie had felt it, too: the need to be close to someone, to return to a sense of togetherness that had vanished when Lucas died. It was an impulse, an almost subconscious act that let her heart lead instead of her head – and when Olly had kissed her it was as if a missing piece fell back into place. 'So, what do we do?'

Wheeling his desk chair across to her, he took hold of her hands. 'Let's just spend time together. We'll get to know each other and have fun, without the pressure of any relationship stuff. And if it eventually feels right to take it to another level, we'll go there. If it doesn't, we stay as friends. Either way, we win. What do you think?'

His suggestion made Elsie happier than she had felt in weeks. 'I think it's just what we need.'

CHAPTER ELEVEN

Stepping out

The following weeks were filled with preparations for The Sundaes' Carnival performance, Elsie and Woody arranging extra rehearsals on Monday evenings to work with the choir. They had settled on a set of three songs for the Carnival: 'What a Wonderful World', 'Forget You' and Woody's ABBA/Deep Purple medley, which had become a particular hit with the male choir members. While the choir busied themselves with performance preparation, Cher appointed herself official press officer for The Sundaes, bombarding the local press with stories and arranging several photo opportunities (always ensuring Sundae & Cher was well positioned in each shot, naturally). Maybe it was her natural knack for promotion, or the signature 'Sundaes Sundae' – a Caramel, Triple Chocolate and Salted Toffee ice cream concoction she had offered solely to local journalists – but her efforts appeared to be bearing fruit.

'Look at this!' Cher spread the latest copy of the free paper out on the table between Elsie and Woody. 'People are talking about us!' She pointed to the Editor's Letter, which carried the headline *Brighton: The UK's New Choir Capital?*

Elsie read it aloud. '. . ."*The recent explosion of new choirs in Brighton can only be a good thing, in my opinion. Music brings people together in ways that nothing else can and in today's society, when so few of us even know the names of our next-door neighbours, ventures like this that encourage interaction must be celebrated. From award-winning show choirs such as The DreamTeam to fascinating community ventures like rock star Woody Jensen's The Sundaes, Brighton is fast becoming a beacon for the uniting power of music . . .*" . . . Blimey, I didn't realise we were part of a social movement.'

'It's what I've been telling you all along, babe. Cometh the revolution.' Woody chuckled. 'That'll ruffle a certain pair of red trousers.'

'Can't say I'm upset about that,' Cher grinned. 'And imagine how they'll be talking about us after the Carnival!'

The mention of their impending performance made Elsie's insides twist. The choir were making progress, but she was acutely aware that more work was needed. Aoife was still struggling to make herself heard, despite encouragement from Woody, Daisy and Irene – and Sasha's growing consternation at her fellow soprano wasn't helping matters.

'Maybe she should join the altos,' she growled one evening, her too-tight ponytail swinging like a bleached blonde pendulum at the back of her head, 'because she's about as useful as a fart in a hurricane at the moment.'

'That's not fair,' Aoife returned, her tiny frame almost shaking with the effort. 'I'm trying to sing louder.'

'We don't need you to *try*, love, we need you to *do it*.'

Elsie groaned and moved in between the two young women who were now glaring dangerously at one another.

'OK, listen. Sasha, I need you to focus on your own performance. Don't worry about what Aoife is or isn't doing. You're far from perfect on song lyrics, so I'd appreciate it if you focused your energies on that, please. Aoife, you're getting stronger every time we do this. Just remember what Woody and I have said about believing in yourself.'

'I just don't want to let you down,' Aoife replied.

'You won't. I want you to enjoy this and have fun, OK? Now, I'll be singing the soprano line along with you and Sasha while I'm conducting, so keep your eyes on me and you won't feel so much on your own.'

'*She* feels alone? Welcome to my world!' Sasha pushed past Elsie and stormed towards the customer toilets, tapping a text message into her mobile as she went.

Elsie groaned. 'Right, everyone take a break for twenty minutes.'

The Sundaes shuffled wearily away to collect their mugs of strong tea and clotted-cream-filled chocolate butterfly cakes from Cher. As Elsie gathered her music together and sat down at her keyboard, a hand gently tapped on her shoulder. She looked up to see the comforting smile of Irene.

'You're doing so well, dear,' she said, sitting on a chair next to Elsie's. 'I think we're sounding lovely.'

'Thanks, Irene. It's down to everybody's hard work.'

Irene folded her hands in her lap. 'Sasha's a good girl. Deep down, I mean. I know she can be difficult, but I'm sure it comes from a good place.'

Elsie stared at Irene. How could she assume that about someone as hell-bent on being the centre of attention as Sasha? 'I want her to do well, really I do, but she's just so hard to reach. She seems to think she's the only person in the choir and she's disruptive when she doesn't get her own way.'

'All the same, that girl needs this choir. And the choir needs her. Now, can I get you tea and one of those delicious cakes, dear?'

Woody sauntered over as Irene left. 'I saw you consulting The Oracle.'

Still unsettled by what Irene had said, Elsie looked at him. 'Sorry?'

'Irene. She's like a diviner of hidden truth, a secret knower of . . . *things*.'

'Right. She thinks Sasha's misunderstood.'

Woody's expression darkened. 'Yeah, well, everyone has off-days.'

'I thought you might say that. The medley sounded good.'

'Progress is happening for sure – we've done good things here.' Leaning towards her slightly, he gave her back a hesitant pat. 'You make me proud, angel.'

Genuinely touched, Elsie nudged him with her shoulder. 'Aw, thanks, dude. The feeling's mutual.'

After their conversation at his office, a wonderful ease settled between Elsie and Olly and they had spent increasingly more time together. Encouraged by this, Elsie decided it was time for Olly's formal introduction to the Maynard family. And so, on the first Sunday in June, Elsie surprised everyone by inviting her family and Olly to her home for a barbecue.

'Are you sure about this?' Olly asked, hovering uncertainly in the small kitchen of the house in Islingword Street with a bottle of wine in his hands as Elsie prepared spiced Quorn burgers for Guin and Jim and pork satay kebabs for everybody else. 'I mean, I know things are going well with us, but is it really time to meet the whole family?'

Elsie giggled. 'They're perfectly harmless. Dad's been

pushing me for a get-together for weeks and my sisters want to meet you. This way we get all the introductions done in one fell swoop.'

'Maybe you're right. Tell me again who's coming?'

His nervousness was endearing and Elsie couldn't hide her smile as she made him sit on a kitchen chair while she opened the wine bottle. 'Dad – who you know well already; my eldest sister Daisy, who is stunningly beautiful and a real sweetie, and her partner André – and, believe me, you're honoured to get to see him, seeing as he is officially the busiest guy on Planet Earth; then there's my middle sister, Guin, who is ridiculously pregnant and likely to cry at just about anything, and her husband Joe, who is the loveliest bloke you could meet.' She handed him a large glass of wine. 'Here, drink this. I think you'll feel better.'

The doorbell rang and Olly sprang to his feet as Elsie walked through to the hall to welcome her family. Daisy and Guin were first into the house, pushing past Jim excitedly and coming to an abrupt halt when Olly appeared.

'Daisy, Guin, this is Olly.' Elsie stood back as her sisters welcomed him.

'Darling, this is a wonderful surprise,' Jim said, kissing her cheek as he entered. 'And the first time we've all been here for a meal since . . . Well, I'm very happy to be here.'

André and Joe squeezed their way into the now cramped hallway, laughing together at the sight of so many people packed into such a small place. Elsie lifted her hand like a tour guide at Brighton Pavilion and shouted above the jovial conversations.

'Let's head out to the garden where we can all breathe!'

'Amen to that!' Guin exclaimed, holding a hand to the small of her back. 'I could really do with sitting down.'

Elsie watched her family filing out to the garden and

166

settling themselves in the selection of garden chairs she had arranged on the small wooden decked area surrounded by rambling roses, tall bamboo and ripening tomato plants. Seeing the house filled with people once more was surprisingly wonderful: it had been a long time since her home had seen such a happy throng. Since she lost Lucas she had always opted for family gatherings at Jim's house, Daisy and André's apartment or Guin and Joe's cottage – anywhere rather than her own home which still echoed with the silence of Lucas' absence.

Daisy appeared by her side and clinked her wine glass against Elsie's. 'Cheers, lovely. This was a brilliant idea.'

'Thank you. I'm so glad André could make it,' Elsie said, looking over to where Daisy's partner was in deep conversation with Olly. 'I thought he'd be too busy.'

Daisy's relationship with property developer André Durand was somewhat of a mystery to the rest of the Maynard family. He was always perfectly charming and polite, but while she liked him immensely, Elsie often felt that something was missing. Guin was less circumspect, comparing him to a building in a Wild West town: 'He's all show on the outside with nothing of substance behind. Daisy's dating a façade.'

'You know what's weird? When I mentioned about today I thought he'd have other things to do, but he accepted straight away,' Daisy said, her eyes wide at her own revelation. 'He's very fond of you, you know. I think he immediately understood how important it was for you to have us all here today.'

'Not to mention wonderful for you.'

Daisy blushed a little. 'I must admit, it is. I've seen so little of him lately.'

'You are talking about me again,' André smiled as he

approached, handing Daisy a fresh glass of wine. 'I do hope your sister is telling you how wonderful I am.'

Elsie threaded her arm through his. 'Of course. It's so lovely to see you, André.'

'And you, *chérie*.' He leaned over and planted a kiss on her cheek. 'I'm pleased I could be here today for this . . . you know.'

'Thank you.' Even though Elsie had become accustomed to half-finished references to her late husband, it still surprised her how few people were confident enough to mention his name. In the early days of her bereavement, this had annoyed her considerably – making her feel as if the man she loved more than anything had suddenly been reduced to an awkward subject. But gradually she learned that the stilted mentions merely revealed how much people had cared for Lucas and that, far from being a sign of dismissal, they were a mark of respect. 'Now, does everyone have enough to drink?'

'I wish I could have wine,' Guin wailed from a brightly striped deckchair beside her sister. 'I tell you, as soon as this baby's out I'm ordering a large one. Intravenously, if possible.'

'Honey, you know what the midwife said,' Joe replied, his auburn curls bobbing as he spoke. 'No alcohol until you finish breastfeeding.'

Guin glared at her husband. 'Well, maybe I've decided to nominate *you* for that task.'

Joe laughed nervously. 'She still has her sense of humour you see, Elsie.'

'Mmm, yes. Good luck with that when Junior arrives!'

'May I propose a toast?' André suggested, his velvety French accent causing the others to turn to listen as he raised his glass. 'To friends, old and new.'

Elsie felt a rush of love as everyone joined in the toast.

'To friends, old and new!'

'And to you, Olly,' Jim said, grinning with pride as Olly slipped his arm around Elsie's waist. 'Welcome to our family. And thank you for making my little girl smile . . .' His eyes welled with tears, which was met with a chorus of *'Dad!'* from his three daughters. 'You'll have to forgive this old sentimentalist. It's just so wonderful to see my girls happy and looked after.' He waved his hand. 'Now, as you were, everybody.'

Olly smiled down at Elsie. 'Thank you for this.'

She leaned against him. 'You're welcome.'

In the following weeks, Elsie felt increasingly surrounded by positivity: the choir, her friendship with Olly and the Maynard family's anticipation of the impending arrival of Guin's baby as she neared the eighth month of her pregnancy.

The box messages from Lucas were also a secret source of strength for her, underpinning the events of her day with his affirmations. Many of them were observations significant only to him and her:

I love you because you watch quiz shows with me, even though you hate them xx

I love you because you make biscuits at midnight xx

I love the way your boobs wobble when you laugh xx

Other messages made Elsie suspect he had perhaps begun to run out of ideas in the admittedly tall task of identifying over thirty reasons why he loved her:

*I love you because of your dad's Sunday
dinners xx*

Occasionally, a message would prove almost prophetic for
the place in which Elsie found herself, taking her breath
away with its pertinence. As summer arrived, one such
message stopped her in her tracks . . .

Sundae & Cher had been particularly busy that week,
the task of speedily serving so many customers further
complicated by Cher accepting a last-minute trip to Cannes
with Jake, leaving Elsie in charge and seriously short-staffed.
Arriving early each morning to bake cookies, mix batches
of ice cream and crêpe batter, and make sure everything
was ready for when the hastily-arranged part-time staff
came in, then leaving late at night after extra rehearsals
with The Sundaes, meant that Elsie didn't have an opportunity to read the latest box message until the Thursday
night. Taking advantage of her rare free evening, Elsie treated
herself to a long bath before snuggling up on the sofa to
watch her favourite film, *The Philadelphia Story*, with a
large helping of roast vegetable lasagne that Jim, concerned
that his daughter was too busy to cook, had made and
smuggled into her fridge the day before.

It was only when she headed up to bed that the silk-
covered box caught her eye. Opening it, she pulled out the
top paper from the stack inside.

*I love that you've read this far. And I love
that your life is moving on so well. Keep
going, beautiful girl. I love you xx*

Stifling a cry with her hand, Elsie burst into tears. Lucas
couldn't possibly have known that she would wait eighteen

months to read his messages, yet his faith in her ability to live without him was perfectly placed for this moment in her life. And, right then, she missed him more than she could bear, the surprise gift of his words both wonderful and devastating.

Lucas was right. She *was* moving on – for the first time in many years Elsie felt the world opening up before her; no certainties, no givens, just possibilities. Before, life with Lucas had always been underpinned by a safe foundation of assumptions: while their circumstances might change, career choices could diversify and homes could move, they would always be together. That was the plan. After he died – for the first year at least – she had felt compelled to carry on as before, her mandate from him to live translating into busyness and routine. But now, it was as if she were lifting her eyes from her immediate surroundings to dare to gaze towards the horizon, where the lay of the land was less certain than that beneath her feet.

And Lucas knew. Because Lucas had known her better than anyone. But the thought of him preparing the box messages as he lay in their bed in his final weeks, accosted by pain on all sides, yet looking forward to a picture of his wife in a future that wouldn't contain him, remained almost too profoundly hurtful for Elsie to comprehend. If she needed any further proof of how extraordinary Lucas had been, this was it.

Lucas believed in her. And that was all she needed to keep moving forward.

'Sage green.'
'Too dull.'
'Clementine?'
'Ugh. Too bright.'

'Duck-egg blue?'

'Too *last year* . . .'

Daisy threw her hands up in frustration. 'Do you want this room repainted or not?'

Cher scrutinised the paint chart in her hand for the millionth time. 'I do.'

'Well, surely you must have some idea of the colour you want?'

Cher raised an eyebrow. 'I thought you were the interior designer.'

'Look, why don't we try to narrow it down?' Elsie suggested, gently removing the chart from Cher's grip. 'Daisy, pop the kettle on. Now you sit here, Cher, and let's think logically about this. It's your bedroom, so what do you have in it that could inform the colour scheme?'

A filthy smirk claimed Cher's scarlet lips. 'Jake Long.'

'For *pity's* sake . . .' Daisy, clearly horrified, escaped to the kitchen.

'You're dreadful,' Elsie giggled. 'But it's good to see you so happy.'

'I am. I really am. He's amazing, Els! You should have seen him in Cannes – so attentive, so chivalrous. Hearing those French words slipping off his tongue was just the *sexiest* thing . . . I can't help it, I think I love the guy! And you know how rare it is for me to admit that.'

'I'm glad. It's about time, too. So, this redecoration – is it for him?'

Cher walked to the window in her small bedroom and lifted the edge of a curtain to inspect it critically. 'Maybe. But more for me. I love my retro stuff and I don't want to change it all, but I reckon it needs a rethink for how I'm feeling now.' She pulled a face. 'I haven't offended Daisy, have I?'

172

'No. She might look like a fragile goddess but she's made of sterner stuff. If I were you, I'd let her design something for you. Trust me, it'll be perfect.'

Half an hour later, Elsie and Daisy waved to Cher as they walked down her garden path.

'I should take you on at the practice,' Daisy said, when she was certain they were out of earshot. 'We've a few awkward clients you could work your magic on.'

'I'll bear it in mind.'

A small child on a blue scooter hurtled towards them on the pavement and the sisters parted to let him through. 'Road-hog!' Daisy called after him. 'Typical male driver.'

'That could be our nephew in a few years' time,' Elsie reminded her. 'Or niece. I still can't quite believe Guin's going to be a mum.'

They reached the end of Cher's road and paused by a small bakery on the corner with a couple of chairs and tables set outside. Daisy checked her watch. 'I've got an hour until André arrives. It's crazy but I always get butterflies when I know he's coming home. The minutes just can't come quickly enough. Fancy a coffee to take my mind off having to wait to see him?'

It was a beautiful Sunday afternoon bathed in sparkling sunshine that glinted along the roofs of the cars parked nose to tail along the road. Children were playing in the front garden of a B&B opposite the bakery and their unbridled laughter instantly reminded Elsie of her own childhood games with Daisy and Guin.

'Remember when we used to invite all the neighbourhood kids round to ours in the summer holidays? Fifteen of us dashing through the house to the garden.'

'More like twenty, one summer,' Daisy said. 'I think that was the time we had a double-glazing salesman measuring up for new windows and he thought all the kids playing in the garden were Dad's. I suppose with Dad's hippy clothes he probably thought we were part of some dodgy commune. Strange to think of a child running around the garden again.' She paused. 'Do you think you and Lucas would have . . .?'

Elsie nodded, inhaling the scent from her espresso and feeling oddly peaceful. 'Lucas wanted to be a thirty-year-old dad. He said he reckoned he would have grown up by then.'

'André mentioned kids the other day.'

Daisy's calm bombshell caused Elsie to almost drop her cup. 'You're joking?'

'That was pretty much my reaction, too. I mean, we see each other maybe ten days a month at the moment, if that? Quite how he thinks that constitutes a relationship constant enough to support a child is beyond me.'

'Do you think he might be hinting at settling down?' Elsie asked.

Daisy raised her eyes heavenwards. 'Who knows? He'll be fifty next year – maybe he's reached that time of life where kids are on the cards. We're not like Guin and Joe, or you and Lucas; we rarely talk about the future. I suppose I'll find out more today.'

'How long is he staying?'

'A whole week. That's practically a lifetime for us. So, cheer me up. How's Olly?'

'Good, I think. He's helping Dad set up the Traders' Association stage for the Carnival next week.'

'No more attempts to jump you, then?'

Elsie laughed. 'You're impossible! *No*, we're staying friends for the time being.'

'Oh, right.' Daisy smirked into her latte. 'For the *time being*.'

* * *

The Sundaes' final rehearsal took place the day before their Carnival debut. A strong sense of urgency filled Sundae & Cher as the choir arrived ready to work. Even Woody withheld his usual lengthy pre-rehearsal pep talk, ushering The Sundaes straight into their first song. Elsie listened intently as she played along, noting the areas that still required work and jotting notes down on a reporter's notebook balanced on the end of her keyboard. Everyone bore a look of grim determination as they progressed twice through the short programme – and Elsie loved them for it.

At tea break – today complemented with double scoops of Cher's latest flavour experiment, Peach and Bacon ice cream, which elicited pleasant surprise from everyone – the visibly exhausted choir gathered together for a halftime post mortem.

'I think we were a bit early coming in on the second song,' Stan said, as Graeme agreed. 'I lost my timing after the chorus, sorry.'

'I'm having trouble remembering the lyrics for "Forget You",' Juliet confessed.

Sheila sighed. 'I don't have any lyrics to remember for that song but I keep getting my oohs and aahs mixed up.'

'People! Chill your collective beans,' Woody said, stepping into the middle of the choir. 'Tomorrow will be the triumphal entry of The Sundaes into the consciousness of this good town. You are the lyrical army I saw in my dream. It's going to be epic!'

'Woody's right,' Elsie agreed.

'He is?' Daisy was incredulous.

'Yes, he is. You've all worked so hard to get these songs ready and it shows. Sure, there may be some tiny details we could still improve on, but you're sounding so good! All I want is for us to get up on that stage and have fun. Do you think we can do that?'

Smiles broke out across the room and Elsie sensed that the weight of worry had been lifted.

'Great. Now let's go through the programme one more time and then call it a night. I think we're ready!'

CHAPTER TWELVE

Welcome to the world

Early next morning Brighton seafront was alive with frenzied activity as stands, stalls and stages were set up. It was already warm, with forecasts of high temperatures and, more importantly, no rain – a perfect day for the Carnival.

Butterflies had begun to bombard Elsie's stomach from the moment she awoke and now, a little after eight a.m., they intensified with the sight of every streamer, string of coloured lights and painted stall she passed. The biannual weekend of Brighton Carnival had always been a highlight of her childhood and now she was about to showcase her very own choir as part of it. Whatever happened today would feel like a glowing achievement.

There was an atmosphere of excitement and expectation pervading the whole town this morning. As she walked, Elsie could almost see the ghosts from Carnivals of years past: herself and Lucas with artfully painted faces, dancing half-drunk with bottles of warm beer as the colour, noise and splendour of the procession passed by. Lucas claimed to be unmoved by the event, but in every photograph Elsie possessed of him at successive Carnivals, his exuberant expression gave the game away.

'Ready for the grand performance?' Olly grinned from the top of a stepladder when Elsie arrived at the small stage. He had a long length of bunting over one shoulder and was fixing it around the metal gantry.

'I think so. How long have you been here?'

'About an hour or so. Jim was panicking it wouldn't be done in time but, as you can see, we're almost finished.'

'That's my Dad,' she grinned. 'Want any help?'

Olly pointed across the stage to two bulging bin bags. 'You could put those balloons up. Sticky tape and scissors should be nearby. Aren't you needed at the café's stall? I thought Cher would be flapping about it.'

Elsie laughed. 'I've just seen her and she's assured me that everything's under control. She's brought enough supplies to feed most of the town by the look of it.'

'Well, if the weather stays like this I reckon she'll have sold out by lunchtime. Even her crazy flavours.'

For the next thirty minutes they worked alongside each other, their conversation jovial and easy. Elsie noticed how much more relaxed Olly was now, his demeanour far less intense than it had been since their heart-to-heart in his office. When the bunting and balloons were all up, they stood back to admire their work.

'How wonderful!' Jim exclaimed, arriving with coffee and doughnuts from a nearby café just in time to see the work completed. 'Glad I have the two of you to help me this morning. What a crack team you make!'

Thanks Dad, Elsie smiled to herself, *subtle as a breeze-block*. 'Do you like it?'

Jim wrapped his arm around her. 'Love it, darling. Olly, your bunting skills are remarkable.'

'Thanks, I'll – er – put that on my CV.'

'Good, good. I'm looking forward to meeting Woody Jensen, I can tell you. His was one of the best gigs of the Eighties – Hellfinger at The Basement, the summer before they hit the charts. I went with your mother, actually. Just before she . . . well, you know.' He pulled a folded list from the back pocket of his jeans, switching the subject before it became too controversial. 'Right, if you'll excuse me I've got to check with the chap from local radio where he wants us to set up microphones.' He shook hands with Olly. 'Thanks so much for your help, mate. And Elsinore – it's going to be fantastic, so don't you worry.'

Olly turned to Elsie, bemused, as soon as Jim had left. 'Elsinore? Is that a nickname?'

Elsie sighed. She hadn't been looking forward to this question. 'No. *That's* my name. Elsinore Galadriel Maynard.'

'No!' He burst into great guffaws of laughter and Elsie waited impassively for him to finish.

This wasn't the first time she had encountered this reaction to the revelation of her full given name. At primary school, after a year of taunting, Jim had informed all of her teachers that they were to refer to her as Elsie immediately, for fear that his daughter would be traumatised by school if her full name continued to be used.

Seeing her expression, Olly's laughter quickly subsided. 'I'm sorry. That was rude of me. I can't believe I've only just found this out about you now. How did you come by that name?'

Elsie sat on the edge of the stage and took the lid off her polystyrene cup to blow on her coffee. 'My mum has an obsessive streak, which is probably a bad thing considering she's an actress. She was cast in *Hamlet* just before she found out she was expecting me, received rave reviews

179

for her portrayal of Ophelia and became obsessed with the play from then on. Hence Elsinore. Then, just before I was born, someone gave her a copy of *The Lord of the Rings*, which she was addicted to until I was born. Hence Galadriel.'

'You're kidding me?'

'Nope. When she was expecting Daisy she became fascinated by *The Victorian Language of Flowers*, so Daisy's middle name is Heartsease. And Guin – or Guinevere Isolde – was named after characters in *Le Morte d'Arthur*, which was her constant companion all the time she was expecting.'

'Wow. My middle name is Henry – I feel positively plain by comparison.'

Elsie grinned. 'You're lucky. I used to dream of changing my name to something really sane – like Jane or Lucy or Kate. Adults think it's cool to be different, but having an unusual name at school means that all your teachers make an effort to learn it, so you can never get away with anything. And when you're fourteen and wanting to fit in unnoticed with everyone else it's a pain in the bum, frankly.'

'No other Elsinores in your class, I take it?'

'Funnily enough, no.'

'Elsie suits you,' Olly said, a self-conscious smile appearing immediately afterwards. 'Which is a good job, obviously, seeing as it's your name.'

By the time Daisy and Woody arrived, the seafront had been transformed into a rainbow-coloured, bustling buzz. Those eager to bag a prime view of the Carnival procession had arrived early to stake their claim, while others spilled out of the pubs onto the street, already lairy, blokes stripped to the waist with T-shirts tied as superhero capes, their half-empty beer bottles clasped like brown glass sceptres. Kids waited impatient and empty-handed as overwrought parents juggled bags, cuddly toys and giant foiled helium-filled

180

balloons from the stalls that lined the seafront. Expectation was in the air as Brighton prepared to display its creative, crazy, colourful best.

Daisy had brought her ludicrously expensive camera – a present from one of André's many Dubai trips – and kept disappearing to snap details of the remarkable sights surrounding them.

'Don't you just love today?' she grinned at Elsie. 'So many photographs waiting to happen! I love Brighton when it's celebrating – there's nowhere on earth like it.'

'So, how was your week?' Elsie asked, keen to hear the details of André's visit.

'Actually, it was surprisingly wonderful,' Daisy replied. 'We spent so much time together, didn't argue once, and to be honest I kept checking that it was my André who had come home and not some rather lovely impostor.'

'Wow. He seems to be making a real effort, then.'

'He does. I don't know whether to be worried by it or just enjoy it while it lasts.'

Elsie nudged her sister. '*Maybe* it's a sign that he's ready to settle down.'

'Mmm, maybe.' Daisy was far from convinced. 'I guess time will tell.'

Woody, meanwhile, was nearby, admiring the intricately painted body of a street performer a little too closely. 'And you have to be *completely* naked when the artist works his magic on you?'

'Pretty much,' the woman giggled, wriggling her upper body to prove – if proof were needed – the very thin layer of colour that was protecting her modesty. 'It's, like, completely sensuous to become a living canvas. It's almost reverent when the paint is applied, you know?'

'I can imagine the *beauty* of that moment, yeah.' Woody's

181

lecherous wink was anything but reverent. 'I'd like to behold the wonder of it sometime.'

A pair of stilt-walkers dressed as lengthy-legged sailors strode past with a gang of whooping and yelling children in their wake. Elsie climbed up on the stage to check her keyboard, her nerves kicking up a gear as she considered the performance The Sundaes would give in little under an hour.

One by one, the rest of the choir arrived, gathering to the right of the stage and chatting nervously. Woody reluctantly allowed the street performer to leave and wandered over to the group.

'OK, people! Cometh the Carnival, cometh the hour.'

'*Freak.*'

Woody surveyed Sasha haughtily. 'I will not rise to ignorance, girl. Today I am above it.'

'Whatever.'

Stan smiled at Elsie as she joined them. 'Think we can do this?'

Elsie squeezed his arm. 'I know we can.'

Waiting backstage for the local radio presenter to announce them was one of the longest twenty minutes Elsie could remember and, judging by the faces of The Sundaes, all were experiencing the same dragging trepidation. Aoife, Danny, Kathy and Dee were huddled together next to Stan, Graeme and Juliet, who didn't look any more confident. Even Sasha was silent. For a split second, Elsie wondered if she had perhaps been too hasty bringing The Sundaes here. Were they really ready to face the sizeable audience? She looked at Woody for reassurance, but he was in the middle of an elaborate pre-gig ritual – eyes closed, head back, shaking his hands like there were no paper towels in the Gents' loo . . .

182

'You're up next,' whispered a gruff-looking radio runner, clipboard clenched tightly against his chest.

Elsie took a deep breath. This was it: the first proper outing of her new venture. Lucas would be beside himself with laughter if he could see her now. Not that he would likely be standing on this stage if he was there: his deep-harboured stage fright was legendary amongst their friends, stemming from the time he had to play the Angel Gabriel at junior school, when his white sheet costume caught on a nail in the school stage and tore almost in half, revealing his very white, well-pressed Y-fronts in front of everyone . . . She smiled at the memory of him recounting the story countless times for friends, the story progressively more embellished and preposterous with each retelling.

'. . . And at that moment, every camera in the school hall flashed. I'm convinced that right across Shoreham-by-Sea there is an abundance of slowly fading photographic evidence of my not-so-tighty-whities . . .'

'Sundaes, onstage *now*,' the radio runner growled.

The choir filed onstage in silent obedience, with Woody leading the way and Elsie bringing up the rear. Just before she stepped out into the blinding Brighton sunshine, Elsie heard a small cheer and calls of '*Wood-ee, Wood-ee!*' from the few Hellfinger faithful who had made a pilgrimage to see their idol.

She imagined Lucas standing beside her in the wings. *Go on, girl. Show 'em what you've got* . . . Smiling at his memory, she strode confidently on stage, taking the microphone by her keyboard.

'Good afternoon Brighton! We are The Sundaes – Brighton's newest choir.' She began to play the opening bars of 'What a Wonderful World' and, nodding at the visibly shaken members of her choir, counted them in . . .

Fourteen impressions of doomed bunnies frozen in approaching truck headlights stared back at her. Elsie's encouraging smile began to pull at the edges. Woody glared at Sasha, who was gawping at the crowd below, her usual brassiness deserting her.

Raising her voice, Elsie began to sing: 'I see . . .'

'. . . fields of blue – *green* . . .' Sasha rushed, unblinking – but Elsie thanked heaven that Sasha had sung anything at all – and, after the impromptu rewrite of the Louis Armstrong classic, she sang with increasing volume and conviction. Behind her, The Sundaes breathed a visible sigh of relief. At the right time the rest of the choir came in, the concentration on their faces almost comical. Elsie made a mental note to talk to them about smiling at the next rehearsal, but right now that didn't matter: they were *singing* – stronger and tighter as the song passed from the chorus to the second verse and headed towards Stan's middle-eight solo. Waving at his wife and son in the audience, he pulled a strong performance out of the bag, his cheeks and balding head reddening with pleasure at the reaction. The choir joined him and completed the first song on a confident note.

Woody cast a glance across the stage and raised his thumbs in a Fonz-like seal of approval. Elsie felt a rush of pride swelling within her as she played the first bar of 'Forget You' and heard a delighted roar as the crowd by the stage recognised it. Danny swapped places with Sasha – the first bit of choreography in the programme – and struck up the chorus. The rest of The Sundaes entered with their *oohs* on time (apart from Sheila who quickly changed her *ahh* to an *ooh* when she realised her mistake). Jim, standing in the audience, started clapping along and some of the people around him joined in. As the Sundaes saw this, their volume soared. They entered the home straight, where all that lay between them and the end of the programme was a questionable Seventies' pop and rock collision . . . Drumming her fingers on the keys for the introduction to the medley, Elsie nodded at Woody, who grabbed the microphone and swung it between his spread legs *á la* Roger Daltrey. Flicking it back to his lips, he pointed out at the crowd: 'Brighton, are you ready to *rock*?'

The sparse Hellfinger faithful yelled, 'Yeah!'

Woody gave a snarling smirk, his snake hips beginning to move to the beat. 'I *said*, are you ready to ROCK?'

'YEAH!' Amused by the ageing rocker with his alarming hip action, more of the crowd shouted back.

'I'm a-gonna need my crew here,' Woody beckoned Stan, Graeme, Lewis and Danny to his side. 'Are you ready, fellas? Take it away!'

To the audience's shock and delight, the men launched heartily into their vocal impression of Ritchie Blackmore's legendary guitar riff, eliciting wolf-whistles and cheers. The female choir members then launched into ABBA's 'Summer Night City' while the men continued the 'Smoke on the Water' riff underneath. Then Irene joined in – and the sight of an eighty-four-year-old lady air-guitaring centre-stage brought the audience's hands clapping over their heads as Elsie played the final bars and The Sundaes lifted their hands in a jazz-style to bring their performance to a thundering finish.

'Let's give it up for The Sundaes!' the radio DJ shouted and Elsie joined the choir on stage for one last bow before they walked off.

'Did you see that?' Lewis said, his eyes wide. 'We were amazing!'

'We were better than that,' Kathy replied, her eyes shining.

Aoife's smile was brighter than Elsie had ever seen. 'I can't believe we did it,' she squealed.

Sasha threw a sunbed-tanned arm around her. 'I actually heard you sing that time, Eef! Who knew you had it in you?'

'You were *awesome*!' Woody stepped into the centre of the choir, who whooped and ruffled his ponytail. 'This is where it starts, people! Choir ninjas called to arms!'

'Er, can you take this offstage?' the radio runner barked.

Giggling like chastened children, Elsie and Daisy led The Sundaes down onto the street and watched as they dispersed to their waiting families and friends. A short, middle-aged blonde-haired woman who bore a striking resemblance to Irene emerged from the crowd and hurried over to Elsie.

'Thank you,' she gushed, shaking Elsie's hand vigorously. 'Mum's gone on about this choir for weeks and it's been so good to see her looking forward to rehearsals. But I never in a million years thought I'd see her playing air-guitar and rocking out in front of everyone!'

'Still got it, dearie,' Irene winked at Elsie, hugging her daughter. 'Thank you, Madame Choirmistress.'

Elsie felt as if her feet were hovering several inches above the pavement. 'It's my complete pleasure, Irene. Thank *you*.'

'Permission to embrace the choral director, ma'am,' Olly's voice said behind Elsie. She turned and smiled at him.

'Permission granted.'

Olly gathered her into his arms and swung her around to face the crowd, where jewel-hued Samba dancers were persuading people to join them as a steel band took the stage. She leaned her cheek against the warm skin of his neck and smiled at the sight of Brighton's revellers as Olly began to sway her gently to the rhythm of the music. Enjoying the sensation of his body next to hers, Elsie leaned in closer, her eyes making a lazy navigation of the street party over his shoulder. She had succeeded: the choir had achieved their first performance and here she was, dancing on Brighton seafront with a handsome man in the Carnival sunshine . . .

Quite without warning, a face summoned her attention in the midst of the partying Carnival-goers.

His dark hair framed his face, his green eyes were fixed on her alone. Slowly, Torin Stewart raised his beer bottle to her as Elsie's stomach tightened. Instinctively, she wrapped her arms further around Olly's neck as Torin turned and disappeared back into the crowd.

'Hey, what's up?' Olly asked, pulling back to scan her face.

'Nothing.' Gazing into his blue-grey eyes, Elsie felt the tension within her subsiding. 'Everything's good.'

'Yes.' He leaned forward and placed the softest kiss on her forehead. 'Yes, it is.'

The thrill of the Carnival performance was exactly what Elsie and the members of The Sundaes needed, uniting them in a way they had never been before. Several of the choir began to visit Sundae & Cher during the week, the ice cream café becoming the unofficial meeting place for both the singers and their friends. Two weeks after the Carnival, Aoife, Lewis and Danny gathered at the counter, following a request from Cher. She emerged from the kitchen with a tray full of small one-scoop tubs, each filled with a different coloured ball of ice cream.

'Right, you lot. Seeing as you're all officially regulars here, I wanted to pick your brains. I take it none of you are averse to eating free ice cream? No, I thought not.'

'What's the catch?' Lewis asked, eliciting a groan from

187

Danny, who was well aware of his devotion to conspiracy thrillers.

Cher was the picture of sincerity. 'No catch. I've just been working on some new flavours and I want to see what reaction they get.'

Lewis shrugged. 'Good enough answer for me. Where do I start?'

Cher's black-brown eyes twinkled and she held out three plastic ice cream spoons. 'Anywhere you like.'

Elsie took a break from cleaning tables to witness Cher's not-so-scientific experiment. 'What happens if they love all of them?' she whispered to Cher.

'Then I'll do a flavour of the month promotion and use all the recipes. See? I've thought of everything.'

'Is this rose-flavoured?' Aoife asked, pleasantly surprised at her first taste.

'Yes. It's Rosewater and Lemon Sorbet. Do you think it works?'

'It's lovely. I'd buy that.'

Cher's smile was pure pride. 'Brilliant.'

'This just looks like vanilla, so it's a safe bet,' Danny said, selecting a pale white scoop. He took a large spoonful and then nearly sprayed his friends and Cher as he was accosted by a violent coughing fit.

Elsie fetched a glass of water as Lewis slapped him on the back and Aoife looked on, concerned. After a couple of sips, a beetroot-faced Danny managed to regain control, his eyes streaming.

'What *was* that?'

'Horseradish,' Cher replied sheepishly.

'Who puts horseradish in ice cream?'

Elsie chuckled. 'Heston Blumenthal.'

Danny groaned. 'That guy is crazy.'

'He's a babe,' Cher argued.

Aoife's disgust was impossible to hide. 'He is not.'

'I wouldn't insult Cher's dream husband if I were you,' Elsie laughed. 'She worships at his Bunsen burner, don't you, hun?'

'Heston happens to be a beautiful man with a brilliant mind. The things he does with liquid nitrogen are enough to make any girl go weak.'

Lewis scrutinised the third flavour with suspicion. 'I'm not sure I want to try this.'

'Oh don't be a baby,' Cher tutted, 'you'll never impress girls if you're scared of ice cream.'

'Nice marketing line,' Elsie grinned. 'I wouldn't use that one if I were you.'

Hesitantly, Lewis lifted the spoon to his mouth. A broad grin spread across his face, fuelled as much by relief as reaction to the new flavour. 'Doughnuts!' he exclaimed. 'It tastes of jam doughnuts!'

'Correct!' Cher said. 'Well, two out of three is encouraging.' An old-fashioned telephone sounded from the kitchen and Cher looked at Elsie, who had resumed her task of clearing tables. 'That's your phone, isn't it? You're popular today, Els.'

Elsie groaned as she walked into the kitchen to answer it. 'It'll probably be someone selling something.' To her surprise, she saw Guin's name flashing on the screen. Quickly, she accepted the call.

'Elsie – I think the baby's coming. I can't get hold of Joe and he has the car. I'm so scared . . . Can you come?'

Shocked, Elsie turned to Cher, who immediately recognised the gravity of the call. 'It's Guin . . .' She grabbed her bag and keys from the kitchen.

'The baby?'

'Yes.'

'Go, go!' Cher practically pushed her out of the door.

Elsie raced up the street towards her car. 'I'm coming. Are you sure it's time?'

'I don't know . . . I had this all planned out and it's not supposed to happen for two weeks yet. I don't have anything ready . . .'

'That's not important, Guin. I'm at the car now. You need to pack a bag for hospital, OK?' There was a loud moan from the other end of the phone. 'Guin? Are you there?'

'Yes . . . I'm here. Please hurry!'

Fifteen minutes later, Elsie pulled up outside Guin's pottery studio in Shoreham-by-Sea and raced around the back to the small fisherman's cottage Guin shared with her husband Joe. Guin was leaning against the kitchen table, bag in hand, breathing heavily. Her tear-stained face broke into a massive grin when she saw her sister.

'Am I glad to see you! It's happening, Els. This is actually happening!'

Tears stung Elsie's eyes. 'I know! Have you reached Joe yet?'

'No, his mobile's off. I can't believe he would turn it off, today of all days . . .' She took a sharp intake of breath and clutched her enormous belly.

Seeing the genuine fear in her sister's eyes, Elsie sprang into action. 'Right, let's go.' She grabbed Guin's bag and supported her as they left the house, gently manoeuvring her into the passenger seat of the car. Then, running round to the other side, she revved the engine into life.

Guin was staring at her, eyes wide. 'Elsie, I'm so scared.'

'You're going to be fine. Just focus on your breathing. Leave the high-speed dash to me, OK?'

Adrenaline pumping madly through her body, Elsie put her foot down and they sped off, taking corners sharply and ducking down side streets whenever traffic loomed ahead. Guin clung onto the door handle, eyes fixed maniacally on the road ahead to divert her from the immensity of the situation.

'I'm going to throttle Joe when I get hold of him,' she swore through gritted teeth. 'I can't believe he's not here. We had a *plan*, Elsie! All those months of preparing and planning and making sure that every last detail was perfect . . .' She broke off as another contraction hit. 'Well, if he thinks I'm *ever* going near him again after this he's got another thing coming.'

Elsie smiled at her sister. 'You don't mean that. One look at your beautiful baby in your handsome hubby's arms and you'll be . . .'

B-A-N-G!

The car veered suddenly to the left and it was all Elsie could do to wrench the steering wheel back. What happened next seemed to take place in ultra-slow-motion . . . Slamming her hand to the dashboard, Elsie hit the hazard lights as the car crossed from the fast lane of the dual carriageway into the nearside lane – thankfully avoiding other motorists, who had witnessed the cause of the noise and moved out of her way. The whole chassis bumped and jerked wildly as Guin screamed, and Elsie prayed fervently that she could stop the car without hurting her sister. Braking had limited effect, the pull on the car from the left front wing too strong for Elsie to fight. Finally, in desperation, she grabbed the handbrake with her left hand and yanked it up as hard as she could, hanging on with all her might while steering with the other hand, until they came to a halt on the hard shoulder.

Silence. Then Guin burst into hysterical tears and Elsie, exhausted, slumped back in her seat.

'We could have been killed! How did nothing hit us? What are we going to do now? We're never going to get there! I'm going to give birth on the A27!'

Shaking, Elsie reached out for Guin's hand. 'No, you're not.'

'I am! And it's all Joe's fault! Because if he'd been with me like he *promised* I wouldn't be in an *exploding car* too far from the *hospital*!'

Elsie faced her sister, panic beginning to gnaw at her stomach. 'Guin, look at me – *look at me* – you have to calm down, for you and the baby. Now come on, breathe with me . . .' She took long, slow, deliberate breaths and nodded at Guin to follow her. Gradually, Guin's breathing began to slow, her tears falling freely as she gripped Elsie's hand.

An HGV thundered past and Elsie suddenly remembered the danger of remaining where they were.

'Honey, we have to get out of the car.'

'No! I'm not going anywhere!'

'Guin, we can't stay here – we're too close to the road. I'm going to get out and take you onto the grass verge, OK? Keep breathing . . .' She puffed her cheeks in and out like a half-crazed nursery school teacher miming breathing for three-year-olds and continued to do it as she climbed out of the car and hurried round to the passenger side.

'What are we going to do?' Guin moaned as Elsie half-walked, half-carried her to the lush green grass a safe distance from the car. As she looked back she could see the shreds of rubber and bare metal where her front left tyre had once been. Leaving Guin, she ducked back into the car to fetch her bag, located Joe's number on her mobile and called it.

Please ring, please . . . she pleaded silently as the call took an age to connect. Then, to her utter relief, a ringing tone sounded, quickly usurped by the frantic voice of her brother-in-law.

'Elsie, what's happening? I can't get through to Guin and she's not at the house.'

'She's with me. We're on our way to hospital, but we've just had a tyre blow out.'

'What? Are you OK? Is the baby . . .?'

'We're all fine. I'm going to call an ambulance . . .'

'Elsie! Someone's stopping!' Guin called and Elsie looked back to see a black Jaguar parking a few feet away from them.

'Listen, Joe – somebody's just stopped. They might be able to help. I'm going to pass you to Guin, OK? Just keep talking to her and for heaven's sake don't let her know you're panicking.'

She hurried over to hand her phone to Guin and ran back towards the black car, waving her hands. The driver's door opened as she approached.

'Can you help us, please? My sister's in labour and I have to get her to the hospit—' Words were snatched from her open mouth in an instant.

'OK, get in the car.'

Shaking her head, Elsie began to back away. 'Actually, we're fine. I'm just going to call an ambulance, so . . .'

'Elsie, your sister's in labour. Now is not the time for avoidance tactics.' Torin walked towards her, his brow heavy and determined.

How could this be happening? Was Torin Stewart some kind of omnipresent entity sent to plague her? 'I'm *calling* an ambulance.'

'No, you're going to help me get your sister into my car and then I'm going to drive you both to the hospital.'

Elsie opened her mouth to protest but Torin was having none of it.

'*Look* at her,' he pointed at Guin, who was half-lying on the verge, sobbing into the phone. 'Now ask yourself: is your stupid issue with me more important than your sister's health and the safe delivery of her child?'

He was right, and everything in her being hated him for it. Guin cried out again and that was all the persuasion Elsie needed. 'Honey, it's OK – this gentleman's going to take us to hospital.'

Guin grasped Torin and Elsie's arms as she struggled to her feet. 'Thank you, thank you so much! I don't know what happened – there was an explosion or something, and then Elsie managed to get us to the side of the road.'

'I was driving on the other carriageway and saw the whole thing. Your sister's reactions were very quick – you were lucky to avoid a serious collision.' He caught Elsie's eye and she looked away.

'She's an amazing person,' Guin gasped, the pain within her building as Torin moved her into the back seat. 'I'd still be terrified at home if she hadn't dropped everything and driven over.'

Elsie fixed her eyes on her sister. 'I didn't want you to be alone. Not coming wasn't an option.'

With Guin safely belted in and Elsie seated resignedly in the soft cream leather passenger seat, Torin started the car.

'I meant what I said. Your driving was impressive. I saw your car go across the lanes and thought I was going to witness a major accident. That's why I pulled off at the next junction and turned round.'

'I just did what I had to.'

'Well, you did it well. You should be proud of yourself.'

'Like I need your permission to do that?' She could feel her fingernails digging into the palms of her hand. *Of all the patronising, moronic things to say . . .*

Torin lowered his voice, his green eyes firmly set ahead. 'I'm trying to pay you a compliment.'

Elsie felt her neck tense. 'I know.' *Trying is the operative word, Torin.*

He sighed. 'Are you OK? No whiplash or anything?'

'I'm fine.' *Of course I'm not fine!* she screamed silently inside. *My car just blew up when I was doing sixty miles an hour, I'm scared we won't make it in time and, to top it all, now I have to sit in a car with you, wishing you were anyone but Torin Stewart . . .*

'All the same, I think we should have someone take a look at you when we get there.' He lifted his chin to peer into the rear-view mirror at Guin. 'How are you doing back there?'

'Not bad, considering. Do you two know each other?'

Elsie surrendered to the inevitable. 'This is Torin Stewart – my shoplifting rescuer.'

'Ha! No way! And your blind date you totally snubbed? That is priceless – *oww . . .*'

'The very same.' Elsie could feel the intensity of green eyes trained on her, but she refused to look at the driver.

Guin's amusement was proving to be a useful distraction from her contractions. 'I bet she floored you when she unleashed the widow line.'

Torin gave a self-conscious cough. 'Er, she did, yeah. Completely.'

'I laughed so much when she told me. To be honest, it sounded like you deserved it. From what she said it sounded like you were being a complete git . . .'

'Guin!'

'I probably was.' He dropped his voice to a barely audible whisper. 'You told her that?'

'I was *upset*,' Elsie hissed back.

'So now I'm the laughing stock of your entire family?'

'Don't flatter yourself.'

'You are unbelievable . . .'

'Can't you go any faster?' Guin called. 'Only I think my passenger is in a hurry to check out the interior of your car.'

The thought of the possible outcome of a birth occurring on the beautiful upholstery of his Jaguar was enough to turn Torin into a contender for the Red Bull Racing Team. He jammed the accelerator and the Jaguar roared towards their destination.

The sight of the hospital caused Guin to burst into tears again and this time Elsie felt like joining her. Ignoring all the No Entry signs, Torin screeched past parked ambulances in the entrance to A&E and parked right by the doors. Two burly paramedics chatting by the open back of an ambulance stood and approached the car, ready for a fight.

'Oi! You can't park here, mate . . .'

Torin jumped out to meet them. 'I have a lady in labour in my car – can you help?'

Their anger gone, the paramedics sprang into action, fetching a foldable wheelchair and helping Guin into it, wrapping a blanket across her. Elsie walked alongside, reassuring her sister. As they reached the automatic doors at the entrance, the taller of the two paramedics grinned at Torin.

'You did well, Mr Knight-in-Shining-Armour. Now move that thing immediately.'

'Sure. Where are you taking her?'

'Maternity, *obviously*. Don't worry, sunshine, your lovely

girlfriends will be there by the time you've found somewhere legal to park.'

'We're *not*—' Elsie began, but Guin started guffawing.

'Girlfriends! Ha! Yes, that's right, both of us are his girlfriends. And it's *his* fault I'm in this predicament!'

Elsie couldn't believe what she was hearing. 'Guinevere!'

'It is, it's all his fault,' Guin continued, halfway between tears and laughter with her contractions. 'That's the last time you have sex with me, mister!' she called over her shoulder.

Thoroughly embarrassed, Elsie kept her head down and didn't look back as the doors slid shut behind them.

The maternity ward was humid and smelled of over-boiled vegetables and disinfectant, its harsh striplights making the backs of Elsie's eyes ache. She shuddered. She had forgotten how much she hated this smell – that caught at the back of your throat and sank itself into your clothes so that you carried it home with you as a constant reminder . . .

The paramedics and nurses bustled Guin into a room and Elsie was left by the nurses' station, the shock of the situation beginning to take hold. Her sister was bringing a new life into the world, a long-awaited member of the Maynard family, which was too fantastic for words. But the car – the possibility of what might have happened had she not controlled the vehicle, of what could have been lost . . . A sudden surge of nausea swept over her and she stumbled towards a row of plastic chairs opposite, breathing heavily. Leaning forward, she hugged her knees, willing the giddiness to pass.

'How are you doing?' asked a friendly female voice.

Slowly, Elsie dared to raise her head and saw a smiling young nurse standing in front of her. 'I feel a bit sick.'

'I'm not surprised. I often say to people that the relatives get the rough deal in births. At least mums know what's happening most of the time. First one, is it?'

Elsie nodded. 'How is she?'

'Midwife's with her now, checking the situation. All standard procedure. Shouldn't be too long and then you can go in, if you like.'

The doors to the maternity unit opened and a wild-eyed, red-haired man rushed in. 'Where is she?' he demanded.

Elsie grabbed her brother-in-law's hand. 'Joe, calm down. She's being examined by a midwife.'

Despite Joe's panic, the nurse's smile never wavered and Elsie was taken back in her mind to a different ward, nearly two years ago. *Don't look at their smiles as an indicator of anything, Els. They're trained to cover all emotion with that smile . . .* In his final hours, Lucas' distrust of the nursing staff's perennial smiles had increased. Trust Lucas Webb to be suspicious of the very people who were trying to help him. But then, he had known his time was coming to an end – his frustrations fuelled by the refusal of the nurses and doctors to confirm the fact. He was in pain and scared, Elsie had explained to one of the nurses, worried that he had offended her. Instead, the nurse had placed a hand on Elsie's shoulder and reassured her that his reaction was more common than she realised. *Compared to some of the things I hear in this job, your husband's a sweetie, love . . .*

'I'll just go and see how they're getting along. Try not to worry.'

Joe sank into the orange plastic chair next to Elsie as the nurse left. 'How, exactly, does she propose I do that? My wife's in there, having our baby!'

Elsie patted his hand. 'Chin up, Daddy. If it helps, she was laughing like a loon when they took her into the room.'

198

'Laughing? After your car accident? Isn't that an indicator of trauma or something?'

'Don't be daft! She'd just accused a random stranger of knocking her up and laughed all the way up here.'

Joe ran a hand through his mussed-up hair. 'Sounds like Guin. Was she really angry with me? We'd planned this out, routes and timings and everything, and you know how hung up on organisation she gets.'

Elsie smiled. 'I think she'll just be glad to see you.'

'Mr Thomas?' A tall Asian doctor in blue scrubs was heading over to them. 'I've just examined your wife and she's progressing well. Baby seems to be comfortable and the heartbeat is strong.'

'How long do you think it will be until . . .?'

'It's difficult to say at this stage. Could be within the next couple of hours or longer. You're welcome to go in and see her, if you like.'

Joe looked at Elsie. 'Do you want to come?'

'I'll stay here a while. I think you and Guin should have some time together. Call me if you need anything.'

'OK, thanks!' Joe was already hurrying away.

The smiling nurse returned to the station and looked over at Elsie. 'How are you feeling now?'

'Much better, thanks. Is there anywhere I can get a coffee?'

'There's a vending machine just out in the corridor, but I wouldn't trust it if I were you. The café is down on the first floor – take the lift just outside the entrance to this unit and you can't miss it.'

Of course there was the café. Elsie knew it well – it had been where they had all gathered after Lucas died. Unable to stay with her husband any longer but unwilling to go home, Elsie had sat on a grey plastic chair in the faceless restaurant, staring at her untouched grey coffee as her family consoled his around her. It was as if the colour had been wrenched from her world, replaced by an indistinct palette of cold greyness under the too-bright striplights . . . Part of her didn't want to go there now, the memory still raw. But her newfound voice of reason intervened. *It's just a place. It doesn't mean anything any more.* Still a little shaky, she made her way out of the ward towards the lift and pressed the call button. The vivid green display counted up from G to 3 and the doors opened to reveal Torin, looking a little stressed, carrying two takeaway cups.

'For you,' he said, handing her a cup and walking past her into the corridor.

'Thank you. I was just on my way to the café.'

'I saved you the journey, then.' Torin sat down on a row of green plastic chairs along the wall opposite the maternity unit entrance and busied himself with emptying two sachets of sugar into his cup.

Elsie remained by the lift doors, unsure whether to sit beside him or go back into the unit. She was too tired for a fight but was aware of his defensiveness, its presence reminding her of her ungratefulness in the car. Stuffing as much of her pride away as she could, she crossed the corridor and sat down, one seat away from him. 'Thank you.'

'You already said that.'

'No, I mean thank you for rescuing me. *Again.* And I'm sorry for being – well, you know. I was just scared and angry at myself and I shouldn't have taken it out on you.'

Her honesty appeared to surprise him and he twisted in his seat to look directly at her. 'Thanks for that.' Lifting his cup, he quickly added: 'I'm afraid I can't vouch for the quality of the coffee.'

Elsie took a sip of the too-hot liquid. 'It's a little better than I remember. A bit too hot, though.'

200

'Drumming up trade for this place, I reckon,' he smiled. 'I wonder if they have a burned-palate ward for hospital coffee-related incidents?'

It was an odd attempt at humour, but in her weary state Elsie smiled regardless. 'Maybe so.'

A moment of silence fell between them. Elsie took another tentative sip and gazed down at her work shoes. In the rush to reach Guin, she had completely forgotten that she was still dressed in her retro waitress uniform. No wonder she had received such strange looks from passing motorists when she pulled the car over!

Torin cleared his throat. 'So, at the risk of sounding cheesy, do you come here often?' Sudden horror immediately painted his face. '*Man*, I'm so sorry. I didn't think . . . That was an incredibly stupid thing to say.'

'It's my first time on this particular floor,' Elsie replied, Torin's utter disgust with his poor-taste joke surprisingly touching. 'How about you?'

'I don't generally make a habit of hanging round maternity wards.' His eyes were very still. 'How's your sister?'

'They say it could be a few hours. My brother-in-law Joe is here, at least, and I called Dad and Daisy as we were walking up to the ward. Guin's doing well, though, so that's a relief.' A thought struck her. 'By the way, I'm sorry about what she said outside.'

'Oh don't worry about that.' A slightly naughty smile began to play at the corners of his mouth. 'Best line I've heard for a while. I'm impressed the paramedics thought me capable of tackling two Maynard sisters at once, actually. Although considering what you're wearing . . .'

'Eeww, that's enough, thank you. I think I liked you better when you were apologising.'

'Elsie, I—'

201

The lift doors opened and Jim appeared, his anxious expression turning to joy when he saw his daughter.

'Dad!' Elsie stood and hurried across the green vinyl corridor floor to greet him.

'Oh, come here, darling! Are you OK after your ordeal with the car? Daisy told me.' He hugged her tightly. 'Such a scary thing to happen!'

'Did you drive here?'

'No, I had a lift. Olly's just parking the car.'

'Olly's here? How come you didn't come in your car?'

'Because I was at his office when you called me and he insisted.' Jim noticed Torin and extended his hand. 'Hello, I'm Elsie's father. Jim.'

Torin stood and shook Jim's hand. 'Torin Stewart.'

Jim's eyebrows made a bid for the white ceiling tiles. 'Ah, the famous Torin! Well, it's a pleasure to finally make your acquaintance.'

Elsie jumped in. 'Dad – Torin was the one who brought us here.'

'Oh, forgive me. Thank you so much for helping my girls. I dread to think what could have happened if . . .'

'No problem. I saw Elsie's tyre blow from the opposite carriageway. Her driving was impeccable,' Torin replied.

'That's my little girl.' Jim hugged Elsie again. 'Is Guinevere well?'

'All good and the baby's fine, too. Joe's in with her.'

'Good, good.' Jim rubbed his hands together. 'All a bit weird, this. I can hardly believe Guin's going to be a mum.'

'And you're going to be a *grandpa*,' Elsie winked as her father visibly cringed.

'I suppose I should call your mother?'

The mention of her mother caused the muscles in Elsie's back to tense. 'She won't come, Dad, you know she won't.'

It had been over a year since she had last heard from her mother: a painfully stilted phone conversation, which mostly revolved around recriminations at the entertainment industry that had overlooked her for years. No questions about Elsie and her sisters, no flicker of any maternal instinct. This came as no surprise to Elsie, having long abandoned any hope of building a meaningful relationship with her mother.

Not that Jim could see it, of course. Despite everything that had occurred between them, he retained a selfless sense of decency towards his former wife and Elsie suspected he still carried a flame for the woman who abandoned him and his family so many years ago.

'All the same, she should know. I'll call her after the baby's born. Do you think they'd mind if I went in to see Guinie?'

Elsie smiled. 'I'm sure they'd be happy if you did.'

'Excellent.' He shook hands with Torin once more. 'Thank you again, for all your help. I hope you know how much my family appreciate it.'

'My pleasure, sir.' Torin had been watching the conversation with passive interest and when Jim had gone he turned to Elsie. 'I take it you're not your mother's biggest fan?'

It was an incredibly personal question to ask, but Elsie had no qualms about answering. 'Not really. She left us when I was two and hasn't had an awful lot to do with us since. We speak occasionally on the phone – at Christmas mainly – but the last time I physically saw her was nearly two years ago, at Lucas' funeral.'

'Wow. That must be difficult, not having a mum around?'

'I don't miss it, really. I've never known her in a maternal capacity. But Dad is fantastic and in many ways he's been both parents to us.'

Torin sipped his coffee. 'So, how come you aren't in with your sister?'

'Sorry?'

'Well, you were out here when I arrived and you've just let your father go in without you.'

Confused by his insinuation, Elsie stared at him. 'She's with her husband and Dad won't be happy until he's seen her. I would imagine the midwives don't want umpteen family members in the delivery room. It's enough for me to know she's here and being cared for.'

He shook his head. 'Forgive me, but I don't think that's the reason.'

What did he think gave him the right to question her motives? 'Well, *forgive me*, but I don't think that's any of your business.'

'Fair enough.'

'Good.'

'Personally, I think you're too scared to go in there.'

'Excuse me?'

'I think this place unnerves you.'

Not again. Disgusted, Elsie stood. 'I am not going to listen to this.'

His voice was velvet-soft but edged with a diamond sharpness. 'I don't want to offend you, Elsie. But I don't imagine that being here is easy for you. I saw your expression when we arrived – for a moment I thought you weren't going to go inside, you looked so fearful.'

'How *dare* you . . .'

'Elsie!' The lift doors closed as Olly emerged. 'Are you OK?'

Heart racing from her exchange with Torin, Elsie hurried into Olly's embrace, the sensation of his protective arms providing a safe place for her whirring mind. 'I'm so glad to see you.'

Surprised, Olly laughed, the rush of his warm breath rustling Elsie's hair as she hugged him. 'Now that's what I call a welcome.' He looked over to Torin. 'Hey, thank you so much for rescuing the girls. I'm glad you were there when they needed help.'

Torin stood and shook Olly's hand as Elsie stepped back. 'It was nothing. Right place, right time.' His eyes met Elsie's. 'Give my regards to your sister.' Digging in his pocket, he produced a business card and held it out to her. 'I don't suppose you'd text me when the baby arrives? I'd like to know the details of my mystery passenger.'

She hesitated for a second. How could he go from challenging her motives to asking her to contact him? But as she stared back Elsie was aware of his earnest expression – as though the card were an olive branch, the gesture an apology. She accepted it, feeling the brief brush of his fingers as he released the card. 'I'll do that.'

'Hope all goes well.' He gave a strange half-smile and walked to the lift.

Olly grinned at her. 'I can't stay long, I'm afraid, but I think we'd better check that your dad isn't pacing the floor before I go. He was a bag of nerves in the car on the way over.'

Agreeing, Elsie walked with him to the maternity unit entrance. Olly went through first and she followed, but as she reached the doors she looked back down the corridor towards the lift. As its steel doors opened, Torin cast a glance back at her, the same earnest expression on his face. Nodding slowly, he stepped into the lift and was gone.

In the seven hours that followed – amid countless coffees, long meandering conversations and false alarms – Elsie thought about her conversation with Torin. How had he recognised the battle in her, when even she had been struggling to define her own emotions?

There had been something in Torin's admittedly hamfisted attempt at broaching the subject – something that unnerved her more than the events unfolding around her. That tone of voice, that unrepentant insight . . .

'You're in denial.'

'I'm not.'

'Yes, you are.'

'Lucas, please drop this. I don't want to fight today.'

'You need to hear it, Els. We have to talk about what the end's going to be like. You have to be ready for it.'

'I know I do, but you only received the diagnosis last week. Can we not just be us for a while longer before this has to take over everything?'

'Of course. I'm sorry, baby.' He had taken her into his arms and held her, the strength of it reassuring. But Elsie had hated that a finite sentence had now been pronounced over even this – that each embrace from that moment on would be one closer to the day when they would cease to be available to her . . .

It was almost midnight when Joe rushed out to Jim, Daisy and Elsie, wearing hospital scrubs and looking as if he'd gone a week without sleep.

'The baby's heart rate has slowed. They're worried about its condition, so they're taking Guin in for an emergency Caesarean. I've got to go back in there. Pray they get through this, OK?'

An hour and forty-five minutes passed, the Maynard family on tenterhooks every time the double doors to the theatre opened. Elsie willed the fear in her heart to subside, trying her best to hold back the ghosts of the past as the nursing staff raced past them. Daisy held her hand, as if reading her mind, and Jim paced backwards and forwards, pausing to check his watch.

Finally, the smiling nurse approached. 'The surgery went well, and mother and baby are fine. You can go in now.'

They crammed into the delivery room, where Guin was sitting up in bed, drained and bruised, cradling a tiny bundle of blankets.

'It's a girl,' she beamed. 'Meet Ottie Rose.'

Hi Torin. Ottie Rose Thomas, born at 1.43am, 6lbs 7oz. Mum, Dad and baby all well. Thank you for helping us. Elsie ☺

Elsie pressed 'Send' and closed her aching eyes. It was nearly light, the birds already filling the neighbourhood with their song, and after a long night at the hospital followed by a taxi ride with Jim to change the tyre on her abandoned car, she was exhausted. In little over an hour and a half, she would have to be up again. Snuggling down into the blissful comfort of her duvet, she was slipping into sleep when her mobile buzzed. Reaching blindly to locate it on her bedside table, she squinted at the screen:

Good news, thanks for letting me know. I'm sorry for pressuring you. Don't hate me? Torin.

Elsie blinked at the message. The apology was certainly unexpected, but why the last sentence? Since when did he care whether she hated him or not? And was she meant to respond to this message? Elsie moaned and rolled over. It was too late and she was far too tired to deal with this now. Torin would have to wait.

CHAPTER THIRTEEN

Take a bow . . .

Morning came far too early and Elsie wearily made her way to work. As usual, she was the first person there but the lack of company proved a relief, given the tiredness weighing heavily in her body. What little sleep she had managed to snatch had been plagued by memories of the day and night before, flitting across her subconscious like blurred, frantic dancers.

At nine-thirty, Cher arrived. In between the usual bartering with Dennis over the number of scoops he could have with his breakfast, a long conversation with Gennaro from the body-piercing and tattoo shop across the street about a possible ice cream discount he could offer his recently punc-tured customers ('Imagine the comfort of your excellent spiced apple cake with a hearty scoop of Toffee Crunch to soothe the pain of their endeavours, ladies!') and the noisy arrival of several regulars from the Vegetarian Shoe Shop for their take-out Almond Milk and Raspberry ice cream, crêpes and chai tea lattes, Cher plied Elsie with countless cups of dark, smoky espresso and sticky, sweet cinnamon and lemon pastries while Elsie recounted the events of the past twenty-four hours.

'How lucky that Torin was nearby when the tyre went,' Cher said, eyes alive with the information Elsie had just presented to her. 'I mean, imagine what could have happened if he hadn't been there.'

'I was about to call an ambulance,' Elsie replied, keen to diminish Torin's hero status. 'I'm sure we would have been fine.'

'And Olly showed up, too? Blimey, I bet you've never felt in so much demand!'

'Hmm.' When faced with the sheer force of Cher's inquiry, Elsie had long ago learned it was best to remain defiantly non-committal. 'But you should see Ottie Rose. I know I'm a biased aunt, but she's the cutest thing you've ever seen.' She reached under the counter for her handbag and flicked through the photos of her new niece on her phone, feeling the rush of love for Ottie Rose all over again.

'Look at that little mop of red curls already!' Cher gushed. 'No prizes for guessing where she got those from.'

Elsie smiled. 'Yes, Joe was very happy to see a redhead for the family. Guin's convinced it'll turn blonde like hers did, but I'm not so sure.'

'Was Torin there when Ottie was born?'

'No, he was long gone by then. I did text him, though – you know, to thank him for everything.'

Cher's eyes narrowed. 'So you have his number?' The question was more heavily loaded than a ten-tonne cannon.

'Yes, I have his number.' She looked over to the door, where a new customer was shaking the rain from his coat. 'And *you* have a customer.'

'Elsie Maynard, you are no fun,' Cher growled, as Elsie hopped down from the stool to head into the kitchen.

Later that afternoon, Woody arrived. He was dressed in a long black leather coat that made him look like a cross between Jack Sparrow from *Pirates of the Caribbean* and Neo from *The Matrix*, and his hair hung lankly from his rain-soaked red skull-print bandana.

'Are you a sight for my weary eyes,' he drawled when Cher met him at the counter. 'An angel in turquoise satin and lace. Tell me what I can say to tempt you away from this place?'

'You can't, you naughty man,' Cher giggled and leaned a little forward to ensure Woody received a full view of the charms of her work uniform. 'Now what can I get you?'

Woody gave her a lascivious wink. 'Arrested?'

'Are you harassing my boss again, Woody?' Elsie grinned, drying the café's oversized coffee cups with a tea towel.

'Nah. She won't let me, angel. Shame, though.'

'Take a seat and I'll bring you a drink over,' Elsie said. 'Cher, is it OK if I take my lunch break?'

'Feel free, sweetie.'

Elsie made two cups of peppermint tea, helped herself to a bowl of butternut squash soup (Cher's latest menu innovation) and took a large slice of dark chocolate and chilli cheesecake from underneath the display dome on the counter. She joined Woody at his table and passed the cheesecake to him.

'There you go, your reward for our recent choral triumph.'

'That, angel, is why the universe brought you to me.' Woody's face lit up and he began to enthusiastically demolish the sweet treat. 'Is this made by the fair lady Cher's delicate hands?'

'It is indeed. So, to what do we owe the honour of your company this afternoon?'

Woody dropped his fork on his empty plate and wiped his stubble-framed mouth with a paper napkin. 'Phase Two.'

'Of what?'

'Of our plan to rock it to this town. See, everything we did before was leading up to the Carnival. They had a purpose. Now they need a new challenge – a righteous cause, if you will – to unite them like the Carnival did.'

Elsie knew he was right, but with no other offers of performance opportunities currently available she didn't know what to suggest. 'I suppose we could ask around to see if there are any amateur concerts we could perform at?'

'Concerts?' Woody scoffed. 'The Sundaes don't do "concerts". We deal in *happenings*, dude.'

'Well, perhaps we'd better ask everyone at rehearsal to get their thinking caps on. I'm sure between us we can come up with something.' She rubbed her forehead. 'I'm sorry, mate. I'll be more on the ball then.'

'Tough night, angel?'

'My sister had her first child in the early hours, so it was a bit of an epic day.'

Woody blew out a whistle. 'Heavy stuff. I wouldn't have guessed she was with child at the Carnival.'

'Not Daisy, you muppet. My middle sister, Guin. You'd like her. She's very – um – *alternative*.'

'Like your dad? That guy is a *dude*, man!'

Elsie suspected that a major reason for Woody's summation of her father was Jim's unfettered admiration for Hellfinger. When they had met at the Carnival, Jim had become a bright-eyed fan, jabbering on for a full thirty minutes about Hellfinger's one and only album and the effect it had on him. Even last night, while Jim, Elsie and Daisy were waiting for news of Guin and the baby, Jim had regaled them with the finer details of the conversation with his rock hero.

'That man is an overlooked lyrical legend,' he had insisted. 'I mean it. So many so-called experts of the day denounced

211

"Hard Rockin' Summer" as a candyfloss-rock ditty, but they failed to see the deeper significance behind the lyrics. Anyone truly worthy of their salt could tell you what that song really means. The industry press didn't know what they were talking about.'

It amused Elsie no end to think of her father bopping around his house to Woody's cheesy rock tunes when nobody was looking. 'We should ask Dad if there are any council-run events coming up where we could sing.'

'It's a start, I guess,' said Woody. 'But hear this, angel, we're meant for bigger things. I sense destiny in the air!'

'It won't work.'

'Open your mind, girl!'

Sasha fixed Woody with a stare that could shrivel steel. 'My mind is always open, thank you very much. We should be singing cool stuff, not random old songs shoved together.'

'The ABBA/Deep Purple medley went down a storm at the Carnival,' Graeme suggested, his round cheeks flushing.

'That's true. People loved it,' Danny agreed.

'It was a fluke. A one-off,' Sasha pouted.

'Could be the first of many,' Daisy said.

Sasha pointed at Woody. 'Or a *one-hit wonder*.'

Woody folded his arms. 'I don't respond to the term "one-hit-wonder". I find it offensive. Hellfinger wrote the definitive rock anthem – so where was there to go from that? We were like the Sistine Chapel, man: nobody ever said to Michelangelo, "We'll only call you a success when you do twelve more like it" . . .'

Elsie took a breath and stepped into the fray. 'Look. Why don't we choose some chart stuff and also work on some of Woody's ideas? We've always said The Sundaes should be about including everyone.'

Sasha gave a loud tut. 'All right.'

At last, some progress! So far this evening the choir rehearsal had been a world away from the happy, post-performance celebration they had enjoyed the week before. A strange atmosphere filled Sundae & Cher that Elsie couldn't quite define: not boredom, or ill feeling, but an odd sense of restlessness, as if their enthusiasm had stalled. Perhaps it was because not all the choir members were there: Aoife was working late at college, Juliet, Sheila and Stan were taking part in a fundraising event for a local under-11s football team, Kathy was away on holiday and Irene hadn't come this week.

The rehearsal came to a quiet end at nine p.m. and, after locking up the café, Elsie and Daisy began to walk home.

'Bit of an odd one tonight,' Daisy said.

'Yes, I thought so. We couldn't sustain the Carnival enthusiasm forever, I guess. I think they're all still happy, though. Even Sasha seemed to be pacified by the end of it.'

Daisy laughed. 'And that's a minor miracle in itself. I think you and Woody are right about us having something else to aim for. I'll ask around to see if anyone knows of anything.'

'Thanks. So, how are things with André?'

'We've both been so busy lately I haven't seen that much of him. But when I do see him it's good.'

Elsie glanced at her sister. 'Are you happy, hun?'

'Of course.' Daisy looked back at her. 'There are things I'd like to change but work's good and I love being part of the choir. You should stop worrying about me and consider your own happiness.'

They had reached Daisy's car and Elsie stopped walking to face her sister. 'What is that supposed to mean?'

Daisy gave her a knowing look. 'Working out what happens with a certain hunky graphic designer we know.'

'We're just getting to know each other.'

'So you said. But I noticed he didn't hang around for long at the hospital.'

'He said he couldn't stay. He had to meet a client.'

Daisy shook her head. 'Or perhaps it was more to do with the fact that you were cool with him.'

Elsie fixed her sister with a defiant stare. 'I was not. We were all concerned about Guin . . .'

'I saw the way you moved away from him. Dad told me how you hugged Olly when he arrived – but when I got there you were standing as far from him as you could. He says he's happy to be friends for now, but I don't know many men who would put up with that amount of uncertainty just for a friend.'

Feeling cornered, Elsie dug her heels in. 'Then you obviously don't have many friends like Olly.'

Daisy opened the car door and sat inside. 'Obviously I don't. Just be careful, Els. I don't want you to get hurt.'

'How am I likely to get hurt when we're just friends?'

Saying nothing else, Daisy closed the door and drove away.

Her words irritated Elsie all the way home. What had she meant by that? If anything, Olly had merely proved what a lovely man he was by the very fact that he was giving her space. To construe all his actions as motivated by a hidden selfish desire to pursue Elsie only cheapened the help he had given and that was unfair. In fact, everything Olly had done since their agreement to get to know one another had endeared him further to her. He had been increasingly present in her thoughts and she found she was beginning to miss his company when they were apart. He never used his actions to demand appreciation from her – unlike Torin, who appeared to use every act that could potentially be classed as good as a reason to make her feel as if she owed him something in return.

She stopped at the entrance to her street and checked herself. Why was she thinking about Torin at all? Yes, she would forever be grateful for his assistance with getting Guin to hospital in time, but his belligerent questioning of her motives and the strange text response afterwards proved – if proof were needed – that he was someone she had no intention of pursuing friendship with.

But had she really been cool with Olly at the hospital? The thought of it sat awkwardly within her as she walked into her house. She went to the kitchen and made herself a mug of tea, pausing to stroke the photograph of Lucas on the fridge as she passed it. Lucas would have understood. He would have understood everything. Cradling her mug, she swallowed back the familiar rush of emotion as she reached out and slid the photograph from its magnetic frame, holding it to her heart as she left the room . . .

Next morning, Elsie woke to the shrill ringing of her mobile beside her bed. Wrestling the duvet away from her arms, she picked it up just as the call ended, but it rang again almost immediately.

'Elsie, it's Danny.' His voice sounded strained, as if speaking was an effort. 'The worst thing has happened – my mum's just told me and . . .' She could hear muffled sobs and the concerned tones of his mother in the background.

'Danny, what is it? Tell me!'

'It's Irene . . . she's . . . oh Elsie, I can't believe it . . .'

Panic gripped Elsie as she waited for Danny to confirm what she now suspected. In the end, it was his mother who gave the news, her son too upset to deliver it.

'I'm good friends with Irene's daughter Lyn and she called

me this morning to say that Irene passed away last night. Apparently it was cancer, but she hadn't told any of her family. It was only after she had died that her doctor confirmed it. She's been battling on her own for a long time.'

Elsie felt the blood drain from her face as inevitable memories from the past joined with her reaction to the news, making her head swim. *Cancer.* The word every person dreads to hear, whether or not they admit it. How could Elsie not have seen the battle in the old lady, when she had spent so much time watching the disease ravaging Lucas? She swallowed hard as a familiar concoction of emotions beset her: guilt, righteous anger, loss . . . Remembering where she was, she forced herself to speak. 'How's Danny taking it?'

His mother's sigh travelled down the line. 'Badly. Irene had become a really good friend lately and he's been talking to her a lot. None of his own grandparents are alive, you see, so I think he saw her as a sort of surrogate grandmother.'

'It's just so awful to think of her suffering alone.'

'I know. Mercifully, the end was quick, according to Lyn. The doctor assured her that Irene wouldn't have known much about it.'

Well, that was a blessing at least. Lucas had fought against the inevitable to his last breath. Elsie blinked away tears as the memory assaulted her, fresh as when it had just happened. 'I'm glad for her family that she didn't suffer at the end. Give Danny a big hug from me, will you?'

'Of course I will, Elsie, thanks.'

'Is there anything I can do for Irene's family?'

'I don't know, but I'll ask Lyn. It's dreadful news, isn't it? You just feel so helpless.'

Elsie wiped the tears from her face. 'I know. Thanks for

telling me. I'll tell the rest of the choir.' Ending the call, she collapsed back into bed, sobbing into her pillow.

Why hadn't Irene told anyone she was ill? It explained why she was often an onlooker at choir rehearsals and in recent weeks both Daisy and Woody had observed privately that she was looking thinner than usual. But they had attributed this to her age and never thought for a second that it could be anything more. All the same, the thought of the lovely lady, who spent so much time giving out to others, concealing a secret so terrible was heartbreaking. Perhaps she had wanted it this way: to squeeze every last drop out of her life without feeling she was a burden to anyone, without having to deal with their pity on top of the battle she was already engaged in.

Lucas had felt this, but his approach had been completely different. To him, other people discovering his condition was unavoidable – especially given his dramatic transformation from a tall, athletic young man to the painfully thin, shaven-headed shadow he became as the cancer laid claim to his body. His way of avoiding others' pity was to face it down. His merciless humour was his weapon of choice and he wielded it with considerable vigour, which only grew as his physical strength diminished.

'The way I see it, I'm being saved from the pitfalls of older life,' he would assert, his face alive with determined mischief. 'I mean, realistically, what would I be missing? I'm saving myself a fortune on the ridiculous sports car I don't need during my mid-life crisis, the reading glasses I would be prescribed in my fifties, the dreadful cruises I'd end up on when I retired. I'll never be forced to play golf, sit on a coach trip or pluck unruly hairs from my ears and nostrils. I won't end up in high-waisted trousers or burgundy-coloured padded gilets I've bought from the back pages of a weekend newspaper magazine. I will never feel the need for a stairlift or those sunglasses that clip over your specs and lift up to make you look permanently surprised. Given all that, do you *still* feel sorry for me?'

It was only to Elsie whom he allowed access to his grief for the pleasures of life he would never see – fatherhood, grandchildren and the prospect of fifty blissful years of marriage to the woman he loved more than life itself. But even then, his grief was short-lived, his need to feel in control of the situation summoning his humour back to the fore. 'Our kids might be completely ugly,' he would joke, tears still running down his lovely face. 'Imagine going through life with kids that look like trolls.'

'They would be gorgeous, just like their dad.'

'So you say. I've seen some of the odd-looking members of my family. If they inherited my granddad's massive ears they would be *terrifying* . . .'

Steeling herself, Elsie began to call the members of The Sundaes, the practicality of the task pushing her emotion to one side.

Cher was already sniffling into a tissue when Elsie arrived for work, the shock of the news still sinking in. And as the day went on, more of The Sundaes gathered – an unplanned meeting to share their grief. As a mark of respect, Cher closed the café at two, allowing The Sundaes to sit quietly together as she made countless pots of tea for everyone. She fussed around, offering slices of chocolate cake, but nobody was hungry. What mattered was that they were together to share in this: to reminisce, to cry, to laugh. As they talked, a surprising picture of Irene began to form. Far from being the shy, disinterested observer she appeared, Irene had been a vital member of the group – a counsellor, confidante and keeper of secrets beyond her own.

'She listened to me,' Lewis said, staring with hollow eyes at the teacup in his hands, 'and that's more than can be said for my family. My mum doesn't know I'm there half the time.'

Aoife nodded. 'I showed her my poems. Some of them I haven't even shown to Danny.' She smiled at her boyfriend, whose red-raw eyes glistened with tears again.

'Irene knew every one of Hellfinger's songs by heart,' Woody said, causing several involuntary laughs from the room. 'No, she did. Quoted them to me every week. That woman was a wonder.'

Elsie bit back tears. 'She knew about me. I . . .' She paused, realising that most of the people in the room actually knew nothing about her own life. 'I lost my husband nearly two years ago. He died of cancer. Irene knew – I'm not sure how. It meant the world to me to know she understood what it was like to lose somebody like that . . .'

The Sundaes stared blankly at her, unsure how to respond to her revelation. Then Lewis nervously stood and crossed the room to give her a stiltedly awkward hug. But the gesture was beautiful and Elsie appreciated it more than she could express.

Sasha, who had been uncharacteristically quiet, raised her hand. All eyes turned to her. 'She knew the truth about me.' The room fell silent. Sasha was suddenly as vulnerable as a child; it was a strange sight to witness the usual embodiment of brassiness reduced to a timid girl. 'I know what you all think about me. You think I'm full of crap, that I'm just a loudmouth. Which I am, but not for the reason you think. At home . . .' She stopped, fear flooding her eyes.

'Go on,' Dee said. 'It's OK.'

Sasha took a breath and stared at The Sundaes. 'At home,

I'm a slave. I don't speak unless I have to. My mum's housebound, has been since I was thirteen. And I'm the only one to look after her. Everyone we've ever trusted has gone away or done the dirty on us. All her boyfriends, my dad . . . even my brother who bogged off five years ago. So, I fight them before they get me. Because if I'm not in control it means people can hurt me. I'm not used to people being nice to me – it doesn't wash, see? Not that it matters much. Most people judge me. But Irene was the first person who listened.'

Silence remained as the shock of Sasha's confession sank in. Daisy, Juliet and Cher exchanged glances, Danny and Aoife stared dumbly at her and Sheila sniffed loudly. To everyone's amazement, it was Woody who spoke first.

'Girl, I've been a fool. I judged you and I shouldn't have.' He opened his arms wide. 'Can you find it in your heart to forgive a prejudiced old rocker?' He stood and approached her.

Sasha rose uncertainly and accepted his stiff but sincere hug. 'Not that I think you're any less of a loser, though.'

'Perish the thought.'

'I'm sorry too,' Elsie said. 'I think we all are.' Around the room murmurs of agreement sounded.

'We should do something to remember Irene,' Stan suggested. 'A song or something.'

Sheila raised a tentative hand. 'Maybe we could do a concert on the pier again?'

'Or we could offer to sing at her funeral,' Danny said. 'My mum could ask Lyn about it.'

Daisy smiled at him. 'I think that's a great idea, Danny. She meant a lot to all of us, so we should do something in her memory.'

And so, on a sunny August afternoon, The Sundaes

220

gathered at the front of the small Methodist chapel where Irene had been a member since childhood and performed a quiet a cappella version of "I'll Walk Beside You" as a small congregation of her family and friends looked on. The notes wobbled a little and several of the choir members missed words, but the heartfelt performance was well received by their audience and they returned to their seats feeling as if they had paid a suitable tribute to their much-missed friend.

After the service, Irene's daughter Lyn came up to Elsie and took both hands in hers.

'I don't think you realise what The Sundaes meant to Mum,' she said, and Elsie could feel Lyn's hands shaking around hers as she spoke. 'You might know that she was a professional singer from the age of seventeen right up to her mid-thirties and she always sang around the house when I was a kid. But she hadn't sung since we lost Dad over ten years ago. Stopped the day he died. And then she joined your choir and was the happiest any of us in the family had seen in a long time. When I saw her on that stage at the Carnival . . .' she pulled a handkerchief from her sleeve and dabbed her eyes '. . . it did my heart the world of good. Thank you so much.'

Elsie was blown away by Lyn's words. She had always wanted The Sundaes to be about fun and acceptance, but she had never expected to create something that could make such a difference to people's lives. To know that the choir she had founded had been the catalyst to encourage Irene to sing again was a phenomenal endorsement of everything they had done so far. Woody, however, was less surprised. When Elsie confided her amazement to him, he merely shook his head.

'I told you – we're the vocal revolution for this town.

We're inspiring song soldiers to seek something greater than themselves, angel. It was bound to happen.'

Losing Irene had been a complete bolt from the blue and for several weeks the choir seemed to be a little lost for direction. Even Woody's usual energetic attitude was lacking. Consequently, the choir's rehearsals became more like social club meetings with the odd song thrown in. Elsie recognised the need for everyone to come to terms with Irene's death, so she encouraged them to talk instead during rehearsals and, as a result, saw them grow considerably closer to one another.

During this time, Elsie found herself turning to Olly more and more. It began on the day she learned of Irene's death, after The Sundaes had left and she was alone in the café with only her conflicted thoughts for company. Without thinking, she had called him and he had hurried to meet her, holding her as she sobbed against him for almost an hour. Then, as the weeks passed, they spent more time together, Olly's gentle sense of humour and sincere concern for her more comforting than she could have imagined.

On the first Friday of September, Olly invited her to his apartment in Kemp Town for dinner after work.

'Nothing fancy, just a Thomasina Miers stew I've been wanting to try out.'

'I'm not sure I want something "trying out" on me, Olly.'

'Trust me, Els, it'll be worth it. And if it all goes pear-shaped, I make a mean omelette.'

Olly's apartment was in a beautiful row of white stucco Georgian houses, with black and white checkerboard steps at each entrance, elegantly curved black iron handrails, and lanterns over the doorways that wouldn't have looked out of place in a BBC costume drama. Elsie loved this part of Brighton – it was the area she had dreamed of living in for a whole summer when she was nine years old after attending a birthday party for a school friend in one of the grand buildings.

Olly was already busy in the kitchen when Elsie arrived, the delicious aromas of roasting meat, herbs and scented steam filling the room.

'I hope you don't mind, I bought wine,' he said, holding a bottle aloft.

'I never mind if there's wine,' Elsie grinned, accepting a large glass and congratulating herself on her decision to walk here this evening.

'So, how is everyone?'

She leant against the large Smeg refrigerator, enjoying the sight of her host dangerously juggling plates and cutlery while trying to appear calm and in control. 'It's taken a while for the news to sink in, obviously. But everyone seems determined to carry on, for Irene's sake. Woody and I just need to come up with something else for them to work towards. I'm wondering if we should put on a concert for Cancer Research or something. In Irene's memory?'

Olly motioned for her to move through into the dining area of his large, open-plan living room. 'That sounds like a great idea. I might be able to get my firm to donate some money towards the venue hire, if you like? And if you need any promotional stuff – you know, posters and flyers – you only have to ask.'

'That would be great. Thank you.'

'My pleasure.' He set out two places at the table and grinned broadly when he caught her eye. 'You know, we should be careful. These meetings are becoming scarily regular for us.'

She tutted. 'I know. Shocking, eh?'

'Right, the food should be ready. Feeling brave?' His eyes twinkled.

Elsie felt a shiver of happiness across her back. 'I think I am.'

CHAPTER FOURTEEN

A night to remember . . .

September arrived with a prolonged spell of wet weather, diminishing the tourist numbers further than the traditional return to school did. Cher took the opportunity to redecorate the kitchen at Sundae & Cher, creating a temporary kitchen in the café while her uncle and cousin replaced worktops and repainted walls and ceilings. For a week, the place was in chaos, but the lack of custom and unusual working conditions proved conducive for Cher and Elsie to talk properly about the events of the past month.

Cher had been spending so much time with Jake lately that Elsie hadn't seen much of her outside of work. Not that Elsie minded; she was pleased that Cher had finally found a decent man after so many dead-end relationships.

'So, how is Mr Wonderful?' Elsie asked, loving the way her boss positively twinkled at the mention of her beau.

Cher gave a little squeal. '*Wonderful!* He's everything I hoped he would be – handsome, loving, sexy *as* . . .'

'No complaints, then?'

'None at all. Apart from how busy he can be, but then he's the senior partner at his firm so it's one of those things, you know. Actually, I'm seeing him tonight for the first time in two weeks and I just can't wait.'

'Has he been away?'

'No, just work at the practice. They've inherited a lot of cases from a rival firm that closed, apparently. Jake's a man in demand, what can I say?'

Elsie giggled. 'Lucky you.'

'Talking of luck,' Cher winked at Elsie, 'how's everything with the lovely Oliver Hogarth?'

'Good, actually.'

'Don't give me that Little Miss Nonchalant act, Els, I'm not buying it. Are you still doing the "just friends" thing or have you finally sacked it off and jumped his bones yet?'

Elsie picked up a cleaning cloth and began to wipe the counter. 'Charming question.'

'No point in skirting the issue. *So?*'

'We're still just friends. But . . .'

Cher whooped and clapped her hands. 'There's a "but"! I knew it!'

'Calm down. All I was going to say is that I like him. A lot. The more time I spend with him, the more I enjoy his company.'

'Not exactly the answer I was hoping for, but it's a start.'

'Thanks for the vote of confidence.'

'No, honestly, I'm pleased that it's going well. There's no rush, so you just enjoy getting to know him. He strikes me as being in it for the long run, if you know what I mean.'

It was a good prospect, even if the mention of the 'long run' did cause Elsie a flutter of anxiety. 'Actually, there was something I've been thinking about that I wanted to run past you.'

'Oh?'

'I've been trying to come up with something The Sundaes

226

can work towards – an event in Irene's memory. And last night I had a brainwave.'

Interested, Cher sat down and motioned for Elsie to join her. 'Go on.'

'I thought we could do a charity night at a pub, where we perform and maybe ask some of the other choirs in the area to come and do a couple of songs. We could charge a small entrance fee and all the money raised could go to Cancer Research.'

What Elsie didn't tell her boss was that the idea had occurred to her in Olly's apartment last night, as he made coffee after another successful Thomasina Miers recipe had been consumed. They had been discussing possible ideas for the choir when Elsie remembered the monthly talent nights at The Feathers and the germ of an idea was born.

'Sounds like you've got it all worked out. Where do I come in?'

Elsie gave a sheepish smile. 'You know how Nick at The Feathers would do anything for you?'

Instantly suspicious, Cher folded her arms. 'Mm-hmm?'

'Well, I might just need to call on your devastating charms . . .'

With no customers left in Sundae & Cher by three o'clock, Cher made an executive decision to close early. Ten minutes later they were standing outside the black and white frontage of The Feathers, gazing up at the painted pub sign that was swinging in the strengthening breeze. Ensuring her blouse was suitably arranged in order to exert maximum influence over her target, Cher exchanged glances with Elsie and they entered.

The pub was quiet, with only the muffled music and flashing lights of the fruit machines providing any movement in its red plush interior. Elsie peered over the bar to see Nick crouching by the other side, restocking the bottles in the line of fridges that ran the entire length of the back wall. Seizing the advantage, Cher leaned provocatively over the bar.

'What does a girl have to do to get your attention?' she purred, her tone low and seeped in suggestion.

Nick almost head-butted the fridge door in his hurry to scramble upright. 'Cher, Elsie! Well, this is a nice surprise. I thought you two would still be beating back the ice cream crowds.'

'Oh if only,' Cher said, lowering her lashes as she spoke. 'I'm having vital renovation work done this week, so our offering is restricted.'

'I wouldn't have thought it was possible to improve on perfection,' Nick grinned, leaning on the bar and fully surveying Cher's assets.

Elsie had to look away when Cher unleashed a Marilyn-esque giggle on her more than willing prey. 'I mean the kitchen, not *me*, silly.'

'Oh, I see. My mistake. So what can I do for you lovely ladies? Bit early for a drink for you, isn't it?'

Cher leaned further towards Nick, the low-cut blouse commanding his full attention. 'We need a favour. A big one.'

The dirtiest smile oozed its way across Nick's lips. 'I see. Well, if it's a *big* one you're after, you've come to the right place . . .'

'*A-a-angel!*' Woody exclaimed in wonderment when Elsie told him the details of the charity open mic night she had arranged to hold at The Feathers. 'It's clear to me that you are the Chosen One I dreamed of.'

'It was mostly Cher, actually,' Elsie replied. 'Nick was only too happy to help after she asked him.'

228

The ageing rocker gave a wry smile. 'I'm guessing *that blouse* might have been responsible for such bewitching.'

'How did you know about that? I thought Cher's persuasion tactics were a closely guarded secret.'

'Believe me, angel, that blouse is legendary in this town for its mystical power over defenceless males. Now tell me, what's your vision for this event?'

The plan was simple: work out a small programme of songs for The Sundaes to perform and invite the other choirs in Brighton to do the same. Cher had balked when Elsie broached the subject of approaching The DreamTeam to participate, but when Elsie explained that they were the most likely to bring a crowd of supporters which increased the potential for raising a decent amount of money, she reluctantly agreed.

'But keep that hideous Jeannette Burton out of my way. If she kicks off, I can't be responsible for what I'll do.'

Elsie called Jeannette later that week and was invited to visit a DreamTeam rehearsal in order to discuss their possible involvement. She arrived at Brighton Electric, an imposing Victorian building that had been converted into a recording studio and rehearsal rooms and was widely acknowledged as the best rehearsal space in town. The room in which the show choir was gathering was an elegant, high-ceilinged space with an enormous oriental rug covering almost the entire floor. A timid-looking woman played an old upright piano at the far end of the room, making hurried notes on her score with a pencil as the members of the choir chatted around her.

Suddenly, the noise ceased and all eyes turned towards the door. For a moment Elsie thought they might be looking at her, but the click of high heels on the polished floor behind made her turn to see a woman dressed entirely in red entering the room. Jeannette Burton certainly knew how to make an entrance. She paused by the piano as her choir respectfully applauded, shaking her shoulder-length mane of platinum-blonde hair in an unconvincing attempt at bashfulness, holding up her hands to halt their adoration. 'Places, darlings,' Jeannette boomed and the choir dutifully filed into place at the far end of the room. Turning, she acknowledged Elsie with what she imagined passed as a genuine smile. 'We have a guest this evening. Choir, let's make Elsie Maynard feel at home.'

A patter of polite applause echoed in the room.

'Elsie leads The Sundaes choir,' Jeannette continued, and Elsie was sure she could see a sneer invading the professional smile. 'She's come to hear us sing, so let's show her what we can do. *June* – a chair for our guest.'

The mousey pianist scurried across the room and placed a wooden chair next to Elsie.

'Sit, sit,' she urged, flashing Elsie the briefest of smiles before hurrying back to her piano stool.

The choir began to sing, the power and unity of their voices filling the space. Elsie had to hand it to Jeannette – she certainly knew how to create a cracking arrangement. They moved as one, sang as one and even smiled as one, all the time maintaining faultless timing and never taking their eyes off their leader.

And yet something about the choir felt wrong. Beyond their uniform smiles and impeccably choreographed movements Elsie sensed little else. No heart, no passion. The Sundaes might not be note-perfect, but their enthusiasm and sheer joy at singing together were plain to see. As she listened to The DreamTeam's performance, Elsie secretly congratulated herself that The Sundaes were nothing like them.

The performance ended and the choir broke into hammy, orchestrated applause, whooping artificially and congratulating one another. Jeannette smiled at Elsie.

'And *that* is how we do it, Miss Maynard.'

After the rehearsal, Elsie and Jeannette stood by the piano as timid June set about making them tea from a small travel kettle on a fold-out table. 'Our idea is to create an evening of music in memory of a lady from our choir who died recently. Irene loved singing, so it seems like a fitting tribute. My lot are really keen to do it and I thought it could be a great opportunity to showcase Brighton's choral talent and raise money for Cancer Research UK.'

Jeannette drummed her long scarlet fingernails on her notebook. 'Excellent. And you've thought about a sound system, engineer, lights?'

Elsie hadn't. 'Um, well I . . .'

Jeannette dismissed this. 'No problem, I'll arrange that. Can't have my choir sounding anything but their best, can I? I take it you haven't started the publicity campaign yet?'

Publicity campaign? This was a charity event at a local pub, not a multi-million-pound performance at the O2! 'No, I was waiting to confirm the programme before . . .'

'Elsie. This event is in three weeks' time. You're already cutting it fine in terms of adequate promotion. We need full coverage – papers, radio, local TV. *June!*' She turned and barked sharply at the timorous lady making tea, who jumped a few feet off the ground and dropped the teaspoon with a clatter. 'Get onto this. I want a press release out first thing tomorrow morning.'

Feeling sorry for the poor put-upon assistant, Elsie offered, 'My friend is a designer and he's offered to provide posters and flyers for the event. Now I know you're on board these can be ready in the next two days, so I'll post some to you.'

'Too long,' Jeannette pronounced. 'You can't trust the post and we can't afford to lose another day. You work with Cher Pettinger, don't you?'

'Yes.'

'Good. June will visit you on Friday morning to collect our allocation.'

'There's no need for her to make a special trip to see us.' Elsie smiled at June. 'If you let me know where you live, I can drop them off on Friday evening.'

June was just beginning to nod when Jeannette interrupted. 'Nonsense! June is more than happy to do it, aren't you?'

'Y-yes, really, i-it's no bother,' June spluttered, head bowing even lower.

'So. All sorted. Any questions?'

Elsie hid her smile. 'No. I think you have everything covered.'

Jeannette grimaced. '*Always*, darling, always.'

At the next rehearsal, Elsie and Woody gathered The Sundaes together to reveal their plans.

'I vote we stick to what we already know,' Daisy suggested. 'We only have three rehearsals – that isn't enough time to start something new.'

Graeme and Sheila agreed, the prospect of having to master new songs anything but attractive.

'But wouldn't it be nice to have something new that people haven't seen yet?' Lewis suggested. 'Especially because we're doing it for Irene. She always loved learning new stuff.'

Elsie raised her hand. 'Whichever way we do this, we

232

have about twenty-five to thirty minutes to fill. It should be something we all enjoy.'

'*E-exactly*,' Daisy agreed. 'Which is why our existing repertoire will work.'

'Rubbish, girl. The Sundaes have to rock it large.'

'I don't have a problem with us rocking anything large provided it's something we already know.'

'But we can give the people so much more . . .'

Danny laughed and pointed to the list of suggestions Woody had given to everyone. 'And what, exactly is a Carpenters/Aerosmith mash-up giving to anyone?'

Woody surveyed him with solemn sincerity. 'Purity and strength, dude. Purity and strength.'

After much discussion, Elsie made an executive decision to include one new song and fill the rest of the programme with songs they already knew. With everyone happy, they embarked on the considerable challenge ahead, determined to make the event the best they could, in honour of Irene.

'At least it'll be a memorable evening,' Elsie said to Daisy, as they walked back to the seafront. But little did she know how true her words would prove to be . . .

Olly arrived at Sundae & Cher the next day, carrying several packages wrapped in brown paper.

'Promotional material,' he announced, struggling through the door as Elsie raced over to help him. 'And, yes, a large mocha latte and ice cream sundae will be perfect as payment.'

Elsie planted a kiss on his cheek. 'Coming up.'

His eyes shone. 'That's why I come to this excellent establishment. How did the rehearsal go last night?'

'Good.' Elsie scooped large balls of rich Dark Chocolate, Cinder Toffee and Butterscotch Pecan ice creams into a large sundae glass. 'It's going to be a lot of work, but it's something everyone seems up for.'

Olly grinned when Elsie handed him the ice cream construction. 'Wow. Where do I start?'

'Wherever you like, it's your sundae.'

'Lucky me! Wait – before I do that, have a look at the posters and flyers.' He began to unwrap the packages and Elsie squealed when she saw his handiwork.

'Olly, they're *perfect*! I love the design.'

The event had been called 'Songs for Irene' and Olly had, with permission, set a recent photograph of Irene in the centre, surrounded by undulating music staves that curled like floating ribbons around her smiling face.

'There are fifty posters and about two hundred flyers here. Will that be enough for you and the other choir?'

'More than enough. Thank you so much.'

'You're welcome.' He took a massive spoonful of ice cream and closed his eyes. 'This is amazing. You know, you could sell these.'

'Do you think so?' Elsie's heart skipped a little as she played along with the joke.

'Absolutely. Mind you, I'd pay just to see you in that outfit.' His eyes widened. 'That came out so wrong! I'm sorry!'

'Oliver Hogarth, I'm shocked! Dismayed!'

He feigned conviction. 'What can I say? I've let myself down. But in my defence you do look amazing.'

Elsie winked back. 'Oh, I know I do. Why do you think I agreed to wear it?'

While it felt a little strange to be indulging in cheeky banter with someone, Elsie found herself enjoying it. As the borderline flirty conversation continued, Cher's words replayed in her mind:

'There's no rush, so you just enjoy getting to know him.'

Cher was right. The thought of spending time getting to know Olly was proving more irresistible by the day.

Just after lunch, the timid pianist from The DreamTeam scurried in.

'I'm June Nunnington, from The DreamTeam. I'm here for the leaflets and posters?' she asked, obviously assuming that Elsie wouldn't remember her.

'Of course. Nice to see you again, June. Would you like a drink?'

June hesitated, her eyes darting left and right as if expecting Jeannette to storm in and drag her off for even considering the offer. 'I'm not really . . . I don't know if . . . Well, maybe just a quick one. Cup of tea would be lovely.'

'Excellent. Take a seat. Have you come far today?'

June sat at the table nearest the counter. 'No. I work mornings at an estate agent's about five minutes' walk from here. My son owns it so I go and help out with paperwork.'

Elsie brought tea to June's table. 'I thought you might like one of these, too,' she smiled, placing a dark chocolate oyster shell filled with Raspberry Coulis ice cream before her. 'It's a shame to come all the way here and then only have tea.'

June gazed at the confection before her with childlike wonder. 'You really are too kind.' She picked up her spoon and demolished the whole thing in what must have been record time, almost as if she was scared it would be taken from her if she ate slowly.

Elsie patiently waited for her to finish and then handed her one of the flyers. 'This is the design for the event.'

'Oh, how lovely. I'm very sorry to hear of your loss.'

'Thank you. I think Irene would be pleased with the event. I hope so, anyway.'

'Jeannette lost her mother last year, you know,' June confided. 'Between you and me, I think she's still trying to cope. Do you know she wouldn't let us sing at the funeral, even though it was what her mum wanted?' She reddened and stared at her teacup. 'Sorry.'

It was an unexpected admission, but Elsie smiled. 'Grief does strange things to people. Maybe she wanted to grieve for her mother privately.'

'Maybe. This is a lovely cup of tea.'

'Thank you.'

'I'll keep you updated on press interest and photo opportunities when they come up. Do you have a card?'

Elsie wrote her phone number on her order pad and tore off the page, handing it to June. 'Anything you need, just call.'

As the choir worked on the programme for 'Songs for Irene' over the next two weeks, Elsie witnessed a significant difference in the group. Since their heart-to-heart in the aftermath of Irene's death, they had become noticeably closer, their camaraderie the underlying tone to all their rehearsals. Even disagreements and the ever-present bickering between Woody and Sasha had a good-natured air. It was almost as if their new understanding of how important the choir was to each other bound them tighter together as a unit.

Elsie and Woody spent several evenings arranging the score for Woody's new medley, which mixed The Carpenters' "Top of the World" with Aerosmith's "Walk This Way". Elsie had to hand it to him – his weird musical vision usually resulted in surprisingly good combinations.

'How do you think of this stuff?' she asked one evening, as she sat at her piano.

'I have a lot of time to think, babe. Comes from being a solitary man,' he replied, stretching out on the small sofa in the corner of the room and kicking off his cowboy boots.

A thought occurred to Elsie. 'I've never actually asked you about your life, have I?'

'Too much to tell,' he grinned. 'When they make a rock biopic of Woody Jensen it'll have to be a trilogy.'

'Must have been exciting, though? All the amazing venues you played, having a hit album – the kind of things people dream about.'

'Ah, the stuff what dreams are made of, to quote the good Bard himself.' He yawned. 'It's true I've seen things most people can only imagine. And I may or may not have thrown the odd TV out of hotel windows. I remember Barcelona, spring of '88, walking onto the stage in front of eighteen thousand and hearing them chanting our name. Good times, babe, good times.'

'Wow.'

'Indeed.'

'Do you miss it? All the rock'n'roll stuff, I mean?'

Woody chewed his gum and considered her question. 'I miss the music, sometimes. I'd say I miss the money, but we never saw much of it. Of course, the perks were *sweet* – the booze, the girls, the somewhat dodgy substances . . . Not that I'd do any of it now, you understand. You see before you a changed man. Can't say that about the girls, obviously, but a gentleman never reveals his dalliances.'

'Anyone special now?' The question was out before Elsie could catch it.

'Why, you interested, babe?' He gave a throaty laugh. 'The look on your face! Don't panic, angel, you just let

Uncle Woody have his joke. Of course, there are always ladies – a man of my charms isn't likely to go unnoticed by the fairer sex. I have companions, so I'm content. Married once in '89. Vegas. Me and Janie Lee, backing singer for our support band on the last US dates. I knew Hellfinger was on the rocks then, you see. Heard the rows, broke up the fistfights. Johnny and Sid were at each other's throats right across the States . . . Janie understood. She was my oasis of calm in the desert of Hellfinger. She was my rock . . .' He checked himself. 'We lasted ten months. After Sid died, everything fell apart. Me and Janie Lee were collateral damage. Still, better to have loved, eh?'

Elsie nodded, the surprise of Woody's sudden candour still sinking in. 'I couldn't agree more.'

'Like you and your man. The one you lost.'

She stared at him. 'Yes.'

He leaned forward, the chains at his wrist tinkling. 'Must have been hard for you, babe, all this stuff with Irene after what you saw.'

'A little. I find it hard to accept that Irene was coping with it all alone. Lucas made sure everyone knew exactly what was happening with him.'

'I think Lucas and I would have been buddies.'

Elsie laughed. 'He would have loved you. And the choir.'

'He knows, you know. I believe it. What we see here – it ain't the end, girl. I reckon your man's smiling at us.'

'I hope so, Woody.'

He gave an awkward smile. 'Now, enough of this slushy crap. Sentimentality's not good for my image and we have world-changing music to arrange!'

A week before Irene's event, Jim invited Elsie, Daisy and Guin to his house for a barbecue. The late summer sun bathed the small garden at the back of his house where the family were gathered together. Guin glowed with pride as Ottie was passed from person to person, the little baby content and gurgling.

Elsie nudged Guin as she sat beside her. 'She's gorgeous, hun.'

Guin smiled. 'I know. I still can't quite believe she's mine. Apart from the three o'clock feeds – *then* I'm in no doubt whatsoever.'

'How's Joe coping with fatherhood?' Daisy asked, bouncing Ottie on her knee.

'He's trying his best, bless him. He's shattered but he loves this one so much. I'm really proud of him.'

'Motherhood suits you,' Elsie smiled.

'Oh shush. Now, please talk to me about something else. Something that doesn't include breastfeeding or nappies or anything baby-related. I love being a mum but it's like my life has just become a single topic. Don't laugh, Els, I'm getting so desperate for conversation that I've started seeking solace in Mr Tumble on CBeebies. I think Joe suspects I'm having an affair with him. So, tell me about this concert. How's it all going?'

'I think we're ready. Rehearsals have been going well and I found out yesterday that some of the younger members have been meeting up to practise at home. It's really helped to have this to work towards and I love that they all want to do it for Irene. It's just so dreadful that we're only now finding out how special Irene was.'

Guin nodded. 'It's sad how often that happens. But I guess the concert will give everyone the chance to thank her, don't you think?'

Butterflies began dancing inside Elsie at the thought of the event. 'I hope so.'

*   *   *

239

'Bring it more to the centre . . . No, not *there*! Do I have to do it myself?'

When Elsie arrived at The Feathers on the day of Irene's concert, Jeannette Burton was a control freak in full flow, sending the techies from the sound company scurrying at her command with foldback speakers and microphones around the small performance space that Nick had cleared at one end of his pub. Nick's face was thunderously stern when he approached Elsie.

'Where on earth did you find this woman?' he asked, ducking as Jeannette barked at someone else. 'She's only been here twenty minutes and already she's half-scared the sound guys. If we're not careful, we'll lose them altogether and then there won't be a concert.'

Elsie patted his shoulder. 'I'm sorry, Nick. Leave her to me.' Preparing herself for battle, she walked over to Jeannette. 'How's everything going?'

'Too slowly! These people are *imbeciles*! Where did the landlord find them?'

'Why don't we go for a little walk?' Elsie gently led Jeannette away as she spoke. 'They're a sound hire company Nick's used for years. And they're doing this for free because it's a charity event. So we probably need to cut them some slack because they volunteered to help us tonight.'

Jeannette stared at her. 'Well, I didn't know that. But the fact remains they don't have a clue how to set up a stage for a choir. My regular sound company would have everything organised by now.'

'I tell you what, why don't I have a word with them and I'll ask Nick to bring you a pot of tea? You need to rest before the big performance.'

This appeared to please Jeannette, who graciously

followed Elsie into the bar and sat down while Elsie went to order refreshments.

'How did you do that?' Nick asked under his breath.

Elsie grinned. 'I opted for the "softly softly" approach. Little trick I learned working with the great British public.'

'I'll have to remember that.'

'Right, so that's tea for our friend the dragon lady and could you bring some out for the sound guys, too? From the look of them I think they're in need of a break. How much is that?'

'Forget it. It's on the house. Anyone who can tame *that thing* deserves free tea as far as I'm concerned.'

With Jeannette safely pacified and the sound guys considerably happier without her interference, the stage soon took shape. When Woody and Cher arrived an hour later, everything was done.

'It looks great,' Cher said, hugging Elsie. 'I can't believe you managed to get everything sorted.'

'This,' Woody said, holding out his arms like a circus ringmaster, 'is the place where magic will happen. It's almost holy ground . . .'

Elsie laughed. 'It's a *pub*, Woody. I doubt The Feathers has ever been called "holy" before.'

The Sundaes and The DreamTeam began to arrive around six-fifteen p.m. and soon the space was filled with excited, chatting people. At six-thirty, Elsie and Jeannette summoned the singers' attention and the room hushed.

'First of all, thank you for being part of tonight,' Elsie said. 'In a moment we'll have a one-song run-through for both choirs, just so we can check the sound levels. But first, I wanted to remind you why we're all here. We lost a very dear member of our choir a few weeks ago and she was suffering in a way that she never shared with us. All she did was encourage her fellow choir members by spending time with them, but Irene Quinn was so much more than a listening ear. She was a real ray of sunlight in The Sundaes. Tonight is about paying tribute to her and filling this space with the music Irene loved so much. All I want for this evening is that we have fun and give the best performance we can. Agreed?'

The choirs broke into sincere applause and even Jeannette Burton managed a small smile.

'Good. Then let's get to work!'

The DreamTeam took to the stage at eight p.m., by which time The Feathers was packed with people. Elsie and Cher stood a little way away from the stage area, watching as the choir launched into their energetic rendition of 'Don't Stop Believing'.

'It's a bit contrived, isn't it?' Cher said.

'The crowd love it, though,' Elsie observed, looking at the audience who were smiling and nodding along. 'And they've been brilliant in getting the word out.'

'Fair enough. But I still think that Burton woman's a bitch. Is Olly not coming?'

'He has a late meeting, so he said he might pop in later. He's done so much already.'

'Well, good evening, lovely ladies!'

Cher and Elsie turned to see Jake approaching. Cher squeaked and rushed over, pulling him to her in a very public display of affection. As they were kissing, Torin stepped from behind his boss and the plush carpet beneath Elsie's feet wobbled a little.

'Great gig,' he called, raising his voice as The DreamTeam's volume increased.

'Thank you.' Unsure what to do next, Elsie turned her attention back to the stage.

Cher was draped around Jake as they joined Elsie and Torin. 'I didn't know you were coming, baby.'

'Couldn't miss this, could I? I know how much you liked the woman,' Jake grinned.

'But aren't you meant to be travelling to Edinburgh tonight? For the client meeting?'

Jake exchanged glances with Torin, who looked down at his pint. 'Don't you worry about that, darling. You're my priority tonight.'

Cher giggled. 'Now that's what I love to hear!'

Elsie was aware of Torin's eyes on her as she kept her gaze firmly on The DreamTeam. After a while, it became too much and she made her excuses, fleeing to the opposite side of the pub where The Sundaes were waiting nervously.

'There are so many people,' Sheila said, twisting the edge of her cardigan around her fingers.

'You'll be fine when you're up there,' Elsie assured her. 'And anyway, this audience isn't anywhere near as big as the one we performed in front of at the Carnival.'

'Take courage, girl. There are many, many people who have come here to hear your voice tonight. This is your moment of truth,' Woody said, his words ill-advised given the look of sheer horror on Sheila's face.

Elsie glared at Woody. 'It's going to be a great night. Everyone just relax and enjoy it.'

The DreamTeam brought their last song to a close and Elsie took the microphone. 'Let's hear it again for The DreamTeam and Jeannette Burton!' The audience applauded. 'Thank you. We're going to break for about twenty minutes and then The Sundaes will be here to entertain you.' She left the stage as the audience dispersed back to the bar, and headed over to Jeannette, who was being congratulated by members of her choir.

'Jeannette, that was great. Thank you so much for being here.'

'My pleasure. I must say I'm intrigued to hear your programme this evening.'

Elsie ignored the note of sarcasm in Jeannette's words and smiled back. 'I think you'll enjoy it. It'll be very different from your material.'

Cher appeared with Jake in tow. 'Elsie, we're getting the drinks in. What will you have?'

'Just an orange juice, thanks. Cher, Jake, have you met Jeannette?'

Jeannette ignored Cher and offered her hand to Jake. 'Well, well, Jake Long. Didn't expect to see you here tonight.'

Jake reddened a little as he shook her hand. 'Another great performance, Jeannette.'

Cher's expression darkened. 'You know each other?'

'Oh, Jake and I go *way* back, don't we?'

Jake muttered something and walked away. Cher folded her arms. 'Small world.'

'It is.'

Sensing an atmosphere brewing, Elsie took Cher's arm. 'We should really go and get those drinks.'

'That woman . . .' Cher growled. 'I swear, if she makes a play for Jake, I'll . . .'

'She won't, don't worry. Just go and help Jake at the bar. There's someone I have to see.'

With Cher safely installed by Jake's side, Elsie walked over to the table where Irene's family was seated. Lyn smiled as Elsie approached.

'It's *wonderful*,' she said. 'Mum would have loved this.'

'I'm so pleased you're enjoying it. I think you'll like the songs we've put together.'

'I hope there'll be air-guitar tonight.' Lyn beamed. 'You know how much my mother loved that.'

'We put some in especially for her. So how are you doing?'

'Oh, you know, day at a time stuff. There's still some of the legal side to sort out but we're slowly making progress. Having this to look forward to has been a great comfort.'

'I'm glad. I know it's not easy. All you can do is hold onto the small glimpses of positivity when they appear. But it does get easier.'

A moment of shared understanding passed between the two women. 'Thank you, Elsie. That means a lot.'

Woody joined them, tipping his Stetson to Lyn and her family. 'Evening. We should gather the troops, babe.'

'Absolutely. Enjoy the rest of the night, Lyn.'

Stan, Lewis, Danny and Graeme were rehearsing their guitar moves as Elsie and Woody joined The Sundaes at the side of the stage. One of the sound technicians raised his thumb and Elsie turned to the choir.

'Right, we're on. Is everyone OK?'

Aoife paled. 'I think I'm going to be sick.'

'You're all going to be great,' Elsie said. 'I'll introduce us and then you guys come on.' Feeling her own nerves start to shiver, she walked up to the microphone. 'Ladies and gentlemen, may I present – The Sundaes!'

A cheer went up from the audience as the choir took their positions on stage. Woody walked on last, tipping his hat to the audience and winking at Elsie as he passed. Elsie raised her hands and the choir began to sing.

This time, Elsie and Woody had chosen to begin the programme with everyone singing – Sasha was still being ribbed for her 'fields of blue' line from the Carnival performance. As Elsie began to play, The Sundaes sang the chorus of Coldplay's 'Paradise', gradually raising their volume and breaking into three-part harmony on the third repeat. Singing together appeared to be combating their nerves as the notes were decidedly less dodgy than their last performance. From there, Sasha stepped forward and started to sing the opening lines of 'You Got the Love'. Elsie nodded at her and she raised her voice even louder as the rest of the choir joined in.

Woody grinned at Elsie and over his shoulder she caught sight of Olly. He was smiling at her and instantly her heart lifted. It felt good to know that he was there. The choir ended the medley as the audience applauded. Elsie nodded at Woody, who took his place in front of the choir to lead his Carpenters/Aerosmith mash-up. Released from her conducting duties for the next two songs, Elsie looked out at the audience as she played. Every person was smiling and it struck her what a huge boost this would be for the choir, especially as this concert meant so much to them. When the boys stepped forward to sing the guitar riff of 'Walk This Way', any reservations she might have had about Woody's crazy song combination disappeared as she saw the reaction of their audience and the delight on the faces of her choir.

And then, in the middle of the smiles, she saw Torin. He was standing next to Jake and Cher and was staring at her, unsmiling. Why was he even here? He seemed so out of place and had hardly spoken three words to her. Why stay where he clearly didn't want to be? Annoyed, she turned her attention back to The Sundaes and resolved not to think about it any more.

The choir's programme ended with Irene's favourite song and Elsie felt tears welling in her eyes as the words of 'I'll Walk Beside You' touched her heart. Several of the choir members were moved, too, and the atmosphere in the pub changed as the audience were touched by the heartfelt performance.

Elsie's thoughts drifted away to a time far back in her memories, long before the diagnosis, when a young couple stood at the altar of Grandma Flo's Methodist church in Hove and made promises to one another. Lucas had insisted on wearing a dark grey Victorian tailcoat, red and grey pinstripe trousers and a tall charcoal velvet top hat – as determined not to conform on this day as much as any – but the emotion in his eyes when he looked at his bride was as old as time itself. Elsie, radiant in a 1920s white lace dress that had once belonged to Jim's great-aunt, gazed up at her handsome Lucas with a heart so full of love it stole her breath. As the minister declared them husband and wife, Lucas leaned close and whispered, 'Forever, Elsinore,' just before he kissed her. There had been so much hope and expectation on that day, so many dreams born and futures foreseen . . .

Smiling at the faces of her choir, Elsie remembered the newest message from the silk box:

I love you because you can always see what's possible, before it even is.
xx

Listening to the voices of The Sundaes now, Elsie realised that, despite the setbacks, fallouts and mishaps, the choir standing beside her was the choir she had envisaged from the beginning. When their song ended, a brief moment of silence ensued before the room erupted with enthusiastic applause. The Sundaes took several bows, surprised and overjoyed by the rush of adrenaline that surged from their audience's reaction.

Woody and Elsie took another bow and Woody grabbed the microphone.

'Thank you, people, for coming out to support us tonight. Irene was a beautiful lady and we hope we've done her justice.'

He passed the microphone to Elsie, who had just been handed a piece of paper by a grinning Nick.

'I'm thrilled to announce that tonight's concert has raised six hundred and fifty pounds for Cancer Research UK. I think you should give yourselves a round of applause.'

The audience did so and Elsie led The Sundaes off the stage. Elsie wiped tears from her face as she watched her choir and Woody held out his arms to her.

'Come here, angel.'

As they were hugging, a loud shout split the air.

'*BITCH!*'

Elsie broke the hug just in time to see Cher launching herself at Jeannette as people pulled back to watch. Shocked, Elsie rushed over and grabbed Cher's shoulders, yanking her back from the furious choirmistress as she kicked and screamed obscenities at her. Jeannette rushed towards Cher, but was halted by a strong pair of arms wrapping around her waist and lifting her bodily away.

'Cher! *Stop* this!' Elsie shouted.

'It's *her fault*,' Cher spat back. 'She was coming on to Jake!'

'I think you'll find it was *him* propositioning *me*!' Jeannette returned. 'Just like the good old days, hey Jake?'

Jake stood in the middle of them, upturned palms signalling his surrender, completely out of his depth.

'Let me go, Elsie, so help me I'll rip that woman's head right off!' As Cher struggled against Elsie's hold, Elsie saw the face of Jeannette's restrainer.

248

'Take her *home*, Jake,' Torin growled, 'this isn't the time or the place.'

'Don't look at me,' Jake replied. 'She's gone nuts.'

'So much for the caring boyfriend, eh, Cher?' Jeannette shouted as she tried to wrench herself from Torin's grip. 'Jake Long will never change. You think you're the only one he's seeing? Dream on!'

Cher broke free and lunged for Jeannette, just as Woody grabbed her. 'Girl, she's not worth it. I'm taking you home.' He looked at Elsie. 'I'll call you tomorrow, yeah?'

Elsie straightened her dress. 'Yes, thanks. Cher, go home and calm down.'

Bursting into tears, Cher held her hand out to Elsie. 'Oh Els, I'm sorry . . .'

Incandescent anger firing through her, Elsie couldn't bring herself to look at Cher. 'Go *home*.' Turning her attention to Jeannette, she shook her head. 'I don't know how, when you knew what tonight was all about, you could let this happen. You call yourself a professional and you constantly tell everyone how superior your choir is. Well, I might be a confirmed amateur, but I would *never* let my choir see me acting the way you just did.' She let out a sigh as Torin released Jeannette. 'I think you should leave.'

Knowing she had met her match in Elsie, Jeannette snatched her pashmina scarf from the floor where it had fallen and, followed by her shocked choir members, left the pub. Breathing heavily, Elsie and Torin faced each other as the onlookers dispersed.

'Thank you.'

'My pleasure. Are you OK? You were incredible just then . . .' He moved towards her and for a moment Elsie thought he was going to offer her a hug.

'Elsie, what happened? Come here.' Olly appeared beside

249

her and gathered her into his arms. As she accepted his embrace, she saw Torin step back. He smiled at her and turned to Jake, who was downing a large whisky by the bar looking as if he'd just been caught in a buffalo stampede.

Elsie broke the hug and stepped back, her mind elsewhere. 'I need to check that Irene's family are OK,' she said, still smarting from the scene Cher and Jeannette had caused. A strange expression on his face, Olly let her pass.

Lyn was gathering her things together when Elsie walked over.

'Lyn, I'm so, so sorry. I have no idea what happened there.'

To her relief, Lyn grinned back. 'Don't worry, Mum would've loved it. She adored drama – whenever there was a family row at Christmas she would be right in the middle of it, laughing her head off.'

'But for it to happen after such a great evening . . .'

'Trust me, Elsie, this is the best way to round off a wonderful night.' She placed her hand on Elsie's arm. 'You've done her proud tonight. Thank you.'

Elsie turned back to smile at Olly, but he was no longer standing where she had left him. She wandered around the pub for a few minutes, even checking outside to see if he was waiting for her there. But there was no sign of him. She reasoned he must have had to go but didn't want to interrupt her conversation with Lyn. *No problem*, she told herself, *I'll text him later*.

Exhausted by the events of the evening, she walked slowly back to the side of the stage to pack her keyboard away. She felt a hand on her shoulder and turned to see Daisy.

'Hey, little sis, that was some impressive crisis management back there.'

'I'm just so angry at them both. What were they thinking?'

250

'They're idiots. But they'll know not to cross you again after that speech of yours.' She hugged Elsie. 'I'm so proud of you, have I told you?'

Elsie gave a weary smile. 'I'm proud of *us*. We sounded amazing tonight.'

'Yes, we did. Now how about I help you pack away and then you come back to mine tonight? André sent a bottle of champagne for us and I can order a takeaway. Bit of Maynard sister quality time. What do you reckon?'

Grateful for the chance to spend time in neutral surroundings, Elsie agreed. 'I think that's a fantastic idea. You're most definitely on!'

Later that evening, relaxing in Daisy's effortlessly gorgeous apartment, Elsie raised her glass. 'I propose a toast: to Irene. For being full of surprises.'

Daisy grinned. 'To Irene!'

But Irene Quinn's surprises were far from over – as Elsie was about to discover.

CHAPTER FIFTEEN

A big ask . . .

Next morning, Elsie woke early. Wrapping herself in the white fluffy towelling robe that Daisy had laid out for her, she walked from the guest room into the large open-plan kitchen and living room overlooking the seafront. Daisy had already made a pot of coffee and Elsie could hear the sound of the shower in the back of the apartment as she poured herself a mug. Taking it, she slid open the concertina-folding doors that wrapped around the front of the property and walked out onto the beechwood balcony, inhaling the tang of fresh sea air. Yachts were already out sailing across the deep blue water and the undulating buzz of early morning jet-skiers floated across the sea.

Elsie had lived all her life with the sea on her doorstep, yet it was only when Lucas became ill that she truly appreciated its beauty. There was something eternal about the never-ending movement of the ocean, its steady rhythm a constant she could rely on. When so much else in her life had been shaken, the sea remained the same – and became a sanctuary for Elsie. She could think here, let her mind relax as she experienced the beauty of the ocean, and be alone with her thoughts for a few precious moments before heading back to the man she loved, to face the challenges renewed.

Lucas had always loved the sea and, long before cancer gate-crashed their lives, he would insist they walked along the beach most days. He had learned to sail as a youngster, taught by his father who was a racing yachtsman in his day, and had become quite proficient. When they first started going out, he would often invite her out on the family yacht at weekends, showing off his mariner skills as he helped his father to unfurl the sails and steer the vessel. When his illness began to limit his strength, they walked to the same bench on the promenade every day, come rain or shine, so that he could watch the movement of the sea that he loved so much.

Elsie gazed out at the sea and for a moment it was as if Lucas was by her side. Closing her eyes, she leaned into the memory of him, a deep peace welling up within her. Instinctively, she curled her left thumb over the third finger of her left hand and felt the drop of her heart as it touched bare skin. Removing her wedding ring had been by far the hardest part of his instructions, but she knew it was what he'd wanted. It now lay in a velvet box in the top drawer of her kitchen dresser, not that she ever looked at it. Knowing it was there was enough – and, as the months passed by, she could feel herself moving further away from the woman she had been when she wore it.

'Morning, gorgeous.'

Elsie turned to see Daisy walking out onto the balcony deck, drying her long blonde hair with a towel. 'Hey, sis.'

'Sleep well?'

'I always sleep well here. It's like living in a magazine room set – I don't know anyone else who puts quite so many cushions on a bed.'

Daisy laughed. 'Oh, stop it. It's just my style.'

'You're *such* an interior designer.'

'I am. So, if I can tempt you into my super-luxe, on-trend, bespoke kitchen, I'll make us a feature-worthy bacon sandwich. Deal?'

Elsie grinned. 'Deal.'

When Elsie arrived at work on Monday morning, Cher was waiting for her. She looked dreadful, the dark circles under her eyes and her lank, lifeless black hair scraped into a limp ponytail so at odds with her usual polished appearance.

'Hi, Elsie.'

'Morning.' Elsie walked past to put her bag in the kitchen.

Cher followed her, wringing her hands. 'I'm so sorry, Els. I was an idiot on Saturday night.'

Elsie tied her apron round her waist and said nothing. She still hadn't really worked out what she was going to say to Cher, the memory of the fight still raw.

'I feel *awful*. I haven't slept. I don't know what came over me – I saw that woman all over Jake and I just went off the edge. I know it was wrong, trust me, I do.'

Keep talking, Pettinger. Elsie pulled a wire tray from the dishwasher and began to unload it.

'Oh, for heaven's sake, say something, Elsie! I'm busting my gut here.'

'You knew how important that night was.'

'Of course I did . . .'

'Not just for me and the choir but for Irene's family. It was *Irene's* night.'

Cher hung her head. 'I feel dreadful about it.'

Elsie stared at her friend. 'I'm not saying it was all your fault, OK? But you should trust Jake enough to not be threatened by some old flame – emphasis on the *old* . . .'

254

Cher looked up with a nervous smile.

'. . . who rocks up and tries to take advantage. Jake was there for *you*, remember? When he had to fly to Scotland next day – even then, he came to support the choir that meets in your café. What does that tell you, hmm?'

'I really am sorry, Els. Forgive me?'

Shaking her head, Elsie hugged her. 'Of course. But do it again and you die, understand?'

'Thank you. Maybe now I can sleep.'

'So, how did you leave things with Jake? He looked pretty shell-shocked when Woody took you home.'

Cher groaned and picked up a handful of cutlery from the dishwasher tray. 'He didn't call till yesterday afternoon, by which time I'd convinced myself I'd blown it with him. Anyway, we talked and it's all good again. He was angry that I didn't trust him enough, which I completely understand. I've just got to hope I don't run into that Burton woman again any time soon.'

'And Woody got you back safely?'

'Oh, he was really sweet. I mean, I was a mess by the time I got home. But he made me a cup of tea and sat with me for over an hour until I'd calmed down enough. Not very rock'n'roll at all. Quite surprising, really.'

'He's a good heart.' Elsie switched on the coffee machine and emptied fresh beans into the grinder. 'You know he has the hots for you?'

'Oh, *shush*,' Cher replied, the pinkness of her cheeks betraying her true reaction. 'A little bit like that gorgeous designer friend of yours. Besotted with you, pure and simple.'

Elsie shook her head. 'I'm not sure . . .'

'Not sure about what? What is there to be sure about? The guy is a walking oil painting, totally gorgeous, laid-back, fun . . .'

'And currently not returning my calls,' Elsie added.

'What? Since when?'

Elsie sighed and flopped onto the stool by the counter. 'Since the concert. I'm not sure what happened: one minute he was hugging me, and the next he disappeared. He hasn't replied to my texts and I only get his voicemail when I try to ring him.'

Cher's brow furrowed. 'Perhaps he's been busy? Or he could have been away with his kitesurfing friends yesterday?'

'Maybe.'

Cher nodded at the café phone. 'Call him now, from here. If he is ignoring you – which I highly doubt – he won't recognise this number and at least you'll have a chance to catch him off-guard.'

Cher was right – she was overreacting. But the memory of Daisy's words a few weeks back and the way he'd disappeared on Saturday night were enough to make her worry. Fetching her mobile, she found the number and dialled from the retro phone mounted on the wall behind the counter.

Sure enough, Olly answered.

'It's Elsie – don't hang up.'

A long sigh came from the other end of the line. 'Why would I hang up?' His words should have comforted her, but his tone made her nervous.

'Can I see you? At lunchtime?'

'Fine. Where?'

'On the beach. By the Fortune of War pub. About twelve-thirty?'

'OK. But I can't stay long.'

Olly was sitting on the bank of shingle about fifty yards from the pub when Elsie arrived on the beach. Around him – at curiously even intervals along the ridge – was an assortment of local couples, enjoying the view of powerful waves pounding the shingle shoreline further down the beach. As soon as Elsie saw his expression she knew all was not well.

'Olly?'

He looked away.

Panic began to squeeze the edges of her insides. 'Olly, talk to me, please.'

Slowly, he raised his eyes to hers and immediately she wished she hadn't seen what they carried. Gone was the smile; the easy comfort of his gaze had become one she didn't recognise – hurt, disappointment and cold resignation. 'I don't understand you,' he said, his voice barely more than a whisper. 'One minute I think you like me, that we have something together, and the next . . . You can't keep doing this to me, Elsie. You can't keep me waiting while you decide whether or not you're ready.'

'I'm – I didn't think I was . . .'

'On Saturday night – after the Cher and Jeannette spat – you pulled away from me as if I was annoying you.'

Elsie stared at him, heart crashing against her chest. 'I didn't. I had to check that Lyn was all right. I can't believe that you thought . . .'

'It doesn't matter what I thought, Elsie. The point is, it's not the only time. We meet, we have fun, we're close and then – then you pull back and I don't know where I stand again. I know I said it was OK to be friends, but don't you see that the more time we spend together the more I'm falling for you?'

'Olly . . .'

He looked away again and for once Elsie was glad of it. 'This is a risk for you, I know; I get it. And I've struggled with how I feel because I wanted to give you space, let you

257

work it out in your own time. But if you aren't into this – into us – then I need to know. I need to know I'm not wasting my time hoping for something that will never happen.'

Taken aback by his words, Elsie scrambled for an adequate response. What did he want her to say? In many ways she couldn't understand her own reticence – after all, wasn't the point of dating to jump in and see what happened? But then if Olly understood her – if he *really* cared for her – surely he could see that this was her first attempt at moving on and, therefore, doubts and fears were bound to rear their heads?

The thunder of waves battering the shingle below them matched the pounding of her heartbeat in her ears as she stood, the wind catching the edges of her scarf as she did so. A large flock of seagulls screeched by overhead, soaring out towards the blackened, stranded skeleton of what was once West Pier, and Elsie felt anger rising from a place deep within.

'I'm sorry I've been a disappointment to you. And I'm sorry you've had to wait for me. But I never asked you to. I don't expect you to understand me, Olly, I hardly understand myself yet. I have no comparative reference for this – no timeframe I can follow.'

Surprised by the force of her response, Olly's expression immediately softened. 'Hey, I know – I know that . . .'

'Maybe I should know what I want now, but I don't. I think perhaps it's best for both of us if I just stay out of your life.' Swallowing back her tears she turned and began to crunch back across the beach towards the promenade steps. She was hurt and angry, although more so by her own inability to take the step she knew she should be taking than by anything Olly had said. He was justified in how he felt – most people in his situation would have complained long before this. As she hurried away, her fingers closed around the latest message from Lucas' box in her pocket:

I love you because you never back away from a battle.
xx

Well, I'm sorry, Lucas, but this time you're wrong. Once I might have waded into the fray, but not since you left. I'm a different woman now.

This time she wasn't just backing away – she was retreating as fast as she could. Was this how it would be from now on, she wondered: running away whenever the opportunity to move on presented itself? When she made the decision to start again she had felt so strong, so full of confidence for the unknown life that stretched out in front of her. Had she been mistaken?

I'm not like that, she argued back, *I'm stronger than this. Aren't I?*

Olly didn't follow her when she walked away. Only when she reached the safety of the promenade did she dare to look back towards the beach, seeing his hunched figure exactly where she'd left him sitting on the shingle ridge, staring out to sea. Nor did he try to call or text her during the following week. The dull ache of their argument hung anvil-heavy on her heart every day, the words of Lucas' note calling like a mockingbird in her mind. Cher noticed the change in Elsie – as did Daisy, Guin and Jim – but something about her mood must have warned them against inquiring further.

In the end, a most unlikely confidant came to her aid.

It was a warm Wednesday afternoon, just over a week

259

since her exchange with Olly, and Elsie had taken advantage of an almost empty Sundae & Cher to claim some outstanding overtime she was owed to head out into the comforting anonymity of Brighton's streets. Walking slowly through the Lanes full of people getting on with their day, Elsie let the rumble of traffic and flow of bodies wash over her, the ordinariness of it all soothing the jumble of questions knotting inside. She crossed a main road without really thinking about where she was and it was only when she was at the other side that she recognised the imposing gated entrance to the Royal Pavilion Gardens. Skirting it, she walked round and into the gardens, the exotic domes and towers of the historic building rising up from very British flowerbeds.

As a child she had often played here with Daisy and Guin, imagining that the Pavilion was Aladdin's palace and they were princesses playing amid its delphinium, rose and lavender beds. Later, she would stroll here with Lucas for tea and cakes at the Pavilion Gardens café on Sunday afternoons in the summer. Recently she hadn't ventured here – largely because it was odd to be in this place without Lucas. Today, it was quiet, save for a group of students lounging on the grass and a lone mandolin busker plucking through a medley of REM songs, his coat spread out before him on the path to catch any change offered. Elsie reached into her pocket and dropped a pound coin into the small pile at his feet. He nodded his thanks with eyes closed, lost in the melodies of his instrument.

Elsie turned towards the café and was about to walk towards it when a familiar voice called her name. Looking around, she eventually traced its owner, sprawled on the grass, his leather jacket folded behind his head and a half-opened six-pack of beers by his side.

Smiling, Elsie lifted her hand to greet him. 'Hey, Woody. Bit early for beer, isn't it?'

He grinned back, his cheeks a little flushed already in the warm sun. 'It's past one o'clock, babe.' He patted the grass beside him. 'Care to join old Woodster for a Wednesday bevvy?'

Finding no good reason to refuse, she stepped over the low wire fence and sat cross-legged on the grass beside him. Woody pulled a bottle from the cardboard holder, levered off its metal cap with a key from his pocket and offered the bottle to her.

'Here's mud in your eye.' He clinked his bottle against hers and they drank. The beer was warm and cheap, but it was a welcome distraction from the muddle of Elsie's head. As she took a swig of it she was aware of Woody's eyes on her. 'Looks like you needed that,' he said, when she lowered the bottle.

'You know what? I did.'

'Sometimes beer is all that's needed,' he chuckled. 'Although judging by your face today, maybe not.'

His insight surprised her and she attempted to shrug it off. 'I'm fine.'

'You're not, though, are you? You've had the weight of the world on you for a while now. Don't look so shocked, babe, you think your Uncle Woody can't see what's happening?'

'Seriously, Woody . . .'

'You can trust me, girl. I mean, who am I likely to tell?'

Elsie observed the ageing musician by her side as if seeing him for the first time. It was terrible to admit, but until now she had assumed the years of rock'n'roll had reduced his mind to the borders of sanity. He had been a fun source of entertainment, with his quasi-spiritual ramblings and belief in himself as some kind of musical guru – but the thought of him being able to perceive changes in someone else had never entered the picture.

'It's Olly – no, it's me . . . Well, it's a bit of everything, really.' She hesitated, unsure whether Woody wanted the details of her life to intrude on his Wednesday afternoon beer session. 'Do you really want to know? I mean, I don't want to spoil your afternoon . . .'

He laughed, a deep guttural guffaw that boomed around the gardens and dislodged some disgruntled pigeons from the top of a Pavilion minaret. 'I have all the time in the world, angel. Explain away.'

So, she told him. About Lucas and The List; about his box of messages that suddenly spoke of a woman she no longer recognised; about Olly's pain and her own frustrations at not being able to jump in where once she would have. Several times she felt tears threatening and she broke off to wash the emotion back down inside with gulps of warm beer. As the mandolin played and groups of people moved slowly through the space, their shadows growing longer in the afternoon sun, Elsie told Woody everything: things she couldn't express to her dad or sisters, things they just wouldn't understand. Woody listened to it all, nodding occasionally and draining one bottle before reaching for another.

When she came to an end, he looked up at the clouds drifting overhead as if seeking some divine insight for the right response. 'You have nothing to reproach yourself for,' he said, finally. 'All the stuff with Irene passing – it'll have raked up the muck again. This journey you find yourself on, it's going to be a rocky one. You can only walk it in your own time, when you're ready – not when anyone else expects you to be. But you'll get there – wherever "there" ends up being.'

Elsie hugged her knees to her chin. 'Do you think I will? Honestly? Because I've never been so unsure of anything.'

Woody sniffed. 'I don't doubt it. Been through it myself, you know: I understand. When Sid died – our drummer – man, I was like an old soul lost at sea. For a long time I didn't even recognise myself in the mirror. Life was useless, pointless. I let friends go and almost drank myself to oblivion. Worst of it was, I never understood how much he meant to me till he wasn't there any more. And I blamed myself for not seeing the signs, you know? He was the most together bloke I ever met – had answers for everything, Sid did. Then we walked into that dressing room in Japan and he was hanging from a beam . . .' He fell silent and Elsie instinctively placed her hand on his knee. Nodding back at her, he downed half a bottle of beer before speaking again. 'Broke me, babe, ripped the heart out from me. Took years to find it again. Difference with you is, your man knew where he was going and believed in you.'

'But what if he was wrong about me?'

Woody shook his head, a smile working its way across his face. 'He wasn't. You just need to trust him, girl. See the strong warrior in you the rest of us see already. Sounds like my kind of bloke, your Lucas. See, you and me aren't so different, angel. We know what it is to have life kick us in the nuts – so to speak. Kindred spirits, that's what we are. Digging through the dirt to get to the diamonds.' He lifted his almost-empty bottle. 'A toast. To the road ahead. However crap it might be.'

Elsie didn't know exactly what this meant, but the welcome lightness within her from this afternoon's unburdening was enough for her to join Woody's toast.

'To the road ahead.'

*   *   *

263

That evening, Elsie arrived at Olly's house without trying to call first. Of course, she risked him not being in, but at least this way she didn't have time to think better of it.

The shock of seeing her on his doorstep was evident in the fact that Olly couldn't speak for a few moments when he opened the door. This was enough of a break for Elsie to take the initiative.

'I'm sorry,' she rushed. 'I'm sorry I hurt you. And I'm sorry I walked away. I know I've probably just confirmed everything you said about me blowing hot and cold, but I didn't know how strongly you felt about all this. The fact is, I like you being in my life, but beyond that I – I just don't have the answers you need. I'll understand if you decide this isn't worth it and, if that's the case, then I'll turn round and walk away and you won't see me again. But I couldn't leave it without saying how much I've appreciated you being my friend.'

He shook his head and held his arms out. 'Come here.'

Heart racing, Elsie stepped into his embrace, feeling the warmth of his arms as they encircled her.

'I overreacted,' he whispered, his breath a summer zephyr in her hair. 'I'm still here.'

Elsie pulled back and gazed into his dark eyes. 'And if I can't promise you what you want?'

'Just you being here is enough for now. Let's deal with whatever whenever we have to.'

'And that was enough to convince him?' Cher asked the next day, as Elsie cut an enormous lemon and ginger cake into slices ready to meet the hungry afternoon tea crowd due to arrive at any moment.

'It seemed to be,' Elsie replied. 'Although I couldn't tell whether he was happy about it or just resigned to wait longer.'

Cher patted her shoulder as she passed her to fetch a new batch of cherry, raspberry and walnut scones from the oven in the kitchen. 'You'll get there.'

'You sound like Woody.'

'Eh?' There was the sound of metal clanking and a barely concealed obscenity.

Elsie looked over her shoulder to see Cher hopping round the kitchen, flapping her right hand wildly. 'Everything all right in there?'

'Peachy, kid. That blasted oven got me again. I think we need to get the door hinge looked at.' She kicked the oven door shut and ran her burned digits under the tap. 'I hope our customers appreciate us risking life and limb for their refreshment provision.'

'I'm sure they do.'

Cher walked back into the café with a basket of scones and placed them on the counter. 'I know they do. I had another proposal this morning.'

'Not Mr Orfanos again?'

'Oh yes.'

'What was it this time? Your devastating wit, personality and ample chest?'

'You'd think so. But I suspect it had more to do with his Maple and Nibbed Sugar Ice Cream Pancake Tower. With extra banana and chocolate sprinkles.'

Several times a week for the past five months, since he and his brother bought the small wine bar in nearby Sydney Street, Mr Dmitri Orfanos had made the short pilgrimage to sample the delights of Sundae & Cher. A divorcee with a love of good food, he had been enamoured first by Cher's infamous blouses, then won over completely by her culinary prowess. As a result, Cher regularly received ever more impassioned proposals of marriage from him – which, while sweet, had become a running joke between her and Elsie.

'Given that much edible temptation, how could the poor guy resist?' Elsie laughed.

Cher raised her head. 'Is that your phone?'

'Ooh, it is.' Elsie pulled her mobile out of her apron pocket. 'Hello?'

'Ms Maynard?'

'Speaking.'

'Good morning. My name is Andrew Delaney and I'm a family law solicitor at Denbigh Associates. I have a matter of probate that concerns you – a will, in layman's terms. I wonder if you could come to our offices to discuss this?'

His formal request threw her for a moment. 'Can I ask whose will it is?'

'Certainly. I am acting for the family of Mrs Irene Quinn.'

Elsie could hardly believe it. Irene had left her something in her will? Why would she do something like that? Intrigued, Elsie replied, 'My day off is tomorrow. Would that be suitable?'

'Perfect. Shall we say nine o'clock?'

'Yes, that's fine.'

'Good. I shall see you then.'

Ending the call, Elsie turned to Cher. 'I've been left something in Irene's will.'

'Seriously? Wow, that's a bit of a surprise, isn't it? I wonder what she's left you.'

Mind whirring, Elsie nodded. 'I guess I'll find out tomorrow.'

I love you because you always
follow your instincts.
　　xx

266

The next morning, with the words of Lucas' message reverberating in her mind, Elsie arrived at the offices of Denbigh
Associates, which were set in a row of elegant black and
white brick buildings. Whatever direction her instincts
might decide on today, they were obviously enjoying a
lie-in, leaving Elsie feeling completely lost. After signing in
with the receptionist she sat alone in the small waiting
area.

As Mr Delaney had given precious few details about the
will, other than Elsie being named in it, she hadn't told
any of The Sundaes, including Daisy and Woody, not
wanting to create any awkward situations with the other
choir members. She felt considerable unease at Irene's inclusion of her, especially in the light of the small amount of
time she had known the elderly lady. Eventually, she had
broken her silence and told Olly after dinner at his house
last night.

'The more I think about it, the more wrong it seems. I
don't think she should have left me anything. I mean, I've
only known her a few months.'

Olly sat beside her on the bench in his back garden, as
the evening light succumbed to petrol-blue darkness, the
smell of sea salt and sun-toasted grass filling the night air.
'From what I know of Irene, I doubt time had any bearing
on her decision.'

'All the same, I'm not sure I can accept her money.'

'Look, there's no point trying to figure this out until you
know the score. She might just want to say thank you for
creating the choir. Why don't you reserve judgement until
you hear what the will actually says?'

She turned to him, gaining strength from his smile, which
was as warm as the autumn evening. 'Maybe you're right.'

'I am. Trust me, Els, you'll be fine tomorrow. Just go

along and see what happens – then deal with whatever you have to.'

The offices were smartly laid out and had a sterile air of professional efficiency about them. Impeccably dressed legal staff scurried from office to office with large folios of papers under their arms. Whenever they passed a colleague, each legal would refer to the other in formal terms, making the general tone of the office sound like a scene from a Jane Austen novel:

'Mr Clark.'

'Miss Westwood.'

'Mr Jevons.'

'Mr Powell.'

'Good day, Mr Guest?'

'Indeed it is, Mr Nicholls.'

Elsie couldn't help but be amused by this archaic communication: not least because it made her remember Number 27 on The List, when she and Lucas had spent an entire day using only Shakespearean language – witnessing the bemusement of others when they ordered coffee, enquired about books in Waterstones and dropped off their washing at the local launderette . . .

'Ms Maynard?'

Elsie returned from her memories to see an impeccably dressed man approaching.

'Yes. Hello.'

'Andrew Delaney. So glad you could come in. Shall we?' He indicated the corridor to the left, along which were several doors leading to frosted-glass-fronted offices.

Elsie followed him to the far end of the corridor and into a bright office that smelled of furniture polish and new paint.

'First of all, please accept my apologies for the rather

cloak-and-dagger approach. As I'm sure you'll appreciate when you hear the stipulations of the will, it was a necessary evil. Would you like coffee before we begin?'

'No, thank you. I must admit, this has all come as a bit of a surprise to me. I've only known Irene for a couple of months.'

The solicitor raised his eyebrows. 'That's not uncommon in matters like this. I once presided over the will of a man who left a considerable sum to his window cleaner, whom he had only met a fortnight before his death. Mrs Quinn sounds a remarkable woman, by all accounts. I haven't seen such a specific will in a very long time.'

Elsie shifted in her seat. If, from his inference, Elsie had been left a considerable amount of money, it would be difficult to accept; and if The Sundaes found out, it could be potentially damaging. 'Specific in what way?'

Mr Delaney's smile was kind and patient. 'A good way, I believe. I think it's best if I read the section of Mrs Quinn's will that concerns you.' He produced a thin folded document, unfurled it and began: '"I wish for the following to be read in its entirety: I would like to mention a wonderful young lady who I have only recently had the pleasure to know. Elsie Maynard, the leader of The Sundaes community choir, has given me a gift greater than I could have imagined: she has given me the opportunity to be part of something, to feel useful once again. It has been many years since I abandoned singing after my beloved George passed away, and I was more or less determined it would stay that way until I died. But, quite by chance, I was invited to attend a new choir meeting, into which I was welcomed unconditionally by all present. In the short time I have been a member of The Sundaes I have regained my love of singing and gained a surrogate family in the process. Each one has shared important details of their lives with me and I have been privileged to be trusted with such information. Which brings me to my desire to reward Elsie Maynard and her lovely choir . . ."' He looked up from the will and smiled at Elsie. 'How are you doing? All making sense so far?'

Elsie's head was swimming. 'A little. Please continue.'

'Good. Here we are: " . . . It has come to my attention that a young member of the choir, Danny Alden, has a dream to propose to his beautiful girlfriend, Aoife McVey, on the Eiffel Tower in Paris. I have been honoured to be party to his ambition, as we have spoken at great length about it. And so I have decided to facilitate this dream for my very special young friend. In order to do this, I am trusting Elsie Maynard to administer my wishes to the letter. I therefore leave a sum of £4,000 to be used specifically to take all members of The Sundaes to Paris for a long weekend (three nights), under the guise of playing a concert in the city. Aoife McVey must **not**, under any circumstances, discover the real reason for the trip. On the second afternoon, the choir is to take a sightseeing trip to the Eiffel Tower and, upon Elsie's signal, begin to sing Aoife's favourite song (Danny to confirm this) as Danny proposes. This is his specific wish, therefore I am merely making it happen. Elsie, I am trusting you to see this through, because both you and I know the importance of real love . . ."' The solicitor stopped reading and observed Elsie closely. 'There is then a personal message to Danny, which I will share with him later this afternoon. I would appreciate it if you could keep the details of this bequest to yourself until he contacts you to discuss plans. Do you understand the terms of the will?'

Numb, Elsie nodded, but a battle had already begun inside her. Thanking Mr Delaney, she walked slowly out of his office, pausing in reception to sit for a moment to take it all in. *Paris.* Why, of all the places in the world that Danny could propose to Aoife, did it have to be Paris? She had no way of shirking this responsibility: it was the final wish of a dear friend, so how could she refuse? And yet, the thought of visiting Paris alone – without the one person in her life who had wanted so much to experience the city with her – was almost too awful to bear.

Lucas had added Paris at Number 51: the only item on The List they were never to fulfil. For, on the day they had planned to go – bags packed, ferry and trains booked and hotel waiting – the vehicle taking them from their little terraced house in Islingword Street was not a taxi but an ambulance, blue lights ablaze and engine roaring as it rushed Lucas to hospital. Elsie had discovered his lifeless body slumped beneath the bathroom sink and, in sheer panic, had dialled 999. The paramedics revived him at the scene but Elsie could tell from their grim determination that this was to be no minor setback for their trip . . .

'Elsie? What on earth are you doing here?'

Heart thudding hard, she looked up. *Please, no. Not today.*

Torin surveyed her, his mild amusement becoming concern when his eyes met hers. He sat quickly beside her. 'Is everything OK? You look terrible.'

'I'll be all right in a minute. I just need to . . . *think.*'

He checked his watch. 'This isn't the place to think, trust me. Look, there's a café not far from here. Why don't we head there?'

'No – no, really, I'm OK.'

'You don't look it.'

Why wouldn't he get the hint? Elsie stared at him for a long time and then, so suddenly she shocked herself, she

271

found herself agreeing – an overwhelming urge within her to be out of Denbigh Associates more compelling than her desire to argue with him. 'I could murder a cup of tea.'

A wry smile broke across his face. 'Good girl. Although, I'd be careful with that gravity of admission in here if I were you.'

He led Elsie out of the law firm's offices, down several back streets until they emerged in a small courtyard with an old-fashioned teashop at the end of it. Despite her internal consternation at her acceptance of Torin's suggestion, the sight of the very British café with its floral tablecloths, handmade bunting hanging around the walls and large, steaming Brown Betty teapots was beautiful to behold. They found a table and Torin ordered a pot of tea and two squares of crumbly Almond Bakewell. Elsie stared out across the teashop to the window beyond, her thoughts far away from its cosy interior.

When their order arrived, Torin poured tea into two bone china cups and passed one across the table to Elsie. The tea was hot and strong, tingling in her throat as she drank.

After observing her for a while, he spoke. 'Is that better?'

'Much. Thank you. Don't you have work to do?'

'Only paperwork. And that can wait. Can I ask why you were at my workplace?'

Great, Elsie thought, for once amused by the coincidence, *trust Torin's law firm to be the one I visit today.* 'I had an appointment with Andrew Delaney.'

His brow furrowed. 'Family law?'

'A will. One I didn't know I was going to be mentioned in, actually. It's come as a bit of a shock.'

'Was it someone you knew well? A family member?'

She gave him a rueful look. 'You ask a lot of questions.'

'Sorry. Par for the course in my line of work, I'm afraid.'

'It was one of the members of my choir, if you must know. Irene – the old lady who did the air-guitar routine when we sang at Brighton Carnival?'

Torin's expression clouded. 'I didn't go to the Carnival this year.'

What was he on about? Elsie had seen him, just after The Sundaes had performed – he knew that. Why deny it when he knew as well as she did that it was a lie? 'Yes, you did. I saw you. I was with Olly . . .'

Obviously he had no intention of admitting it, for whatever strange reason. 'I must have a doppelgänger in Brighton.'

His odd denial irritated her, but the last thing on her mind today was trying to understand the mind of Torin Stewart. 'Maybe so.'

Torin looked away. 'Were you close? To the lady, I mean?'
Was he blushing?

'I didn't think I was, but Irene had other ideas. She's left me a whole list of crazy instructions in her will and I have no idea how I'll be able to do it.'

'You can always decline. It's very simple: you either appoint another person to carry it out for you or renounce the responsibility altogether.'

'That's not an option. I've been asked to organise something for someone else. If I don't do it, they'll lose out. I don't have a choice.'

'Elsie, there's always a choice.'

She was about to reply when she noticed something on the table. 'Wait – is that a *Filofax*?'

Torin looked down at the black leather organiser. 'Yes.'

Forgetting her cautiousness, Elsie laughed out loud. 'Wow. I never had you pegged as a *Filofax* kind of guy.'

Torin placed his hand protectively on it. 'I love this. My mum bought it for me when I started with the firm.'

'Oh my goodness, it has your initials on it, too. In gold!'

'OK, now you're just being insulting.'

'T.H.S. What does the "H" stand for? Harry? Herbert?'

Torin groaned. 'Hamish.'

'Nice name.'

'Thank you.' He smiled. 'Listen, you can tell me about the terms of the will, you know, if you want to. I'd be happy to advise you.'

'No. But thanks for offering. I think I need to wait until the other person gets in touch and then I can start to arrange things.' She wished with all her might that she couldn't see the sting of her refusal in his eyes. Raising her teacup, she smiled at him. 'Great tea, though.'

'I'll take that as a compliment. Even if you did diss my personal organiser.' He paused, his eyes still as they had been in the maternity ward a few weeks ago. Then, he clapped his hands together and stood. 'Now I really have to get back to work. Tea's on me, so stay as long as you need to.' He made to leave, then hesitated and turned back. 'Give my regards to your sister – and Ottie Rose.'

A strange undulation of surprise appeared in Elsie's stomach as Torin left. He made no sense at all: one minute combative and full of his own importance, the next almost human. Whatever the truth about him, today wasn't the day to find it. She had far more pressing issues to deal with – and all of them were now inextricably linked with the one city she had vowed never to visit after Lucas died: Paris.

They had talked about it endlessly for eleven and a half months, so Elsie knew by heart what Lucas wanted them to see in the French capital: the Louvre, Montmartre, Notre

274

Dame. And, finally, going up to the second stage of the Eiffel Tower as the sun set across the city. Not the first, not the third, but the second. Lucas had visited Paris with his grandmother at the tender age of ten and they had shunned the elevators to climb the metal staircases. As it was a windy day, the top tier of the famous tower had been closed, so his first glimpse of Paris from the Eiffel Tower was from the second level – as high as the steps reached.

'That's the best view,' he maintained, although Elsie always suspected this stemmed from his grandmother's effort to lessen his disappointment on the day. 'We have to stand at the railing, kiss and shout out, "*C'est magnifique!*" over Paris. Even if there's a coachload of tourists there. In fact, *especially* if they're there, because then we can be eccentric English tourists and not care a bit about what everyone else is thinking. Once we've done that, Number 51 can be ticked and it will all be done.'

In the months that had passed since his death, Elsie often wondered if Lucas had always known his chances of fulfilling the final List item were slim. His insistence that The List must be completed in chronological order confirmed that Paris would happen in his last weeks – days, even. Several times during his final month, Elsie had begged him to reconsider Number 51, but he was adamant it should remain. Even now, she couldn't explain why this had been so important to him, but she had, of course, laid her arguments aside in the face of his granite-like determination.

Number 51 had confirmed to Elsie that Paris should be struck forever from the list of places she would like to visit. The thought of walking its streets, viewing its sights and experiencing its heart without the love of her life was just too painful. But now, the only thing that stood between the fulfilment of Irene's final wish – and Danny's dream proposal – was Elsie's decision . . .

Perhaps Torin's suggestion was the answer here: to renounce the responsibility and find someone more suitable to the task of making it happen. But could she really live with this decision, knowing that Irene had placed so much trust in her, despite the small amount of time they had been acquainted?

Or maybe she could organise everything from home? It would be easy to book transport, Channel crossings, accommodation and food provision from Brighton, and Woody and Daisy were more than capable of leading the trip once these details were arranged. But after all her hard work to bring The Sundaes together as a tightly-knit community, could she *really* desert them at their most important performance so far?

After leaving the teashop, Elsie wandered aimlessly around the town, paying little attention to the time or the streets she followed as her inner battle ensued. By the time dusk began to fall, a storm had blown in from the sea, causing tourists to scuttle for the safety of hotels, pubs and B&Bs, while a few hardy locals defiantly fought their way along the wind-battered seafront, the famous British spirit in the face of inclement weather still alive and well in Brighton. Elsie joined them, the growing ferociousness of the wind no match for the typhoon raging in her mind.

Tired and beset by memories, she left the promenade, buffeted by gusts of wind as she made her way onto the beach. Her blonde hair flapped violently around her face and the strong wind almost took her breath away. But all of this was immaterial: she needed to make sense of her feelings without having to give account to anyone else. Jim would only worry, Daisy would demand that she share every detail and Olly wouldn't understand without a long, drawn-out explanation that she just couldn't endure right now.

What was worse was that Elsie suspected even Lucas wouldn't understand her gut reaction to this situation. She could almost see him now, stomping along the pebbled beach beside her, vehemently making his point over the roar of the wind and waves.

'What's your problem, Elsie? You've never let fear hold you back in the past – why start now?'

'I'm not afraid, Lucas.'

'Yes, you are. But I don't understand why. I never said you couldn't go to Paris without me, did I?'

'I'm not saying you did. I just don't want to see it now.'

'This had better not be some lame attempt to immortalise Paris in my name.'

'Don't be ridiculous.'

'I'm not the one being ridiculous. Paris is an amazing city, Els! You should see it. And you won't be alone. Plus, you'd be making that lad's dream come true. Consider all the facts for the moment. Now tell me, honestly, do you still have a good enough reason for not going?'

Standing at the water's edge, Elsie watched the foam whipping over the pebbles at her feet. All of it was true and unavoidable, but deep down she knew the real reason for her reticence: by visiting Paris, she would be completing The List. Even though she had argued with Lucas about the existence of Number 51, its unfulfilled presence had somehow been comforting. If she saw Paris – and climbed the Eiffel Tower – it was the final step in letting Lucas go. She had achieved so much and yet, even now, she knew the final goodbye had not been said.

'This is too hard, Lucas!' she shouted out over the raging,

windswept sea, her heart breaking all over again. 'It's too much to ask of me!'

There was no reply, only the wind lashing at the waves as graphite clouds skidded across the sky. The salt spray hit her face meeting her tears and she cried out again as an overwhelming sense of aloneness crashed over her. She knew what she had to do – her decision was already made. It was impossible to avoid, stubborn in its immovability – almost as if Lucas had engineered it himself. But could she see it through? Could she stand being in Paris without him?

CHAPTER SIXTEEN

Something like a plan

Danny called the next day and Elsie agreed to visit him at home after work. When she arrived, his mother met her at the door.

'Isn't this just lovely? I couldn't believe it when Mr Delaney read out Irene's plan. Come in, come in!'

Danny jumped out of his chair when his mother ushered Elsie into the lounge. 'Hey, Elsie.'

'Hi, Danny.'

Danny's mum smiled nervously. 'Right. Well. You two have a lot to talk about, so I'll just . . .' She backed out of the room and shut the door.

Danny grimaced. 'Sorry about Mum. She's really excited, you know.'

'It's nice.'

Remembering his manners, Danny pointed at the sofa. 'Please – sit down. Can I get you anything? Cup of tea?'

Triple vodka? 'No thanks. So . . .'

'Yeah. Major stuff.'

'I have to admit, it was a bit of a shock. I never expected to be arranging a Paris trip for the choir.'

Concern filled Danny's eyes. 'But you'll do it, right? You'll help me?'

Swallowing hard, Elsie hoped her smile was convincingly confident. 'Of course I will. But we need a plan. You heard what Irene said – Aoife can't suspect a thing. So I have an idea and I'll need you to get behind it one hundred per cent.'

'You know I will.'

'Because it's going to feel like you're lying to her for the next couple of weeks, and that could be hard.'

Danny took a deep breath. 'I know. But it's worth it for what I'll be able to do. I'm ready.'

The first part of the plan was easy enough to achieve. Between them, Elsie and Danny concocted a cover story that they shared with the choir at the next rehearsal.

'I have some exciting news,' Elsie told The Sundaes as they sat together in Sundae & Cher. 'We've been offered a gig.'

The Sundaes looked at each other in surprise.

'How did that happen?' Daisy asked.

'It was someone who came to Irene's concert last week. They called me yesterday and made the offer.'

'I didn't think we were that good,' Sasha said.

'Well, *obviously* we were if someone's booked us,' Lewis returned.

Sheila raised her hand. 'So, where is it?'

Elsie glanced at Danny. 'Paris.'

A shocked murmur went round the group. Woody leaned forward. 'Hold on there, angel. You're messing with us, right?'

'Nope. We have, if we want it, the opportunity to sing in an open-air concert in Paris.'

'When?' Daisy asked.

'That's the slightly problematic thing: it's in three weeks' time.'

Suddenly, everyone was talking at once. Elsie made several attempts to speak before a loud whistle from Woody finally restored order to proceedings.

'Let the lady speak! The floor's yours, angel.'

'Thank you. I believe we can do this, but it's going to take commitment from everybody.'

Stan coughed. 'I probably can't go.' All eyes swung to him. 'It's the money, you see. Things are tight enough for the missus and me as it is. But Paris? It's an expensive city. I don't have that kind of money. I'm sorry, everyone.'

'Stan, it's fine. The organisers have offered to pay our expenses. That means travel, accommodation and food. So the only thing you need is a free weekend in three weeks' time.'

Surprise reverberated round the room. Danny caught Elsie's eye and nodded. 'That sounds great. Er, actually, Els, I'm afraid Aoife and I have to shoot off.'

Aoife looked at him. 'We do?'

'Yeah, sorry, hun. Mum's car's playing up again and I said we'd take her to the supermarket. She's buying us tea.'

'But you'll both come to Paris?' Elsie asked, playing her part. 'It won't be the same if you two aren't there.'

Aoife's smile lit up the room. 'I wouldn't miss it, Elsie! I have always, *always* wanted to go there!'

'Excellent. See you two next rehearsal. I'll text you the dates we agree tonight, OK?'

Danny and Aoife said their goodbyes and left. Once the door was shut, Elsie grinned at the choir. 'Right. This is the *real* reason we're going to Paris . . .'

With the rest of The Sundaes in on the surprise, rehearsals began immediately. Elsie had arranged a schedule of fake rehearsals where Danny and Aoife would be present and real rehearsals where The Sundaes could rehearse the song for Danny's proposal without them. It was a big commitment but everyone was so amazed by Irene's generosity and thrilled by the prospect of fulfilling Danny's wish that they threw themselves into rehearsals with renewed vigour.

Meanwhile, Elsie began to research the logistics of getting The Sundaes to Paris. Not all of the choir could come: Dee was too young, Kathy was working that weekend and Juliet had already arranged to visit her sister in Vancouver. This meant that Elsie was now looking at a party of eleven for the trip. Focusing on the practicalities helped her to ignore the insistent pull of her heart at each mention of the French capital. She made countless lists, gathered quotes and scoured the web for hotel deals. When she wasn't planning she was rehearsing or working – but keeping busy was essential to keep her from thinking about the trip.

A week into rehearsals, almost everything was planned except the transport. Flights for ten people turned out to be prohibitively expensive, so a road and ferry combination seemed the only option. Hiring a minibus was relatively straightforward, but Elsie wasn't sure who would be nominated as drivers. She didn't relish the prospect of doing it herself, having never driven on the Continent before, yet it seemed too big an ask to expect anyone else to take on such a responsibility.

The issue was playing on her mind when she arrived at her father's house for tea. As they tucked into homemade lentil and chickpea dahl, Jim cast a concerned glance at his daughter.

'I'm worried about you.'

'Dad, don't worry. I just wish I could finalise all the

details for this trip. Everybody else is putting so much work into rehearsals that I feel like I'm letting them down.'

Jim put his fork down and placed his hand on hers. 'Stop that, young lady! You're doing more than enough to make this happen. With no thought for your own feelings, I might add. And don't give me your "oh Dad" look, I know what Paris means to you. Don't think for a moment that I've missed the significance of you going there. I think it's one of the most selfless acts I've ever seen someone do.'

'I'm just trying not to think about actually going,' she confessed, feeling the sting of burgeoning tears. 'What's important for now is getting everybody there, making sure they have somewhere to sleep and keeping the real reason for our visit a secret from Aoife.'

'How are the plans going?'

'Not too bad. I've found a good hotel near Montparnasse station, which puts us in the right place to get to the Eiffel Tower, and I've been quoted a great price on group ferry tickets. The only thing left now is to decide who is going to drive the minibus.'

'Do you have a minibus?'

Elsie smiled. 'Technically, not yet. But I have had some quotes. I was hoping to book one with a driver but it was just working out too expensive. It's been a bit of a headache to be honest with you.'

Jim sat back in his chair. 'I might know someone, actually.'

Elsie's heart flipped. 'Who?'

He spread his hands wide like a magician at the end of a trick. 'Me.'

It took a few seconds for this to sink in. 'Really?'

'Yes, really. I have a friend who has a vehicle hire business – I'm pretty sure he has a minibus or mini-coach or whatever they're called these days. When you, Daisy and Guin were little I used to drive over to France a couple of times a year to buy furniture at the flea markets out there, do you remember? Your Grandma Flo used to come and look after you and Uncle Frank and I shared the journey.'

Elsie blinked. 'I never realised that was what you were doing. I just thought Grandma Flo was coming to stay for fun.'

'She was,' Jim chortled. 'My mother used to encourage Frank and me to go more often because she loved playing mum to you three. She'd be so proud to see what you're planning now.' He sniffed. 'So what do you say, eh? Fancy your old Dad driving you to *gay Paree*?'

'Wow, Dad, I don't know what to say. Yes! I'd love you to be our driver.'

'But I have one condition.'

'Name it.'

A huge grin appeared on Jim's face. 'That you let me be part of The Sundaes, just for the trip. To be honest, I've been dying to see you at work, but I didn't want you feeling like your daft old Dad was cramping your style.'

Jumping up from her chair, she flung her arms round Jim and hugged him as hard as she could. 'Yes, Dad! The answer is yes!'

'This song is *well* lame,' Sasha moaned, as Elsie played through Danny's choice of song for the big proposal. 'I can't believe this is Aoife's favourite.'

'It's the one that Danny's picked,' Elsie said, weariness beginning to shorten her temper. 'We don't have time to debate the merits of it.'

'I think it's lovely,' Sheila ventured, instantly incurring a scowl from Sasha. 'Anyway, this is for Danny, not for you, so you're just going to have to like it or lump it.'

The rest of The Sundaes stared in surprise at Sheila's outburst. In all the time the choir had been together, Sheila had been one of the quietest members, her nerves always getting the better of her whenever she tried to speak. 'What's the matter? Why are you all looking at me like that?'

Woody strode over to her and slung his arm round her shoulders. 'Well said, girl.'

Sasha mimed being sick and slunk back into place.

'Thank you. Any other problems I should know about? Anyone? Good, let's get back to it, then.' Elsie saw Jim grin at her as she began to play. His introduction into the choir had gone smoothly, Elsie choosing to tell all of The Sundaes that he had joined as a permanent member of the choir. It was easier this way, with less pertinent details for The Sundaes to remember in order to keep Aoife from asking too many questions. As for her father, he was in his element, singing with gusto beside Stan and Graeme, and taking every opportunity to hang out with Woody.

After the secret rehearsal, Elsie called Danny from home to update him on their progress.

'How's it going with Aoife?' she asked.

'Good so far, although I feel dreadful about lying to her. I'm scared she'll see through my story and think I'm cheating on her or something.'

'Just try to stay calm and remember why you're doing this, OK? You're going to ask Aoife to marry you in just over a week's time – surely that's worth a few more days sticking to your cover story?'

'You're right, I'm sorry. I just want it all to be perfect, Els.'

'I know. And I'm going to do everything I can to make sure it is. I promise.'

Ending the call, she threw her mobile to the far end of her bed and let the emotion that had building for two weeks finally break over her. The fear of standing on the Eiffel Tower was looming over her, larger than the famous structure itself. Despite her best efforts to keep it at bay, the prospect of it was never far from her mind, hiding in the shadows like an assailant awaiting his victim's arrival. It brought back all the feelings of helplessness she had encountered during the final weeks of Lucas' life. Last time she had been losing Lucas; this time she was on the brink of letting his memory go.

She rolled over on her bed and picked up the framed photograph of him that she had taken on their honeymoon years before. It was her favourite image of Lucas – leaning on the edge of the balcony of their hotel room in Malta, staring out across the Mediterranean Sea, the summer breeze blowing his dark hair back from his face and his eyes reflecting the setting sun. This was how she loved to remember him, not how he had been at the end.

Several of The Sundaes had expressed confusion at Irene's decision to keep her illness from them, but Elsie completely understood. Having lived with someone facing cancer, she knew how important it had been to Lucas to keep as much of his life as normal as possible. While he was open about his condition with anyone who asked, he had done all he could to maintain a sense of normality in his final months.

Lucas never really talked much about dying, apart from in jest, although Elsie knew this was his defence mechanism kicking in to avoid being the object of pity. There was only one time that he mentioned it, about four months after his diagnosis.

They were sitting on a seafront bench, dressed in charity shop clothes, feeding the seagulls – Number 19 on The List:

19. Dress up as old people and feed seagulls on the prom (shouting at them obligatory).

The reasoning behind this was that, for as long as Elsie had known him, Lucas had a stock answer when anybody asked him what his life ambition was:

'I want to shout at seagulls when I'm ninety.'

It had been a long-standing joke between him and Elsie – one that gained a heavy irony following his diagnosis. Number 19 was all about helping him to fulfil his professed life ambition. So, they had visited several charity shops to create the perfect old people's outfits. Lucas wore a flat cap, white and green checked shirt, sports jacket (complete with suede-effect elbow patches), tan shoes and baggy grey trousers three sizes too big for him, while Elsie was a picture in a pale blue silk turban hat, abstract-patterned polyester dress, knitted cardigan and the kind of thick-soled beige sandals Grandma Flo used to call 'slippers with straps'. All of which made the conversation even more of an unlikely bolt from the blue when it came.

'I don't think this is it,' he said, suddenly.

Elsie had turned to face him. 'Should we have done the facepaint wrinkles? I knew we should have gone the whole hog . . .'

'No.' His dark brown eyes had been fixed on the far horizon, a translucent wash of somewhere else over them. 'I mean *this* – life. I don't think it ends here. Do you?'

Blindsided, Elsie had stammered to reply. 'Well, I haven't – I mean I don't . . . Let's not talk about this now.'

'At some point we should, don't you think?' He closed his eyes. 'Don't answer that, I'm sorry.'

Heart contracting, Elsie reached for his hand. 'Tell me what you're feeling, Lucas.'

'I think about it, you know? I try not to but it's sort of inevitable.' Opening his eyes, he made a startling confession. 'I saw a priest yesterday.'

If Lucas had admitted to being an alien life form, Elsie couldn't have been more surprised at that moment. 'Really?'

'Yep. I went to see Mum and stopped in the village pub on the way home. Father Andrew was in there and – surprisingly – we got chatting. He's a sound guy. Didn't judge me, didn't try to drum up Sunday business, he just listened. Turns out he lost his daughter last year to non-Hodgkin's lymphoma, so we had more in common than I was expecting. You'd have laughed, Els. Me and a priest talking afterlifes in The Queen's Arms over a pint of IPA.'

'That's a mental picture I'm having trouble processing.'

'Just a little gift from me to you, baby. It was cool, though, and it made me think a lot. The thing is, I can't imagine everything just stops – at the end, I mean. I'm not sure what's next, but I think there must be something else. Strange to think I'm going to find out soon . . .'

'Lucas, *please* . . .'

'Let me say this and I won't mention it again, I promise. Here it is: I'm not scared of it. I don't want to lose you and it's far too early to be bowing out, but I can't stop it happening. I just need you to know that I think I'm reconciling myself to it. And I'm not afraid.' He grabbed a handful of seed from the crumpled white paper bag in his lap and threw it at a gaggle of competitive gulls flapping by the bench. 'Have you not eaten half your bodyweight of this stuff already?' He grinned at Elsie and she sensed the subject had been closed. 'Ungrateful little blighters. Think we should start shouting at them yet?'

Had Irene felt the same way? Elsie wondered now. The thought of the lovely old lady carefully planning other people's futures knowing she would never see the outcome was heartbreaking. Looking at her husband's sun-kissed face in the photograph she held, Elsie made a silent promise. Lucas had been unafraid: now it was her turn.

The next day, Elsie found herself in charge of Sundae & Cher. Cher, after being surprised with a dinner reservation at one of Brighton's hottest restaurants by Jake, had arranged an 'emergency hair appointment', taking the afternoon off to prepare herself for her special night. The café was moderately busy, mostly with regular customers, so Cher's absence posed no particular problems for Elsie. She took the opportunity to make up a batch of gingerbread and vanilla swirl cookies, which she would later ice with cream cheese frosting and decorate with jelly shapes for the children who often came in with their parents after school and at weekends. This was one of the aspects of her job that she loved the most – batch-baking trays of biscuits and cakes to be sold alongside the ice creams. It made her remember Saturday afternoons with Jim, up to her little elbows in flour with more of the cake mixture on the kitchen worktops than in the bowl as her father revelled in the sight of his youngest daughter's first forays into baking.

She was mixing up a batch of cream cheese frosting when the brass bell above the door rang out. To her surprise, Torin approached the counter.

'Now, before you say anything about me not being allowed in here again, let me defend my actions.'

'Go on.'

'I happened to be passing and I thought it would be entirely wrong of me to do so without saying hello, if you had seen me pass by your window.'

Elsie wiped her hands on her apron. 'I suppose it would have been. If I'd seen you passing by.'

'You didn't see me?'

'Sorry.' Elsie indicated the bowl she had been mixing. 'My attention was taken by this.'

'Ah. Then my being here is a bit awkward, isn't it?'

'It is.'

He flashed a broad smile at her. 'OK, cards on the table – I wanted to see how you were after your meeting at my law firm. I've been debating whether or not to visit and today I ran out of reasons not to. So, how are you?'

Still a little stunned by his sudden arrival, Elsie shrugged. 'Good. Thanks for asking. Would you like a drink while you're here?'

He brightened. 'I would. Pot of tea would be great. And one of those chocolate and hazelnut pastry twists if it's not too much trouble.' He watched Elsie as she filled a small teapot with hot water from the coffee machine. 'I take it Cher recovered from her run-in with the choirmistress?'

'She did.' Elsie placed a teacup and the teapot on the counter in front of him and filled a small jug with milk. 'But she was really upset. I think Jeannette was a little too tactile with Jake.' She placed a pastry twist on a plate and handed it over.

'She was a little. Nothing more tragic than watching a desperate woman fling herself at a man who clearly isn't interested.'

'Do you think Jake wasn't interested? I mean, those things that Jeannette said about him, they weren't true, were they?'

Torin stirred his tea. 'Of course not. It was just the ramblings of a desperate single woman.' Seeing Elsie's concern for her friend, his green eyes softened. 'Jake's a good guy. I have a lot of time for him. He might have had a bit of a reputation for being one for the ladies in the past, but he seems to really care about Cher.'

'Honestly? You know him better than I do, Torin. If you thought for a moment there was anything true in what Jeannette said to Cher, you'd tell me?'

'Of course.' He poured his cup of tea. 'And how's the other thing going?'

'Oh. Fine.'

'You decided what to do about it?'

'Yes. I'm going ahead as requested. Thank you for your help that day, by the way, it meant a lot.'

He smiled. 'I'm glad I could help. Like I said, if there's ever anything I can advise on . . .'

'Thank you. I'll bear that in mind.'

'Good.'

'So he just turned up, no warning or anything?' Daisy asked, her eyeballs on the verge of leaving her head altogether.

'Yes. He came in, asked about me and Cher, had a cup of tea and left.'

Guin stuck her head through the bead curtain in Jim's kitchen. 'What are you two whispering about?'

'It's nothing,' Elsie began, but Daisy was too interested in the conversation not to include their middle sister.

'Torin Stewart turned up at Elsie's work today,' she said.

Guin gave a delighted whoop and hurried into the kitchen. 'Ha! Gossip! Tell me!'

Elsie sighed. 'There really isn't much to tell. He came in to ask how I was, which was a bit of a shock, but nice of him, I suppose.'

'Nice? You're using the words "Torin" and "nice" in the same sentence? May I remind you this is the man you hated so much that you almost had me giving birth on the verge of the A27 because you didn't want us to get in his car?'

'I'm not saying I like the guy, but he has helped me twice in the last month.'

'The fact of which he is bound to parade triumphantly in front of you for months to come,' Daisy added.

Hearing their sister's sudden harsh critique of Torin made Elsie and Guin stare at her.

'I thought you said you liked him when you met him?' Guin asked.

Daisy raised her eyebrows. 'Well, I did, but I've had time to think about it since then and now I think he's a bit too self-congratulatory for my liking.'

'He wasn't that obnoxious this time,' Elsie offered, surprised to hear herself defending the man.

'Be careful, Els,' Guin warned, a conspiratorial glint in her eyes, 'at this rate you might end up liking him.'

'I can categorically confirm that will *never* happen,' Elsie replied. 'All I'm saying is that he helped to break Cher and Jeannette's catfight apart and he offered advice when I'd heard about Irene's will. And at least he bothered to check if I was OK.'

Olly parted the bead curtain and peered in. 'Sorry to interrupt, but your dad says he's ready to go when you are.'

Elsie linked her arm with his as they all walked to the front door, where Jim was waiting. He carried a towel and was dressed in a tracksuit that looked like he'd bought it in the early 1980s. The sight of him made his three daughters burst out laughing and he held up his hands to stop them.

'OK, enough of that. We need to get a move on if we're going to make it in time.'

Joining the choir, if only as a cover story for Paris, had

292

brought a new confidence out in Jim, evident in his recent participation in new activities. He had joined an art class at the local community centre, signed up for a business supper club in the town and was even embarking on a distance learning course in Hindi. But even given all of this, it had still come as a surprise to his family when he accepted an invitation from his business partner to join a five-a-side football game.

'I can't believe we're about to watch our own father trying to play football,' Guin whispered to Elsie and Daisy as they sat in the back of Jim's people-carrier. 'I thought Dad was allergic to sport.'

'Don't be so mean,' Daisy whispered back. 'Olly's uncle invited him to play five-a-side. I think it's sweet. Even if that tracksuit is the single most unflattering outfit I've ever seen him wear.'

'It must have been fashionable at one time,' Elsie suggested. 'Perhaps he's waiting for it to come back into fashion again?'

Daisy pulled a face. 'Trust me, there's no way *that* is ever going to be in fashion again. I can't believe it ever was.'

Once inside the leisure centre, Olly sat next to Elsie on the raised tier of seats overlooking an artificial pitch.

'How long has it been since Jim last played football?'

'Longer than I've known him. I hope your uncle goes easy on him.'

Olly laughed. 'Uncle Marty's not much fitter. This is just a bunch of blokes he knows having fun. They meet once a month for a bit of a kick-around so they can tell their wives they've exercised. I don't think it's a competitive thing.'

Jim was shaking Marty's hand in the middle of the pitch as the other men jogged over to greet him. The group separated into two teams and Jim accepted an orange bib, putting it over his head and raising his thumb to his family as the referee blew his whistle to start the game.

Olly nudged Elsie. 'It's nice to see you, even if it is with our families present.'

Elsie leaned against his arm. 'It is. I'm sorry I've been so busy, we've just been working to get everything ready for Paris next weekend.'

'And have you?'

'I think so. Everything's booked, the song is all prepared for the big question and Aoife is none the wiser. Oh, and Dad's going down a storm with the rest of the choir. I'm thinking I might let him stay on after the Paris trip.'

Olly smiled. 'I think he'd like that.' He rose to his feet as his uncle took a shot at goal, groaning when the ball ran wide of the net. 'No! Did you see that? *So close . . .*' He sat down again. 'So, Paris, eh? Can't help thinking Danny's a bit young to be proposing to anyone.'

'He's nineteen. I wasn't much older when Lucas proposed.' Elsie saw Olly's reaction and smiled at him. 'It's OK, we *were* quite young. But at the time, it felt like we'd waited forever for it to happen.'

One of the players fell over in a highly dramatic attempt to win a penalty. Elsie and Olly both shouted out at once and turned to look at each other, laughing.

'I'm not sure this is a particularly relaxing spectator sport,' Olly smiled. 'I'm exhausted already.'

'Me too. Aw, look at Dad. He's been running around for ages and hasn't managed to come near the ball yet.'

'He'll get there. Go on, Jim!'

Jim looked up at the stand and grinned, his face beetroot-red from the exertion.

'He looks happy,' Elsie said.

Olly waved at Jim. 'I really like him. He's become a good

friend lately.' He took a sideways glance at Elsie. 'I'm quite fond of his daughter, too.'

Elsie looked up at him as his hand found hers. Suddenly, a shout went up from the pitch and they turned to see Jim lying on the ground, clasping his ankle. Elsie left Olly and hurried down, closely followed by Guin and Daisy. The other players were gathered round Jim as he writhed on the floor.

'What happened?' Daisy demanded.

'He got caught in a bad tackle,' Marty said, kneeling down by Jim's side. 'Mate, do you think you can walk on it?'

Jim shook his head and let go of his ankle. The onlookers gasped as the protruding bone came into view. Shocked, Guin began to shoo the other players away as Elsie grabbed her mobile to dial 999.

Two hours later Elsie, Guin, Daisy and Olly were sitting still stunned in the A&E department waiting room, waiting for news.

'I hope he's all right,' Elsie said. 'That break looked horrendous.'

'It did,' Olly nodded. 'They'll probably have to X-ray it and then set it. That's what's taking the time.'

'At least they took him straight through,' said Guin, checking her watch. 'Look, this is going to sound awful, but would you mind if I call Joe to collect me? Ottie's due a feed soon and I didn't prepare any bottles.'

Daisy hugged her. 'We don't mind at all. You go.'

Thanking them, Guin gathered her belongings and left.

'How long has he been in there?' Elsie asked.

Olly checked his watch. 'A couple of hours. Try not to worry, Els.'

But Elsie was worried. Not only had she just witnessed

her dad in pain – and the horrific injury he had sustained – but she now faced the prospect of having to drive The Sundaes to Paris herself. She felt awful for even thinking about it, but with the trip now only days away this new development was not a welcome one. Not to mention the fact it had brought her back to a hospital waiting area – and all the unwelcome memories that accompanied it.

A male nurse pushed through the double doors and checked the file in his hand. 'Mr Maynard?'

Daisy, Elsie and Olly stood and the nurse walked over. 'Hi. We've just got the X-ray back and the first thing you need to know is that it's a clean break, which is good news. It looks a lot worse than it actually is, so we're going to set Mr Maynard's ankle and then you'll be able to take him home.'

'Is he OK?' Daisy asked.

The male nurse smiled. 'He's fine. He's been joking away in there since he arrived. I wish more of our patients were as cheerful. Should be about another forty minutes or so.'

Almost an hour later, Jim emerged, his right foot encased in white plaster, walking shakily with the aid of crutches. 'Just call me Hopalong!'

Daisy rushed over to help him. 'Dad, be careful!'

'I'm fine, stop fussing. Well, this is a bit of a pickle, isn't it? I always knew exercise was bad for my health!'

Olly laughed. 'Trust you to be joking when you've broken your ankle. How long do you have to keep the cast on for?'

'The doctor reckons eight weeks for this cast, then they change it for a walking cast, whatever that is. It could be several months till I'm walking on it again.' He turned to Elsie. 'Darling, I'm so sorry.'

'Don't apologise, Dad, it wasn't your fault.'

'But the trip . . .'

'I'll sort something, don't worry.'

As they all walked out to the car park, Olly caught Elsie's hand. 'I'll drive.'

'Oh, cheers.' Smiling, Elsie handed him the keys to Jim's car. Olly shook his head and gave them back to her.

'Not now. I mean for Paris. I can't sing, obviously, but I'll drive the minibus – if you like?'

Elsie could hardly believe it. 'Would you do that? Really?'

'I'd love to. I've driven abroad quite a bit – I hired a minibus last summer and drove a few of the guys down to the South of France for a stag do. But I've never been to Paris. It would be great to see it with you – and the choir. What do you think?'

Elsie raised herself on her tiptoes to plant a kiss on his cheek. 'I think I've found the perfect driver!'

Exhausted by the emotional rollercoaster of the day, Elsie opted for a long bath and early night, snuggling into bed at just after ten p.m. Knowing that all the details for the Paris trip were arranged, she felt that a good night's sleep was guaranteed. And it was, until the incessant ringing of her mobile phone caused her to wake with a start. Scrambling upright, she blinked the sleep from her eyes as she answered the call.

'Hello?'

'Elsie – it's me. Can you . . . I'm so sorry, I didn't know who to . . .'

'Cher? What's the matter?'

'I've just . . . I'm so, so sorry to call you . . .'

'Don't worry about that. What's happened?' There was no answer, just the muffled sound of sobbing. Clambering out of bed, Elsie grabbed her jeans and struggled into them as she held the phone to her ear with her shoulder. 'Right, tell me where you are.'

'At home . . . but . . .'

'OK, stay there. I'm coming over.'

When Elsie parked her car outside Cher's house she had barely clambered out when a sobbing Cher flung open the front door. Her usually perfectly set hair hung in tangled clumps and mascara was smeared down her cheeks. Shocked at her friend's appearance, Elsie ushered her back inside and set about making strong, sweet tea as Cher huddled tearfully on the sofa.

'There,' she said, handing Cher a mug.

'Thank you. Oh Els, I feel so dreadful dragging you out at this time of night.'

'Stop apologising. This was my idea, remember? Now tell me what happened.'

Cher took a long glug of tea and wiped her eyes with the back of her hand. 'I spoke to Jake earlier and he said he was going to be out this evening but that he would love to chat when he got home. And I don't know why, Els, but I took that as an invitation. So I went to his house and let myself in with the spare key he keeps under the planter by the front door. I wanted to surprise him, you know?'

Elsie nodded, but a heavy sense of foreboding was already laying claim to her stomach. 'Go on.'

'I was fully prepared to give him a *big* surprise, if you know what I mean . . . I'm talking the full deal – red lacy underwear, high heels—' She broke off and sobbed again. 'And I waited there for nearly an hour. I sent him a text and he replied that he was on his way home from a client meeting and couldn't wait to speak to me, so I was thrilled to think he'd find me, in his favourite chair, just like that scene from *Pretty Woman* where she's only wearing a tie . . .'

Elsie shuddered at the mental picture, which would have been excruciatingly embarrassing at the best of times but practically unfathomable at two thirty-five a.m. 'What happened?'

'I heard his car pull up, the key in the lock . . . and I prepared myself with a big smile . . . the living room door opened and . . .' she let out another sob '. . . and he walked in snogging the face off some slutty twenty-something.'

'Oh, Cher . . .'

'And there I was, draped across the chair in my undies, looking and feeling every one of my forty-one years. I wanted to die.' She turned her tear-stained face to Elsie. 'And he said *nothing*. Just stood there with lipstick all over his face, staring at me like I was some random intruder . . .' she sobbed '. . . in cut-price lingerie!'

Elsie wrapped her arms around Cher. 'Oh honey, I'm so sorry. I thought he was different. Torin said . . .' Realising what she had said, she fell silent.

'Torin said what?'

Indignation rising, Elsie felt her nerves fizz with building rage. 'I saw Torin a couple of days ago and I asked him straight out if Jake could be trusted. After what Jeannette said, I wanted to be sure. And he assured me that Jake was a changed man. I believed him. I'm so sorry.'

Torin *must* have known the truth about Jake, Elsie reasoned – surely that kind of thing was a well-known topic of office gossip? And if so, why had he insisted his boss was trust-worthy? If he really wanted Elsie to like him, as he'd seemed to suggest when he visited her, why would he lie to her? Once again, he had switched personalities – from sanctimonious lawyer to potential friend to downright liar. As she fumed silently, Elsie realised she knew no more about Torin now than she did when he had first arrived unannounced into her life.

Cher broke the hug and sniffed. 'Then Torin is as bad as his spineless, cheating toe-rag of a boss. You were right about him from the beginning, Els. I should never have set you up on that date.'

They shared rueful smiles.

'From now on, girl, we make a pact: any man in Brighton *apart* from solicitors.'

Head still reeling, Elsie shook hands with Cher. 'Deal.'

CHAPTER SEVENTEEN

A sentimental journey . . .

By the time the morning of the Paris trip arrived, Elsie had begun to worry about Olly's inclusion in the party. Olly had been so happy when they travelled back to Jim's house from the hospital that Elsie had been swept up in the apparent perfection of it all. But later, when Elsie was alone, she began to see cracks appearing in the plan. Where having Jim by her side would have been a great support, with Olly it was a different story. Jim knew a lot of what she had endured with Lucas and he knew the significance of the final item on The List. But the thought of explaining every little detail to Olly filled her with dread.

Daisy recognised the battle in her sister as soon as she saw her, taking her to one side in the car park where The Sundaes were excitedly gathering with packed bags. 'Elsie, stop it.'

'Stop what?'

'Stop talking yourself out of inviting Olly. He offered, remember?'

Elsie was on the verge of tears after a sleepless night. 'But Paris . . .'

'I know, my love, but this was always going to be hard for you. Olly is a good man – a good friend – and he's doing this for you. It's a positive thing, believe me. I'll be there, remember, and you don't have to explain yourself to anyone.'

Fear reverberating through her body, Elsie nodded and sank into her sister's welcome embrace. 'Thank you.'

'You're welcome, lovely. Now,' she broke the hug and held Elsie at arm's length, 'let me look at you. You're amazing, Elsie Maynard, and you've come so far this year. All that lies ahead of you is promise and possibility. You just have to be brave enough to grab it. Ready to go?'

Elsie took a deep breath and summoned up a smile. 'Ready as I'll ever be.'

'That's all the luggage packed,' Olly called. 'Right, you lot, let's get going!'

Whopping and cheering, the Sundaes clambered into the minibus. Elsie twisted in the front seat to look back at the elated faces of the choir.

'Where to, guys?'

A chorus of voices rang out: 'PARIS!'

Twenty-five minutes later, the port of Newhaven came into view. Elsie and Woody went to sort out the tickets, leaving the rest of the choir in the minibus singing snippets from their fake new programme. The cross-Channel ferries loomed large and white ahead, and Elsie's stomach somersaulted when she saw them.

'You nervous of the crossing, angel?' Woody asked.

'No, it's just been a while since I travelled on a ferry,' Elsie lied. While she knew Woody would have understood had she told him about her trepidation, she had made the decision this morning to keep her feelings to herself. It was easier that way: she didn't want anyone worrying about her when they were all so excited about the trip.

Tickets all in order, they boarded the ferry, eventually gathering in the seating area that wrapped around the bows of the ship.

Elsie addressed the grinning choir. 'I suspect you all have different things you'd like to do now we're here, so let's just meet back here half an hour before we're due to land in Dieppe.'

The choir dispersed, Woody heading for the duty-free shop, the younger members of the choir seeking out the onboard entertainment and Stan, Graeme and Sheila wandering off to find food. Olly volunteered to find tea and Daisy and Elsie agreed, finding a table surrounded by three comfortable armchairs.

'Feeling OK, Els?'

'I think so. Better now we've set off.'

'Good. Keep me posted if things change.' She checked her watch. 'Actually, I'm just going to have a look in the shop. Won't be long.'

Left alone, Elsie retrieved a book from her bag and settled down to read. Losing herself in someone else's world was certainly preferable to pondering her own, at least for the next couple of hours. The piece of paper marking her place was the newest message from the silk-covered box – Elsie feeling comforted by the presence of Lucas' handwriting on the journey to the place he had dreamed most about:

I love you because you make every day feel like the greatest adventure.
xx

'There.'

Elsie jumped as a pale pink tissue-wrapped package landed in her lap. Daisy was smiling as she sat next to her.

303

'What's this?'

'Open it and you'll see.'

Casting a wary glance at her sister, Elsie carefully pulled away the expensive-looking ribbon that held the package together and unfolded the tissue paper to reveal a long, delicate silk scarf. It was the colour of a summer blue sky, dotted with tiny, pale pink cherry blossoms.

'Oh, wow, it's gorgeous! You didn't have to get me this.'

'Yes, I did.' Daisy's smile said it all. 'I thought you needed something brand new to remind you of Paris.' Her eyes glistened in the bright lights of the ship's lounge. 'Now, if you don't mind, I think I'll skip tea and go for a wander instead. I haven't found my sea legs yet and I'm better when I'm moving. Will you be OK?'

Elsie hugged her. 'I'll be fine. Thank you so much.'

'You're welcome, lovely. See you later.'

Touched by her sister's thoughtful gift, Elsie ran her fingers across the printed flowers on the scarf, folding it carefully before putting it in her bag and opening her book again.

When Olly returned he motioned for her to carry on reading, which was a relief. Elsie relished the opportunity to be quiet, especially knowing that as soon as they landed she would have little chance for aloneness for the rest of the trip. Olly produced a newspaper and sat next to her, close enough to reassure her yet removed enough to give her space. Any concerns Elsie had prior to today were instantly laid to rest with this one simple action and she found herself enjoying the unspoken companionship.

Lucas always loved his Sunday papers – even from the very early days of their relationship – and his favourite thing to do was find a café, preferably with a view of the ocean, order a full English breakfast and relax while he and Elsie shared the various sections in comfortable silence. For the last three years of his life, his café of choice was the boardwalk café where Elsie had inadvertently embarked on her new role as a choirmistress – and that fact had been another reason for her confidence in accepting Woody's offer. Lucas found peace in moments like these, sneaking glances at Elsie over the top of the *Times 2* section that she pretended not to see, her heart thudding at the intimacy of it.

'I love Sundays. Me, you, ten-tonne weekend papers and copious gallons of tea by the sea – just about as near to perfection as you can get!'

Throughout their last year together, Elsie and Lucas had religiously observed their Sunday ritual, the need for normality increasing in importance as the months passed. Towards the end, when Lucas was too tired to make the journey out, Elsie would wake early to run to their local newsagent's and prepare breakfast to recreate the boardwalk café experience in the small bedroom of their home. The look of pure peace on his face when they sat reading together made all her effort worth it. When he died, one of the things Elsie missed the most was the simple act of sitting alongside someone without speaking, relaxing in the knowledge that words were unnecessary.

After an hour, Olly nudged her. 'Good book?'

If she was completely honest, Elsie's mind had been wandering more than absorbing the words on the pages, but to admit this would open an unwelcome line of explanation. 'Yes, thanks. Good paper?'

His smile was slow and easy. 'About as good as newspapers ever are. But it's good to rest when I have the long drive ahead of me.'

'Thanks so much for doing this, Olly. I'm glad you're here.'

'I'm glad I'm here, too.' His hand was warm and welcome when it took hers and brought it up to meet the gentle softness of his lips.

The ferry steamed into a grey, drizzly Dieppe harbour just after four p.m. and Olly drove the minibus through the rain out of the ferry terminal. The Sundaes were in high spirits, not least Woody, who had brought two bulging carrier bags from the duty-free shop and was already making progress through a large bottle of bourbon. They chatted loudly, occasionally breaking into song, as the minibus passed through distinctly Gallic towns and countryside.

'This gig is going to be *epic*,' Lewis said. 'I hope the French are ready for some Sundaes magic.'

'We'll be a vision,' Woody proclaimed, holding his dwindling bottle aloft, 'a glimpse of musical destiny, man!'

'You are such a freak.'

'A freak I may be, Sasha, but at least I'm free.'

'Oh, for heaven's sake, you two,' Sheila said, glaring at Woody and Sasha. 'I thought you'd buried the hatchet after our heart-to-heart?'

'I have no quarrel with her,' Woody replied blithely.

Sasha glowered back. 'I don't have a problem with him, Sheila. I'm just stating the obvious. The man is a freak of nature.'

'Let's sing again!' Graeme shouted, the after-effects of his liquid lunch on board the ferry beginning to reveal themselves. 'Gaga, on the downbeat . . .'

Daisy raised her eyes heavenwards as the choir launched into a rowdy rendition of their by now infamous Lady Gaga medley, the expansive fields of Northern France flying past the minibus windows. As the time passed, the fields gave way to woodland, low hills rising beyond as the road snaked its way through towns of whitewashed and redbrick buildings clustered along the road. Driving on, tall trees rose at either side of the carriageways, seemingly for miles as they began the long approach to Paris.

By half past six, the choir had quietened, with Woody, Aoife and Stan fast asleep in their seats and the others reading, listening to MP3 players or staring out of the windows. Olly pointed ahead to a road sign as they emerged from a long, orange-lit tunnel.

'Here we are, folks. Welcome to Paris.'

Elsie's heart bumped against her chest as they drove into the city she'd vowed she would never see. Despite her anxiety, she couldn't help but be captured by the elegant beauty of the architecture and the distinctively Gallic air of their surroundings. The previously cloudy skies that had met them in Dieppe were now clear and bright, the deepening blue overhead heralding the slow approach towards sunset. Golden sunlight bathed the tall white buildings rising on both sides of the tree-lined avenues with their corner cafés beneath, packed with people reading newspapers, smoking cigarettes and conversing over small cups of coffee and low glasses of red wine. Elsie looked back at the choir, who were all wide awake now and pressed up against the windows, drinking in the sights.

Although she had never been here before, Elsie began to recognise the architecture, streets, vehicles and pedestrians from the countless photos of Paris scenes in the guidebooks Lucas had lost himself in almost every day towards the end of his life. The trees proudly framing the streets, the crazy disorganised chaos of Parisian drivers, and even the pace the city's citizens walked at, was somehow uniquely French. All around her, Elsie experienced the beauty of the city, almost as if she were watching an impressionist painting coming to life: from the elegantly moulded rooflines of tall buildings, to muted colours of shop windows and the nonchalant style of the people who breezed along the streets. The minibus came to a halt at a road junction and Olly opened the driver's door window, bringing in a sudden rush of noise as a rich tang of cooking food wafted in from a corner bistro.

I wonder how Lucas would have reacted. Of course, he would have been like an overexcited child, pointing at everything he saw and hugging Elsie. He had been most animated during their last year together whenever he spoke about Paris. 'Montparnasse Cemetery – really that's where you should put me, amongst all the artists, composers and writers,' he would joke, showing her a plan of the famous French graveyard. 'Right on rue Anglais, somewhere between Alain Lorraine and our mate Jacques Offenbach.'

Offenbach's famous *Barcarolle* was the piece of music Lucas always chose to listen to when he was talking about how they would fulfil Number 51 – it was one of his favourite pieces of classical music despite, as he put it, 'being forced to murder the violin with it' while he was at school. As the lilting music played on a small CD player by their bed, Lucas would describe, in detail, how they would climb to the viewing platform on the second tier of the Eiffel Tower, kiss and shout '*C'est magnifique!*' over the city.

'We have to look towards the Montparnasse Tower over the Champ de Mars when we do it – gazing out over the most beautiful city in the world. And I know you think I'm being a sap for wanting to do this, but *just imagine* it, Els! Me and you and the whole of Paris: for that one moment the city will be ours. And then it doesn't matter what we face when we leave because we'll always have that moment.'

The image of them being there together had always been irresistible when Lucas described it. But to stand there – tomorrow – without him? Elsie closed her eyes as the excited chatter of The Sundaes continued behind her.

'This is it,' Olly said, as the minibus pulled into a car park. 'Welcome to Hotel Saint-Louis!'

The Sundaes piled out, stiff and aching from the journey. Grabbing their luggage, they walked to the front of the hotel and stopped in their tracks. Above them rose a seven-storey building, sweeping magnificently round the corner of a street, the clotted-cream stone of its frontage studded with elegant ironwork-topped, intricately carved stone balconies. Ivy and carefully clipped box trees framed the row of balconies on the second and fourth storeys, while arched windows peeked out from the grey tiled roofline on the highest floor. Everything about the building embodied Paris. It was exactly the kind of grand Parisian structure that Lucas loved so much and Elsie felt herself torn between admiration and an unfathomable sense of loss.

As they walked into Hotel Saint-Louis's reception, Elsie felt a gentle hand at the small of her back and turned to see her sister.

'We're here, then.'

'Yes, we are.'

'How do you feel?'

'A bit shaky. But I'm glad you're here.'

Daisy hugged her. 'Of course I'm here. This is going to be a very special weekend, you'll see.'

Danny grinned as he walked up to them. 'I'm so excited! Aoife has no idea.'

'That's great,' Elsie replied, the thought of Aoife's surprise tomorrow strengthening her resolve.

The smartly dressed lady at reception smiled politely when Elsie approached the desk.

'*Bonjour, j'ai une réservation pour six chambres, s'il vous plait? Je m'appelle Elsie Maynard.*'

'*Ah, oui. Bonjour,* Miss Maynard. Welcome to Paris. I trust you had a good journey?'

'Wonderful, thank you.'

'*Bon.* I will sign you in and assign your key cards and then Franc will take you to your rooms.'

'*Merci.*'

Woody stood next to Elsie as the receptionist arranged key cards on the desk. 'Bit nifty with the old *Français*, aren't you?'

'Not really. I just made sure I knew a couple of key phrases before we came here. My school French is decidedly rusty.'

'Been a few years since I set foot in the City of Light myself. There are some old haunts of mine I've a hankering to return to – for old times' sake, you understand.'

'Well, we're here till Sunday afternoon, so we should have plenty of time for everyone to do what they want.'

Woody clapped his hands together. 'Sweet!'

A gangly young man dressed in the smart hotel uniform arrived by the reception desk.

'*Bonjour.* I am Franc. Please follow me.'

Daisy and Elsie had agreed to share, so after the others had been taken to their accommodation, the sisters arrived at their room. Walking inside, Daisy whooped at the sight of the over-the-top interior, complete with Toulouse-Lautrec-inspired mural on the wall behind the twin headboards, sumptuous drapes at the tall windows and two small crystal chandeliers over the beds.

'It's so camp it's delicious!' she exclaimed, snapping images on her iPhone as she moved about the room. 'André would be horrified! I wish he could be here. It doesn't seem right being in his city without him.'

Elsie kicked off her shoes and sank into one of the beds. 'I know, hun.' She closed her eyes, succumbing to the weariness of her body, and slowly the sound of Daisy unpacking drifted into the distance.

A knock at the bedroom door suddenly roused Elsie and she was surprised to discover that she had slept for over an hour. Daisy opened the door and Olly entered.

'Your room is cool,' he grinned, flopping down on the bed beside Elsie.

'How's yours?' Elsie asked.

'Nice. I don't think I'll have any problems getting to sleep tonight, mind you. Although I am sharing with Woody, so anything's possible.'

Elsie laughed as she hugged her knees up to her chin. 'Don't worry, I think his trashing hotel room days are well and truly over.'

'Good.' He laughed when he saw Daisy's trusty travel kettle on the mahogany dressing table. 'Blimey, you two are organised, aren't you? I didn't think of bringing a kettle.'

'Ah, well, that's what happens when you travel as much as I do,' Daisy replied. 'It's rare to find one in Paris hotels. Fancy a cuppa?'

'Do I ever! I was on the brink of calling room service for a coffee.' He turned to Elsie. 'So, what's the plan for this evening?'

'I think we should find somewhere to eat and explore the streets a little. It'll be good for everybody to relax tonight: tomorrow is going to be pretty full on.'

Daisy's phone beeped and she laughed. 'I sent pictures of our room to André earlier and he's just replied: "Escape while you can!"'

'Well, that's what comes of living in five-star luxury

whenever he's away,' Elsie grinned. 'He misses out on delights like this room.'

'Indeed,' Daisy replied. 'Mind you, it would have been hilarious to see his reaction. Maybe next time we visit Paris I should book us in here!'

An hour later, The Sundaes gathered in the hotel lobby and set off into the warm evening to find a bistro recommended by the Hotel Saint-Louis's receptionist.

'How far is it?' Danny asked, as they walked along the wide pavement of the rue des Écoles, past antique bookshops, pavement restaurants and florist stores.

'Not far,' Elsie said. 'It's meant to be really good.'

'But we've passed three bistros already,' Sasha moaned. 'Why can't we go to one of those?'

Daisy groaned. 'Sasha, you're in Paris, one of the world's most beautiful cities. Can you not just relax for once and take it all in? We're heading for a gorgeous little bistro in an historic part of the city. Trust me, it'll be worth the walk.'

It was almost dark and lights blazed from every window of the tall, carved stone buildings along the Latin Quarter boulevards. Above them, the clear evening sky was dotted with tiny stars, making the avenue resemble a Van Gogh café scene.

From the rue des Écoles they turned onto the boulevard Saint-Michel, passing art bookshops, galleries and restaurants, the wonderful scent of food filling the air. The Boulevard was packed with students, Parisians and tourists taking advantage of the pleasant Friday evening, while laughter and loud conversation emitted from customers seated on the wicker seats of the street cafés under jewel-coloured awnings. Elsie felt the lustre of Paris by night wrapping itself around her heart and she began to relax.

312

In all the time she had spent thinking about this trip, she had never paused to consider how beautiful the city might be – and it was utterly breathtaking. Lucas would have loved this. He would have insisted that they walk arm-in-arm, pausing to peer into windows of the restaurants, patisseries, bookshops and bars, soaking up the unique atmosphere of the area. Now, she was walking streets he'd described in such breathless detail it was almost as if she had been here many times before.

But the best was yet to come. As they passed a very non-Parisian Gap store, the pavement suddenly widened out into a stunning cobbled square, framed by trees filled with tiny white lights. At its head rose a beautiful, classically styled building, floodlit in golden light from all sides, its dark dome crowned with a white stone cross reaching up into the night sky. Two rectangular carved stone fountains with rows of bubbling white water led from the building to a large octagonal ornamental fountain surrounding the tallest water column, and all were bathed in the white glow of streetlamps that edged the square, reflected on damp cobbles beneath. Restaurants and bars were all around, their chairs and tables spilling out into the square. Elsie's breath caught in her throat. Against the indigo-black night sky, the place de la Sorbonne glowed as bright as a sunlit day.

'What do you think?' Olly's arm was as warm as a blanket as it circled Elsie's shoulders. 'Is this place stunning or what?'

'It's amazing,' Elsie breathed, her eyes barely believing its utter beauty.

'And that,' Daisy said, pointing at the bright yellow awning of the largest bistro on the square, 'is where we're having dinner this evening.'

The Brasserie Monique was warm and buzzing with voices, music and movement. Brass lamps shone from every wall and beautiful coloured glass partitions separated three distinct dining areas. Laid-back jazz music drifted through the packed interior from a quartet playing near the bar, a saxophone solo eliciting a round of applause from Woody as a professionally nonchalant waiter led them to a row of tables pushed together at the back of the restaurant and handed out menus with practised detachment. Elsie sat between Woody and Olly, laughing at Woody's doomed attempts at eliciting a smile from the waiter. It was good to see The Sundaes relaxed and happy. Wine arrived first, followed half an hour later by their orders. The food was magnificent – creamy artichoke soup with crunchy slices of stone-baked baguette, steak that melted in the mouth, buttery oysters and crayfish served with rustic chunks of onion and roasted garlic and bowls of hot, salty *frites*.

When they had finished eating, Elsie tapped her glass with a spoon, bringing all eyes to her.

'Here we are, then,' she smiled. 'I'd just like to say a massive thank you to all of you, for the hard work you've put in for this concert. I'm so proud to be part of The Sundaes and I love how we've become such an awesome team, especially since Irene left us. I know we all wish she was here, but somehow I think she probably is.' The choir members nodded and Sheila sniffed loudly.

'I also think we owe Olly a round of applause for getting us here safely.'

The choir whooped and applauded, causing the diners around them to stare at the rowdy English party. Olly took a bow and grinned at Elsie.

'My pleasure. I'm looking forward to seeing the performance.'

'Make him sing!' Sasha called, followed by whistles from the choir.

Olly's face was a picture. 'No fear! The moment I opened my mouth we'd be drummed out of Paris for crimes against music.'

'He's here to drive and nothing else,' Daisy said, ducking as Olly threw a napkin at her.

'Do we need to have another rehearsal?' Lewis asked, wincing as Stan jabbed him in the ribs with his elbow.

Elsie hoped her expression was as relaxed as she wanted it to be. 'Actually, I think we've rehearsed enough. We ought to enjoy the city tonight after all the hard work we've put in. Added to that, we're booked on a sightseeing tour tomorrow before the concert, so we wouldn't have time to rehearse anyway. Don't worry, though. I believe we're ready.'

Aoife raised her hand. 'What will be seeing on the tour?'

Elsie grinned. 'Pretty much all the classic sights – the Champs-Elysées, Arc de Triomphe, Notre Dame, Luxembourg Gardens, the Eiffel Tower . . .' She paused as she saw Aoife's face light up. 'I thought it would be good for us to see the city without Olly having to navigate it.'

Olly laughed. 'I second that thought. I'm looking forward to being chauffeured!'

'While we're making speeches,' Woody said, lifting his glass, 'I vote we raise a toast to our esteemed choirmistress. This wonderful angel has made all of this happen. Without her we wouldn't be here. Elsie, babe, you're a top chick. To Elsie!'

All around the improvised group table glasses were raised and Elsie felt her face flushing red as The Sundaes cheered around her.

After their meal, Elsie and the choir walked slowly through the Latin Quarter, their spirits boosted by considerable amounts of wine. Everything Lucas had dreamed about this city seemed to be coming true: Paris was magical at night. The boulevards and small alleyways were framed with streetlights and music drifted on the night air, giving the city a timeless, otherworldly atmosphere. After a while, Elsie wasn't even aware of the constant hum of traffic, her mind ablaze with the sights, sounds and aromas of the City of Light.

Seeing Olly walking alone at the back of the group, Elsie drew back to walk with him.

'Hey you.'

'Hi.'

'You're not too tired for this, are you? I wasn't sure whether you needed an early night after driving us here.'

He smiled, his handsome features bathed in the soft glow of lights from the bars and bistros they were passing. For the first time since they arrived, Elsie was acutely aware of how attractive he was – the realisation shocking her. Maybe it was the magic of the city working its spell on her, or maybe she was only now understanding what Oliver Hogarth meant to her – and *could* mean to her in future . . .

'I'm fine. I like hanging out with you all. It's fun – and this city should be fun. I can sleep later.' He offered her his hand and, after contemplating it for a moment, she took it, the warmth of his skin on hers a perfect accompaniment to their progress through the Parisian streets. For this evening at least, thoughts of Lucas could wait: there would be more than enough time to consider everything tomorrow.

They followed the boulevard Saint-Michel until they reached the quai des Grands Augustins. Aoife squealed and grabbed Danny's hand.

'It's the Seine, Danny!'

Smiling at the young couple, Daisy turned to the others. 'Fancy a walk along the river?'

Olly squeezed Elsie's hand. 'Great! I've always wanted to see the Seine. Shall we?'

Heart thumping, Elsie nodded, following The Sundaes across the busy road and down a steep ramp onto the cobbled walkway alongside the river.

'Ooh, it's like *An American in Paris*!' exclaimed Sheila, linking arms with Graeme. 'Now you can be Gene Kelly and I'll be Leslie Caron.'

Graeme chuckled and launched into a bumbling waltz with her, singing 'Our Love Is Here to Stay' as Sheila giggled like a teenager and Daisy, Aoife, Danny and Lewis cheered.

Woody sniffed, 'That was my old mum's favourite film, you know. Classic Kelly magic.'

Shimmering with reflections of lights from the city streets surrounding it, the River Seine flowed hypnotically beside them as they walked past the barges and houseboats moored by the banks. Here by the riverside the buzz of Paris became a muted hum, the constant lap of water against the moored vessels mingling with the sounds of music and laughter from barges converted into bars. Elsie watched the group, enjoying the sight of their excitement at everything.

'Which bridge is this?' Lewis asked, when they neared the arched white stone structure.

'It's Pont Neuf,' Daisy informed him.

'I never thought I'd say this,' said Sasha, 'but that is one beautiful bridge.'

Woody let out a gravelly laugh. 'She's mellowing at last!'

'I am not. I just think the bridge is cool.'

Olly bent down to pick up a stone from the cobbled walkway and offered it to Elsie. 'Here. Make a wish.'

'What?'

317

'Hold the stone in your hand, make a wish and throw it into the Seine.'

Elsie stopped walking and stared at him. 'Are you serious?'

'Deadly.'

'Is this some strange French tradition you know about?'

Olly shrugged. 'Not that I'm aware of. Just do it because it's Paris and it's a gorgeous night and it's the kind of thing you do to remember memorable nights.' He sighed. 'I can tell you think I'm insane.'

Confused as she was by his suggestion, Elsie was touched by the reasoning behind it. Taking the stone, she held it in her palm, feeling its coolness against her skin. She closed her eyes and the image of the Eiffel Tower flashed into her mind. Silently, she made her wish. Opening her eyes again, she walked to the water's edge and threw the stone out over the dark waters. As it arced across the river it caught the light from Pont Neuf before disappearing into the depths of the Seine.

Olly was smiling when she turned back. 'Hope it comes true.'

Two hours later, the weary group arrived back in the softly lit lobby of the Hotel Saint-Louis. Daisy, who still managed to look flawless even considering the late hour, stretched her arms out over her head. 'Guys, it's late. We have to find breakfast and get over to the coach tour meeting point for eleven tomorrow morning, so can I suggest we call it a night?'

Agreeing, the choir members stood and said their good-nights, making their way up the marble staircase to their rooms. Woody yawned at the door to his and Olly's room, a few steps down the corridor from the room Elsie and Daisy were sharing.

'Anyone for a nightcap?'

Elsie laughed. 'You are a wonder, Mr Jensen. I don't know how you do it.'

'You never lose the skill,' he replied, tipping the brim of his Stetson over his eyes. 'Rock'n'roll, babe – it's in my *soul*.'

Olly said goodnight to Daisy as she headed down the corridor to the room before turning to Elsie.

'Big day tomorrow.'

'Yes indeed. I'll be glad when we've done it, to be honest. There's been so much planning to get here that it'll be good to enjoy the results. I do hope Aoife says yes.'

'She will. Paris isn't the kind of place that lets you get away with maybes.' His eyes fixed hers as she felt his arms encircling her. 'Maybe another *maybe* might become a yes here.' He looked away, embarrassed by his own words. 'Man, that was lame. I meant . . .'

'It's OK, I know.' Taking a deep breath, Elsie pushed the gathering questions within her away. 'Maybe it will.'

Daisy looked up as Elsie entered the room. 'Good night?'

'Daisy Heartsease Maynard, if ever there was a loaded question!'

Her sister was unrepentant as she unfolded her pyjama bottoms. 'It's not against the law or anything, is it?'

Elsie poked her tongue out and took off her shoes. 'Stop stirring and do something useful. Tea, no sugar, thanks.'

'Oh, *charming*! All I am is a refreshment machine to you . . .' She picked up the travel kettle and headed into the tiny en-suite bathroom to fill it. 'Have you spoken to Dad yet?'

'Yes, I phoned him when we arrived. He's missing us – although he mentioned that *Louise* was helping him?'

'Which Louise?'

319

'That's what I asked him. Apparently when he was being plastered in A&E he procured the phone number of one of the nurses who, it appears, lives three doors away. Turns out she's been popping in to keep him company most of the evenings this week.'

Daisy reappeared, agog at the news. 'You're joking?'

'Nope. He only felt brave enough to tell us when we were the other side of the Channel.'

She shook her head. 'Well I never, the sly old devil. Good for him. About time he looked out for himself instead of fussing over us three. I'm wondering if this weekend is going to turn out be surprising all round.'

'What is that supposed to mean?'

'It's *supposed* to mean exactly what you think.' She sat on the edge of Elsie's bed as the kettle began to boil. 'What's happening with Olly and you? Why are you still waiting?'

Feeling cornered, Elsie turned her eyes towards the view of the street from their window. 'I'm not . . . I'm just . . .'

'Scared, I know. But he's more than proved himself, hasn't he? And you like him – that's plain to see. I watched the two of you when we were walking by the Seine tonight. There's so much chemistry there and I really think he could make you happy, Els. I think he deserves you to give him a shot. And I know you have so much going on right now in that head of yours, but this was what you said you wanted, remember? It's what Lucas wanted for you . . .'

This was too much. 'Would you just stop hassling me? I can't think about that now – *here*. So please, I'm begging you, don't ask me. It's been a great evening and we're here to do something truly wonderful for two of our friends. Can that not be enough for tonight?'

Stunned by Elsie's response, Daisy took a step back. 'Hey, I'm sorry. I won't mention it again.'

320

They prepared for bed without speaking further, the aftermath of Elsie's words hanging like gunsmoke over their heads. Elsie immediately regretted her outburst, but weariness from the long day, together with the conflict of emotions still raging within, robbed her of sufficient words to repair the damage. After thirty minutes of enforced silence as they lay in their beds reading, Daisy lowered her book and held out her hand to Elsie.

'Sweets, I'm sorry. I just want you to be happy.'

Relieved by the break in hostilities, Elsie reached across to hold her hand. 'I know. I didn't mean to shout . . . It'll be better after tomorrow.'

'It will. Sleep well.' Daisy placed her book on the bedside table, switched off her light and settled down under the sheets.

'You too.' Elsie watched her sister for a long time, the buzz of nerves still claiming her insides. Then, her eyes heavy, she clicked the switch on her bedside light and fell into a deep slumber.

CHAPTER EIGHTEEN

A beginning and an end

'It's official: I'm moving to Paris for the breakfasts!' Danny exclaimed next morning, in between mouthfuls of freshly baked pastries. Having woken early and begun their journey towards the meeting point for their forthcoming coach tour, The Sundaes had discovered a small café a few blocks away and were now sitting around outside tables pushed together under the pale green awning, indulging in large helpings of baked goods and strong black coffee.

Elsie, her mind preoccupied by the day that lay ahead, let her attention drift from the group to the other customers. The café was like Paris personified this morning. A group of older men huddled over their cigarettes nearby, a single newspaper spread over the table unread, catching croissant crumbs and falling ash. At the next table, two women who could have been anything from early twenties to mid-forties (in Paris it was almost impossible to tell), were debating some emotive topic, shielding their eyes from the pale morning sun with expensive sunglasses. A young man, perhaps a student, was engrossed in an antiquated copy of Proust, his coffee virtually untouched as he avidly turned the pages. The interior of the café was decorated in dark wood, with bare, polished floorboards and simple tables and chairs surrounding a glass counter not unlike the one in Sundae & Cher. Gilt-framed sepia photographs of Old Paris were clustered together around the walls and small brass lamps illuminated the customers as they enjoyed their morning meals.

In typical French style, the only unwelcome detail of the café was the downright rude attitude of the staff. Even Daisy, a seasoned traveller and frequent visitor to the French capital with André over the past few years, appeared to be taken aback by their dismissive looks and complete absence of respect for the customers they purported to serve.

'I have to say, these *pains au raisin* are excellent,' Stan agreed, polishing off his third helping. 'I could eat more of those.'

Daisy caught the waiter's attention and he approached, his scowl as obvious as the long apron he wore at his waist.

'*Oui?*' he snarled.

She smiled and ordered another basket of pastries in flawless French. Observing her as if she were a bug floating in his soup, the waiter tutted and flounced off to the kitchen.

Olly watched him leave. 'All we've had since we arrived are surly looks and muttered insults. It's like they think they're doing us a favour letting us eat here.'

'Nah, man, it's always like this,' Woody said. 'Exactly the same attitude I got when I was last here with Hellfinger . . .'

Another waiter, who was clearing plates from the next table suddenly turned, eyes wide open and rushed forward to shake Woody's hand, much to everybody's shock. '*C'est* Hellfinger, *non?* "Hard Rockin' Summer"!'

'Oh *spare* us,' Sasha moaned, watching the waiter who

was now attempting to sing Woody's seminal hit, as the former frontman looked on amused.

The waiter stopped singing and gazed at Woody as though he had just received a year's wages as a tip. 'It is an honour to have you in this café!' He shook Woody's hand so enthusiastically that Woody had to raise his other hand to prevent his Stetson from toppling off his head. 'I am Henri Renard and I am in love with your music!'

Even Woody appeared to be a little taken aback by the waiter's recognition. 'Always good to meet a fan.'

'You are here for a rock concert, yeah? It is your comeback tour?'

'If only, Henri,' Woody replied. 'But this concert is a little more . . . *low key* . . . if you get my meaning.'

'*Ah oui.*' The waiter leaned closer and tapped the side of his nose. 'Hush-hush. *D'accord.*'

'We're a choir,' Sasha interjected, keen to burst Woody's bubble. 'Woody's one of our leaders.'

Woody shrugged. 'New direction, you know.'

'I see. So if you are a choir you must sing something!'

Sheila looked worried and Graeme dropped half of his croissant.

'It's a little early . . .' Stan began.

'This is not early for Paris,' Henri scanned their faces, then threw his hands in the air. 'OK. If you sing, I will lose your bill. We have a deal?'

This was all the justification anyone needed for an impromptu performance. Everyone turned to Elsie for direction.

'Right, ABBA/Deep Purple?'

Song choice thus agreed, Henri called the other members of staff into the café from the kitchen and a young waitress who had been serving at the counter joined them to listen as The Sundaes launched into their favourite mash-up medley, incurring the mystified looks of local customers whose quiet *petit déjeuners* were being rudely interrupted. Stan and Lewis did their best to air-guitar while still holding half-eaten croissants and Graeme had to pause for a swig of coffee when he was hit by an attack of hiccups, but the enthusiasm of the elated choir carried them through it. The performance ended with applause from the suddenly less threatening café staff.

'*Bravo!* It is magic!' Henri exclaimed. 'And as a reward, you shall have *crêpes*!'

Almost an hour later, The Sundaes said goodbye to the still-smiling unlikely Hellfinger fan and struggled out of the café.

'I am *never* eating again,' Daisy moaned. 'I can't remember when I ever ate that much for breakfast.'

Olly patted his stomach. 'Awesome *crêpes*, though. I should hang out with this choir more often if it means free food like that!'

Elsie smiled to herself as the others laughed and joked around her. The events of the morning so far had proved a pleasant distraction. Before leaving her hotel room, Elsie had taken a moment to prepare for what lay ahead – slipping a couple of important items into her coat pocket. Now, she was reassured by their presence as her fingers closed around them, while around her the good-natured banter of her friends filled the air.

What had begun as a sunny morning was fast becoming overcast and a strong breeze had sprung up, sending leaves skidding along the pavement from the autumnally-dressed trees above. Elsie could see Danny's concern as he looked up at the leaden sky and instantly her mind returned to the day Lucas proposed to her . . .

They say you can tell when a man is about to ask you to marry him because he begins to act very strangely. In Lucas' case this was certainly true. He and Elsie were providing backstage assistance for a friend who was putting on an amateur production of *Romeo and Juliet* in a community theatre space near the centre of town. It was the dress rehearsal and tempers were fraying as overwrought actors clashed with lighting and set technicians in the old converted flour warehouse. Elsie remembered suddenly becoming aware of Lucas fidgeting as they waited for the next scene change. He must have looked at his watch twenty times in the space of five minutes, huffing each time he did. This was the first oddity that she noticed – Lucas rarely wore a watch at all and his relaxed attitude to timekeeping was nigh on legendary amongst their families and friends. It was a standing joke that when anyone invited him anywhere they had to observe the real time for the event and 'Lucas-time', which was at least half an hour before his presence was actually required. Elsie had bought him a watch for their first anniversary of going out, but he chose to wear it only for special occasions and job interviews. Therefore seeing it in a setting that was neither of the above was remarkable.

When she questioned him about it, he had glared at her and stomped off into the backstage gloom, returning only as the scene change approached. As was usually the case when he fell into a mood, Elsie ignored it: she had learned from experience that it was far better to refuse to rise to his behaviour than attempt to challenge it. By the time the actors and technicians broke for refreshments, Lucas had practically worn a trench pacing the concrete floor behind the wooden flats of the set.

Irritated by her boyfriend's behaviour, Elsie had joined

the rest of the theatre group at the front of the stage for coffee and was in half a mind to abandon the rehearsal – and Lucas – altogether for the night. Just as she was describing his weirdness to a friend, a bright follow-spot blazed into life, causing the company to follow its beam to the set's Act II, Scene II balcony. Standing there, with a bunch of red roses clamped between his teeth, was Lucas. Elsie stared blankly at him, as the others cheered and wolf-whistled.

He had swung his legs over the edge of the wooden balcony – revealing that he had changed into a pair of bright red tights and green breeches, although his favourite black Doc Marten boots were still very much part of his outfit. Grasping the set's rope ladder disguised as an ivy length, he made a decidedly wobbly descent down the side of the painted flat, looking considerably more confident once he landed on the stage. Elsie, who was still coming to terms with the ridiculous spectacle of her boyfriend cavorting about in quasi-Elizabethan garb, could only watch in disbelief as he sashayed towards her. Dropping the bouquet to one hand in a single movement, he faced her in the middle of the stage.

'I have a little something for you,' he grinned, gyrating his velvet breeches as wolf-whistles sounded again.

'What are you *doing?*' she hissed under her breath, the avid scrutiny of the theatre company beginning to make her face burn.

'Fair maiden, wilt thou hearest my dearest plea-eth?'

'*Lucas . . .*'

And then, he dropped to one knee as everyone in the performance space drew a collective breath, producing a black velvet box from the pocket of his breeches and revealing a ring that Elsie now kept in the kitchen dresser with the small gold band that was to follow. They were both in tears before Elsie even accepted; by the time Lucas placed the ring on her finger most of their friends in the room had joined them, leading Lucas in later years to proclaim the scene as 'worthy of a *Dynasty* season finale' for its need of tissues.

That moment now seemed a lifetime away as Elsie and The Sundaes neared the starting point of the tour that would ultimately lead to another proposal.

'Elsie! Do you have the tickets?' Daisy called from the front of the group.

'Of course I have.' As she was speaking, a large white coach pulled up beside them and a slightly harassed-looking woman with a clipboard and a chignon so tight she could hardly move her face hurried out from the tour company's office.

'*Bonjour.* You are here for the tour, yes? *Bon.* Follow me, if you please.'

'More than happy to follow *her* anywhere,' Woody winked at Elsie as they climbed into the luxury coach. 'Bossy ladies make this rocker a happy man!'

'*Psst!* Elsie!' Lewis hissed, already midway down the coach seats.

Pausing to allow Sheila room to remove her coat and store it overhead, Elsie made her way over. 'What?'

'Just wanted to let you know, we all remembered to—' He pulled down the neck of his hoodie to reveal his choir T-shirt. 'When you give us the nod, we'll all strip off.'

'Easy, tiger,' Sasha giggled from the seat next to him. 'Bet you never realised you had such power, eh, Els?'

Enjoying the lightness of the atmosphere, Elsie played along. 'I *knew* there was a reason I came to Paris.'

Armed with cameras, the members of the choir sat on

the edge of their seats as the coach tour began. Yvette, the uptight tour guide, produced a microphone and launched into a suitably bored commentary on the history of the city, her eyes barely looking at the landmarks that drew the enthusiastic clicking of camera shutters from her guests. It amused Elsie to think of the poor woman delivering the same 'interesting, informative facts' (as the brochure had termed it) day in, day out.

'Do you think she books informative coach tours when she's on holiday?' Elsie whispered to Olly, who was sitting behind her and Daisy.

'Probably. Can you imagine her talking you through her holiday snaps, though? Purgatory personified!'

The night before, Elsie had anticipated the entire coach tour being a constant source of nostalgia for her, each new landmark summoning a bittersweet picture of Lucas as she ticked it off the mental list of places they had discussed. But today, with the jewels of Paris passing slowly by, she found the experience calming – as if each new sight was a further step in the journey she had been making over the last six and a half months.

'Do you think we'll see it soon?' Aoife asked Danny, as the coach drove round the Arc de Triomphe.

'Wait! I just saw it! I saw the Eiffel Tower!' Danny yelled and every head turned to look – apart from Elsie's.

As the coach continued round the landmark, the celebration soon faded as the buildings and trees of the roundabout obscured the tower from view. Elsie breathed a sigh – she knew the moment would soon be here but she was determined not to seek it until the last possible moment. Finally, when every other landmark in the tour itinerary had been visited, Yvette stood to address the party. 'And now, we arrive at our final destination – La Tour Eiffel!'

Applause reverberated through the air-conditioned body of the coach. With her heart crashing loud in her ears, Elsie raised her head.

And there it was – rising majestically from four enormous iron-girded feet and soaring proudly into the graphite sky. The scale of it was stunning, far greater than she had anticipated, the effect evident in the reverent hush that settled around her. Yvette continued her deadpan commentary as the coach slowly navigated the line of identical-looking vehicles, but nobody was listening. Instead, all eyes were trained on the magnificent structure, following its criss-crosses of wrought iron towards its summit.

'Isn't it awesome?'

Elsie wrenched her eyes away to look back at Olly. 'Yes, it is.'

'It's one of those landmarks everybody knows, but somehow that doesn't prepare you for actually seeing it. And I never thought an iron tower could be a thing of beauty – but this is.'

'So, *Mesdames et Messieurs*, I will escort you to the entrance where we will be admitted to the Tower. Please be aware that there may be a small wait for the elevators. We have approximately ninety minutes here. Please return to the coach no later than three p.m. Follow me, if you please.'

Crowds of tourists swarmed like picnic ants around the base of the famous landmark, with long queues stretching away from the entrances. Yvette led Elsie and The Sundaes past the lines of disgruntled visitors, checking them in at a different entrance. Leaving her behind at the gate, the group then gathered around Elsie and Woody.

'Do we queue for the lift or tackle the stairs?' Aoife asked.

Not wanting to give the game away at the last moment, Danny stared pointedly at Elsie. 'I don't mind either way.'

'Although,' Elsie interjected, right on cue, 'it might be worth waiting for the lift so we can have more time to enjoy the view up there.'

'You know, Els, I think that's a good point,' Danny agreed.

'I'm down with that,' Woody said. 'Besides, I don't do stairs. Not the ones you can see through, at any rate.'

Their decision made, they joined the queue for the elevator. Olly nudged Elsie's arm.

'This is it, then?'

Calling on every last ounce of resolve, Elsie smiled back. 'Here at last.'

Ten minutes later, they were ushered into the lift and Elsie felt her nerves lurching as the ascent to the second tier began. Through the windows Elsie could see the ground disappearing and the almost hypnotic passing of the Tower's ironwork frame as Paris fell away. When the elevator doors opened, a sharp blast of cold wind blew in. Slowly, everyone filed out, the surprising height of their new surroundings impressing each one as they instinctively gravitated towards the railings at the edge of the platform. The crowded tier was a mass of grinning people – posing for photographs and jostling for the best views. Danny exchanged looks with Elsie and led Aoife a little way away from the rest of the choir.

'How long is it going to be before he does the deed?' Sasha asked.

'I think they're going to look at the view for a bit,' Elsie replied. 'Everyone just stay within sight of Woody and me and we'll give the signal.'

Sheila shivered. 'Should I take my sweater off now? Only it is a little breezy up here.'

'No need for your striptease just yet, girl,' Woody leered. 'Leave that particular delight until I give you the eye, if you get me.'

Sheila reddened and gave a nervous laugh. Maintaining a line of sight to Elsie and Woody, each of The Sundaes moved away. Daisy and Olly pretended to pose for each other's photographs, Graeme and Stan moved to the railing to survey the view, while Lewis, Sasha and the other young members of the choir huddled together a little way from the edge. Woody pulled a tobacco pouch and rolling paper from his jacket pocket and began to roll a thin cigarette as he and Elsie maintained a respectful distance from Danny and Aoife, who were standing hand in hand by the view overlooking the Seine.

At least it's not the Champ de Mars side, Elsie thought, one of her anticipations about this moment now laid to rest, *and at least it's not sunset*. She could see the nervous glances of the choir and feel her anxiety building as the moment approached.

Ten minutes passed. Sasha and Lewis were getting jumpy, twice misinterpreting Woody's encouraging smile for the signal to reveal their choir T-shirts and having to scramble back into their top layer garments when they realised their mistake. Determined to stay calm, Elsie maintained her watchful vigil on the young couple now entwined by the wooden railings.

Hurry up, Danny. What are you waiting for?

And then, it happened. Danny looked over his shoulder at Elsie and gave a single, slow nod. Elsie smiled at Woody and they both made eye contact with the choir. Suddenly, every member was struggling out of coats and shrugging off sweaters and hoodies, the discarded top layers ultimately winding up with Olly, who was thus unanimously appointed Guardian of Surplus Garments. Proudly sporting their choir T-shirts, The Sundaes headed towards Woody and Elsie. As they drew level, Elsie hummed the opening note and counted them in.

They began to sing, ignoring the startled glances of the international visitors they passed. Nearing Danny and Aoife, the volume of their song increased, causing Aoife to turn round in surprise.

'Guys, what are you doing?' she laughed, seeking answers from her boyfriend only to discover that he, too, had abandoned his jacket to reveal his Sundaes T-shirt and was joining the singing.

As they reached the first chorus of 'Umbrella', The Sundaes began to clap in time and sway from side to side, much to the amusement of the gathering crowd around them. Some of the onlookers began to sing along, while others filmed the scene on their phones and camcorders. Delighted with the response and thrilled by the sheer temerity of the moment, the choir threw themselves wholeheartedly into the song. Elsie could feel tears building and when she looked across at the others she saw that she was not the only one. Knowing that they were doing it for Danny – and for Irene – only deepened the impact of this amazing moment.

At the right time, as the choir dropped their voices to hummed harmonies, Danny lowered himself slowly onto his right knee. A loud cheer broke out from the crowd surrounding them and Aoife's hands flew to her face as he opened a small blue box and held it up to her.

'Aoife Mary McVey, I love you. I can't imagine my life without you in it. So that's why we've come all this way – because I wanted to show you how much I love you. I love you with everything I am. Will you marry me?'

Reaching the end of their song, The Sundaes paused as the large crowd around them waited for Aoife's response.

'Yes!'

Bursting into tears, Danny kissed her and slipped the ring onto her outstretched hand, barely completing the task before the members of the choir launched themselves at the happy couple in an energetic dog-pile of congratulations, as the onlookers applauded and photographed the celebrations.

Laughing uncontrollably, The Sundaes pulled back, revealing a very dishevelled young couple wearing matching grins.

'Go, Danny boy!' Stan exclaimed, catching Danny in a headlock and ruffling his hair.

'I can't believe you all did this for me,' Aoife said, wiping tears from her face and hugging every member of the choir. 'So I take it the other concert isn't happening?'

'Hey, angel, there was only ever one show on our Paris tour,' Woody replied, 'and that was all for you.'

Danny hugged Elsie, Daisy and Woody in turn. 'Thank you. You were amazing.'

'Was it like you planned it, Danny?' Daisy asked.

'No. It was *better*.'

Aoife kissed Danny and beamed at the choir. 'And you knew my favourite song, too! That was so amazing. When did you get to practise it?'

'Whenever D-Boy took you home early,' Sasha grinned.

Aoife gave Danny a playful punch. 'I *wondered* why we kept having to give your mum lifts everywhere! Is there actually anything wrong with her car at all?'

Danny shook his head and yelped when Aoife hit him again. 'She was in on it, sorry! We needed a plausible excuse to take you away from choir practice.'

'No way!' A look of horror spread across Aoife's elfin

features. 'I've been saying the *worst* things about your mum the last few weeks! I'm going to have to apologise to her when we get home.'

'I think she'll forgive you. Especially now you've said yes to her son,' Elsie smiled.

'You're all awesome. And I now hate you all for being so sneaky!'

As The Sundaes gathered around, congratulating Danny and Aoife, Elsie pulled back a little, accepting her coat from Olly and putting it on to keep the chilly wind at bay.

'I think we should find a bar when the coach drops us back and start the celebrations,' Stan said, flushing with pride when his suggestion was deemed brilliant by all.

Olly noticed that Elsie was hanging back. 'Are you coming, Els?'

Her joy giving way to deep stillness as she contemplated what lay ahead, Elsie declined. 'You go on. I'll be down soon.'

'You sure? I don't mind staying with you if you want to look around a bit more?'

'I'm sure.' For a horrible moment, Elsie could see Olly insisting on accompanying her, which would mean having to explain it all to him to get him to leave. But Olly merely shrugged and rejoined the others, leaving Elsie alone amid the crowd.

The strong breeze had become great gusts that swirled around the heads of the visitors, whistling through the wrought-iron latticework as Elsie neared the steps to the raised viewing platform. She could feel her limbs shaking as she reached into her coat pocket and pulled out her iPod – the first item she had hidden from the others. Placing the earphones in her ears, she selected the track she had uploaded back in Brighton, the night before the journey to Paris. At the time she hadn't been able to bring herself to listen to it and now, as she pressed Play and grasped the handrail to ascend the steps to the viewing platform, the opening bars of *Barcarolle* caused her heart to shatter.

It was as if time itself began to slow as she approached the side overlooking the Champ de Mars, with Paris stretching away towards Montparnasse and beyond. The darkening sky had caused some of the lights far below to flicker into life and, as Elsie reached the railing, the tiny pinpricks of light became sunbursts through her tears. Suddenly, she was aware of no one around her – just her trembling fingers as they rested on the cold polished wood of the railing and the splendour of Paris beneath her feet. *Barcarolle* lilted and swelled in her ears as she pulled the second item from her pocket.

The passport photo had been taken six months after they were married, Lucas pretending he needed one for a job application before dragging Elsie into the booth just as the first picture was taken. They were laughing, their eyes full of love, the frozen moment capturing the very essence of a young couple with their whole lives together ahead of them, long before the cruel shadow of cancer fell. It was how Elsie always wanted to remember them – so much in love that everything else was meaningless. Gazing at their smiles now, as strong gusts of wind pressed her body against the railing, she was arrested once again by the force of love his gorgeous face evoked in her heart. He had been the love of her life, the one she intended to grow old with, the perfect complement to her personality – *her* Lucas.

Her face was stinging where the cold wind met the trails of salt water that ran down her cheeks as the moment she had dreaded arrived. *Barcarolle* was building to its crescendo and Lucas was waiting for her to fulfil her promise . . .

The very last words he had spoken had been about this moment. His breathing laboured, he had moved his lips without sound for several minutes, his tired eyes relentless in their hold of hers. Sensing his urgency, Elsie had leaned closer, pressing her face to his to hear what he was trying to say.

'I love you,' he whispered, each word an achievement as he fought for control of the body that was deserting him.

'I love you, too. Don't leave me.'

'I love you,' he said again, his eyes glistening. '*C'est magnifique*, Elsie . . . *Say it* . . .'

Pain and emotion choking her voice, she had cupped his face in her hands and looked deep into his eyes for the last time. '*C'est magnifique*, Lucas.'

He had closed his eyes and tilted his chin a little, his fingers finding her cheek as their lips met. Elsie felt the sigh leaving his body and the heaviness of his hand against her face, her muffled cry causing her father and sisters to rush to her side as his family broke down around the small hospital room . . .

It was time. Time to complete The List that had bound her to Lucas for so long. She had accomplished everything he asked – and now he was urging her to move into whatever life had planned. This was what he wanted – and in that moment it was as if his presence with her was more tangible than at any other time since his death.

Gazing at the photograph in her hands, Elsie sobbed as the impending parting bore down on her as it had in his hospital room two years ago. She stroked the contour of his face with numbing fingers and lifted it to her lips. Then, throwing back her head, with the spread of Paris as her witness, she shouted:

'*C'est magnifique*, Lucas! *C'est magnifique!*'

Opening her raised hand, she let go of the photograph as the music drew to a close, watching as the wind caught the small square and carried it up into the dark grey sky and then out towards the city Lucas had finally seen through Elsie's eyes. And as it disappeared from view, swirling on the air currents rising around the Eiffel Tower, Elsie felt a sudden lightness dawning inside, as if the responsibility of his wishes had been lifted from her soul.

'I'm trusting you, Elsie Maynard, to live your life for every second it's yours. I won't accept anything but the best for you. Promise me you won't hold back.'

I won't hold back, Elsie promised herself, wiping her eyes and taking one last look across the city before making her way towards the lift entrance. Tired but strangely comforted, she entered the elevator and leant against its side as it made its descent to her waiting friends.

CHAPTER NINETEEN

You ain't seen nothing yet . . .

After more than one celebratory drink to toast the happy couple The Sundaes dispersed into the city to pursue their own agendas for the rest of the afternoon. Woody went off in search of his old haunts, while Sasha, Sheila and Lewis had shopping in mind. Stan and Graeme headed off in search of souvenirs for their families, Danny and Aoife went for a romantic stroll through the Latin Quarter's narrow streets and Daisy and Olly took the Metro to the Louvre. Leaving them at the Metro station, Elsie caught a Metro train in the opposite direction to return to the hotel. Despite the train being packed, she felt cocooned by her thoughts from the noise, the jostling bodies and the strong scent of stale cigarettes. She was more than grateful for the solitude, the need for her own stillness and silence suddenly great.

Leaving the Metro station, she booked a table for the choir at a restaurant on the nearby rue de Médicis for later that evening and walked the three blocks back towards the hotel, enjoying the sights of the Montparnasse streets. Elegant honey-stone buildings surrounded her, each one beautifully carved, proudly displaying the *Tricolore*. At the end of almost every block of buildings were tiny parks fringed with iron railings and framed by trees. Clipped bay trees planted in dark blue ceramic planters were arranged outside each restaurant, as lines of bicycles formed two-wheeled guards of honour at the side of the roads. Above her head, window boxes filled with ivy and red pelargoniums graced every window and it felt as if the whole of the city was marking the significance of this day.

When she arrived at the Hotel Saint-Louis, Elsie climbed two flights of the winding, ornate iron-railed staircase to her room. The stillness of her surroundings was a blessed relief to the noise and activity of her day, her mind now at rest and more than ready to relax. Discarding her shoes, she sank her toes into the lush pile of the bedroom carpet and wandered into the bathroom to run a bath. While the tub was filling, she switched on the television to find a black and white French film for background noise and made herself a cup of tea.

She didn't quite know how she would feel after her visit to the Eiffel Tower, but the calmness in her soul was an unexpected discovery. Since her fulfilment of The List she sensed that walls had been broken down, even though as yet she was unsure how this would be revealed in the life that lay ahead of her. For now, it felt as if her heart had been revealed like soft new skin after a wound heals – fragile but somehow infinitely better than before.

After a long bath, she dried herself and pulled on a pair of skinny jeans with a long-sleeved top and the new scarf that Daisy had given her. As she lay on her bed watching the elegant French cast of the 1940s movie, she drifted away into a blissfully peaceful sleep.

Several hours later, she stirred just as Daisy opened the door, sitting up in bed to greet her sister.

'How was the Louvre?'

'Awesome. I've visited so many times over the years but it never ceases to amaze me. The simple lines, the marriage of glass and stone – beautifully stark yet utterly compelling, the ultimate showcase for art.' Laughing at her own gushing summation, Daisy flopped down on her bed, kicked off her shoes and leaned down to massage her toes. 'But for all its beauty this city *kills* your feet. I knew I should have worn trainers today.'

'Ah, the price of maintaining your fashion icon status,' Elsie grinned, leaving her bed to refill the kettle.

'Tell me about it. I took a tonne of photos to show you. You'd love it. I'm going to show them to André, too.' She sighed and looked at the ceiling. 'I love Paris, but it's so strange being in André's home city without him. I tried calling him all afternoon, but his phone was constantly busy. Luckily Olly didn't seem to mind me checking my mobile like a lunatic every five minutes. He's a lovely bloke, Els. We had a real giggle this afternoon.' She smiled at her sister. 'You look great, by the way. I knew that scarf would be perfect on you. Did you manage to catch up on some sleep?'

'Yes. And I had a bath. I feel so much better.'

'About being here?'

'About everything. It was so important for me to go to the Tower today.'

Daisy's eyes misted over. 'I know, petal. And did you – you know – do what you had to up there after we left?'

Elsie nodded and Daisy rose to give her a long hug. 'It's done.'

'And now you can move on?'

'Now I can *carry on* moving on,' Elsie smiled. 'Oh blimey, listen to me: I sound like a self-help book.'

Daisy placed her hands on Elsie's shoulders. 'You know what we need, my lovely?'

'What?'

'Wine. And copious amounts of the stuff. We have another whole day and night in this gorgeous city and nothing else we have to do. So tonight we enjoy refined dining, fabulous company and *lots* of luscious *vin*.'

Elsie felt her heart lifting at the thought. 'Now *that* is the best suggestion I've heard all weekend.'

Spirits were high when The Sundaes reconvened in the darkly welcoming bar of Bistro L'Artiste on rue de Médicis at eight p.m. Tiny lights framed the trees in the park opposite the restaurant and a smiling accordion player strolled slowly back and forth on the pavement outside. Aoife was proudly displaying the small solitaire diamond ring to anyone who would look and Danny was in grave danger of pulling muscles in his face from smiling. Sasha had already taken a shine to the barman efficiently serving drinks, doing her best to engage him in pigeon-French conversation. Woody was yet to arrive and speculation as to his current whereabouts was rife amongst the choir.

'I reckon he's visiting a former groupie from his Hellfinger days,' Lewis grinned.

Olly smiled. 'Or his French children, who he's secretly been supporting for years.' Seeing Elsie's despairing expression, he held up his hands. 'What? You know what they say about these ageing rock stars – I'd lay odds on there being several love-children with Jensen blood across the world.'

'He's probably in some seedy bar,' Daisy said, enjoying the opportunity to take part in the light-hearted attack on Woody in his absence. 'Reminiscing about old times with a barman who used to be a roadie.'

342

'That sounds like the kind of tragic thing he would do,' Sasha laughed. 'Anyway, forget the ageing rock freak. Let's enjoy this wine!'

By nine p.m. they were seated at their table in the packed restaurant but Woody had still not surfaced and everyone was complaining of hunger. Making an executive decision, Elsie decided to go ahead with the meal, sending Woody a text to let him know.

The meal was a bit of an extravagance but a wonderful way to celebrate the events of the day. Provençale chicken, roasted duck, melt-in-the-mouth rainbow trout and bowls of *moules marinière* elicited squeals of delight from The Sundaes as the wine flowed. Elsie loved the ambiance of L'Artiste and the effect it was having on the choir – the dark wood meeting subdued lighting from candles and wall lamps, while the buzz of conversation mingled with the music floating around the red gingham-covered tables. As beautifully crafted *crème brûlée*, *tarte tatin* and *îles flottantes* were served, she leaned across to Daisy.

'You were absolutely right, Dais. Tonight is fantastic.'

'Which just goes to prove you should always trust your eldest sister.'

'Did I mention your eldest sister almost walked my poor feet off?' Olly interjected.

'I did not!'

'Seriously, Els, she is the fastest walker I've ever met. We were doing *circuits* of the Louvre, like some kind of fine art-themed gym class.'

Daisy giggled and for the first time Elsie noticed how fond of Olly her sister appeared to be. Their afternoon together had clearly brought them closer and, just like Jim, Daisy was relaxed in his company. 'The thing is, Els, I don't reckon Olly is as fit as he likes to think he is. I haven't been to the gym for months but I was leaving him for *dust*.'

Olly feigned offence, folding his arms and sticking out his chin. 'You see what she's like?'

'I think that from now on I ought to make sure I always accompany you,' Elsie smiled, enjoying the thrill of her own flirtatiousness and the effect it had on Olly's expression.

'I think maybe you should,' he replied, returning her smile. 'Just for my own protection, of course.'

'Consider myself your personal bodyguard.'

'I will. And, if I may say so, *what* a body to be guarded by.'

'Oliver Hogarth, you incorrigible flirt!'

Olly's smile sparkled with mischief. 'Admit it, you wouldn't have it any other way.'

Feeling a thrill ricocheting to her toes, Elsie grinned back. 'Absolutely.'

By ten p.m., Elsie was in the middle of settling the evening's bill when her mobile began to ring. Leaving Daisy to assume bill-paying duties, Elsie hurried out to the lobby.

'Hello?'

'A-a-angel.'

'Woody? Where are you? You've missed dinner.'

'Yeah, I know, babe. I'm starving.'

Elsie sighed. 'Right, we're at the rue de Médicis – I put the address on one of the ten texts I sent you. Just make your way back here and we can try to find you food nearby. Failing that, we could always order something from room service back at the hotel, just for tonight.'

'Sweet. *Slight* complication with that plan, though.'

'What? You've been gone for ages, Woody. How hard can it be to get here?' A thought occurred to her and she instinctively lowered her voice, even though none of the

344

customers at the pavement tables were likely to eavesdrop. 'Have you run out of money?'

'No, angel.'

'OK. So what's the problem? Why can't you get here?'

She could hear a long, nicotine-gravelled sigh on the other end of the call.

'Because I'm in jail, babe.'

The next thirty minutes were a blur of frenzied activity, as Elsie, Daisy and Olly drove the minibus around the streets of Paris, which all appeared to have become identical, in search of the police station where Woody was being held. Stan and Graeme had been left in charge at the hotel, gathering the choir together in their room to wait for news, the revelation leaving all of them in shock.

'What do you think it is?' Daisy asked as Olly attempted to follow the directions quickly scribbled on a sheet of Hotel Saint-Louis notepaper by the helpful receptionist.

Elsie stared at the road ahead, her mind swimming. 'I don't know. I'm just hoping it's some language-barrier misunderstanding thing that we can clear up quickly. Although my GCSE French didn't cover dealing with the Parisian police force.'

'Why don't you let me do the talking?' Daisy said. 'I might not have every word but I'm pretty certain I can cobble the right sentences together.'

'There!' Olly pointed at a large building ahead. 'I think that's it. I'll drop you guys off and try and park somewhere.'

Elsie and Daisy hurried from the minibus into the police station. Daisy waited by the main desk but it was several minutes before anyone came over. Finally, an unsmiling hulk of a policeman approached. Elsie stood by, helpless, as Daisy engaged in quiet, fast French conversation, the desk sergeant making occasional notes as they spoke. After a couple of minutes, he gave a nod and disappeared.

'Well?'

Daisy's face said it all. 'It's not good. Woody was arrested as part of a major drugs raid on a bar on the Left Bank.'

'What? But how . . .?'

'The sergeant doesn't know the details. He's gone to check them out.'

Elsie couldn't believe what she was hearing. 'Has Woody been charged?'

'He didn't seem to think so.'

'Right.' A million and one thoughts raced through Elsie's mind. 'What do we do in this situation? Should we try to find a lawyer, or call the British Consulate, or what?'

Daisy placed her hand on Elsie's arm. 'Calm down. He was only arrested an hour ago, so they're probably still processing him. Let's just wait to see what they tell us before we start to panic.'

Ten minutes later, the desk sergeant returned and spoke to Daisy. Turning to Elsie, she shrugged. 'He said the ten people they arrested all have to be questioned, so we should be prepared for a wait. I asked him about the British Consulate and he said they would be notified in due course.'

'Anything else?'

'He told me the coffee in the machine isn't great but it's cheap. And he said my French was very good.'

Elsie had to smile at that one. 'Oh well, Woody may be facing prosecution, but at least you know your French is passable.'

Daisy grinned. 'I told him I was dating a Frenchman. I think he approved.'

Olly arrived soon after, a little flustered after driving around to find a suitable space. 'It'll be a mistake,' he assured them. 'Woody might be a little eccentric but he's not an idiot.'

Right at that moment, Elsie begged to differ. She was angry with Woody – whether he was in the wrong place at the wrong time or something worse, he *should have* been at the bistro with the choir he was partially responsible for, not being hauled into a police station in the middle of Paris.

Hours passed. The desk sergeant ended his shift and handed over to another equally bulky officer who wasn't impressed by anything and seemed happier to ignore the three English visitors who were drinking sub-standard coffee and suffering the overzealous French air-conditioning in the waiting area into the early hours of the morning. Elsie made several phone calls to the waiting choir to keep them updated, eventually telling everyone to go to bed as the realisation that she wouldn't see her own tonight dawned upon her. People came and went – tramps and bloodied youths, efficient-looking duty lawyers and a succession of shady characters were shuffled through the security doors by disinterested policemen.

Just before four a.m., a man in his forties wearing a suit hurried in and spoke in flawless French to the desk sergeant, who gave a disgruntled nod in the direction of Elsie, Daisy and Olly. The man approached them with a brief smile.

'You're here for Walter Jensen?'

Elsie and Daisy exchanged glances at the revelation of Woody's Christian name. 'Yes – he goes by the name of Woody,' Elsie said.

'Right. I'm Charles Ross, from the British Consulate. The police informed me of Mr Jensen's arrest.'

'Thank you so much for coming,' Elsie replied, shaking his hand. 'We don't know what's happening.'

'I understand. What I can do is see Mr Jensen and try

to establish the current situation regarding his arrest. If it looks likely that they will charge him, I can advise you of our list of suitable lawyers and translators. But I shouldn't worry about that yet. Let me talk to the police and to Mr Jensen and I'll let you know what I discover.'

They watched as Charles was admitted into the body of the police station. Olly stretched and yawned and Daisy braved another mud-like coffee from the coffee machine.

'Why don't you go back to the hotel?' Elsie asked Olly. 'There's no need for all of us to be here.'

He stared at her. 'Do you want me to leave?'

'No, that's not what I'm saying. You look shattered and I don't know how long we're going to have to wait.'

'I'm going to stay here until the Consulate bloke tells us what's happening. It might be that we have to leave him here anyway and in that case I want to make sure that you and Daisy can get back to the hotel.'

Elsie rubbed her eyes, her need for sleep weighing heavily. 'OK. I didn't mean to suggest that we didn't need you, Ol.'

'I know. Fancy a hug?'

Gratefully, Elsie accepted, leaning her head against the soothing heat of his chest as his arms folded round her. She remained there, losing track of time – so much so that when Charles returned almost an hour later, it was Olly's gentle shaking of her shoulders that made her realise she'd fallen asleep in his arms. Blinking the sleep away in the harsh striplight of the waiting area, she sat upright and tried her best to focus on what Charles was saying.

'Mr Jensen has been questioned for an hour and I'm afraid he was less than co-operative, which has not helped his case at all. However, I have since spoken with him and he has given me the name of a legal firm in England who will represent him. I secured a phone call for him and I understand a solicitor is travelling to Paris this morning. Mr Jensen has still not been formally charged, but this is usual in cases such as these. They are holding him in the cells tonight and will recommence questioning at nine a.m. when his legal representative arrives.'

'Did you get any idea of what is likely to happen to him?' Daisy asked.

'Not really. We're limited in terms of what we can do, I'm afraid. But the police have assured me that he will be treated fairly and that they will afford him every opportunity to explain his actions, provided he curbs his temper and language – both of which, I have to say, were not in check when I arrived. Naturally, I have advised him to co-operate fully. Beyond that, there isn't much I can do. He sends his sincere apologies to you all, by the way. I think the thought of you waiting for him has done much to suppress his anger.'

'Well, at least that's something,' Elsie said. 'Thank you for your help, Charles.'

'My pleasure. I would advise you all to return to your hotel for now – the police don't expect to be making a decision either way before midday, so there really is little point in waiting for hours. I wish you all the best.'

Daisy turned to Elsie and Olly after Charles had left. 'Right, you heard the man: let's go back to the hotel.'

Elsie hated leaving Woody at the police station, but a part of her argued that a night in the cells might just persuade him to be willing to work with the police in the morning. None of them spoke much on the journey back to Montparnasse, weariness claiming their full attention. It was five-thirty by the time they wandered back into the reception lobby, heading straight to their rooms without conversation to fall into bed.

Next morning, The Sundaes gathered in a café across the street from Hotel Saint-Louis to discover the details of Woody's arrest. Strong coffee was all that anyone could stomach this morning – the basket of pastries they had ordered lay untouched in the middle of the table.

'Man, I know he's a freak but I never thought he'd be into that kind of dodgy stuff,' Sasha said, shaking her head.

'He isn't into any of it,' Elsie returned, the four hours of sleep she had managed to steal on her return barely enough to allow her to function this morning. 'I'm convinced it's a mistake.'

'All the same, what do we know about him, really?' Stan asked, as several of the choir murmured their agreement. 'We know he lived the rock'n'roll lifestyle before – what's to say he doesn't still indulge in the odd illegal substance? You've heard some of the stuff he comes out with. It makes sense when you look at it.'

Danny nodded. 'And we have a ferry to catch tomorrow. What happens if they want to keep him here and we all have to surrender our passports?'

'It won't come to that, Danny.'

'With respect, Ol, how do you know?'

Sasha raised her hand. 'I vote we leave him here.'

Elsie could hardly believe what she was hearing. 'Sasha! That's a dreadful thing to say.'

'Is it? Well, I'm sorry, but he showed us no consideration yesterday, did he? It was Danny and Aoife's day and last night should have been about *them*. If he has so little respect for us, why should we hang around for him?'

Everyone began to talk then, some agreeing with Elsie but most voicing support for Sasha's argument. Finally, Elsie gave a loud shout and all fell silent.

'OK, listen everyone. Woody is one of us – whether he

remembered that fact last night or not. He's partly the reason we exist as a choir and he's worked hard too to get our performance ready for what we did yesterday. He hasn't been arrested on purpose and while I agree that he is an idiot for getting caught up in the middle of a drugs raid, the fact remains that we are a team. And teams don't just break apart at the first sign of trouble.' She let out a sigh. 'I don't like this any more than you do. But at least we have today and tonight in Paris. Our ferry ticket is an open return, so we won't be rushing back to Dieppe in the morning. Woody's solicitor is coming today and if the worst comes to the worst and he has to stay in France we'll head home and help where we can from England. Daisy, Olly and I are going back to the police station in a while, so I suggest the rest of you make the most of your last day here. I'll let you know if we have any news. There's no point in all of us hanging around.'

Touched by her words, The Sundaes agreed and they left the café to go their separate ways. Making sure they had water and food with them this time, Elsie, Daisy and Olly climbed into the minibus and retraced their steps from last night. In the daylight, the roads were much more distinctive, brought alive by the bustling businesses open along the route. Olly dropped the sisters outside the police station once again.

'Look on the bright side,' Elsie said to Daisy as they walked through the front doors, 'at least we won't have to drink that awful coffee again.'

'Thank heaven for small mercies,' Daisy grinned, walking up to the desk and blessing a different officer with her now confirmed excellent French.

'What did they say?' Elsie asked when Daisy rejoined her in the small waiting area.

'His lawyer is in with him now and should be able to advise us soon.'

Elsie pulled her book from her handbag. 'Might as well settle in for a few hours then, eh?'

Daisy retrieved a copy of French *Vogue* from her own bag and smiled back. 'No harm in being prepared.'

Three chapters of Elsie's book, half of French *Vogue* and two bottles of water later, they were summoned by a whistle from the desk sergeant. The door they had seen Charles disappearing through hours before opened and Woody's solicitor walked through to greet them.

'Well, this is an interesting place to meet, isn't it, ladies?'

Elsie stared in disbelief as Torin kissed Daisy's cheek. *How on earth . . .?* 'You're Woody's lawyer?' she repeated, as if somehow saying it out loud would disprove the fact. It didn't. Torin Stewart was there, in a central Paris police station, looking like the only hope for Woody's release.

'Technically, no. But my father is good friends with Woody's former manager, so when I heard of his arrest I was only too happy to represent him.' He leaned towards Elsie to kiss her cheek but she stepped back. Confused, he did the same, his green eyes full of questions. 'I take it you had a long wait last night?'

'We did. How is he?'

'As well as can be expected. They've asked him a lot of questions, many – it has to be said – that are irrelevant to the case. I'm glad I was here to advise, or else his frustrations could have caused considerable problems.' He smiled at Elsie despite her not returning it. 'Try not to worry.'

'Easier said than done.'

'So, what happens now?' Daisy asked, as Olly walked into the waiting area and joined them on the uncomfortable red plastic seats.

'Sorry, only just got parked,' he said, planting a kiss on Elsie's head.

352

The merest flicker passed across Torin's expression. 'They're still interviewing the other suspects, so they won't be talking to Woody again for at least an hour. Oliver,' he extended his hand, which was politely received.

'Torin. Never expected to see you here.'

'It's a bit of a shock to be here, if I'm honest,' he replied. 'How about we try to find a bar or a restaurant nearby and I can talk you through the details? I haven't had a decent coffee since I arrived this morning.'

Walking out into bright October sunshine, they found a small, cheerfully painted café one block away amid a row of second-hand art book stores. They ordered coffee and bowls of bubbling *tartiflette* and to Elsie's surprise she discovered that she possessed quite a hunger. As they ate and drank, Torin explained the situation in full, both from the police standpoint and Woody's version of events. It transpired that Woody had travelled to the Left Bank to a bar he had visited when Hellfinger toured the French capital in 1988, remembering the wild night he had spent there with his bandmates in their last summer before their friendship soured. In its Eighties heyday, the bar had been *the* venue of choice for the hip set in Paris but now, unbeknownst to Woody, it had deteriorated into a seedy den of dodgy characters and questionable trade.

'From what I can work out, Woody was just unlucky with his timing. The French drugs squad have been carrying out surveillance on the place for the past two years and last night was to be their big raid. They arrested pretty much everyone in the club, hence the considerable time they spent interviewing overnight and this morning. Woody said he had just arrived when the police burst in and all hell broke loose.'

'Do you think the police believe him?' Elsie asked.

'I think they're maybe beginning to,' Torin replied, 'but he's not out of danger yet. He was very agitated when they brought him in and then spent the best part of three hours denouncing everything in France. This did nothing to endear himself to them, as you can imagine.'

Daisy groaned. 'Idiot! I don't even play the anti-French card when I'm arguing with André. Some things are sacrosanct to the French – their national pride is one of them.'

'So, what's the plan?' Olly asked.

'I'll argue for a case of mistaken identity,' Torin replied. 'They have very little evidence to suggest otherwise, so it'll come down to how determined they are to hold a grudge against him.'

Olly looked at Daisy and Elsie. 'Then should we wait? I mean I'm sure all of us are willing, but if we can't be of any practical use then perhaps we should consider catching up on our sleep back at the hotel before the journey home tomorrow? I don't know how long I can leave the minibus where I've parked it – the restrictions are a bit contradictory around here. We don't need to be slapped with a parking fine on top of everything else.'

Torin shrugged. 'I see no reason for you all to stay. It could well be a couple more hours before I can even get back in to restart negotiations.'

Daisy agreed. 'Amen to that. I'm so tired I can hardly think straight. I want a shower and then bed. You look tired too, Els.'

Despite her weariness, Elsie was reluctant to leave until she knew for sure whether Woody would be travelling back with them tomorrow or not. She had meant what she'd said to The Sundaes over breakfast: Woody was part of the team and she wasn't ready to abandon him when he needed her support.

'I think I should stay,' she said.

Olly shook his head. 'You heard what Torin said, there's no need.'

Elsie put her hand on his arm. 'To be honest, I don't think I'd rest much if I went back to the hotel now. I put this trip together: it's up to me to make sure everyone comes home safely.'

'Then I'm staying,' Olly stated resolutely. Elsie could see the dark circles forming beneath his eyes as he fought against his weariness.

'Ol, you have a long drive back for us tomorrow. You need to make sure you're fully rested.' She kissed his cheek. 'I'll just stay until I know what's going on, then I'll catch the Metro back.'

Still unsure, he frowned at her. 'Promise?'

'I promise.'

He cast a cursory glance at Torin, then back at Elsie. 'Text me when you know anything, OK?'

She smiled at his concern. 'Of course I will.'

At the door of the café, Olly grabbed her hand and walked her a little way from Daisy and Torin. 'I don't like leaving you with him. He's a wind-up merchant and you don't need any more stress.'

'Seriously, I can handle Torin Stewart,' she assured him. 'I just want to make sure Woody's all right.'

'Fine.'

'Thank you for worrying about me. It's nice.'

His eyes lit up. 'It is?'

She nodded. 'Yes.'

'I want to make you feel cared for all the time,' he whispered, gently pulling her close to him. 'And I know we're taking it slowly and you've had things you wanted to deal with, but I just want you to know that you only have to say the word and . . . I'll *be* there.'

His words sent tingles over her skin. 'You will?'

He bent his head and planted a long, slow kiss on her cheek, his lips so close to hers that she almost forgot to breathe. 'Like a shot.'

As he and Daisy said goodbye and walked away, Elsie took a deep breath and turned back towards Torin.

'Fancy another coffee while we're waiting?' he asked, his smile annoyingly exultant. 'Not that I think it's a patch on Sundae & Cher's, of course.'

Irritation building within her, Elsie faced him. 'Let's just get one thing perfectly clear. I'm here because I care about Woody, and no other reason.'

Taken aback, he raised one eyebrow. 'So is that a yes to coffee or not?'

'Yes, I think we should have another coffee to avoid the awful stuff at the police station, but only because I value the welfare of my stomach.'

The green stare narrowed. 'Fine.' He walked to place an order at the bar as Elsie returned to their table, fuming quietly. After the experience of comforting Cher following Jake's blatant infidelity, she hadn't considered what she would say to Torin the next time she saw him, but the very sight of him this morning had confirmed to her just how angry she still was.

He returned and opened his briefcase, slapping the bulging personal organiser Elsie had found so amusing before him on the table with a thud. 'I wish I knew what your problem is with me,' he blurted suddenly.

'My problem? My problem is that I never know where I am with you! One minute you're cocky as hell, the next you're trying to be my friend.'

'Excuse me?'

Aware that she had already said too much, Elsie folded

her arms. 'Forget it. We're here to help Woody – it doesn't matter what we think of each other.'

'No, Elsie, *I* am here to help Woody because that is my job. And to suggest that how much we like or dislike each other might have a bearing on that fact is to call my professional integrity into question. I won't stand for that, from you or anyone else.'

Elsie snorted. This was rich coming from him, considering the ease with which he had withheld the truth about Jake's philandering. 'Well, all I can say is that it's a good job Woody is your client and not your friend.'

'*Deux cafés.*' A waiter served coffee and beat a hasty retreat.

'All right, I give up! What have I done?'

Elsie placed a sugar lump in her coffee and stirred it, wishing her anger would dissipate as quickly. 'I don't want to fight, Torin. I just want to get Woody out and go home.'

'*Tell* me.'

Raising her head, Elsie fixed him with a stare. 'Jake Long.'

'What about him?'

'He's been cheating on Cher. She caught him in the act, last week. She was devastated, Torin! I had to go to her house in the middle of the night and hold her while she sobbed her heart out over him.'

'That's terrible, but how is that my fault?'

'I asked you about him! I asked you to tell me if you knew he was cheating and you assured me he wasn't. I trusted you to tell me the truth and when I needed to hear it most, you lied to protect your boss.'

He opened his hands. 'I had no idea . . .'

'Oh, of course you did! That kind of behaviour is always the talk of offices – you must have known it was still going on.'

'I can't believe you think me capable of lying to you.' She noticed him fiddling with the spoon in his coffee cup saucer.

'Why not? You've lied to me before.' Was he lying to her now?

She could see the sting of injustice in his stare, but the words were out now and she knew she would have to back them up.

'When? When did I lie to you?'

Closing her eyes to shut his face from view, she lowered her voice. 'When you said you weren't at the Carnival this year. You *were* there: I saw you. And you saw me, too.'

He was silent for a long time. Elsie opened her eyes and stared at the rich darkness of her coffee, contrasting against the stark whiteness of the coffee cup, the bright yellow of the café walls around them and the pristine white cloth that covered the table.

'Fine, I lied. I saw you with Olly. And I didn't want to intrude,' he said, finally. 'When you mentioned it, I panicked. What was I supposed to say?'

'The truth?'

'Yes, well, not all of us can be perfect like you. I mistakenly thought it would better to deny it. Clearly, that was wrong.'

'That makes no sense,' she said slowly.

'Nothing much makes sense to me where you're concerned.' His eyes met hers. 'But I honestly didn't know Jake was cheating on Cher.'

'Maybe you panicked then, too? You must have heard rumours about him?'

'I didn't think it was my place to speculate. Yes, he's always had a bit of a reputation but I respect the guy and I didn't want to suggest he might be playing around without

358

any evidence. Also, he's my boss. He seemed genuinely interested in Cher, so I didn't think he'd be looking else-where. But I can tell you don't believe me, so really what's the point in trying to convince you?'

The conversation felt like they were navigating a narrow path around a dangerous cliff and Elsie was scared one wrong word could send her plummeting. She changed tack. 'Realistically, what can you do for Woody?'

'I'm going to do all I can to ensure he is on the ferry with you all tomorrow.'

Her anger under control, Elsie nodded and drank her coffee. 'We should get back.'

'We should.'

As soon as they entered the police station, Torin switched into lawyer mode, striding through the doors and gaining entry to the interview rooms immediately. Elsie resumed her vigil in the uncomfortable waiting area, settling down with her book. But her mind was distracted from the pages lying open in her lap, straying instead to the exchange with Torin and her growing disquiet at his being here. Had he really answered her accusations about Jake and Cher? Or admitted he knew more than he'd revealed? And what about his admission that he lied about the Carnival? What was that supposed to mean?

As the minutes turned to quarter hours and half hours, a slow realisation began to dawn on Elsie: the reason for her hurt whenever Torin was around was that, deep down, she wanted to trust him, and she didn't want to see his every motive through cynical eyes.

Elsie disliked the constant lurching between anger and surprise whenever she met Torin. Not knowing how to feel about someone was an alien experience to her, yanking the carpet of her foundations from under her feet.

'Elsie.'

She jumped and looked up to see Torin standing beside her. He was smiling but his eyes betrayed the after-effects of intense activity and stress.

'What it is it? What's happening?'

'They're dropping all charges. He'll be free to go in half an hour.'

'Oh, that's wonderful!' Sheer relief overwhelming all other emotions, Elsie stood and hugged Torin for all she was worth. This must have come as a surprise to him because he took a few moments to respond, his arms eventually moving to encircle her. For a while, they remained, Elsie feeling the sharp rise and fall of his chest against her cheek and hearing the insistent thud of her own heart as she closed her eyes, surrendering to her relief.

And then, it passed, Elsie breaking away with a self-conscious smile.

'Thank you.'

'You're welcome. In reality they knew they had no evidence against him, so it was only a matter of time before they released him.'

Elsie shook her head. 'I don't think it was as clear-cut as that. You're the reason he's coming home with us. I really appreciate what you've achieved.'

He looked away and made some excuse about an important call he had to make, hurrying outside. Elsie sank back onto the chair, tears welling in her eyes as she called Daisy.

'We're bringing him back!' she said, laughing at the huge cheer that went up from The Sundaes, who were gathered around her sister on the other end of the line.

Woody emerged, thirty minutes later, looking tired but relieved, carrying his personal belongings in a clear plastic bag.

He held out his hands to Elsie as he and Torin walked towards her.

'Babe, what can I say? Can you ever forgive an old fool who can't let go of his glory days?'

Elsie hugged him. 'I can if you promise to never do something as stupid as that again.'

'I'm a slave to the whims of rock, babe, I can't say what she will have me do,' he replied, his grin fading when he saw Elsie's expression. 'But I'll do my best to reason with her.'

'Make sure you do.'

'I think my work here is done,' Torin said. 'Will you be able to get back to your hotel OK?'

Elsie smiled. 'Yes, there's a Metro station not far from here.'

'Excellent. Well, Woody, take care.' He held out his hand but Woody refused it.

'You're not leaving?'

'I am. I've done what I came to do.'

'You can't vanquish the feds and leave without being rewarded,' Woody replied. 'You must allow me to buy you a drink at least? Or better still, join us for dinner.'

'Well, I . . .' Surprised, Torin looked at Elsie, as if seeking her permission.

'You should come for dinner. If you don't have to get back soon.'

'I didn't book a return because I wasn't sure how long negotiations would take. Are you sure?'

'Totally, man,' Woody insisted. 'You'll be our guest of honour.'

The Sundaes were waiting in the lobby of Hotel Saint-Louis when Elsie, Torin and Woody arrived, greeting their choir leader like a celebrity. After much embracing and congratulations, they moved to the comfort of a nearby bar. Olly sat next to Elsie as the choir commandeered a large section of tables.

'Are you OK?' he asked.

'I'm fine now Woody's out.'

'Good.' He shot a sideways glance at Torin. 'He obviously knows his stuff.'

'Yes. He tried to play it down but I think the battle to persuade the police to drop the charges was tougher than he was letting on.'

Olly reached over and took her hand. 'I felt so useless, Els. I wanted to make everything OK for you.'

'Oh, I was fine. I just didn't want to leave until Woody was free.'

'Fair enough.' His eyes told a different story.

Wanting to reassure him, Elsie smiled. 'You were wonderful, driving us through lesser-known bits of Paris in the dead of night and having me fall asleep on you.'

His smile reappeared. 'Well, there was that, I suppose. Actually, I was pretty awesome, wasn't I?'

'Don't get too chuffed with yourself,' she laughed.

'So, there I was, everybody speaking French over my head, thinking my days were numbered . . .' Woody, seated in the middle of the group, was weaving his questionably accurate version of events like a master storyteller. 'And the cops were shouting at me, worse than the crowd in Vienna '86 who started a riot. I'm not ashamed to say, I thought Lady Luck had finally packed her bags and left me.'

'You must have been so scared!' Sheila squeaked.

'Scared? No, girl. When you've lived as much as I have everything becomes merely one more step on the road of life.'

362

'I bet he was crapping himself,' Sasha said.

'Apprehensive I may have been, but no rocker worth his salt gives in to fear like that,' Woody returned. 'Besides, at that very moment, my young champion appeared.'

Torin looked more than a little uncomfortable with this description. 'Hardly, Woody . . .'

The waiter brought wine and they raised their glasses to toast Woody's freedom. Enjoying the lifting of tension from their final day in Paris, the conversation flowed.

Olly moved seats to speak to Woody as Elsie was talking to Aoife.

'That's such a pretty ring. He did well, didn't he?'

Aoife smiled. 'He certainly did. I think I'm still in shock, though. I keep checking to make sure it's there, like I'm going to discover I was dreaming or something. What I can't work out is how Irene planned all of this when she was so ill.'

'It was amazing – you should have heard the instructions she left for me. This trip was something she had obviously thought about a great deal.'

'I wish she could have seen it.'

Elsie smiled. 'I think she was there, checking up on us.'

Danny beckoned Aoife over to the other side of the bar where he was chatting with Lewis. 'Oh, my *fiancé's* calling me,' she grinned. 'Better not keep him waiting.'

It was good to see Aoife and Danny so happy in love and Elsie was relieved that the events of the past twelve hours hadn't dampened the thrill of their engagement.

'I hear they're the reason for your trip.'

Elsie turned to see Torin sitting in the vacant seat next to her. 'They are. Danny's proposal was wonderful.'

'Can I ask if this was linked to the request in the will?'

'You can and it was.'

363

'So why were you thinking of renouncing the responsibility?'

Elsie looked away. 'It's a long story. The point is, I'm glad I didn't. Yesterday was very special.'

'And you had Olly there, so I imagine it was pretty romantic.'

What was that supposed to mean? 'Everyone was there and it was an honour to be part of Danny and Aoife's special moment,' she replied carefully.

'I'm sorry, I just wondered.'

'Wondered what?'

'How serious you are about him.'

'Torin, I'm not sure what you're trying to say.'

'You and me both.' He rubbed his forehead and Elsie was intrigued to see a glimpse of him without the control he usually hid behind. 'I'm sorry. It's just that every time I've seen you and him together, I haven't been able to work out what the deal with you two is. I mean, you strike me as someone who knows exactly what she wants, but when you're with him it's like you don't know your own mind.'

Elsie stared at him. 'That isn't any of your business. And you don't really know me that well, so I'm not sure why you think you can pass judgement on my life.'

'I see that you're not someone who is going to settle for anything less than the best,' he continued, ignoring her reaction. 'You told me your husband was the love of your life – surely that sets the bar for your future relationships?'

Elsie couldn't believe what she was hearing. 'Not that it concerns you, but I will never find another man like Lucas. And I'm not looking for that. If I decide to pursue a relationship with Olly it will be because of who he is, not who I've lost.'

'Which is all well and good, but can he really challenge you in the way I'm guessing Lucas did?' His casual mention of Lucas' name infuriated Elsie, but Torin was far from finished. 'Sure, he's a great bloke, but is he enough of a match for you? Or is he just a pleasant presence in your life? He's besotted with you – that's plain enough to see – but I don't see the same emotion in you for him.'

He had crossed a line. 'How *dare* you even presume to understand me? I can't believe you're trying to have this conversation now . . .'

'Now's as good a time as any. I don't understand the guy. He doesn't seem to be good enough to make you commit to something with him.'

Aware that she didn't want to cause a scene, Elsie's voice became a harsh whisper. 'What Olly and I do is none of your business.'

He held up his hands. 'It's just an observation – don't be offended. I'm sorry. It can't be easy starting again after losing someone so important in your life. Look, you can ask me anything in return. How's that? Might even be fun?'

Elsie cast her gaze around the bar. All of the choir were engaged in conversation, the atmosphere relaxed as they chatted and laughed together. The chance to get her own back was too appealing to refuse. 'Fine. I want to know what her name is.'

'Sorry? Whose name?'

'Whoever it was that made you so cynical about relationships. I'm guessing there had to be a woman who betrayed your trust.'

Torin sat back, a look of wounded admiration on his face. 'Wow. And I thought I was direct.'

'You said to ask anything. So that's my question.'

He admitted defeat. 'Cass. Her name was Cass.' As he spoke, Elsie was intrigued to see him touch the third finger of his left hand – a reflex action that revealed more than he could have intended.

'And how long were you married?'

'Have you ever considered changing careers? You'd fit into the law community incredibly well.' He shook his head. 'Just over a year. She left two days after our wedding anniversary with some guy she'd picked up at the hotel where she worked as Assistant Manager. But plenty of guys my age are divorced, right?'

'So I hear.'

'Marriage was another task ticked off my wife's list of things she wanted to achieve before she was thirty. It felt like a constant compromise. That's why I won't settle next time. Living with a less-than-perfect relationship is worse than being on your own.'

Elsie stared at Torin, her anger beginning to ebb a little. It was strange to be having this conversation now with the man who had once prided himself on his ability to sum others up on sight. 'How long ago were you divorced?'

He sipped his wine. 'A year ago. We don't keep in touch, unsurprisingly. After everything that happened we've nothing left to say to each other. Since then, I've had the odd date here and there but nothing serious. How about you?'

'I'm just beginning again.'

'And Olly?'

Her defences suddenly rising, Elsie looked away. 'Olly's a great friend and I love spending time with him.'

'Not exactly promising for the start of a relationship, is it?'

'It's a start. And it's also none of your business.'

Torin stood. 'As you've already said. I have to make a phone call, so if you'll excuse me . . .'

Frustrated by his attitude, Elsie drank the rest of her wine and moved over to the younger members of the choir, letting their effervescent chatter put Torin's words out of her mind.

At six p.m. the choir moved back to the hotel to get ready for dinner. When they walked into the hotel lobby, the receptionist beckoned Elsie over.

'I have a message for one of your party, Madame.' She handed Elsie a white envelope.

Daisy, seeing her sister's expression, hurried to her side. 'What is it? Not more trouble?'

'You tell me,' Elsie replied, handing the envelope to Daisy. 'It has your name on it.'

Daisy stared at the handwriting for a moment, before carefully opening the envelope and taking out a single sheet of paper. Her eyes widened and, without another word, she pushed past Elsie and hurried towards the hotel's drawing room.

'Daisy! What's the matter?' Filled with concern for her sister, Elsie followed her, coming to a halt as she reached the entrance to the sumptuously decorated room. Daisy was standing still, the envelope and letter still in her hand, the only movement the rapid rise and fall of her shoulders. Looking beyond her sister, Elsie caught her breath as she recognised the man standing at the far end of the room, a single red rose held tentatively in his hands. In all the years she had known him, Elsie had never witnessed André Durand so seemingly out of his depth, yet here he stood, his expensive suit, white open-collared shirt and bespoke black brogues at odds with the vulnerable smile and quickening breath of the man who now faced Daisy.

'What are you doing here?' Daisy breathed, the

unmistakeable quiver of emotion at the edge of her voice. 'I thought you were in Dubai . . .'

'As you see, I am not,' he replied, amusement at his own uncharacteristic spontaneity lighting up his eyes.

'I – I don't understand . . .'

André took a step towards her. 'Don't you understand? You are in my home city – my beautiful Paris – and yet I was not by your side. I was in my office and I suddenly thought how wrong this is.'

'But I would be coming home tomorrow,' Daisy said. 'How is being here without you this time so wrong?'

'*Mon amour*, I don't mean just this visit. I mean it is wrong for me to be anywhere without you. We have spent too much time apart, don't you think?'

'Well, I . . .'

He walked across the room towards her and held out the rose. 'I have been the biggest fool. We have lost so much time over the years and for what? You are the love of my life. You always have been.'

Slowly, he dropped to one knee as Daisy and Elsie gasped in unison.

'Let's get married, start a family, as soon as possible.'

'But – your business, all the time you have to spend away,' Daisy protested. 'I can't be without you for months on end. I just won't do it, André. I've waited for you long enough.'

'I'm selling my business interests in Dubai. I have found a buyer who will pay a good price. We can buy a home together and I'll begin again in England. It's all arranged.' He smiled up at the woman he loved, tears glistening in his pale blue eyes. '*Marry me*, Daisy Maynard.'

Sasha, Sheila, Aoife, Danny and Woody had now joined Elsie in the doorway and spontaneously burst into applause as Daisy flung her arms round André's neck and he rose to his feet, lifting his new fiancée from the ground and spinning her round. And then the drawing room was filled with laughing, congratulating, noisy Brits and one ecstatic Frenchman, as the elegant Parisian staff and guests looked on, bemused. Elsie's tears flowed as freely as Daisy's, thrilled at the sight of her sister's surprise.

To celebrate this surprising new development, together with Woody's release and Danny and Aoife's recent happy news, André called in some favours and arranged for them to dine in one of his favourite restaurants on the roof of a five-star hotel on avenue Montaigne, as his treat.

'I think your man might be a keeper!' Sasha exclaimed when André revealed the news to the excited choir.

La Fantasmagorie was every inch the chic Parisian venue, with its stunning views across the rooftops of Paris, to the Dôme des Invalides and the Eiffel Tower glowing gold against the darkening sky in the distance. Floor-to-ceiling green-tinted glass doors allowed the best view for the restaurant guests, leading out to a beech deck inset with white lights round its edges. Large white porcelain planters of French lavender infused the elegant space with heavenly scent and white canvas canopies draped over the outdoor area gave the effect of sails suspending the restaurant high above the beautiful rooftops of La Ville-Lumière.

'I feel like a celeb!' Sheila squealed, as the waiter led them to their table on the open terrace. 'This is too gorgeous for words!'

'How did André swing this?' Elsie asked her sister.

Daisy giggled. 'It never ceases to amaze me just how many people he knows. He stays in a hotel nearby when he comes on business here and I think that's how he got

369

to know the owner of La Fantasmagorie. Believe it or not, they share a love of Arsenal football club.'

'This is going to cost him a fortune, though.'

'He said money was no object. I'm not sure how to deal with this new André,' she said, looking for the millionth time at the large diamond ring she now wore on her left hand.

Elsie hugged her. 'Are you happy?'

'I am,' Daisy replied, and Elsie noticed genuine peace in her sister's expression.

Elsie smiled as Daisy turned back to André, their whispered conversation and intimate body language mirroring that of Danny and Aoife across the table. At the far end, Sasha and Woody were laughing together, while Lewis, Stan and Graeme toasted each other's health with expensive red wine. Maybe Paris was a magical city after all, Elsie thought to herself, and subconsciously she turned to Olly who was sitting beside her. He was smiling at the others, and Elsie was immediately struck by how much he was a part of them now. It felt good to be beside him, his constant faith in her reassuring and strong. Through all the emotion of this weekend – apart from the one time she needed to be alone – Olly had stood beside her. It seemed like an age since she had felt that kind of security with someone. Torin was wrong: Elsie didn't need a challenge; she needed to feel safe in someone's love. Just as her sister had demanded from André before she accepted his proposal, constancy and reliability were what she needed in her life now . . . weren't they?

Realising the dangerous lurch of her train of thought, Elsie bundled the questions to the back of her mind, took a deep lungful of Parisian rooftop air and settled herself to enjoy the meal as a string quartet began to play.

Tonight, she was here with good friends in a stunning restaurant in a beautiful city. Questions could wait for England.

They were treated to the kind of cuisine usually reserved for television shows like *MasterChef*: classic French cuisine served across four delicious courses, each flavour delicately balanced and every portion judged to perfection. Fresh asparagus with anchovy butter, shellfish and sea urchin to start; red snapper, pan-roasted scallops and langoustines for a fish course; veal, duck and rib-eye steak for mains; followed by desserts laced with brandy, cassis and champagne – every course was perfect.

The wine and conversation flowed easily as The Sundaes revelled in the luxury of their surroundings. Elsie was aware of Torin's eyes as they occasionally caught her attention during the meal. He looked apologetic, as if his impertinent questioning of her earlier that day was a source of great embarrassment to him now. She smiled back, determined to enjoy this remarkable evening without further controversy.

During dessert, Olly nudged her with his elbow. 'You know, I could get used to this.'

'It's certainly a great way to end our trip,' Elsie agreed, her eyes drifting across the Paris skyline to the glow of the Eiffel Tower. 'I don't think I'll ever forget it.'

'Ah, that's the City of Light for you,' Olly smiled. 'It's impossible to resist its magic. *Anything* can happen in Paris.'

'As Woody now knows,' Daisy laughed.

While they waited for coffee, Elsie picked up her glass of wine and walked to the edge of the roof terrace, leaning against the glass-panelled barrier to gaze at the view. A cool calm had settled within her, and seeing the Eiffel Tower again reminded her of the significant step she had taken this weekend. Lucas would be smiling at her now, she thought.

He would point at the happy members of her choir, with Woody safely back at its heart:

'Look at them, Els – all the pieces are falling into place for you. And this could only happen because you were brave enough to come here. What does the future hold for you, my darling? Only possibility and promise. I'll be watching . . .'

At that very moment, the Eiffel Tower began to shimmer and sparkle on the far horizon, as tiny blue twinkling lights flashed up and down its height. Elsie's heart skipped a beat and tears of surprise filled her eyes. The Sundaes saw it, too and, whooping, grabbed their phones and cameras to capture the spectacle. For ten minutes they watched, transfixed by its beauty, until the light show ended and the restaurant diners broke into delighted applause.

'How amazing was that?' Daisy exclaimed, as Elsie returned to her place at the table. 'The waiter said that happens every hour during the evening. Oh, Els, you're crying . . .'

Elsie's heart was beating fast as she wiped the tears from her eyes. 'I'm fine. It just happened at the right time. All of this trip happened at the right time.' She nodded at André. 'Especially for you.'

Daisy pulled her sister to her, kissing the top of her head. 'And you have your whole life ahead of you, to do with it what you will, darling. I reckon Lucas is loving all this. And I'm so proud we could be here together – I love you, little sister.'

When the meal was over, the group made their way to ground level, assembling on the pavement as Torin prepared to leave.

'Woody, it's been fun,' he smiled, offering his hand to the ageing rocker and laughing in surprise as Woody flung his arms around him in an enormous hug.

'You're a gent, brother,' he exclaimed. 'I won't forget what you did for me in that place.' Depositing a slightly crumpled solicitor back on the pavement, he slapped his back. 'Any time you need old Uncle Woody's assistance, you just call.'

'Erm, thanks – I'll bear that in mind.' He turned to Olly. 'Good to see you again, mate. Take care of this lot tomorrow, yeah?'

Olly shook his hand. 'I will. I appreciate your help with the police.'

'It's what I do, so no problem.' He smiled at The Sundaes. 'Nice to meet you all. Keep Woody out of any more trouble, won't you?' He checked his watch and looked at Elsie. 'I should go. Can I have a word?'

Nodding, she followed him a little way down the street. When they were a sufficient distance from the rest of the group, he stopped, his eyes assuming their strange stillness that she had witnessed before.

'I know this is probably not the time, but please let me say this. I'd like to think we could be friends one day – real friends – after everything that's been said today. I'd hate it if my overactive gob and rash opinions have jeopardised any chance I have of getting to know you.'

It came from nowhere, but Elsie found herself warming to his newfound openness. 'They haven't. I think if we could manage an entire conversation without either of us taking offence it might be a start.'

'Like this one, for example?'

Uncertain in this new territory, she smiled. 'Possibly.'

He took a breath. 'What are you doing Tuesday evening after work?'

Elsie thought for a moment. 'Nothing, as far as I'm aware.'

'Then have a drink with me? I'd like to give our non-confrontational experiment a try. And if it fails spectacularly, we can admit defeat and give up there and then.'

Elsie could think of no good reason to refuse. She was keen to see if she could shake off the inner cynicism, which even now was screaming belligerent questions at her. After all he had done for Woody this weekend, she felt she should at least try to be friends with him.

'OK, let's give it a go. But I'm paying.'

Torin smiled as he hailed a taxi. 'Then I wouldn't dream of refusing.'

Buzzing from their unexpected exchange, Elsie rejoined the others and they began to walk to the Metro station.

'I think I'm going to sleep like a baby tonight,' Stan said, stretching his arms overhead as he walked.

'I don't care how you sleep as long as you don't snore,' Graeme joked. 'It's like sharing a room with a pneumatic drill!'

'*Attendez, s'il vous plaît!*'

They turned to see a waiter from La Fantasmagorie running down the street after them, waving something in his hand. When he reached the group, he handed Elsie a small, black leather-covered object and she recognised it immediately.

'A gentleman from your party left this on the table,' the waiter explained.

'Oh, *merci, Monsieur*,' Elsie said.

'*Je vous en prie, Mademoiselle. Au revoir.*'

'What is it?' André asked as the choir gathered round.

'It's Torin's Filofax.'

Danny and Lewis sniggered. Olly shook his head. 'I didn't think high-flying lawyers still had those.'

'I know. Go figure,' Elsie replied. 'I'll make sure he gets it back.'

'People, may I announce that there is a brand new bottle of bourbon in my room, which I will gladly share for a nightcap when we reach our lodgings,' Woody announced. 'I reckon on our last night in Paris we should all get a little rock'n'roll, eh?'

'Woody Jensen, I think walking into a major drugs raid and being incarcerated in a French police station overnight is more than enough rock'n'roll for anybody,' Elsie laughed.

'Fair do's, babe. But you'll still partake of it with me?'

Happier than she had felt in a long time, Elsie linked arms with him. 'Just you try and stop me!'

CHAPTER TWENTY

Back to the future

Next morning, The Sundaes bid a fond farewell to Paris, with Daisy staying behind to travel home with André.

'Are you *sure* you're going to be OK without me?' Daisy asked, her face a picture of worry, 'because I can tell André to make his own way home if you like.'

'Stop talking, Dais. We'll be fine. Now, we have a ferry to catch and you, I believe, have a set of future in-laws to meet.'

André circled Daisy's waist from behind and grinned at Elsie over her shoulder. 'My mother has been waiting a long time for this. She will hold us hostage at her house until she has heard every detail.'

It was so good to see her eldest sister glowing and happy. If it was possible for Daisy Maynard to become more beautiful, she did so now, safe in the arms of her handsome fiancé. Elsie hugged them both and climbed into the passenger seat of the minibus beside Olly.

'Now, do what I suggest and take the scenic route out of the city,' Daisy said, leaning in to direct her comment at Olly. 'It would be wrong not to make the most of Paris as you leave.'

Olly saluted her. 'Yes, ma'am,' he replied.

'Have a safe journey!' Daisy called as they drove away.

So they passed the Louvre, the Luxembourg Palace, the Sorbonne and the Seine, glimpses of the Eiffel Tower never far from sight. It surprised Elsie how quickly she had become accustomed to the beauty of this city, its elegant stone buildings, vivacious streets and breathtaking vistas both majestic and familiar to her now. So much had happened here in such a short amount of time, and Elsie knew, as they skirted the city's famous landmarks, that she would return here often. Paris had been a place of memory and rebirth: it would always now have a place in her heart.

Reluctantly leaving the city they began the long journey towards Rouen and on to Dieppe. They arrived in time to board the mid-afternoon ferry crossing and Elsie joined the others to wander around duty-free, buying a bottle of Jim's favourite aftershave and Cher's beloved Chanel No5, together with an Yves Saint-Laurent *Touche Éclat* as a treat for Guin. Olly was a little quiet, but Elsie assumed it was due to tiredness from the journey.

They arrived back in Brighton just before six p.m. and reluctantly said goodbye to one another. Woody almost crushed Elsie with the strength of his embrace.

'Give me a few days to recover from my adventure and then we're back on it, babe. I've been dreaming about our next project and I reckon a flashmob ninja attack is well overdue. We start small – Brighton Pavilion, maybe – and then build up to something bigger than the Eiffel Tower. I'm thinking the music of Marley, The Rasmus and Pink colliding in a world-class venue. How do you feel about a Sundaes campaign in *London*?'

'After this weekend I can honestly say anything's possible,' Elsie replied.

Casting a surreptitious glance around him to make sure none of the other choir members were in earshot, Woody moved a little closer to Elsie. 'Actually, old Woodster's been meaning to ask you something.'

'Ask away.'

'The lovely Lady Cher. Is she – is *that dude* still hanging around?'

Elsie shook her head. 'Oh no. That *dude* is long gone.'

Woody's eyes twinkled. 'So – hypothetically, angel – if a certain Brighton figure was to, you know, pursue a certain line of action that might be agreeable to the lady . . .'

'I think she'd say yes,' Elsie replied, '*hypothetically*.'

'Sweet,' he nodded, a treacle-slow smile appearing as he raised his Stetson to her and sauntered away. Elsie grinned to herself, secretly delighted at the prospect of a Woody–Cher collaboration. Cher had no idea what she was in for . . .

Danny walked over and hugged Elsie. 'Thanks again for everything you've done. You totally made it happen for us.'

'You're welcome. You two just be happy, OK?'

'We will,' Aoife beamed, slipping her arm round Danny's waist. 'We'll see you at rehearsal on Wednesday?'

Elsie smiled back. 'Wouldn't miss it for the world.' As they walked away, she turned to Olly. 'You've been a star this weekend. Thank you for everything.'

'I did it for you,' he said, suddenly. 'Because I want to be part of your life.'

'Oh, Olly, you are . . .'

'Look, don't be mad at your sister, but she told me – about The List.'

'What?' Of course it was something Elsie planned to share with Olly – but the knowledge that Daisy had furnished him with the details already was inexplicably unsettling.

'I was worried about you when we left you up on the Eiffel Tower. You looked so lost and I didn't want you to be on your own. I was all ready to come back up, but Daisy explained about Number 51. I know what you were doing up there and I think it's amazing. No – let me say this, OK? I don't want to take Lucas' place – I know I'll never come close to being the kind of man he was. But I think we could be happy together, Elsie. I think we have a chance. And Paris made me realise that I don't want to wait around any more. You asked us to be friends, and we have been friends, and it's been wonderful. But everything within me wants us to start discovering how it could be for us right now – no more delays. So here it is: I am yours, wholeheartedly, completely, if you want me.' He stopped, his face flushed and his breath coming fast. 'I should get the minibus back. Promise me you'll think about what I said?'

Numb from his passionate declaration, Elsie promised. 'I will.'

He nodded, climbed into the minibus and sped away. Elsie stood alone in the middle of the car park, breathing the familiar sea air of home but feeling as if she was standing on another planet entirely. Her limbs were heavy with travel weariness and she could feel the need for sleep pulling at the corners of her eyes. She needed to put all the pieces from the weekend into their rightful places and see what picture was revealed. Only then could she decide the way forward, once and for all . . .

Jim's budding relationship with his new lady friend turned out to be far more serious than he had suggested in his phone call. When Elsie arrived at his house that evening, things were decidedly cosy between her father and Louise, the A&E nurse. Elsie noted with interest the sudden proliferation of female toiletries in the family bathroom and the arrival of several pots of orchids on the kitchen window ledge.

'This woman is an *angel*,' he told her happily as Louise fussed around him in his armchair. 'She's been looking after me so well, Els.'

'Your dad's a poppet,' Louise smiled. 'He's no trouble. Although I can't promise I'll ever love vegetarian food as much as he seems to do.'

'I don't think *anyone* loves it as much as Dad,' Elsie smiled, accepting a mug of tea from the forty-something bottle-blonde.

'So, how was Paris?' Jim asked, leaning forward as far as his raised plastered leg would allow.

'Gorgeous,' Elsie replied truthfully. 'I wasn't expecting to love it as much as I did, but I think I might go back there again. Daisy was mentioning I could go on a springtime trip there next year with her and André.'

'I wonder if Lucas knows what he's started?'

'I wonder too. So come on, be honest, what's happening with you two?'

Jim flushed and took Louise's hand when she stood by his chair. 'I think I might have stumbled across a very special lady, pardon the pun.' They giggled together and Elsie was thrilled to see Jim looking so happy. Quite what Daisy and Guin – who were far harsher critics of their dad than she was – would make of his new girlfriend remained to be seen, but Elsie loved this new development in Jim's life. After everything he had done for his daughters, a shot of happiness of his own was more than deserved. When Louise left the room, Jim patted the empty chair next to his and Elsie moved to his side.

'Now talk to me, littlest one. How are you feeling?'

'Odd, to be honest. I finished The List.'

Jim's eyes blinked his understanding. 'And now?'

Elsie took a deep breath. 'Now, I don't know. So much has changed during the past year and I feel as if I'm learning every day about what my life is going to look like. It's immensely scary but I can't help being fascinated by it, too. Lucas was right about me finding my own way forward; I'm still just working out how to do that.'

'You'll do it, Elsinore. I know you will.' He smiled in the direction of the kitchen, where Louise was busying herself to allow him time alone with his daughter. 'Life rarely throws you a challenge you can't find a way to handle. You just need to keep your mind open to consider the twists and turns ahead.' He stroked her hair, the way he used to when she was a little girl, and Elsie was immediately soothed by it. 'You are my fighter, darling, you always were. I wish for all the world that you hadn't had to go through all you did with Lucas, but I can see you're so much stronger for it. Right from when you were the tiniest toddler, you always worked out a way to do things. I used to joke with your mother that you were destined to be an inventor, a problem-solver. It was almost as if we could see your brain whirring. What I'm trying to say – in a very "your Dad"-like way – is that you'll work this out. When the next step comes, you'll find yourself taking it.'

Elsie wrapped her arms round her father. 'Thanks, Dad. I love you.'

'I love you too, my darling little one. Great things are a breath away.'

When Elsie arrived at Sundae & Cher next day, Cher greeted her at the door like a long-lost sister.

'I can't wait to hear all about Paris!'

Elsie laughed. 'You will, I promise. Can I just make it through the door, please?'

Sheepishly, Cher stepped back and Elsie walked into the kitchen to hang up her bag. She was just tying on her apron when a familiar voice spoke behind her.

'*A-aangel.*'

'Woody! You nearly scared me half to death! Don't let Cher find you back here, you know how she feels about café customers stepping behind the counter.'

'I think for this one I might make an exception,' Cher replied, as she walked into the kitchen and Woody slung a lazily affectionate arm round her shoulder. A smudge of flour was streaked across his cheek and, if Elsie didn't know better, she could swear his self-satisfied smile bore smudges of what looked suspiciously like Cher's favourite shade of lipstick . . .

Despite her 'hypothetical' conversation with Woody yesterday, Elsie wasn't expecting to witness this scene quite so quickly. 'Blimey, you didn't hang about, did you?'

'Elsie, time is a mere fly in the ointment of happiness when matters of the heart are involved,' Woody replied. 'I had a lot of time to ponder my future in that prison cell and all I could think of was this heavenly creature.' He gazed lovingly at Cher's greatest assets as she wiggled them saucily at him.

Elsie couldn't repress the shudder as she smiled back. 'Well, I'm very happy for the pair of you. Just one piece of advice, Cher: if he takes you out on a date, make sure you choose the venue. His judgement of happening night spots isn't so hot.'

Woody clutched at his heart. 'You cut me deep, angel!'

Pushing him away, Cher chuckled as she pulled the blackboard menu from the hooks in the wall by the counter and chalked up today's list of ice cream flavours. 'I bet this one had you scared for a while.'

'He did. I had visions of us all being investigated as collaborators. One thing's for sure, I won't be recommending the French police station as a must-see Paris landmark!'

'Little wonder.' Her smile faded as she faced Elsie. 'So how about Olly?'

'Olly was amazing. He drove us back and forth to the police station, kept me calm and was there when we needed him. Not to mention driving the choir all the way to Paris and back.'

Cher's eyes narrowed. 'That's great, but it wasn't what I meant.'

Elsie carried a large chocolate vanilla marble fudge cake from the catering fridge into the café, placing it carefully on a 1950s cut-glass cake stand on the counter. 'He told me that he's mine if I want him.'

'Oh, Els, that's amazing! Isn't it?'

Elsie had thought of nothing else all last night, any chance of sleeping denied by the urgency of her thoughts. Instead, she had taken her duvet downstairs and huddled on the sofa, watching the BBC News channel with the sound off as she tried to make sense of her feelings.

Olly was a wonderful man – there were countless reasons why she should throw caution to the wind and run into his arms. He cared for her, he was there when she needed him and, until his outburst in the car park, he had never once demanded anything in return. Being in his arms at the police station had felt like the safest place. His kisses at the beginning of their friendship *had* been fantastic – there was no denying the chemistry between them. Her family adored him – especially Daisy, who seemed to have become his biggest fan in Paris – and the choir now loved him too. There was every reason in the world for Elsie to fall in love with him.

And yet . . . try as she might, she couldn't escape the feeling that something was missing. In recent months, she had put this down to the inevitable comparisons she was making with Lucas – a contest Olly could never hope to win. Perhaps, she had thought, her reticence was borne out of trepidation about loving someone again, of starting at page one of a new book after reading *War and Peace*. But for all her reasons and all her excuses, one unavoidable fact remained: that if she felt for Olly even a fraction of what he professed to feel for her, there would have been no hesitation whatsoever. Lucas had known it – in his many attempts to talk about the relationships Elsie would have after him, he had insisted that she would know without doubt when to fall in love.

'Your instinct is stronger than anyone else I know. I can't see you being in two minds about this, even if the thought of it terrifies you. One of the things I admire the most about you is your resolve, Els. It's like a beacon of surety within you and it's led us well all the time we've been together. When you fall in love again, that will be your best guide.'

When I fall in love . . .

'Can I take an extra hour at lunchtime?' she asked Cher, who immediately understood the reason behind her request.

'Of course, lovely. You take all the time you need.'

They met in BiblioCaff, the familiar surroundings providing a suitably neutral venue for the conversation Elsie was now dreading. Olly had ordered coffee and sandwiches, which neither of them managed to touch – and from the way he was observing her it was as if he already suspected the outcome of their meeting.

'Busy day?' Elsie asked, trying her best to keep her voice steady.

'Not bad. We've won a couple of good pitches with new customers, so that should keep us occupied well into next year. You?' Today he seemed more handsome than ever, his fitted blue and white striped shirt and dark blue trousers matching the colour of his eyes.

'Trade's falling off a little now. But Cher has plans for Bonfire Night and Christmas promotions, so that might tempt more people in.' She took a breath. 'Olly . . .'

'Wait – before you say anything, I just wanted to apologise for what I said yesterday evening. It was completely out of order and the last thing I wanted to do was to put you on the spot.'

'Olly, it's fine. I'm not quite sure where to start . . . I want you to know that I think the world of you . . .'

Olly's head dropped. 'No, don't say it . . .'

'I have to, I'm sorry! I love spending time with you and it's true that I'm very attracted to you. Everything you've done for me, all the time you've waited when you shouldn't have had to . . . it's all been completely wonderful and I love having you in my life. But I can't be the woman you want me to be. And believe me, I wish with all my heart that I could. You deserve the best, Olly – the best that there is. You deserve someone who won't need a reason to fall in love with you . . .'

'Maybe you just need time,' he argued, stubborn hope still burning in his eyes as they met hers. 'I rushed you – I made you decide too early . . .'

'No, I should have decided the moment we kissed. I should never have made you wait so long, when all you've ever done is be honest with me about how you feel.'

'Elsie, please, let me be the judge of that.' The pain in

385

his eyes broke her heart and she hated herself for being the cause of it.

'I have to follow my heart,' she said. 'I can't do anything else.'

He stared at her for a long time, his eyes impossibly sad. Then, he reached across and took her hand. 'Then you shouldn't have to. Just don't disappear from my life completely, will you?'

'Not if you don't want me to.'

'I might need to take some time away from this – just to get my head round it all. But I'll get over it. You haven't seen the last of me, Elsie.'

'I know. I really am sorry, Olly.'

'I expect we'll laugh about this one day.' He didn't look convinced by this. 'So, friends, then?'

Elsie smiled and squeezed his hand. 'Friends.'

Walking back to Sundae & Cher, Elsie felt as if she'd gone ten rounds with a heavyweight boxer, but she knew her decision was the right one. Olly's reaction confirmed this – although his utter decency in the face of her rejection was further proof of the calibre of the man she was refusing. In the late October afternoon she let the familiar sights and sounds of her home town soothe her battered spirit. Brighton knew her better than anyone – even Lucas. Despite everything that had happened in her life, this town had been her constant companion; her highest and lowest days had been set with its Pier, sea, promenade, Royal Pavilion, gardens and Lanes as a backdrop. Today, as the few remaining tourists braved the autumnal temperatures along the seafront and local people went about their daily business around her, she felt certain that Brighton was going to witness her future, too. Whatever that was.

Cher asked few questions about Elsie's meeting with Olly:

the expression she had worn when she returned had obviously answered any questions her boss might have had. After an uneventful afternoon with few customers, Cher closed the shop as Elsie changed into a long white and silver Indian print tunic, skinny jeans and black boots for her meeting with Torin. As a final touch, she wound the summer-blue, cherry-blossom-print silk scarf from Daisy round her neck, which had retained the orange blossom scent of the drawer liners in the hotel room in Montparnasse. Wearing it reminded her of the newness she had felt after her visit to the Eiffel Tower and the peace she had encountered on the roof terrace of La Fantasmagorie.

'Wow, you look different,' Cher remarked, when Elsie emerged from the staff toilet. 'Is this your new Parisian look?'

Elsie smiled. 'You could say that.'

Cher kissed her cheek. 'Have fun tonight. I will expect *details* tomorrow, Madame Maynard. Don't let him get away with being a cocky so-and-so, OK?'

'*Mais naturellement, ma chérie. À bientôt!*'

Perhaps wisely, given the debacle with Jake and Cher, Torin had decided against The Feathers as a venue for their early evening drink and Elsie was glad of this. Everything around her felt new since she returned from Paris, so new surroundings seemed fitting for their first non-confrontational meeting.

Added to this, Torin's choice of venue couldn't have been more uniquely Brighton: The Fortune of War pub, on the seafront, summed up the town perfectly. Its beautiful wood-lined bar, shaped to resemble an upturned boat, and the large seating area on the beach itself had been a favourite haunt of Jim in his teenage years and the place where Elsie bought her first pint on her eighteenth birthday. Eccentrically British with all the flamboyance Brighton was famed for, the pub was the perfect setting.

When Elsie arrived, the seats on the beach and across its frontage were already filled, despite the cool October evening. Torin, dressed in a black shirt, indigo fitted jeans and blue Converse sneakers, was waiting at a table under the front canopy and stood as she approached.

'I would have ordered a round of drinks, but I seem to remember you insisting that you were paying,' he said as they sat down.

'That's what I said. So what can I get you?'

'Bottle of lager, thanks.'

'Coming up.' Elsie wandered into the bar and returned a few minutes later with Torin's order and a glass of red wine for herself.

'Is this table good? I thought it would give us a good view of the beach, although if it gets too chilly we can always go inside.'

'This is fine. You know, I haven't been in here for years. Nothing seems to have changed much, though.'

Torin smiled and Elsie noticed how relaxed he seemed this evening. 'I come here occasionally with my mates from the rugby club. So, what's with the red wine? Did Paris rub off on you?'

'I just fancied it. And this is Bulgarian, so it's a little different from the stuff we all became very accustomed to this weekend. Plus, the plastic glass sets it apart, don't you think?'

'I'll say. Although the wine at La Fantasmagorie was something else.'

'It was.' The mention of the rooftop restaurant prompted Elsie to pick up her bag. 'That reminds me, you left

388

something behind up there.' She handed him his Filofax and, completely taken aback, he accepted it from her.

'Oh, thank heaven! I turned my house upside down last night looking for this. My whole life is in this organiser.'

'I had a feeling you might say that.'

'Where did I leave it?'

'On our table on Sunday night. One of the waiters noticed it and brought it down to us.'

'Stunning, simply stunning,' he breathed, gazing at the slightly battered leather folder as if it were a priceless artefact in the British Museum. 'Thank you.'

'You're welcome.'

The conversation between them ebbed as a crowd of rowdy students began to mock one of their number on the beach. Overhead, the sky began to redden as gilt-edged clouds glided along the line where the ocean met the sky.

'I'm impressed – with us, I mean,' Torin remarked, causing Elsie's eyes to return to him. 'Almost fifteen minutes in and no sign of conflict yet.'

'Mind you, it's still early. Things could change at any time.'

'True. Forgive me, I'm curious: what made you agree to try this?'

Elsie shrugged as she swallowed a mouthful of wine. 'No reason.'

He frowned. 'No, I'm not having that. Something must have changed your mind.'

'Careful, Mr Stewart, or we might not make it to twenty conflict-free minutes.'

'Good point. So, did everyone arrive home safely?'

'Yes, thank goodness. Olly brought us all back in one piece.'

Torin's expression flickered. 'Olly. Listen, I'm sorry about what I said on Sunday. You were right: it wasn't my place to pass judgement.'

'No, it wasn't.' The mention of Olly's name made a knot appear in Elsie's stomach. 'But you were right.' It was more candid than she had planned to be this evening, but felt like the right thing to share.

He blinked. 'Sorry?'

'You were right about him and I. He challenged me about where we stood when we arrived home yesterday and today I told him I couldn't be any more than friends.'

'Wow.'

'So, there it is.'

'How did he take the news?'

Her discomfort returned. 'How do you think? Anyway, it's done and there really isn't anything else to say about it.'

Receiving the message loud and clear, Torin picked up a menu from the table. 'I'm starving, aren't you?'

Nice side step, Mr Stewart. 'Not particularly. But you go ahead.'

He grinned back. 'I would hazard a guess that if I order a bowl of chips you'll help me eat them.'

'There's only one way to find out.'

'Excellent. Back in a tick.'

Elsie watched him disappear into the pub and took a deep breath. Spending so much time with him without their usual default of conflict felt strange – like the feeling you get when you take a stone out of your shoe and walking without it feels alien for a while. At least during arguments Elsie's quick mind could see where to head next. Now, she found herself daunted by the prospect of an entire evening of non-contentious conversation. Torin Stewart without his preferred armour of smugness and superiority was a strange animal indeed.

Of course, this was only their first attempt, she reminded herself, and so far their conversation had remained carefully within the boundaries of small talk. How they would fare when approaching anything deeper remained to be seen. But it felt good – and Elsie couldn't deny how much she was enjoying the experience. Torin returned with a wooden table number and their careful conversation continued. They talked about work, the experience in the police station, The Sundaes, their families and even their plans for Christmas. The bowl of chips arrived and, just as Torin had predicted, Elsie dipped into them as the conversation began to veer into slightly more personal areas – Torin's divorce and Lucas' illness.

'How did you discover he was ill?'

'He started complaining of pains in his lower abdomen about six months before he was eventually diagnosed and lost a lot of weight quite quickly. Our doctor tested him for lots of different things, but all the results were inconclusive. The cancer he had is really rare in people of his age, so I don't think the doctors even considered it for a long time. In the end, it was a new specialist we saw who decided to run the test, just to rule it out.'

'I'm so sorry, Elsie.'

'What for?'

'For your loss. He sounds like a wonderful guy.'

She smiled. 'He was.'

'I suppose after losing someone like that you can't ever imagine loving anyone else.'

Elsie bit into a hot chip, the steam warming her lips. 'Not straight away, no. But Lucas kept telling me I would find someone else. Even when I didn't want to hear it. He was stubborn like that. So that's where I'm at now – thinking about dating, looking to the future. I will fall in love again.'

His eyes grew still. 'Will you? And how will you know when you do?'

A shiver passed across Elsie's skin. The thought of this had been on her mind since she left the Eiffel Tower. 'I'll know. I'm looking forward to it, actually. When Lucas and I married I never thought I'd feel that first thrill with anyone else. But now I'll get to experience it again.'

'I can't even remember what it's like – with Cass every good memory was obliterated by all the acrimonious fallout.'

'It's wonderful,' Elsie breathed. 'There's this moment, just before it happens, when everything around you goes still. It's like that moment you get just before it snows – like nature is holding its breath . . . And in that moment, anything is possible, and everything you know is called into question. Believe me, I'll know when that moment comes.'

He was staring at her now. 'And when it does?'

'Then I'll close my eyes and jump.'

He fell silent, his gaze drifting away to the beach beyond.

In an attempt to drag the conversation back to safer territory, Elsie added, 'But, you know, that's just me. I guess it's different for everyone.' She looked down at the near-empty basket between them. 'I'm sorry, I appear to have eaten a lot of your chips after saying I wasn't going to.'

'Not a problem.' He stood, popping the last two chips into his mouth. 'Another drink?'

'Why not? Same again, please.'

The sun was starting to dip in the sky, its perfect circle increasing in size as it slipped slowly down. As Elsie watched, the colours deepened – gold, red, pink and purple, with ice-blue clouds floating across the wide expanse of sky. After the excitement and undeniable beauty of Paris, it was wonderful to be home.

A gaggle of seagulls took off from the roof of the pub

and coasted on air currents overhead. The students on the beach had begun singing a Bon Jovi classic, adding some air-guitar that Woody himself would have been proud of. And Elsie felt an air of serenity touching everything.

'Excuse me, are these finished with?' a barman asked, bringing Elsie's attention back to the pub.

She looked down at the empty chip basket and collection of plastic glasses on the table. 'Yes, thanks.'

He put down the large round tray he was carrying to load it with the glasses, but as he lifted it away the tray caught the clasp on Torin's organiser, sending it flying off the edge to burst open on the concrete floor beneath the table.

'Oh, man, I'm so sorry,' the barman stuttered, shoving the tray onto the table and bending down to scoop up the organiser's contents that had spilled out. Still apologising, he handed it all back to Elsie before hurrying away.

Smiling at the amount of detritus Torin had managed to pack into his organiser, Elsie put the pile of paper scraps on the table and began to place them carefully back into the black folder. She'd never pictured him as a hoarder before, but the evidence on the table now proved otherwise. He had kept a matchbook from La Fantasmagorie and a small paper doily from the saucer of his coffee cup in the café with the bright yellow walls near the police station in Montparnasse. There was a full sugar packet from BiblioCaff and a Sundae & Cher business card . . . Elsie froze as a thought began to form in her mind.

No – that's not possible. Is it?

Leafing through the rest of the papers she discovered a receipt from the café Torin had taken her to on the day Irene's will was read, a flyer for The Sundaes' concert at The Feathers, a pay-and-display car park ticket from the

Royal Sussex County Hospital and a scrap of notepaper from an order pad of the Scandinavian interiors store in Croydon. And last of all, folded up in a handwritten receipt from a high street chemist in Brighton, was the twenty-pound note Elsie had shoved into his hand on the very first day they met.

A chair scraped along the concrete floor and Elsie raised her head to see Torin standing there, drinks in hand, a look of pure horror on his face.

'What's all this?' she asked slowly.

He didn't move, his eyes frantically scanning the damning evidence lying across the metal table. 'It's not what you think,' he said, quickly.

'I don't know what to think,' she replied, looking at him, then back at the table.

'How did you – *why* did you open it?'

'I didn't. A barman knocked it off the table and everything fell out.'

'Right.'

'OK, I think you should put the drinks down and talk to me.'

He did as he was told, sitting down slowly while keeping his eyes on the table. Elsie had never seen him like this – suddenly so unsure of himself, stripped of his usual arsenal of comebacks by the truth of his motives now lying bare before her.

'Everything here is to do with me,' she said, slowly.

'Yes.'

'So every time we met you kept a souvenir?'

'It's not what you think.'

'Answer me.'

He closed his eyes. 'Yes.'

'Why?'

394

'It doesn't matter.'

'I think it does. Why keep this stuff? You always seemed so intent on having the upper hand, and being the one in control. I thought you were amused by me. I thought you enjoyed pointing out my failings.'

'It was never like that. And certainly not recently.'

Elsie's mind was whirring as she processed it all. And then, quite without warning, she began to laugh. Torin stared at her in disbelief as she threw her head back and let out great, breathless guffaws that caused the students on the beach to abandon their songs and air-guitaring to stare at her, too. Tears began to stream from her eyes as the absurdity of the situation dawned upon her – that all the time she was assuming Torin was out to make her life difficult, he was actually carefully preserving the memory of their every meeting.

Thoroughly embarrassed and irritated by her response, Torin went on the defensive. 'I might have known this would be your reaction. You're loving this, aren't you? I can tell. Mocking the man who you've waited the best part of a year to get the upper hand on. Well, thanks for showing me your true colours, Elsie Maynard. I'm glad how I feel is such a source of amusement to you.' He pushed back his chair and stormed off over the beach.

Elsie stopped laughing and stared at the items from his abandoned organiser on the table. For a moment, she didn't move as a truth began to dawn.

No – surely not . . .

Scooping the souvenirs back into the organiser and snapping the clasp shut, she flung it into her bag and ran out onto the shingle of the beach. The red-gold sun was halfway into the sea now, its rays painting a line of ripples towards the shore as the sky flamed around it. To her left, the multi-coloured strings of lights on Brighton Pier were reflected in the dark waters beneath the vintage structure.

Torin was striding ahead down the shingle ridge of the beach, his figure cast into silhouette against the sunset sky. Elsie raced towards him, her feet sending showers of pebbles along the beach as she ran. Skidding down the steep pebble ridge, Torin reached the shoreline and stopped abruptly, running his hand through his dark hair and bowing his head. Elsie slowed as she neared him, stopping a few feet away.

'You forgot this,' she called, taking the organiser from her bag and holding it out to him.

'Keep it,' he called back, refusing to turn round. 'I don't need it now.'

Elsie took a breath and walked to his side. 'That's not good enough, I'm afraid,' she said, raising her voice over the noise of the waves breaking by their feet. 'I still haven't had an explanation.'

He let out a long groan and turned to face her. 'It's hardly rocket science, is it? I'm sure you can work it out.'

'You *like* me,' Elsie made no attempt to hide her smile.

'Would you just leave me alone?'

'But you don't just like me. You *really* like me . . .'

'Great. Now we've established that fact you can go home happy and laugh at me all you want.'

'In fact, you like me so much you've been carrying round mementoes of me. In your *retro organiser* . . .'

He shoved his hands in his pockets and glared at her. 'Fine. Mock me.'

Her smile faded. 'And all this time, when I thought you were laughing at me, when I dreaded seeing you because I knew we would end up fighting, you *wanted* to see me . . .'

'OK, for the love of all things sacred, enough! Of course

I like you! I fell for you the moment I saw you standing in the rain with that security guard and those ridiculous items in your hand. And I couldn't stop thinking about you after you walked away. I didn't engineer every meeting, but I found myself hoping for another opportunity to see you again. And it happened, time after time. But it was always so much of a battleground when we met and I didn't know how to deal with it . . .'

'Torin . . .'

'How could you be so easy with everybody else, yet never more than three sentences away from a fight with me? It's pretty clear what you think of me and now I have my answer I can walk out of your life for good . . .'

'Torin.'

'*What?*'

Elsie shook her head. 'Shush.'

'What is that supposed to m—' He stopped, mid-sentence, as Elsie moved forward and kissed him.

It was a moment when reason was discarded and her heart took control; when the final piece of the puzzle clicked into place; when the world around them stood still. Then, his arms were wrapping round her, pulling her body tight against his as he returned her kiss. And Elsie felt her heart softening as the truth of Torin's love for her began to open doors she had never noticed before . . .

The last message in the silk-covered box read:

I love you because, after all the crazy things I've asked you to do for me, after all the pain and heartbreak you've endured, and after bravely stepping out into your new life without me, you're every

*bit the wonderful, courageous, perfect
woman that I spent my whole summer
holiday trying to blag a date with.
I will always love you. Be happy, gorgeous.
Lucas xxx*

**NOT THE END,
BUT A BEGINNING . . .**

Please read on for all
51 items on The List

The List

<u>Three rules for The List:</u>
1. Nothing overly sentimental
2. Nothing expensive
3. Nothing predictable

1. *Sneak into Brighton Library and stick smiley-face Post-its into dreary books.*
2. *Spend the night in a treehouse.*
3. *Buy embarrassing fridge magnets from seaside towns and display on home fridge.*
4. *Paddle in Victoria Fountain wearing wellies.*
5. *Dress up as our favourite Pixar characters.*
6. *Tap-dance along Brighton Pier.*
7. *Lie in the back garden and count shooting stars.*
8. *Decorate the rubbish bins on the promenade with tinsel in July.*
9. *Dance in the rain, wearing sunhats.*
10. *Have a picnic on Brighton beach wearing a ballgown (you) and black tie (me).*

11. Do 'The Birdy Song' in the veg aisle at Sainsbury's.
12. Kidnap a garden gnome for a night.
13. Buy spacehoppers and race along Islingword Street (I will whop your 'hopper ass, by the way, but don't let me win just because I'm dying).
14. Count jet-skiers for an afternoon and do a robot dance for every ten you see.
15. Sneak into Brighton Home Stores at night and rearrange the cushions on all the sofas (to freak out Jim).
16. Spend the day calling each other Bert (you) and Ernie (me).
17. Watch Seven Brides for Seven Brothers five times in a row (dressed as cowboys, singing every song).
18. Wear rockstar mullet wigs for a day but don't refer to them at all.
19. Dress up as old people and feed seagulls on the prom (shouting at them obligatory).
20. Eat ice cream listening to Bob Dylan songs.
21. Buy a waffle iron (just because I've always wanted one) and throw a 'Make Your Own Waffle' party.
22. Walk backwards across zebra crossings for a day.
23. Find the biggest puddle and jump in it.
24. Buy an ice cream every time we see an ice cream van (chase it down the streets if necessary).
25. Find a field of sheep and baa at them.
26. Spend a whole day in bed together.
27. Speak in Shakespearean English for an entire day.
28. Walk round Brighton with bunches of gladioli in our back pockets (to make Morrissey proud).
29. Have a pillow fight around the house (and continue in the street if I'm not winning!)
30. Go into the Pound Shop and ask the assistants how much everything costs.

31. *Buy a bunch of helium balloons from the balloon seller near the Pier who never smiles and release them one by one as we walk along the beach.*
32. *Do 'The Monkees' cross-leg dance all the way from Brighton Station down Queen's Road to the seafront.*
33. *Hire a tandem and whistle the theme tune to 'The Great Escape' whenever we ride it.*
34. *Sit and kiss on every bench we can find.*
35. *Play 'Strip Jenga'.* ☺ ☺ ☺
36. *Wear matching outfits for a night at the pub.*
37. *Go to the cinema when it opens and watch back-to-back films all day.*
38. *Have afternoon tea dressed as clowns.*
39. *Watch 'The Matrix' and high-five every time someone says 'Neo' or 'Mister'.*
40. *Sneak onto a kids' playground after dark and play on the swings.*
41. *Waltz around the Royal Pavilion Gardens.*
42. *Do a forfeit every time you say YES or I say NO for a whole day.*
43. *Borrow in-line skates and travel up and down Gardner Street (since neither you or I can skate, this will be hilarious).*
44. *Do an interpretive dance at a bus stop (and don't laugh . . .)*
45. *Hold hands from the moment we wake till the moment we go to bed.*
46. *Stay up all night watching Katharine Hepburn and Spencer Tracy films.*
47. *Spend a day quoting as many song lyrics as we can.*
48. *Hand out lollipops to random strangers.*
49. *Fill the house with fairy lights and candles – no standard lights allowed.*

50. *Read the box messages – all of them.*
51. *Visit Paris, stand on the second tier of the Eiffel Tower, kiss and shout 'C'est magnifique' over the city.*

Reading Group Questions

Did you feel the author's own experience influenced the themes in this book?

Most romantic fiction suggests that there is only one true love for each of us. How does *When I Fall in Love* conform to or challenge that idea?

The unpredictability of life is a key theme in *When I Fall in Love*. How does the book present the idea of overcoming situations?

How has Elsie's early life experience of being abandoned by her mother affected her view of life? Do you think she might have approached the situations in the story differently if Moira had still been part of her life?

How do think Jim's commitment to his daughters has influenced the lives of Elsie, Daisy and Guin?

How do the worldviews of the people in Elsie's life support or challenge her own?

What part do you think *The Sundaes* play in helping Elsie to step into her 'unexpected life'?

How does Woody influence Elsie?

How have Woody's outlandish music suggestions and flamboyant philosophies on life been influenced by his experience of brief stardom, the death of his bandmate and the acrimonious break-up of Hellfinger?

How do Olly and Torin reflect different sides to Elsie's character?

'I don't want that kind of memorial.' How does the representation of loss differ in this book from others you have read?

How important is it for Elsie to follow – and complete – The List?

What does Paris represent in Elsie's life, and why is it so important for her to do what she does at the Eiffel Tower?

What do the box messages mentioned throughout the story reveal about the person who wrote them?

Do you think the Eiffel Tower is an allegory for the importance Elsie has placed on the fifty-first item of The List? If so, why?

What are the key lessons Elsie learns during the course of the story?